Jora, who knew the tune well, hid under the stairs the moment she heard the first notes. While his colleagues broke down Rath's door, a soldier wielding a flashlight paced nervously back and forth at the main entrance. The torch's beam cut through the darkness, barely missing Jora's worn grey shoe. Yudel grabbed her with such animal fear that Jora had to bite her lip in order not to cry out in pain. The soldier came so close to them that they could smell his leather coat and the cold metal and oil of the gun.

A loud shot rumbled down the stairwell. The soldier interrupted his search and rushed upstairs to his companions who were yelling. Jora lifted Yudel in her arms and went out into the street, walking slowly.

Juan Gómez-Jurado is a journalist who has worked on radio and television. He has also been a director of several large corporations. He has won several prizes for his journalism. He lives with his wife and daughter in Spain.

CONTRACT WITH GOD

Juan Gómez-Jurado

Translated by A.V. Lebrón

An Orion paperback

First published in Great Britain in 2009
by Orion
This paperback edition published in 2010
by Orion Books Ltd,
Orion House, 5 Upper St Martin's Lane,
London WC2H 9EA

An Hachette UK company

1 3 5 7 9 10 8 6 4 2

A CIP catalogue record for this book
is available from the British Library

ISBN 978-0-7528-8431-8

Printed and bound in the UK by CPI Mackays, Chatham, Kent

The Orion Publishing Group's policy is to use papers
that are natural, renewable and recyclable products and
made from wood grown in sustainable forests. The logging
and manufacturing processes are expected to conform to
the environmental regulations of the country of origin.

www.orionbooks.co.uk

For Matthew Thomas, a greater hero than Father Fowler

How to Create an Enemy

Start with an empty canvas
Sketch in broad outline the forms of
men women and children

Dip into the unconsciousness well of your own
disowned darkness
with a wide brush and
strain the strangers with the sinister hue
of the shadow

Trace onto the face of the enemy the greed,
Hatred, carelessness you dare not claim as
Your own

Obscure the sweet individuality of each face

Erase all hints of the myriad loves, hopes,
fears that play through the kaleidoscope of
every infinite heart

Twist the smile until it forms the downward
arc of cruelty

Strip flesh from bone until only the
abstract skeleton of death remains

Exaggerate each feature until man is
metamorphosed into beast, vermin, insect

Fill in the background with malignant
figures from ancient nightmares – devils,
demons, myrmidons of evil

When your icon of the enemy is complete
you will be able to kill without guilt,
slaughter without shame

The thing you destroy will have become
merely an enemy of God, an impediment
to the secret dialectic of history

from *Faces of the Enemy*
by Sam Keen

The Ten Commandments

I am the Lord thy God.
Thou shalt have no other gods before me
Thou shalt not make unto thee any graven image
Thou shalt not take the name of the Lord thy God in vain
Remember the Sabbath day, to keep it holy
Honour thy father and mother
Thou shalt not kill
Thou shalt not commit adultery
Thou shalt not steal
Thou shalt not bear false witness against thy neighbour
Thou shalt not covet thy neighbour's house

Prologue

Am Spiegelgrund Children's Hospital

VIENNA

February 1943

Arriving at the building where a large flag with a swastika was flapping overhead, the woman could not suppress a shiver. Her companion misinterpreted and drew her closer to him in order to warm her. Her thin coat offered meagre protection against the sharp afternoon wind, which warned of an approaching blizzard.

'Put this on, Odile,' the man said, his fingers trembling as he unbuttoned his coat.

She loosened herself from his grip and hugged the package closer to her chest. The six-mile walk through the snow had left her exhausted and numb from the cold. Three years ago they would have made the trip in their Daimler with a driver, and she would have been wearing her fur. But their car now belonged to a Brigadeführer and her fur coat was probably being shown off in a theatre box somewhere by some Nazi wife with painted eyelids. Odile composed herself and pressed the buzzer forcefully three times before answering him.

'It's not because of the cold, Josef. We don't have much time before curfew. If we don't return in time ...'

1

Before her husband could reply, a nurse suddenly opened the door. As soon as she took one look at the visitors, her smile disappeared. Several years under the Nazi regime had taught her to recognise a Jew immediately.

'What do you want?' she asked.

The woman made herself smile, even though her lips were painfully cracked.

'We want to see Dr Graus.'

'Do you have an appointment?'

'The doctor said he'd see us.'

'Name?'

'Josef and Odile Cohen, Fräulein.'

The nurse took a step back when their surname confirmed her suspicions.

'You're lying. You don't have an appointment. Go away. Go back to the hole you came from. You know you're not allowed here.'

'Please. My son is inside. Please!'

Her words were wasted as the door slammed shut.

Josef and his wife looked helplessly at the huge building. As they turned away, Odile suddenly felt weak and stumbled, but Josef managed to catch her before she fell.

'Come on, we'll find another way to get in.'

They headed over to one side of the hospital. As they turned the corner, Josef pulled his wife back. A door had just opened. A man wearing a thick coat was struggling to push a cart filled with rubbish towards the rear of the building. Keeping close to the wall, Josef and Odile slid up to the open doorway.

Once inside, they found themselves standing in a service hall leading to a maze of stairs and other corridors. As they proceeded down the hallway, they could hear distant muffled cries that seemed to be coming from another world. The

2

woman concentrated intently, listening for her son's voice, but it was useless. They went through several corridors without running into anybody. Josef had to hurry to keep up with his wife who, compelled by sheer instinct, moved forward swiftly, stopping only for a second at each doorway.

Before long they found themselves peering into a dark L-shaped ward. It was full of children, many of whom were strapped to their beds and whimpering like wet dogs. The acrid-smelling room was stifling and the woman began to sweat, feeling a tingling in her extremities as her body warmed up. She paid no attention to this, however, as her eyes raced from bed to bed, from one young face to the next, searching desperately for her son.

'Here's the report, Dr Graus.'

Josef and his wife exchanged looks as they heard the name of the doctor they needed to see, the person who held their son's life in his hands. They turned towards the far corner of the ward and saw a small group of people gathered around one of the beds. An attractive young doctor was seated at the bedside of a girl who looked about nine years old. Next to him an older nurse held a tray of surgical instruments while a bored-looking middle-aged doctor took notes.

'Dr Graus ...' said Odile hesitantly, steeling herself as she approached the group.

The young man gestured dismissively to the nurse without taking his eyes from what he was doing.

'Not now, please.'

The nurse and the other doctor stared at Odile in surprise, but said nothing.

When she saw what was taking place, Odile had to grit her teeth in order not to scream. The young girl was deathly pale and appeared to be semi-conscious. Graus was holding her arm over a metal basin as he made small cuts with a scalpel. There was hardly a place on the girl's arm that hadn't been touched by the blade and the blood flowed slowly into the basin, which was almost full. Finally the girl's head slumped to one side. Graus held two slender fingers to the girl's neck.

'Good, she has no pulse. The time, Dr Stroebel?'

'Six thirty-seven.'

'Almost ninety-three minutes. Exceptional! The subject remained awake although her level of consciousness was comparatively low, and she showed no signs of pain. The combination of laudanum and datura is undoubtedly better than anything we've tried up to now. Congratulations, Stroebel. Get the specimen ready for dissection.'

'Thank you, Herr Doktor. Right away.'

Only then did the young doctor turn towards Josef and Odile. In his eyes was a mixture of annoyance and disdain.

'And who might you be?'

Odile took a step forward and stood next to the bed, trying not to look at the dead girl.

'My name is Odile Cohen, Dr Graus. I am Elan Cohen's mother.'

The physician looked at Odile coldly and then turned to the nurse.

'Get these Jews out of here, Fräulein Ulrike.'

The nurse grabbed Odile's elbow and with a rough push positioned herself between the woman and the doctor. Josef rushed to help his wife and struggled with the hefty nurse. For moments they formed a bizarre trio, pushing in different directions without anyone gaining ground. Fräulein Ulrike's face grew red from the effort.

'Doctor, I'm sure there's been a mistake,' said Odile, fight-

4

ing to get her head past the nurse's broad shoulders. 'My son is not mentally ill.'

Odile managed to free herself from the nurse's grip and turned to the doctor.

'It's true that he hasn't talked much since we lost our house, but he's not mad. He's here because of a mistake. If you let him go . . . Please let me give you the only thing we have left.'

She placed the package on the bed, making sure she didn't touch the body of the dead girl as she carefully removed the newspaper wrapping. Despite the dimness of the ward, the golden object cast its glow on the surrounding walls.

'It's been in my husband's family for generations, Dr Graus. I would rather have died than give this up. But my son, Doctor, my son . . .'

Odile began to cry and fell to her knees. The younger doctor barely noticed since his eyes were transfixed by the object on the bed. However, he managed to open his mouth long enough to destroy any hope the couple had left.

'Your son is dead. Go away.'

As soon as the cold air outside hit her face Odile regained some strength. Holding on to her husband as they hurried away from the hospital, she was more fearful than ever of the curfew. Her mind was concentrated solely on getting back to the far side of the city, where their other son was waiting.

'Hurry, Josef. Hurry.'

They quickened their pace through the steadily falling snow.

In his hospital office, Dr Graus hung up the phone with a distracted air and caressed the strange gold object on his desk. Minutes later, when the sirens from the SS vehicles reached him, he didn't even look out of the window. His assistant said something about fleeing Jews, but Graus paid no attention.

He was busy planning young Cohen's operation.

Main Characters

Clergy

FATHER ANTHONY FOWLER, agent working with both the CIA and the Holy Alliance.

FATHER ALBERT, ex-hacker. Systems Analyst with the CIA and liaison with Vatican intelligence.

BROTHER CESÁREO, Dominican. Curator of Antiquities at the Vatican.

Security Corps for Vatican City

CAMILO CIRIN, Inspector General. Also Head of the Holy Alliance, the Vatican's secret intelligence service.

Civilians

ANDREA OTERO, reporter for the newspaper *El Globo*.

RAYMOND KAYN, multimillionaire industrialist.

JACOB RUSSELL, Kayn's executive assistant.

ORVILLE WATSON, terrorism consultant and owner of Netcatch.

DR HEINRICH GRAUS, genocidal Nazi.

Personnel on the Moses Expedition

CECYL FORRESTER, biblical archaeologist.

DAVID PAPPAS, GORDON DURWIN, KYRA LARSEN, STOWE ERLING and EZRA LEVINE, assistants to Cecyl Forrester

MOGENS DEKKER, chief of security for the expedition.

ALOIS GOTTLIEB, ALRYK GOTTLIEB, TEWI WAAKA, PACO TORRES, LOUIS MALONEY and MARLA JACKSON, Dekker's soldiers.

DR HAREL, physician on the excavation.

TOMMY EICHBERG, head driver.

ROBERT FRICK, BRIAN HANLEY, administration/technicians.

NURI ZAYIT, RANI PETERKE, cooks.

Terrorists

NAZIM and KHAROUF, members of the Washington cell.

O, D and W, members of the Syrian and Jordanian cells.

HUQAN, head of the three cells.

1

RESIDENCE OF
BALTHASAR HANDWURZ

STEINFELDSTRAßE, 6
KRIEGLACH, AUSTRIA

Thursday, 15 December 2005. 11:42 a.m.

The priest wiped his feet carefully on the welcome mat before knocking on the door. After tracking the man for the past four months, he had finally discovered his hiding place two weeks ago. He was now sure of Handwurz's true identity. The moment had come to confront him.

He waited patiently for a few minutes. It was noon and Graus would be having his customary midday nap on the sofa. There was hardly anyone in the narrow street at that hour. His neighbours on Steinfeldstraße were at work, unaware that at Number 6, in a small house with blue curtains at the windows, a genocidal monster was peacefully dozing in front of his TV set.

Finally the sound of a key in the lock warned the priest that the door was about to open. The head of an elderly man with the venerable air of someone in an advertisement for medical insurance appeared from behind the door.

'Yes?'

'Good morning, Herr Doktor.'

The old man looked the person who was addressing him up and down. The latter was tall, thin and bald, about fifty years of age, with a priest's collar visible under his black coat. He stood on the doorstep with the rigid posture of a military guard, his green eyes observing the old man intently.

'I think you're mistaken, Father. I used to be a plumber, but now I'm retired. I've already contributed to the parish fund, so if you'll excuse me . . .'

'You aren't by any chance Dr Heinrich Graus, the famous German neurosurgeon?'

The old man held his breath for a second. Aside from that, he did nothing that might give him away. However, that small detail was enough for the priest: proof positive.

'My name is Handwurz, Father.'

'That's not true and we both know it. Now if you'll let me in, I'll show you what I've brought with me.' The priest raised his left hand, in which he held a black briefcase.

The door swung open in response and the old man limped quickly towards the kitchen, the ancient floorboards protesting with each step. The priest followed but paid little attention to the surroundings. He had peered in through the windows on three separate occasions and already knew the location of each item of cheap furniture. He preferred keeping his eyes fixed on the old Nazi's back. Even though the doctor walked with some difficulty, the priest had seen him lifting sacks of coal from the shed with an ease that a man decades younger might have envied. Heinrich Graus was still a dangerous man.

The small kitchen was dark and smelled rancid. It had a gas stove, a counter on which sat a dried-up onion, a round table, and two unmatched chairs. Graus gestured for the priest to sit down. The old man then rummaged through a cupboard, took out two glasses, filled them with water and set them on the table before taking a seat himself. The glasses remained untouched as the two men sat there, impassive, regarding each other for over a minute.

The old man was dressed in a red flannel bathrobe, cotton shirt, and worn trousers. He had started going bald twenty years earlier, and the little hair he had left was completely white. His large round glasses had gone out of style before the fall of communism. The relaxed expression around his mouth lent him a good-natured air.

None of this fooled the priest.

Dust particles floated in the shaft of light created by the weak rays of the December sun. One of them landed on the priest's sleeve. He flicked it away without taking his gaze from the old man.

The smooth certainty of the gesture did not go unnoticed by the Nazi, but he'd had time to recover his composure.

'Aren't you going to have some water, Father?'

'I'm not thirsty, Dr Graus.'

'So you're going to insist on calling me by that name. My name is Handwurz. Balthasar Handwurz.'

The priest paid no heed.

'I have to admit you're pretty sharp. When you got your passport to leave for Argentina, no one imagined that you'd return to Vienna a few months later. Naturally it was the last place I looked for you. Only forty-five miles from Spiegelgrund Hospital. The Nazi hunter, Wiesenthal, searched for years in Argentina, unaware that you were a short ride away from his office. Ironic, don't you think?'

'I think it's ridiculous. You're American, aren't you? You speak German well, but your accent gives you away.'

The priest lifted his briefcase onto the table and removed

11

from it a worn folder. The first document he held up was a photo of a younger Graus, taken at the hospital at Spiegelgrund during the war. The second was a variation of the same photo, but with the doctor's features aged thanks to a software program.

'Isn't technology great, Herr Doktor?'

'That doesn't prove a thing. Anyone could have done that. I watch television too,' he said, but his voice betrayed something else.

'You're right. It doesn't prove anything, but this does.'

The priest took out a yellowing sheet to which someone had stapled a black-and-white photo, on top of which was written in sepia letters: **TESTIMONIANZA FORNITA**, next to the stamp of the Vatican.

'"Balthasar Handwurz. Blond hair, brown eyes, strong features. Identifying marks: a tattoo on his left arm with the number 256441, put there by the Nazis during his stay at the concentration camp at Mauthausen." A place you never set foot in, Graus. Your number is a false one. The person who did your tattoo made it up on the spot, but that's the least of it. Until now, it's worked.'

The old man touched his arm through the flannel bathrobe. He was pale with anger and fear.

'Who the hell are you, you bastard?'

'My name is Anthony Fowler. I want to cut a deal with you.'

'Get out of my house. Right now.'

'I don't think I'm making myself clear. You were second in command at Am Spieglgrund Children's Hospital for six years. It was a very interesting place. Almost all the patients were Jewish and they suffered from mental illness. "Lives not worth living", isn't that what you called them?'

'I don't have the slightest idea what you're talking about!'

'Nobody suspected what you were doing there. The experiments. Cutting children up while they were still alive. Seven hundred and fourteen, Dr Graus. You killed seven hundred and fourteen of them with your own hands.'

'I told you—'

'You kept their brains in jars!'

Fowler smashed his fist on the table so hard that both glasses toppled over and for a moment the only sound was that of the water dripping onto the tiled floor. Fowler took a few deep breaths, attempting to calm himself.

The doctor avoided looking into the green eyes that seemed ready to cut him in half.

'Are you with the Jews?'

'No, Graus. You know I'm not. If I were one of them you'd be dangling from a noose in Tel Aviv. My . . . affiliation is with the people who facilitated your escape in 1946.'

The doctor repressed a shiver.

'The Holy Alliance,' he muttered.

Fowler did not reply.

'And what does the Alliance want from me after all these years?'

'Something in your possession.'

The Nazi gestured at his surroundings.

'As you can see, I'm not exactly a rich man. I have no money left.'

'If I were after money, I could easily sell you to the Attorney General in Stuttgart. They're still offering 130,000 euros for your capture. I want the candle.'

The Nazi stared at him blankly, pretending not to understand.

'What candle?'

13

'Now you're the one being ridiculous, Dr Graus. I'm talking about the candle you stole from the Cohen family sixty-two years ago. A heavy candle without a wick, covered with gold filigree. That's what I want and I want it now.'

'Take your bloody lies elsewhere. I don't have any candle.'

Fowler sighed, leaned back on his chair and pointed at the upturned glasses on the table.

'Do you have anything stronger?'

'Behind you,' Graus said, nodding towards a cupboard.

The priest turned and reached for a bottle that was half full. He picked up the glasses and poured two fingers of bright yellow liquid into each. Both men downed the drinks without making a toast.

Fowler grabbed the bottle again and poured another round. He took a sip then said: '*Weizenkorn*. Wheat schnapps. It's been a long time since I tasted this.'

'I'm sure you haven't missed it.'

'True. But it's cheap, isn't it?'

Graus shrugged his shoulders.

'A man like you, Graus. Brilliant. Vain. I can't believe you drink this. You're slowly poisoning yourself in a dirty hole that smells of piss. And you want to know something? I understand ...'

'You don't understand a thing.'

'Pretty good. You still remember the techniques of the Reich. Officers Regulations. Section Three. "In the event of capture by the enemy, deny everything and give only short answers that will not compromise you." Well, Graus, get used to it. You're compromised up to your neck.'

The old man pulled a face and poured himself the rest of the schnapps. Fowler watched his opponent's body language as the monster's resolve slowly crumbled. He was like a painter, stepping back after a few brush strokes to examine the canvas before deciding which colours to use next.

The priest decided to try using the truth.

'Look at my hands, Doctor,' said Fowler, placing them on the table. They were wrinkled, with long delicate fingers. There was nothing strange about them except for one small detail. At the top section of each finger near the knuckles was a thin whitish line that continued right across each hand.

'Those are ugly scars. How old were you when you got them? Ten? Eleven?'

'Twelve. I was practising the piano: Chopin Preludes, Opus 28. My father came over to the piano and without any warning he slammed the lid of the Steinway down as hard as he could. It was a miracle I didn't lose my fingers, but I was never able to play again.'

The priest gripped his glass and seemed to lose himself in its contents before going on. He had never been able to acknowledge what had happened while looking another human being in the eye.

'From the time I was nine years old my father ... forced himself on me. That day I told him I was going to tell someone if he did it again. He didn't threaten me. He simply destroyed my hands. Then he cried, asked me to forgive him, and called on the best doctors money could buy. No, Graus. Don't even think about it.'

Graus had slid his hand under the table, feeling for the cutlery drawer. He quickly withdrew it.

'That's why I understand you, Doctor. My father was a monster whose guilt went beyond his own capacity to forgive. But he had more guts than you. Rather than slowing down in the middle of a sharp curve, he stepped on the gas and took my mother with him.'

'A very moving story, Father,' Graus said in a mocking tone.

'If you say so. You've been hiding in order to avoid facing your crimes, but you've been found out. And I'm going to give you what my father never had: a second chance.'

'I'm listening.'

'Give me the candle. In turn you'll get this file containing all the documents that would serve as your death warrant. You can go on hiding out here for the rest of your life.'

'And that's it?' said the old man incredulously.

'As far as I'm concerned.'

The old man shook his head and stood up with a tight smile. He opened a small cabinet and pulled out a large glass jar filled with rice.

'I never eat grains. I have an allergy.'

He emptied the rice onto the table. There was a small cloud of starch and a dry thud. Half buried in the rice was a package.

Fowler leaned forward and reached for it, but Graus's bony paw grabbed his wrist. The priest looked at him.

'I have your word, right?' said the old man anxiously.

'Is it worth anything to you?'

'Yes, as far as I'm concerned.'

'Then you have it.'

The doctor let go of Fowler's wrist, his own hands trembling. The priest carefully brushed off the rice and lifted out the dark cloth package. It was tied with twine. With great care he undid the knots and unwrapped the cloth. The faint rays of the early Austrian winter filled the filthy kitchen with a golden light that seemed at odds with the surroundings and the dirty, grey wax of the thick candle lying on the table. At one time the candle's entire surface had been covered by a thin sheet of gold worked in an intricate design. Now, the

16

precious metal had almost disappeared, leaving only traces of filigree on the wax.

Graus smiled sadly.

'The pawnshop took the rest, Father.'

Fowler didn't reply. He took out a lighter from his trouser pocket and flicked it on. Then he stood the candle upright on the table and brought the flame to the top of it. Although there was no wick, the heat of the flame began to melt the wax, which gave off a nauseating smell as it slid down towards the table in grey drops. Graus looked on with bitter irony, as if he enjoyed being able to speak as himself after so many years.

'I find it amusing. The Jew at the pawnshop has been buying Jewish gold for years, thereby supporting a proud member of the Reich. And what you're witnessing now proves your search has been completely pointless.'

'Appearances can be deceptive, Graus. The gold on this candle is not the treasure I'm after. It's only a distraction for idiots.'

Like a warning, the flame suddenly sputtered. A pool of wax had accumulated on the cloth below. At the top of what remained of the candle, the green edge of a metallic object was just about visible.

'Good, it's here,' said the priest. 'Now I can leave.'

Fowler stood up and folded the cloth around the candle once more, being careful not to burn himself.

The Nazi watched in astonishment. He was no longer smiling.

'Wait! What is that? What's inside?'

'Nothing that concerns you.'

The old man stood up, opened the cutlery drawer and pulled out a kitchen knife. With trembling steps he made his way around the table towards the priest. Fowler watched him, motionless. In the Nazi's eyes burned the crazed fire of someone who had spent whole nights contemplating that object.

'I have to know.'

'No, Graus. We made a deal. The candle for the file. That's all you get.'

The old man raised the knife, but the expression on his visitor's face made him lower it again. Fowler nodded and threw down the file on the table. Slowly, with the cloth bundle in one hand and his briefcase in the other, the priest backed towards the kitchen door. The old man picked up the file.

'There are no other copies, right?'

'Only one. The two Jews waiting outside have it.'

Graus's eyes nearly leapt out of their sockets. He raised the knife again and advanced towards the priest.

'You lied to me! You said you'd give me a chance!'

Fowler looked at him impassively one last time.

'God will forgive me. Do you think you'll have as much luck?'

Then, without another word, he disappeared into the hallway.

The priest walked out of the building clutching the precious package to his chest. Two men in grey coats stood guard several feet from the door. Fowler warned them as he passed: 'He has a knife.'

The taller of the two cracked his knuckles and a small smile played on his lips.

'Even better,' he said.

2

ARTICLE PUBLISHED IN EL GLOBO

17 December 2005, Page 12

AUSTRIAN HEROD FOUND DEAD

Vienna (Associated Press)

After evading justice for over fifty years, Dr Heinrich Graus, 'the butcher of Spiegelgrund', was finally located by the Austrian police. According to the authorities, the infamous Nazi war criminal was found dead, apparently of a heart attack, in a small house in the town of Krieglach, only 35 miles from Vienna.

Born in 1915, Graus became a member of the Nazi party in 1931. By the beginning of the Second World War, he was already second in command at the Am Spiegelgrund Children's Hospital. Graus used his position to conduct inhumane experiments on Jewish children with so-called behavioural problems or mental deficiencies. The doctor stated on several occasions that such behaviours were hereditary and the experiments he conducted were justified since the subjects possessed 'lives not worth living'.

Graus vaccinated healthy children with infectious diseases, performed vivisections, and injected his victims with different mixtures of the anaesthesia he was developing in order to measure their reaction to pain. It is believed that close to a thousand murders occurred within the walls of Spiegelgrund during the war.

After the war, the Nazi fled, leaving no trace except for 300 children's brains preserved in formaldehyde. Despite the efforts of the German authorities, no one was able to track him down. The famous Nazi hunter, Simon Wiesenthal, who brought over 1,100 criminals to justice, remained intent until his death on finding Graus, whom he called 'his pending assignment', hunting the doctor tirelessly throughout South America. Wiesenthal died in Vienna three months ago, unaware that his target was living as a retired plumber not far from his own office.

Unofficial sources at the Israeli embassy in Vienna lamented that Graus had died without having to answer for his crimes, but nonetheless celebrated his sudden demise, given that his advanced age would have complicated the extradition process and trial, as in the case of the Chilean dictator Augusto Pinochet.

'We cannot help but see the hand of the Creator in his death,' stated a source.

3
KAYN

'He's downstairs, sir.'

The man in the chair shrank back a little. His hand trembled, although the movement wouldn't have been noticeable to anyone who didn't know him as well as his assistant.

'What's he like? Have you investigated him thoroughly?'

'You know I have, sir.'

There was a deep sigh.

'Yes, Jacob. My apologies.'

The man stood up as he spoke and reached for the remote control that regulated his environment. He pressed down hard on one of the buttons, his knuckles turning white. He had already broken several remotes and his assistant had finally given up and ordered a special one made out of reinforced acrylic that conformed to the shape of the old man's hand.

'My behaviour must be trying,' said the old man. 'I'm sorry.'

His assistant didn't respond; he realised that his boss needed to let off steam. He was a humble man yet very aware of his position in life, if those traits could be said to be compatible.

'It pains me to sit here all day, you know? Each day I find less pleasure in ordinary things. I've become an insignificant old idiot. When I go to bed each night I say to myself:

tomorrow. Tomorrow will be the day. And the next morning I get up and my resolve has vanished, just as my teeth are doing.'

'We'd better make a start, sir,' said the assistant, who had heard countless variations on this theme.

'Is it absolutely necessary?'

'You're the one who requested it, sir. As a way of controlling any loose ends.'

'I could just read the report.'

'It's not just that. We're already at Phase Four. If you want to be a part of this expedition, you'll have to get used to being around strangers. Dr Hocher was very clear on that point.'

The old man pressed a series of buttons on his remote control. The blinds in the room came down and the lights went out as he sat down once again.

'There's no other way?'

His assistant shook his head.

'Very well, then.'

The assistant headed for the door, the only remaining source of light.

'Jacob.'

'Yes, sir?'

'Before you leave . . . Would you mind letting me hold your hand for a moment? I'm frightened.'

The assistant did as he was asked. Kayn's hand was still trembling.

4

$\mathcal{H}$EADQUARTERS OF $\mathcal{K}$AYN $\mathcal{I}$NDUSTRIES

NEW YORK

Wednesday, 5 July 2006. 11:10 a.m.

Orville Watson was nervously drumming his fingers on the bulging leather portfolio on his lap. He had been sitting on his well-padded rear end in the reception area of the 38th Floor of Kayn Tower for the last two hours. At 3,000 dollars an hour, anyone else would have been happy to wait until Judgement Day. But not Orville. The young Californian was growing bored. In point of fact, the fight against boredom was what had made his career.

His college studies had bored him. Against his family's wishes he had dropped out during his second year. He had found a good job at CNET, one of the companies on the cutting edge of new technologies, but once again boredom had set in. Orville was constantly hungry for new challenges and his real passion was for answering questions. By the turn of the millennium, his entrepreneurial spirit had prompted him to leave his job at CNET and start up his own company.

His mother, who read in the newspapers each day about the failure of yet another dot-com, objected. Her worries didn't deter Orville. He packed his 220-pound frame, blond ponytail, and a suitcase full of clothes into a dilapidated van and drove right across the country, ending up in a basement apartment in Manhattan. Thus Netcatch was born. His slogan was 'You ask, we respond'. The whole project could have remained nothing more than the crazy dream of a young man with an eating disorder, too many worries, and a singular understanding of the Internet. But then 9/11 happened, and straight away Orville understood three things that it had taken the Washington bureaucrats much too long to figure out.

First, that their methods of handling information had been obsolete for thirty years. Second, that the political correctness brought on by eight years of the Clinton administration had made it even more difficult to search for information, since you could only count on 'reliable sources', which were useless when dealing with terrorists. And third, that the Arabs were turning out to be the new Russians when it came to espionage.

Orville's mother, Yasmina, was born and had lived in Beirut for many years before marrying a handsome engineer from Sausalito, California, whom she met while he was working on a project in Lebanon. The couple soon moved to the United States, where the lovely Yasmina educated her only son in both Arabic and English.

Adopting different identities on the web, the young man found out that the Internet was a paradise for extremists. It didn't matter physically how far apart ten radicals might be; online, the distance was measured in milliseconds. Their identity might be secret and their ideas insane, but on the Net they could find people who thought just like them. In a matter of weeks, Orville had accomplished something that nobody in Western intelligence could have achieved by conventional means: he had infiltrated one of the most radical networks in Islamic terrorism.

One morning towards the beginning of 2002, Orville drove south to Washington with four boxes of files in the boot of his van. Arriving at CIA headquarters, he asked for the person in charge of Islamic terrorism, stating that he had important information to divulge. In his hand was a ten-page summary of his findings. The lowly official who met with him made him wait two hours before even bothering to read his report. When he had finished reading, the official was so disturbed that he called in his supervisor. Minutes later four men showed up, threw Orville to the floor, stripped him, and dragged him into an interrogation room. Orville smiled inwardly throughout the humiliating procedure; he knew he'd hit the nail on the head.

When the big shots at the CIA grasped the magnitude of Orville's talent, they offered him a job. Orville told them that what was in the four boxes (which eventually produced twenty-three arrests in the United States and Europe) was just a free sample. If they wanted more, they should contract the services of his new company, Netcatch.

'Our prices are very reasonable, I should add,' he said. 'Now, may I please have my underwear back?'

Four and a half years later, Orville had put on another twenty pounds. His bank account had also gained some weight. Netcatch now employed seventeen full-time workers who produced detailed reports and information searches for the main governments of the Western world, mostly on security-related issues. Orville Watson, now a millionaire, was once again beginning to grow bored.

Until this new assignment came up.

Netcatch had its own way of doing things. All requests for its services had to be made in the form of a question. And this latest question came with the words 'budget unlimited' attached. The fact that it came from a private company, and not a government, also aroused Orville's curiosity.

Who is Father Anthony Fowler?

Orville got up from the plush waiting-room sofa in an attempt to ease the numbness in his muscles. He put his hands together and stretched his arms behind his head as far as he could. A request for information from a private company, especially one such as Kayn Industries, which was ranked among the top five of the *Fortune 500*, was unusual. Especially such a strange and precise request about an ordinary priest from Boston.

... about a seemingly ordinary priest from Boston, Orville corrected himself.

Orville was in the middle of stretching his upper limbs when a dark-haired, well-built executive dressed in an expensive suit entered the waiting room. He was barely thirty years old, and was regarding Orville seriously from behind his rimless glasses. From the orange tint of his skin, it was clear that he was no stranger to using a sunbed. He spoke with a clipped British accent.

'Mr Watson. I'm Jacob Russell, executive assistant to Raymond Kayn. We spoke on the telephone.'

Orville tried to regain his composure, with little success, and extended his hand.

'Mr Russell, I'm very happy to meet you. Sorry, I ...'

'Don't worry. Please follow me and I'll take you to your meeting.'

They crossed the carpeted waiting room and reached a set of mahogany doors at the far end.

'Meeting? I thought that I was supposed to explain my findings to you.'

'Well, not exactly, Mr Watson. Today Raymond Kayn will hear what you have to say.'

Orville was unable to respond.

'Is there a problem, Mr Watson? Aren't you feeling well?'

'Yes. No. I mean, there's no problem, Mr Russell. You simply took me by surprise. Mr Kayn . . .'

Russell pulled a small knob on the frame of the mahogany door and a panel slid open to reveal a simple square of dark glass. The executive placed his right hand on the glass and an orange light appeared, followed by the brief sound of a buzzer and then the door opened.

'I can understand your surprise, given what the media has said about Mr Kayn. As you probably know, my employer is a person who values his privacy . . .'

He's a fucking hermit, that's what he is, thought Orville.

'. . . but you needn't worry. Ordinarily, he doesn't want to meet strangers, but if you follow certain procedures . . .'

They walked down a narrow hall, at the end of which loomed the bright metallic doors of a lift.

'What do you mean, "ordinarily", Mr Russell?'

The executive cleared his throat.

'I should inform you that you will be only the fourth person, aside from the top executives of this firm, to have met Mr Kayn in the five years I've worked for him.'

Orville let out a long whistle.

'That's something.'

They reached the lift. There was no up or down button, only a small numerical pad on the wall.

'Would you kindly look the other way, Mr Watson?' Russell said.

The young Californian did as he was told. There was a series of beeps as the executive punched in a code.

'You can turn around now. Thank you.'

Orville turned back to face him again. The doors of the lift opened and the two men stepped in. Again there were no buttons, only a magnetic card reader. Russell took out his plastic card and slid it briefly into the slot. The doors closed and the lift moved smoothly upward.

'Your boss certainly takes his security seriously,' Orville said.

'Mr Kayn has received quite a few death threats. In fact, some years back he suffered a rather serious attempt on his life and was lucky to emerge unharmed. Please don't be alarmed by the mist. It's absolutely safe.'

Orville was wondering what on earth Russell was talking about, when a fine mist began to fall from the ceiling. Looking up, Orville observed several devices that were spewing out a fresh cloud of spray.

'What's going on?'

'It's a light antibiotic compound, absolutely safe. Do you like the smell?'

Hell, he even sprays his visitors before he sees them to make sure they're not going to give him their germs. I've changed my mind. This guy's not a hermit, he's a paranoid freak.

'Mmmm, yes, not bad. Mint, right?'

'Essence of wild mint. Very refreshing.'

Orville bit his lips to suppress a reply, and concentrated instead on the seven figures he'd be billing Kayn once he emerged from this gilded cage. The thought revived him somewhat.

The lift doors opened on to a magnificent space filled with natural light. Half of the thirty-ninth floor was a giant terrace enclosed by glass walls, providing a panoramic view of the Hudson River. Straight ahead was Hoboken and over to the south, Ellis Island.

'Impressive.'

'Mr Kayn enjoys remembering his roots. Please follow me.' The simple décor stood in contrast to the majesty of the view. The floor and the furniture were all white. The other half of the floor, with a view of Manhattan, was separated from the glassed-in terrace by a wall, also white and with several doors. Russell stopped in front of one of them.

'Very well, Mr Watson, Mr Kayn will see you now. But before you go in, I'd like to outline a few simple rules for you. First of all, do not look directly at him. Second, do not ask him questions. And third, do not attempt to touch him or go near him. When you enter you'll see a small table with a copy of your report and a remote control for your Power Point presentation which your office provided us with this morning. Remain by the table, do your presentation, and leave as soon as you've finished. I'll be here waiting for you. Is that clear?'

Orville nodded nervously.

'I'll do the best I can.'

'Very well then, go on in,' said Russell, as he opened the door.

The Californian hesitated before entering the room.

'Oh, one more thing. Netcatch has discovered something interesting in a routine investigation we did for the FBI. There are indications to suggest that Kayn Industries could

29

be targeted by Islamic terrorists. It's all in this report,' said Orville, handing the assistant a DVD. Russell took it with a worried look. 'Consider it a courtesy on our part.'

'Thank you very much indeed, Mr Watson. And good luck.'

5

$\mathcal{H}$OTEL $\mathcal{L}$E $\mathcal{M}$ERIDIEN

AMMAN, JORDAN

Wednesday, 5 July 2006. 6:11 p.m.

On the other side of the world, Tahir Ibn Faris, a minor official in the Ministry of Industry, was leaving his office a bit later than usual. The reason was not his dedication to his job, which was in fact exemplary, but his desire to avoid being seen. It took him less than two minutes to reach his destination, which was not the customary bus stop but the luxurious Meridien, the finest five-star hotel in Jordan, which was currently lodging the two gentlemen who had requested this meeting through a well-known industrialist. Unfortunately, this particular intermediary had made his reputation through channels that were neither respectable nor clean. Tahir therefore suspected that the invitation for coffee might have shady undertones. And although he was proud of his twenty-three years of honest work at the Ministry, he was beginning to have less use for pride and more for hard cash; the reason being that his eldest daughter was about to get married, and that was going to cost him.

On his way to one of the executive suites, Tahir examined his reflection in the mirror, wishing he had the look of a greedier man. He was barely five feet six inches tall, and his belly, greying beard, and increasing baldness made him look

31

more like an affable drunk than a corrupt government employee. He wanted to erase the slightest trace of integrity from his features.

What more than two decades of honesty couldn't give him was the correct mind-set for what he was doing. As he knocked on the door, his knees made their own percussion. He managed to calm himself down an instant before entering the suite, where he was greeted by a well-dressed American who looked about fifty. Another much younger man was seated in the spacious living room and was smoking as he talked on his mobile phone. When he noticed Tahir, he ended the call and stood up to greet him.

'*Ahlan wa sahlan*,' he welcomed him in perfect Arabic.

Tahir was taken aback. When, on various occasions, he had refused bribes to reclassify land for industrial and commercial use in Amman – a veritable gold mine for his less scrupulous colleagues – he had not done so out of a sense of duty, but because of the insulting arrogance of westerners who, within minutes of meeting him, would drop wads of dollar bills on the table.

The conversation with these two Americans couldn't have been more different. Before Tahir's astonished eyes, the older one sat down in front of a low table, where he had prepared four *dellas*, Bedouin coffee pots, and a small coal fire. With a sure hand he roasted fresh coffee beans in an iron frying pan and let them cool. He then ground the roasted beans with more mature ones in the *mahbash*, a small mortar. The whole process was accompanied by a steady stream of conversation, except when the pestle was rhythmically striking the *mahbash*, since this sound is considered by the Arabs as a kind of music whose artistry should be appreciated by the guest.

The American added cardamom seeds and a pinch of saffron, meticulously brewing the mixture according to a tradition that went back centuries. As was customary, the guest – Tahir – held the cup, which had no handle, while the American filled it halfway, for it was the host's privilege to serve the most important person in the room first. Tahir drank the coffee, still slightly sceptical about the results. He thought he wouldn't have more than one cup since it was already late, but after tasting the brew he was so delighted that he drank four more. He would have ended up having a sixth cup, were it not for the fact that it was considered impolite to drink an even number.

'Mr Fallon, I never imagined that someone born in the country of Starbucks could perform the Bedouin ritual of *gahwa* so well,' said Tahir. He was by now feeling quite comfortable and wanted them to know, so that he could find out what the devil these Americans wanted.

The younger of the hosts extended a gold cigarette case to him for the umpteenth time.

'Tahir, my friend, please stop calling us by our surnames. I'm Peter and this is Frank,' he said as he lit yet another Dunhill.

'Thank you, Peter.'

'Good. Now that we've relaxed, Tahir, would you consider it bad manners if we discussed business?'

The ageing civil servant was again pleasantly surprised. Two hours had gone by. An Arab doesn't like to discuss business before half an hour or so has passed, but this American was even asking his permission. At that moment Tahir felt ready to reclassify any building they were after, even King Abdullah's palace.

'Absolutely, my friend.'

'Good, this is what we need: a licence for Kayn Mining Company to dig for phosphates for one year, starting from today.'

'That is not going to be so easy, my friend. Almost the entire Dead Sea coast is already occupied by local industries. As you know, phosphates and tourism are practically our only national resources.'

'No problem there, Tahir. We're not interested in the Dead Sea, only in a small area of roughly ten square miles centred on these coordinates.'

He handed Tahir a piece of paper.

'29° 34' 44" north, 36° 21' 24" east? You can't be serious, my friends. This is just north-east of Al Mudawwara.'

'Yes, not far from the border with Saudi Arabia. We know, Tahir.'

The Jordanian looked at them in confusion.

'There are no phosphates there. It's desert. The minerals there are useless.'

'Well, Tahir, we have great confidence in our engineers, and they feel they can extract a significant amount of phosphates in that area. Of course, as a gesture of our good will, there will be a small commission for you.'

Tahir's eyes grew wide as his new friend opened his briefcase.

'But that must be . . .'

'Enough for the wedding of little Myesha, right?'

And a small beach house with a double garage, Tahir thought. *These damned Americans probably think they're sharper than anyone else and can find oil in that area. As if we haven't searched there countless times. Anyway, I'm not going to be the one to ruin their dreams.*

'My friends, there is no doubt that you are both men of

great worth and knowledge. I'm sure your business will be welcomed in the Hashemite Kingdom of Jordan.'

Despite Peter and Frank's sugary smiles, Tahir kept racking his brain as to what it all meant. What the hell were these Americans looking for in the desert?

As much as he wrestled with the issue, he never came close to guessing that in a few days this meeting was going to cost him his life.

6

$\mathcal{H}$EADQUARTERS OF
$\mathcal{K}$AYN $\mathcal{I}$NDUSTRIES

NEW YORK

Wednesday, 5 July 2006. 11:29 a.m.

Orville found himself in a darkened room. The only light came from a small lamp shining at a lectern ten feet away on which his report sat along with a remote control, just as the executive had told him. He walked over and picked up the remote. As he examined it, wondering how to begin the presentation, he was suddenly startled by a bright glow. Not six feet from where he was standing was a large screen twenty feet wide. On it was displayed the first page of his presentation, with the red Netcatch logo.

'Thank you very much, Mr Kayn, and good morning. Let me begin by saying that it's an honour—'

There was a small buzz and the image on the screen changed, revealing the title of his presentation and the first of the two questions:

WHO IS FATHER ANTHONY FOWLER?

Clearly, Mr Kayn valued brevity and control, and had a second remote to hand in order to speed up the process.

OK, old man. I get the message. Let's get down to business.

Orville pressed the remote to bring up the next page. It showed a priest with a thin, craggy face. He was balding and whatever hair he had left had been cut very short. Orville began speaking to the darkness before him.

'John Anthony Fowler, alias Father Anthony Fowler, alias Tony Brent. Born 16 December 1951 in Boston, Massachusetts. Green eyes, roughly 175 pounds. Freelance agent for the CIA and a total mystery. Solving this mystery took two months of research carried out by ten of my best investigators, who worked exclusively on this job, as well as a considerable amount of cash in order to grease the palms of some well-placed sources. That explains in large part the three million dollars it cost to produce this report, Mr Kayn.'

The screen changed again, this time displaying a family photo: a well-dressed couple in the garden of what looked like an expensive home. At their side, an attractive, dark-haired boy about eleven years old. The father's hand seemed to be squeezing the boy's shoulder and all three wore tense smiles.

'The only son of Marcus Abernathy Fowler, business magnate and owner of Infinity Pharmaceuticals. Today it's a multimillion-dollar biotechnology company. After his parents died in a suspicious automobile accident in 1984, Anthony Fowler sold the company, along with the rest of their assets, and donated everything to charity. He held on to his parents' mansion in Beacon Hill, renting it out to a couple with children. But he kept the top floor for himself, and had it converted into an apartment containing some furniture and a whole bunch of philosophy books. He stays there every once in a while, whenever he's in Boston.'

The next image showed a younger version of the same

woman, this time on a college campus and dressed in a graduation gown.

'Daphne Brent was an expert chemist who worked at Infinity Pharmaceuticals until the owner took a liking to her and they got married. When she fell pregnant, Marcus turned her into a housewife overnight. That's all we know about Fowler's family, except that young Anthony went to Stanford instead of attending Boston College like his father.'

Next slide: young Anthony, looking not much older than a teenager, with a serious expression on his face, standing beneath a banner that read '1971'.

'He graduated magna cum laude at the age of twenty with a degree in Psychology. The youngest in his class. That photo was taken a month before classes ended. On the last day of the term, he collected his things and walked into the university recruitment offices. He wanted to go to Vietnam.'

An image appeared on the screen of a worn yellowed form that had been filled out by hand.

'This is a photograph of his AFQT, his Armed Forces Qualifying Test. Fowler scored ninety-eight out of one hundred. The sergeant was so impressed that he immediately sent him to Lackland Air Force Base in Texas where he went through basic training, followed by advanced parachute regiment instruction for a Special Ops unit that retrieved downed pilots behind enemy lines. While at Lackland, he learned guerrilla tactics and became a helicopter pilot. After a year and a half of combat, he returned home a lieutenant. Among his medals is a Purple Heart and an Air Force Cross. In the report you'll find details of the actions that earned him those medals.'

A snapshot of several men in uniform at an airfield. At the centre stood Fowler dressed as a priest.

'After Vietnam, Fowler entered a Catholic seminary and was ordained in 1977. He was assigned as military chaplain to Spangdahlem Air Force Base in Germany, where he was recruited by the CIA. With his language skills it's easy to see why they wanted him: Fowler speaks eleven languages fluently and can get along in fifteen others. But the Company is not the only outfit that recruited him.'

Another photo of Fowler, in Rome, with two other young priests.

'At the end of the seventies, Fowler became a full-time agent for the Company. He retains his status as military chaplain and travels to a number of Armed Forces bases all over the world. The information I've given you so far could have been obtained from any number of agencies, but what I'm going to tell you next is top secret and was very difficult to come by.'

The screen went blank. In the light from the projector Orville was just about able to make out an easy chair with someone sitting in it. He made an effort not to look directly at the figure.

'Fowler is an agent for the Holy Alliance, the Vatican's secret service. It's a small outfit, generally unknown to the public, but active. One of its accomplishments is having saved the life of former Israeli president, Golda Meir, when Islamic terrorists came close to blowing up her plane during a visit to Rome. The medals were awarded to Mossad, but the Holy Alliance didn't care. They take the phrase 'secret service' literally. Only the Pope and a handful of cardinals are officially informed of their work. Among the international intelligence community, the Alliance is respected and feared. Unfortunately, I have little to add about Fowler's history with this institution. As for his work with the CIA, my professional ethics and my contract with the Company don't allow me to reveal anything further, Mr Kayn.'

Orville cleared his throat. Even though he didn't expect an answer from the figure sitting at the end of the room, he paused.

Not a word.

'As to your second question, Mr Kayn . . .'

Orville wondered for a moment if he should reveal that Netcatch was not responsible for finding this particular piece of information. That it had come to his office in a sealed envelope from an anonymous source. And that there were other interests involved who clearly wanted Kayn Industries to have it. But then he recalled the humiliating spray of mentholated mist and simply went on talking.

On the screen a young woman appeared with blue eyes and copper-coloured hair.

'This is a young journalist named . . .'

7

$\mathcal{E}$DITORIAL $\mathcal{O}$FFICES OF
$\mathcal{E}$L $\mathcal{G}$LOBO

MADRID, SPAIN

Thursday, 6 July 2006. 8:29 p.m.

'Andrea! Andrea Otero! Where the hell are you?'

To say that the newsroom fell silent at the sound of the Editor-in-Chief's shouts would not be entirely accurate, for the newsroom of a daily paper is never quiet one hour before going to press. But there were no voices, which made the background noise of telephones, radios, televisions, fax machines and printers seem like an uneasy kind of silence. The Chief was carrying a suitcase in each hand, and had a newspaper tucked under one arm. He dropped the suitcases at the entrance to the newsroom and walked straight over to the International section, to the only empty desk. He banged his fist on it angrily.

'You can come out now. I saw you duck under there.'

Slowly a mane of coppery-blonde hair and the face of a young blue-eyed woman emerged from beneath the desk. She tried to act nonchalantly, but her face was tense.

'Hey there, Chief. I just dropped my pen.'

The veteran newsman reached up and adjusted his wig. The issue of the Editor-in-Chief's baldness was taboo, so it certainly wouldn't help Andrea Otero that she had just witnessed this manoeuvre.

'I'm not happy, Otero. Not happy at all. Can you tell me what the hell's going on?'

'What do you mean, Chief?'

'Do you have fourteen million euros in the bank, Otero?'

'Not the last time I looked.'

In fact, the last time she checked, her five credit cards were seriously overdrawn, thanks to her insane addiction to Hermès bags and Manolo Blahnik shoes. She was thinking of asking the accounts department for an advance on her Christmas bonus. For the next three years.

'You'd better have a rich aunt who's about to pop her clogs, because that's how much you're going to cost me, Otero.'

'Don't get angry with me, Chief. What happened in Holland won't happen again.'

'I'm not talking about your room service bills, Otero. I'm talking about François Dupré,' said the editor, slamming the previous day's newspaper on the desk.

Holy shit, that's what this is about, thought Andrea.

'One day! I take off one lousy day in the last five months, and all of you screw up.'

In an instant the entire newsroom, down to the last reporter, stopped gaping and turned back to their desks, suddenly able to concentrate on their work once more.

'Come on, Chief. Embezzlement is embezzlement.'

'Embezzlement? Is that what you call it?'

'Of course! Transferring a huge amount of money from your clients' accounts into your personal account is definitely embezzlement.'

'And using the front page of the International section to

trumpet a simple mistake made by the principal stockholder in one of our major advertisers is a royal fuck-up, Otero.'

Andrea swallowed, feigning innocence.

'Principal stockholder?'

'Interbank, Otero. Who, in case you didn't know, spent twelve million euros last year on this newspaper and was thinking of spending another fourteen this coming year. *Was* thinking. Past tense.'

'Chief . . . the truth doesn't have a price.'

'Yes, it does: fourteen million euros. And the heads of those responsible. You and Moreno are out of here. Gone.'

The other guilty party walked in dragging his feet. Fernando Moreno was the night editor who had cancelled the harmless story about an oil company's profits and replaced it with Andrea's bombshell. It was a brief attack of courage that he now regretted. Andrea looked at her colleague, a middle-aged man, and thought about his wife and three children. She swallowed again.

'Chief . . . Moreno had nothing to do with it. I'm the one who put in the article just before going to press.'

Moreno's face brightened for a second then returned to its previous expression of remorse.

'Don't fuck around, Otero,' said the Editor-in-Chief. 'That's impossible. You don't have the authorisation to go into blue.'

Hermes, the computer system at the paper, worked on a system of colours. The newspaper pages appeared in red while a reporter was working on them, in green when they went to the managing editor for approval, and then in blue when the night editor passed them to the press for printing.

'I got into the blue system using Moreno's password, Chief,' Andrea lied. 'He had nothing to do with it.'

'Oh yes? And where did you get the password? Can you explain that?'

'He keeps it in the top drawer of his desk. It was easy.'

'Is that right, Moreno?'

'Well ... yes, Chief,' said the night editor, trying hard not to show his relief. 'I'm sorry.'

The Editor-in-Chief of *El Globo* was still not satisfied. He turned so quickly towards Andrea that his wig slid slightly on his bald head.

'Shit, Otero. I was wrong about you. I thought you were just an idiot. Now I realise you're an idiot *and* a troublemaker. I will personally make sure that no one ever hires a sneaky bitch like you again.'

'But, Chief ...' said Andrea, starting to sound desperate.

'Save your breath, Otero. You're fired.'

'I didn't think—'

'You're so fired that I don't see you any more. I don't even hear you.'

The Chief strode away from Andrea's desk.

Looking around the room, Andrea saw nothing but the backs of her fellow reporters' heads. Moreno came and stood next to her.

'Thanks, Andrea.'

'It's all right. It would be crazy for both of us to get fired.'

Moreno shook his head. 'I'm sorry you had to tell him that you broke into the system. Now he's so mad he'll make things really difficult for you out there. You know what happens when he gets on one of his crusades ...'

'Looks like he's already started,' Andrea said, gesturing to the newsroom. 'Suddenly, I'm a leper. Well, it's not as if I was anyone's favourite before this.'

'You're not a bad person, Andrea. In fact, you're quite a

gutsy reporter. But you're a loner and you never worry about the consequences. Anyway, good luck.'

Andrea swore to herself that she wouldn't cry, that she was a strong and independent woman. She gritted her teeth while Security placed her things in a box, and with a great deal of effort was able to keep her promise.

8

ANDREA OTERO'S
APARTMENT

MADRID, SPAIN

Thursday, 6 July 2006. 11:15 p.m.

The thing that Andrea hated the most since Eva had gone for good was the sound of her own keys when she came home and deposited them on the little table next to the door. They made an empty echo in the hallway that, to Andrea, seemed to sum up her life.

When Eva had been there, everything was different. She would run to the door like a little girl, kiss Andrea, and start babbling about the things she'd done or the people she'd met. Andrea, overwhelmed by this whirlwind that prevented her from reaching the sofa, would pray for some peace and quiet.

Her prayers had been answered. Eva had left one morning, three months ago, the same way she had shown up: suddenly. There was no sobbing or tears, no regrets. Andrea had said practically nothing, was even somewhat relieved. She'd have plenty of time for regrets later, when the faint echo of keys broke the silence of her apartment.

She had tried to deal with the emptiness in different ways: leaving the radio on when she left the house, putting the keys back in the pocket of her jeans as soon as she walked in, talking to herself. None of her ruses was able to mask the silence, for it came from within.

Now as she entered the apartment her foot shoved aside her latest attempt at not being lonely: an orange tabby. At the pet shop the cat had seemed cute and loving. It took Andrea almost forty-eight hours to begin hating it. That was fine with her. You could deal with hatred. It was active: you simply hated someone or something. What she couldn't deal with was frustration. You just had to put up with that.

'Hi, LB. They've fired Mummy. What do you think about that?'

Andrea had given him the name LB, short for Little Bastard, after the monster had got into the bathroom and managed to hunt down and rip apart an expensive tube of shampoo. LB did not appear to be impressed with the news that his mistress had been fired.

'You don't care, do you? You should, though,' Andrea said, pulling a can of Whiskas out of the refrigerator and spooning its contents on to a dish in front of LB. 'When there's nothing left for you to eat I'll sell you to Mr Wong's Chinese restaurant on the corner. Then I'll go and order chicken with almonds.'

The idea that he would become part of the menu at a Chinese restaurant didn't curb LB's appetite. The cat had no respect for anything or anybody. He lived in his own world, ill-tempered, apathetic, undisciplined and proud. Andrea hated him.

Because he reminds me so much of myself, she thought.

She looked around, annoyed at what she saw. The book-cases were covered in dust. There were leftovers on the floor, the sink was buried under a mountain of dirty dishes, and the manuscript of a half-finished novel that she had started three years ago was scattered over the bathroom floor.

Fuck. If only I could pay for a cleaning lady by credit card . . .

The only place in the apartment that was neat and orderly was the huge – *thank god* – wardrobe in her bedroom. Andrea was very careful with her clothes. The rest of the apartment looked like a war zone. She believed her messiness had been one of the main reasons for the break-up with Eva. They had been together for two years. The young engineer was a cleaning machine and Andrea had affectionately dubbed her The Romantic Vacuum Cleaner because she loved tidying the apartment to the accompaniment of Barry White.

At this point, as she surveyed the disaster that was her apartment, Andrea had a revelation. She'd clean up the pigsty, sell her clothes on eBay, find a well-paid job, pay off her debts, and make up with Eva. She now had a goal, a mission. Everything would turn out perfectly.

She felt a rush of energy through her body. This lasted precisely four minutes and twenty-seven seconds, the exact time it took her to open a rubbish bag, fling in a quarter of the leftovers on the table along with a few dirty dishes that were beyond salvaging, move haphazardly from one spot to another, then knock over the book she'd been reading the night before so that the photo inside fell to the floor.

The two of them together. The last one they'd taken.

It's useless.

She dropped onto the sofa, sobbing, as the rubbish bag disgorged part of its contents onto the living-room rug. LB came over and nibbled on a slice of pizza. The cheese had started to turn green.

'It's obvious, isn't it, LB? I can't escape the person I am, at least not with a mop and broom.'

The cat didn't pay the least attention but ran over to the apartment entrance and began rubbing itself against the door frame. Andrea stood up mechanically, realising that some-body was about to ring the bell.

What kind of lunatic would come over at this time of night?

She threw the door open, surprising her visitor before he could ring.

'Hey there, beautiful.'

'I guess news travels fast.'

'Bad news does. If you start crying, I'm out of here.'

Andrea stepped aside without rubbing the expression of disgust from her face, but secretly she was relieved. She should have guessed. Enrique Pascual had been her best friend and shoulder to cry on for many years. He worked for one of the big radio stations in Madrid, and every time Andrea stumbled Enrique showed up at her door with a bottle of whisky and a smile. This time he must have thought that she was especially needy because the whisky was twelve years old and to the right of his smile was a bouquet of flowers.

'You had to do it, didn't you? The super-reporter had to fuck with one of the paper's major advertisers,' Enrique said, going down the hall and into the living room without tripping over LB. 'Is there a clean vase in this dump?'

'Let them die and give me the bottle. Who cares! Nothing lasts for ever.'

'Now you've lost me,' Enrique said, ignoring the problem of the flowers for the moment. 'Are we talking about Eva or getting fired?'

'I don't think I know,' Andrea muttered, appearing from the kitchen with a glass in each hand.

'If you'd hooked up with me, maybe things would have been clearer.'

Andrea tried not to laugh. Enrique Pascual was tall, attractive, and ideal for any woman for the first ten days of the relationship, then a nightmare for the next three months.

'If I liked men you'd be in my top twenty. Probably.'

It was now Enrique's turn to laugh. He poured two fingers of whisky neat. He had hardly taken a sip before Andrea had emptied her glass and was reaching for the bottle.

'Take it easy, Andrea. It's not a good idea to end up in Casualty. Again.'

'I think it would be a fucking great idea. At least I'd have somebody to look after me.'

'Thank you for not appreciating my efforts. And don't be so dramatic.'

'You think it's not dramatic losing your lover and your job in the space of two months? My life is shit.'

'I'm not going to argue with you there. At least you're surrounded by what's left of her,' Enrique said, waving disgustedly at the mess in the room.

'Maybe you could become my cleaning lady. I'm sure it would be more useful than that bullshit sports programme you pretend to work on.'

Enrique's expression didn't change. He knew what was coming next and so did Andrea. She buried her head in a cushion and screamed with all her might. After a few seconds her scream turned into sobs.

'I should've brought two bottles.'

Just then a mobile phone rang.

'I think it's yours,' Enrique said.

'Tell whoever it is to go fuck themselves,' Andrea said, her face still buried in the cushion.

Enrique snapped open the phone with an elegant gesture.

'A Torrent of Tears. Hello ...? Hold on a moment ...'

He handed Andrea the phone.

'I think you'd better handle this. I don't speak foreign languages.'

Andrea took the telephone, wiped away her tears with the back of her hand and tried to sound normal.

'Do you know what time it is, you idiot?' Andrea said through gritted teeth.

'I'm sorry. Andrea Otero, please?' said a voice in English.

'Who is it?' she answered in the same language.

'My name is Jacob Russell, Ms Otero. I'm calling from New York on behalf of my boss, Raymond Kayn.'

'Raymond Kayn? Of Kayn Industries?'

'Yes, that's right. And you're the same Andrea Otero who pulled off that controversial interview with President Bush last year?'

Of course, the interview. That interview had had a big impact in Spain and even in the rest of Europe. She had been the first Spanish reporter to get inside the Oval Office. Some of her more direct questions – the few that had not been agreed beforehand and she had managed to sneak in – had made the Texan more than a little nervous. That exclusive interview had relaunched her career at *El Globo*. At least briefly. And it seemed to have rattled some cages on the other side of the Atlantic.

'One and the same, sir,' Andrea replied. 'So tell me, why does Raymond Kayn need an excellent reporter?' she added, sniffing quietly, pleased that the person on the phone couldn't see the state she was in.

Russell cleared his throat. 'Can I count on you not to tell anyone at your paper about this, Ms Otero?'

'Absolutely,' Andrea said, amused at the irony.

'Mr Kayn would like to give you the greatest exclusive of your life.'

'Me? Why me?' Andrea said, making a writing motion to Enrique.

Her friend extracted a notebook and pen from his pocket and handed them to her with a questioning look. Andrea ignored him.

'Let's just say he likes your style,' Russell said.

'Mr Russell, at this point in my life it's hard for me to credit that someone I've never met is calling me up with such a vague and probably unbelievable offer.'

'Well, let me convince you.'

Russell spoke for quarter of an hour, during which the astonished Andrea continuously scribbled down notes. Enrique tried reading over her shoulder, but with Andrea's spidery writing it was no use.

'. . . that's why we're counting on you to be at the site of the excavation, Ms Otero.'

'Will there be an exclusive interview with Mr Kayn?'

'As a general rule, Mr Kayn doesn't give interviews. Never.'

'Maybe Mr Kayn should find a reporter for whom rules matter.'

There was an uncomfortable silence. Andrea crossed her fingers, praying that her shot in the dark would hit its target.

'I suppose there could always be a first time. Do we have a deal?'

Andrea thought about it for a few seconds. If what Russell was promising was really true, she'd be able to get a contract with any media company in the world. And she would send that son of a bitch editor at *El Globo* a copy of the cheque.

Even if Russell's not telling the truth, there's nothing to lose.

She didn't give it another thought.

'You can make a reservation for me on the next flight to Djibouti. First class.'

Andrea hung up.

'I didn't understand a single word except "first class",' Enrique said. 'Can you tell me where you're going?' He was surprised by the obvious change in Andrea's mood.

'If I said the Bahamas, you wouldn't believe me, right?'

'Very nice,' Enrique said, half annoyed and half jealous. 'I bring you flowers, whisky, I scrape you off the floor and this is how you treat me ...'

Pretending she wasn't listening, Andrea went into the bedroom to pack.

9

RELICS CRYPT

VATICAN CITY

Friday, 7 July 2006. 8:29 p.m.

The knock at the door startled Brother Cesáreo. Nobody came down to the crypt, not only because access was restricted to a very few people, but also because it was damp and unhealthy, despite the four dehumidifiers that hummed constantly in each corner of the enormous space. Pleased to have company, the old Dominican friar smiled as he opened the security door, standing on tiptoe to embrace his visitor.

'Anthony!'

The priest smiled and embraced the smaller man.

'I was in the neighbourhood . . .'

'I swear by God, Anthony, how did you manage to get this far? This place has been monitored by cameras and security alarms for some time now.'

'There's always more than one entrance if you take your time and know the way. You taught me, remember?'

The old Dominican massaged his goatee with one hand and patted his large belly with the other, laughing heartily. Under the streets of Rome was a system of more than three hundred miles of tunnels and catacombs, some of them over two hundred feet beneath the city. It was a veritable museum, a maze of winding, unexplored passages that linked almost every part of the city, including the Vatican. Twenty years earlier, Fowler and Brother Cesáreo had dedicated their spare time to exploring those dangerous and intricate tunnels.

'It looks like Cirin will have to revisit his flawless security system. If an old dog like you can slip in here ... But why not use the front door, Anthony? I hear that you're no longer *persona non grata* with the Holy Office. And I'd love to know why.'

'Actually, now I may be a little too *grata* for some people's taste.'

'Cirin wants you back in, doesn't he? Once that low-rent Machiavelli gets his teeth into you, he doesn't let go easily.'

'And old guardians of relics can be stubborn too. Especially when speaking of things they're not supposed to know about.'

'Anthony, Anthony. This crypt is the best kept secret in our tiny country, but its walls echo with rumours.' Cesáreo waved his arms at the surroundings.

Fowler looked up. The ceiling of the crypt, supported by stone arches, was black from the smoke of the millions of candles that had illuminated the space for almost two thousand years. In recent times, however, a modern electrical system had replaced the candles. The rectangular space was roughly two hundred and fifty feet square, part of which had been hewn from the living rock by pickaxe. On the walls, from ceiling to floor, were doors that concealed niches containing the remains of various saints.

'You've spent too much time breathing in this horrible air, and it certainly doesn't help your clients either,' said Fowler. 'Why are you still down here?'

It was a little known fact that for the past seventeen hundred years in every Catholic church, no matter how humble, a relic from a saint had been hidden in the altar. And this site housed the largest collection of such relics in the world. Some of the niches were almost empty, containing only small fragments of bone, while in others the whole skeleton was intact. Each time a church was built anywhere in the world, a young priest would pick up a steel suitcase from Brother Cesáreo and travel to the new church to deposit the relic inside the altar.

The old historian took off his glasses and wiped them with the hem of his white habit.

'Security. Tradition. Stubbornness,' said Cesáreo in answer to Fowler's question. 'The words that define our Holy Mother the Church.'

'Excellent. Besides the damp, this place reeks of cynicism.'

Brother Cesáreo tapped the screen of his powerful MacBook Pro on which he had been writing when his friend arrived.

'Locked in here are my truths, Anthony. Forty years of work cataloguing bone fragments. Have you ever sucked on an ancient bone, my friend? It's an excellent method for determining if a bone is fake, but it leaves a bitter taste in your mouth. After four decades I'm no closer to the truth than when I started.' He sighed.

'Well, maybe you can go into that hard disk and give me a hand, old man,' Fowler said as he handed Cesáreo a photo.

'Always the business at hand, always—'

The Dominican stopped in mid-sentence. For a moment he stared myopically at the photograph, and then went over to the desk where he worked. From a pile of books he pulled out an old volume in classical Hebrew that was covered in pencil marks. He leafed through it, checking various symbols against the book. Startled, he looked up.

'Where did you get this, Anthony?'

'From an ancient candle. A retired Nazi had it.'

'Camilo Cirin sent you to recover it, didn't he? You have to tell me everything. Don't leave out a single detail. I need to know!'

'Let's say I owed Camilo a favour and I agreed to carry out one last mission for the Holy Alliance. He asked me to find an Austrian war criminal who had stolen the candle from a Jewish family in 1943. The candle was covered with layers of gold and the man had had it since the war. A few months ago I caught up with him and retrieved the candle. After melting the wax, I discovered the copper sheet that you see in the photo.'

'Don't you have a better one with a higher resolution? I can barely make out the script on the exterior.'

'It was rolled up too tightly. If I had completely unrolled it, I could have damaged it.'

'It's a good thing you didn't. What you would have ruined is priceless. Where is it now?'

'I turned it over to Cirin and didn't really give it much thought. I figured someone at the Curia wanted it. Then I went back to Boston, convinced that I had repaid my debt—'

'That's not quite true, Anthony,' a calm, unemotional voice interjected. The owner of the voice had managed to slip into the crypt like a master spy, which was exactly what the squat, plain-faced man dressed in grey was. Sparing of word and gesture, he concealed himself behind a wall of chameleon-like insignificance.

'It's bad manners to enter a room without knocking, Cirin,' said Cesáreo.

'It's also bad manners not to respond when summoned,' said the Chief of the Holy Alliance, staring at Fowler.

'I thought we were done. We agreed on a mission – only one.'

'And you've carried out the first part: recovering the candle. Now you have to make sure that what it contains is used correctly.'

Annoyed, Fowler didn't answer.

'Maybe Anthony would appreciate his assignment more if he understood its importance,' Cirin continued. 'As you now know what we're dealing with, Brother Cesáreo, would you be so kind as to tell Anthony what that photo you've never seen depicts?'

The Dominican cleared his throat.

'Before I do so, I need to know if it's authentic, Cirin.'

'It is.'

The friar's eyes lit up. He turned to Fowler.

'This, my friend, is a treasure map. Or to be precise, half of one. That is, if my memory doesn't fail me, because it has been many years since I held the other half in my hands. This is the piece that was missing from the Copper Scroll of Qumran.'

The priest's expression darkened considerably.

'You're telling me—'

'Yes, my friend. The most powerful object in History can be found through the meaning of these symbols. And all the problems that come with it.'

'Good Lord. And it has to show up at this precise moment.'

'I'm glad you finally understand, Anthony,' Cirin broke in. 'Compared with this, all the relics that our good friend keeps in this room are nothing more than dust.'

'Who put you on the trail, Camilo? Why now, after all this time, did you try to find the person from whomever you recovered this?' asked Brother Cesáreo.

'The information came from one of the Church's bene-factors, a Mr Kayn. A benefactor from another faith and a great philanthropist. He needed us to find Dr Graus, and personally offered to finance an archaeological expedition should we could recover the candle.'

'Where to?'

'He hasn't revealed the exact location. But we know the area. Al Mudawwara, Jordan.'

'Great, then there's nothing to worry about,' Fowler inter-rupted. 'Do you know what's going to happen if anyone gets even a sniff of this? Nobody on that expedition will live long enough to lift a shovel.'

'Let's hope you're wrong. We're going to send an observer with the expedition: you.'

Fowler shook his head. 'No.'

'You're aware of the consequences, the ramifications.'

'My answer is still no.'

'You can't refuse.'

'Try stopping me,' said the priest, heading for the door.

'Anthony, my boy.' The words followed him as he walked towards the exit. 'I'm not saying I'm going to try to stop you. You must be the one who decides to go. Luckily, over the years, I've learned how to deal with you. I had to recall the only thing you value more than your freedom, and I found the perfect solution.'

Fowler stopped, still with his back to them.

'What have you done, Camilo?'

Cirin took a few steps towards him. If there was anything he disliked more than talking, it was raising his voice.

'In speaking to Mr Kayn, I suggested the best reporter for his expedition. Actually, as a reporter she's fairly average. And not too pretty, or sharp, or even overly honest. In fact, the only thing that makes her interesting is that once you saved her skin. How do you say it – she owes you her life? So now you won't be making a dash to hide yourself in the nearest soup kitchen, because you know the risk she's running.'

Still Fowler didn't turn around. With each of Cirin's words, his hand had begun closing a little more until it was clenched in a fist, his fingernails digging into his palm. But the pain wasn't enough. He slammed his fist into one of the niches. The impact made the crypt shake. The wooden door of the ancient resting place splintered and a bone from the desecrated vault rolled out onto the floor.

'St Soutiño's kneecap. Poor man, he limped his entire life,' said Brother Cesáreo, bending down to pick up the relic.

Fowler, by now resigned, finally turned to face them.

Excerpt from
Raymond Kayn: The
Unauthorised Biography

BY ROBERT DRISCOLL

Many readers might ask how a Jew without much of a background, who lived off charity during his childhood, managed to create such a vast financial empire. It is clear from the previous pages that prior to December 1943, Raymond Kayn did not exist. There is no record of his birth certificate, no document that confirms he's an American citizen.

The period of his life about which most is known began when he enrolled in MIT and amassed a sizable list of patents. While the United States was embracing the glorious 1960s, Kayn was reinventing the integrated circuit. Within five years he owned his own company; within ten, half of Silicon Valley.

This period was well documented in *Time* magazine, along with the misfortunes that destroyed his life as a father and husband ...

Perhaps what most troubles the average American is his invisibility, this lack of transparency that transforms someone so powerful into a disturbing enigma. Sooner or later, someone must lift the aura of mystery that surrounds the figure of Raymond Kayn ...

ON BOARD THE BEHEMOTH

THE RED SEA

Tuesday, 11 July 2006. 4:29 p.m.

... someone must lift the aura of mystery surrounding the figure of Raymond Kayn ...

Andrea smiled broadly and set aside the biography of Raymond Kayn. It was a lurid, biased piece of shit and she'd been completely bored by it as she flew over the Sahara desert on her way to Djibouti.

During the flight Andrea had had time to do something she rarely did: take a good long look at herself. And she decided that she didn't like what she saw.

As the youngest of five siblings – all male except for her – Andrea had grown up in an environment in which she felt entirely protected. And which was utterly banal. Her father was a police sergeant, her mother a housewife. They lived in a working-class area and ate macaroni most nights, chicken on Sundays. Madrid is a beautiful city, but for Andrea it served only to highlight her family's mediocrity. At fourteen she swore that the minute she turned eighteen she'd be out the door and would never come back.

Of course the arguments with Dad about your sexual orientation sped up your departure, didn't they, honey?

It had been a long journey from the time she left home –

they threw you out – until her first real job, with the exception of the ones she had had to take in order to pay for her Journalism studies. The day she started at *El Globo* she felt as if she had won the lottery, but that euphoria didn't last long. She bounced from one section of the paper to another, each time feeling as if she was falling upwards, losing her sense of perspective as well as control of her personal life. She had ended up in the International section before leaving . . .

They threw you out.

And now this impossible adventure.

My last chance. The way things are going for reporters in the labour market, my next job will be as a supermarket check-out girl. There's just something about me that doesn't function. I can't do anything right. Not even Eva, who was the most patient person in the world, could stand being with me. The day she left . . . What did she call me? 'Recklessly out of control', 'emotionally frigid' . . . I think 'immature' was the nicest thing she said. And she must have meant it, because she didn't even raise her voice. Fuck! It's always the same. I'd better not screw up this time.

Andrea shifted mental gears and turned up the volume on her iPod. The warm voice of Alanis Morissette calmed her spirits. She leaned her seat back, wishing she was already at her destination.

Luckily, First Class had its advantages. The most important one was being able to get off the plane ahead of everyone else. A young, well-dressed black driver was waiting for her next to a clapped-out jeep at the edge of the runway.

Well, well. No Customs, right? Mr Russell has arranged everything, Andrea thought as she descended the staircase from the plane.

'Is that it?' The driver spoke English, pointing to Andrea's carry-on bag and backpack.

'We're heading out to the fucking desert, aren't we? Drive on.'

She recognised the way the driver was looking at her. She was used to being stereotyped: young, fair, and therefore stupid. Andrea wasn't sure if her carefree attitude to clothes and money were her way of burying herself still further in this stereotype, or were simply her own concession to banality. Maybe a mixture of both. But for this trip, as a sign that she'd left her old life behind, she'd kept her baggage to a minimum.

While the jeep travelled the five miles to the ship, Andrea took photos with her Canon 5D. (It wasn't really *her* Canon 5D but the one that belonged to the paper, which she had forgotten to return. *They deserved it, the pigs.*) She was shocked at the extreme poverty of the land. Dry, brown, covered in stones. You could probably cross the entire capital on foot in two hours. There seemed to be no industry, no agriculture, no infrastructure. The dust from the wheels of their jeep coated the faces of the people who stared at them as they sped by. Faces without hope.

'The world's in a bad way if people like Bill Gates and Raymond Kayn earn more in a month than this country's Gross National Product in a year.'

The driver shrugged in response. They were already at the port, the most modern and well-maintained part of the capital, and virtually its only source of income. Djibouti profited from its favourable location within the Horn of Africa.

The jeep swerved to a sudden stop. When Andrea regained her balance, what she saw made her jaw drop. The *Behemoth* was nothing like the ugly freighter she had expected. It was a sleek modern vessel whose enormous hull was painted red and its superstructure a blinding white, the colours of Kayn Industries. Without waiting for the driver to help her, she grabbed her things and ran up the gangplank, wanting to start her adventure as soon as possible.

Half an hour later the ship had raised anchor and was underway. One hour later Andrea confined herself to her cabin, intent on vomiting in private.

After two days, during which the only thing that she could handle was liquids, her inner ear called a truce and she finally felt brave enough to step outside for a little fresh air and to get to know the ship. But first, she decided to toss *Raymond Kayn: The Unauthorised Biography* overboard with all her might.

'You shouldn't have done that.'

Andrea turned from the railing. Walking towards her on the main deck was an attractive, dark-haired woman of about forty. She was dressed like Andrea, in jeans and a T-shirt, but over them she wore a white jacket.

'I know. Pollution is a bad thing. But try being locked up for three days with that crappy book and you'll understand.'

'It would have been less traumatic if you had opened the door for something other than getting water from the crew. I understand that you were offered my services ...'

Andrea fixed her eyes on the book that was already floating far behind the moving ship. She felt ashamed. She didn't like people seeing her when she was sick, and hated feeling vulnerable.

'I was fine,' Andrea said.

'I understand, but I'm sure you would have felt better if you'd taken some Dramamine.'

'Only if you wanted me dead, Dr . . .'

'Harel. You're allergic to dimenhydrinates, Ms Otero?'

'Among other things. Please call me Andrea.'

Dr Harel smiled and a series of wrinkles softened her features. She had beautiful eyes, the shape and colour of almonds, and her hair was dark and curly. She was two inches taller than Andrea.

'And you can call me Dr Harel,' she said, offering her hand.

Andrea looked at the hand without extending hers.

'I don't like snobs.'

'Me neither. I'm not telling you my name because I don't have one. My friends usually call me Doc.'

The reporter finally reached out her hand. The doctor's handshake was warm and pleasant.

'That must break the ice at parties, Doc.'

'You can't imagine. It tends to be the first thing people remark on when I meet them. Let's walk around for a bit and I'll tell you more.'

They headed towards the bow of the ship. A hot wind was blowing towards them, causing the ship's American flag to flutter.

'I was born in Tel Aviv shortly after the end of the Six-Day War,' Harel went on. 'Four members of my family died during the conflict. The rabbi interpreted this as a bad omen, so my parents didn't give me a name, in order to deceive the Angel of Death. They alone knew my name.'

'And did it work?'

'For Jews a name is very important. It defines a person and it has power over that person. My father whispered my name in my ear during my *bat mitzvah* while the congregation was singing. I can never tell anyone else.'

'Or the Angel of Death will find you? No offence, Doc, but

that doesn't make much sense. The Grim Reaper doesn't look you up in the phone book.'

Harel let out a hearty laugh.

'I often come across that kind of attitude. I have to tell you I find it refreshing. But my name will remain a secret.'

Andrea smiled. She liked the woman's easygoing style, and stared at her eyes perhaps a little longer than was necessary or appropriate. Harel looked away, slightly startled by her directness.

'What's a doctor without a name doing on board the *Behemoth*?'

'I'm a substitute, last-minute. They needed a doctor for the expedition. So you're all in my hands.'

Beautiful hands, Andrea thought.

They had reached the bow. The sea slid away below them and the afternoon shone majestic and bright. Andrea looked around.

'When I don't feel as if my guts are in a blender, I have to admit that it's a beautiful ship.'

'*His strength is in his loins, and his force is in the navel of his belly. His bones are as strong pieces of brass; his legs are like bars of iron,*' the doctor recited in a lively voice.

'There are poets among the crew?' Andrea laughed.

'No, dear. It's from the Book of Job. It refers to the huge beast called the Behemoth, Leviathan's brother.'

'Not a bad name for a ship.'

'At one point it was a Danish naval frigate in the *Hvidbjornen* class.' The doctor pointed to a metal plate about ten feet square that had been welded on to the deck. 'That's where the only gun used to be. Kayn Industries bought this ship for ten million dollars in an auction four years ago. A bargain.'

'I wouldn't have paid more than nine and a half.'

'Go ahead and laugh if you like, Andrea, but the deck on this beauty is two hundred and sixty feet long; it has its own heliport and it can sail eight thousand miles at fifteen knots. It could travel from Cadiz to New York and back without refuelling.'

At that moment the ship cut through a formidable swell and the vessel lurched slightly. Andrea slipped and almost went over the railing, which at the bow was only a foot and a half high. The doctor grabbed her by the T-shirt.

'Watch out! If you fell in at this speed you'd either be shredded to pieces by the propellers or drown before we had the chance to rescue you.'

Andrea was about to thank Harel, but then she noticed something in the distance.

'What's that?' she asked.

Harel squinted, holding up a hand to shield her eyes from the glare. At first she saw nothing, but five seconds later she could make out a shape.

'At last we're all here. It's the boss.'

'Who?'

'Didn't they tell you? Mr Kayn is going to supervise the whole operation in person.'

Andrea turned around open-mouthed. 'You are joking?'

Harel shook her head. 'It'll be the first time I've ever met him,' she replied.

'They promised me an interview with him, but I thought that would come at the end of this ridiculous charade.'

'You don't believe the expedition will succeed?'

'Let's say I have my doubts about its real purpose. When Mr Russell recruited me, he said that we were after a very important relic that had been lost for thousands of years. He wouldn't go into the details.'

'We're all in the dark. Look, it's getting closer.'

Andrea could now make out what appeared to be some sort of aircraft about two miles off the port bow. It was approaching fast.

'You're right, Doc, it's an airplane!'

The reporter had to raise her voice above the roar of the aircraft and the sailors' cheers as it swooped in a semicircle around the ship.

'No, it's not a plane – look.'

They turned to follow it. The plane, or at least what Andrea thought was a plane, was a small aircraft, painted with the colours and logo of Kayn Industries but its two propellers were three times the normal size. Andrea watched, amazed, as the propellers began to turn up on the wing and the plane stopped its circling of the *Behemoth*. Suddenly it was hanging in the air. The propellers had made a ninety-degree rotation and, like a helicopter, were now holding the aircraft still as concentric waves fanned out on the sea below it.

'That's the BA-609 TiltRotor. The best in its class. This is its maiden voyage. They say it was one of Mr Kayn's own ideas.'

'Everything this man does seems impressive. I'd like to meet him.'

'No, Andrea, wait!'

The doctor tried to hold Andrea back, but she slipped away into the group of sailors who were leaning over the starboard railing.

Andrea went onto the main deck and down one of the gangways under the superstructure of the ship that connected with the poop deck where the aircraft was now hovering. At the end of the corridor she found her way blocked by a six foot two blond sailor.

'That's as far as you go, Miss.'

'Pardon me?'

'You can have a look at the plane once Mr Kayn is in his cabin.'

'I see. And what if I want to have a look at Mr Kayn?'

'My orders are to let no one go astern. Sorry.'

Andrea turned away without a word. She didn't like being refused, so she now had twice the incentive to fool the guard.

Slipping into one of the hatchways on her right, she entered the main area of the ship. She would have to hurry before they took Kayn below. She could attempt to climb down to the lower deck, but there would surely be another guard posted there. She tried the handles on a few doors, until she found one that was not locked. It was some sort of recreation lounge with a sofa and a dilapidated ping-pong table. At the end was a large open porthole with a view of the stern.

Et voilà.

Andrea put one of her small feet on the corner of the table and the other on the sofa. She put her arms through the porthole, then her head, and slid her body through to the other side. Less than ten feet away, a sailor wearing an orange vest and protective headphones was signalling to the pilot of the BA-609 as the wheels of the aircraft hit the deck with a squeal. Andrea's hair blew about in the wind from the rotor blades. She crouched down instinctively, even though she had sworn countless times that if she ever found herself under a helicopter she wouldn't imitate the characters in films who ducked their heads even though the blades were almost five feet above them.

Of course, it was one thing imagining a situation and another being in it . . .

The door of the BA-609 started to open.

Andrea sensed movement behind her. She was about to turn around when she was thrown to the ground and pinned against the deck. She felt the heat of the metal against her cheek as someone sat on her back. She twisted with all her strength but couldn't free herself. Although she was finding it difficult to breathe, she managed to peer at the aircraft and saw a tanned, handsome young man wearing sunglasses and a sports jacket exit the plane. Behind him came a bull of a man weighing about 220 pounds, or so it seemed to Andrea from the deck. When the brute looked at her she registered no expression in his brown eyes. An ugly scar ran from his left eyebrow to his cheek. Finally there followed a thin, small-ish man, dressed completely in white. The pressure on her head increased and she could barely distinguish this last passenger as he crossed her limited field of vision – all she could see were the shadows of the slowing rotor blades on the deck.

'Let me go, OK? The fucking crazy paranoid is already in his cabin, so get up off my back, damn it.'

'Mr Kayn is neither crazy nor paranoid. I'm afraid he suffers from agoraphobia,' her captor replied in Spanish.

His voice was not that of a sailor. Andrea remembered well that educated, serious tone, so measured and aloof, that had always reminded her of Ed Harris. When the pressure on her back eased, she jumped to her feet.

'You?'

Standing before her was Father Anthony Fowler.

12

OUTSIDE THE OFFICES OF NETCATCH

225 SOMERSET AVENUE, WASHINGTON, DC

Tuesday, 11 July 2006. 11:29 a.m.

The taller of the two men was also the younger, so he was always the one who fetched the coffee and the food, as a sign of respect. His name was Nazim and he was nineteen years old. He had been in Kharouf's group for fifteen months and he was happy, for finally his life had found meaning, a path.

Nazim idolised Kharouf. They had met at the mosque in Clive Cove, New Jersey. It was a place full of 'westerniseds' as Kharouf called them. Nazim enjoyed playing basketball near the mosque, which was where he had got to know his new friend, who was twenty years older than him. Nazim had been flattered that someone so mature, and a college graduate besides, would speak to him.

Now he opened the car door and struggled into the passenger seat, which is not easy when you are six foot two inches tall.

'I only found a burger bar. I got salads and hamburgers.' He gave the bag to Kharouf, who smiled.

'Thanks, Nazim. But I must tell you something, and I don't want you to become angry.'

'What?'

Kharouf took the hamburgers out of their boxes and threw them out of the window.

'Those burger bars add lecithin to their hamburgers and there's a chance they could contain pork. That's not *halal*,' he said, referring to the Islamic restriction on pork. 'I'm sorry. But the salads are fine.'

Nazim was disappointed but at the same time he felt reassured. Kharouf was his mentor. Whenever Nazim made a mistake, Kharouf corrected him respectfully and with a smile, which was the complete opposite to the way Nazim's parents had treated him over the past few months, constantly yelling at him ever since he'd met Kharouf and started attending another mosque that was smaller and more 'committed'.

In the new mosque the imam not only read from the sacred Koran in Arabic, but also preached in that tongue. Despite the fact that Nazim had been born in New Jersey, he read and wrote the prophet's language perfectly. His family was from Egypt. Through the hypnotic preaching of the imam, Nazim began to see the light. He broke away from the life he had been leading. He got good grades and could have begun studying engineering that year, but instead Kharouf found him a job in an accounting firm run by a believer.

His parents disagreed with his decision. They also didn't understand why he locked himself in the bathroom to pray. But as painful as these changes were, they slowly accepted them. Until the incident with Hana.

Nazim's remarks were becoming increasingly aggressive. One evening his sister Hana, who was two years older than him, came in at two in the morning after having drinks with her friends. Nazim was waiting for her and scolded her about the way she was dressed and for being a little drunk. The insults went back and forth. Finally their father stepped in and Nazim pointed his finger at him.

'You're weak. You don't know how to control your women. You let your daughter work. You let her drive and you don't insist that she wear a veil. Her place is in the home until she has a husband.'

Hana started to protest and Nazim slapped her. That was the last straw.

'I may be weak, but at least I am master of this house. Get out! I don't know you. Leave!'

Nazim went to Kharouf's with only the clothes on his back. That night he cried a little, but the tears didn't last. Now he had a new family. Kharouf was both his father and his older brother. Nazim admired him a great deal because Kharouf, who was thirty-nine, was a real jihadist and had been in training camps in Afghanistan and Pakistan. He shared his knowledge with only a handful of young men who, like Nazim, had suffered countless insults. In school, even on the street, people mistrusted him the instant they saw his olive skin and hooked nose and realized he was an Arab. Kharouf told him it was because they feared him, because Christians knew that the Islamic faithful were stronger and more numerous. Nazim liked that. It was time that he commanded proper respect.

Kharouf raised the window on the driver's side.

'Six minutes and then we'll go.'

Nazim gave him a worried look. His friend noticed that something wasn't right.

'What's the matter, Nazim?'

'Nothing.'

'It's never nothing. Come on, you can tell me.'

'It's nothing.'

'Is it fear? Are you afraid?'

'No. I'm a soldier of Allah!'

'Soldiers of Allah are allowed to be afraid, Nazim.'

'Well, I'm not.'

'Is it firing the gun?'

'No!'

'Come on, you've had forty hours of practice at my cousin's slaughterhouse. You must have shot more than a thousand cows.'

Kharouf had also been one of Nazim's shooting instructors and one of the exercises had been firing at live cattle. On other occasions the cows were already dead, but he'd wanted Nazim to get used to firearms and to see what bullets did to flesh.

'No, the practice sessions were good. I'm not afraid of firing at people. I mean, they're not really people.'

Kharouf didn't answer. He leaned on the steering wheel, staring straight ahead and waiting. He knew that the best way to get Nazim to speak up was to allow a few moments of uncomfortable silence. The kid always ended up spilling out whatever was bothering him.

'It's just . . . well, I feel bad about not saying goodbye to my parents,' he said finally.

'I see. You still blame yourself for what happened?'

'A little. Am I wrong?'

Kharouf smiled and placed a hand on Nazim's shoulder.

'No. You're a sensitive and loving young man. Allah gave you those qualities, blessed be his name.'

'Blessed be his name,' Nazim repeated.

'He also gave you the strength to overcome them when you need to. Now take Allah's sword and do his will. Rejoice, Nazim.'

The young man attempted to smile, but the result was more of a grimace. Kharouf increased the pressure on Nazim's shoulder. His voice sounded warm, loving.

'Relax, Nazim. Today Allah is not asking for our blood. He is asking for that of others. But even if something were to happen, you've videotaped a message to your family, haven't you?'

Nazim nodded.

'Then there's nothing to worry about. It could be that your parents have become slightly westernised, but deep in their souls they are good Muslims. They know the reward for a martyr. And when you reach the Next Life, Allah will allow you to intercede for them. Just think how they'll feel.'

Nazim imagined his parents and his sister kneeling in front of him, thanking him for their salvation, begging him to forgive them for being wrong. In the gauzy mist of his fantasy, this was the most beautiful aspect of the next life. He finally managed to smile.

'That's the way, Nazim. Your face has the *bassamat al-farah*, the smile of a martyr. It's part of our promise. Part of our reward.'

Nazim slipped a hand into his jacket and gripped the handle of the gun.

Calmly he and Kharouf got out of the car.

On Board the Behemoth

Tuesday, July 11, 2006. 5:11 p.m.

'You!' Andrea said again, with more anger than surprise.

The last time they'd seen each other, Andrea had been perilously balanced thirty feet above the ground, pursued by an unlikely enemy. Back then Father Fowler had saved her life, but he had also prevented her from getting *the* great story of her career, the kind most reporters only dream about. Woodward and Bernstein had done it with Watergate, and Lowell Bergman with the tobacco industry. Andrea Otero could have done the same, but this priest had got in the way. At least he got her – *I'll be damned if I know how*, Andrea thought – an exclusive interview with President Bush, thanks to which she was now onboard this ship, or so she surmised. But that was water under the bridge and right now she was more concerned with the present. Andrea wasn't going to let this opportunity slip away.

'I'm happy to see you too, Ms Otero. I see that the scar is barely a memory.'

Andrea instinctively touched her forehead, the place where Fowler had caused her to have four stitches sixteen months ago. A thin pale line was all that remained.

'You're a safe pair of hands, but that's not why you're here.

Are you spying on me? Are you aiming to screw up my work again?'

'I'm on this expedition as an observer for the Vatican, nothing more.'

The young reporter eyed him suspiciously. Due to the extreme heat the priest was wearing a short-sleeved shirt with his clerical collar and sharply pressed trousers, all in the usual black. Andrea looked at his tanned arms for the first time. His forearms were huge, with veins as thick as a ballpoint pen.

Those are not the arms of a Bible-basher.

'And why does the Vatican need an observer on an archaeological expedition?'

The priest was about to answer when a cheerful voice interrupted them.

'Great! The two of you have already been introduced?'

Dr Harel appeared at the stern of the ship, flashing her lovely smile. Andrea did not return the courtesy.

'Something like that. Father Fowler was about to explain to me why he was pulling a Brett Favre on me a couple of minutes ago.'

'Ms Otero, Brett Favre is a quarterback – he doesn't do much tackling,' Fowler explained.

'What happened, Father?' Harel asked.

'Ms Otero came back here just as Mr Kayn was getting out of the aircraft. I'm afraid I had to restrain her. I was kind of rough. I'm sorry.'

Harel nodded. 'I understand. You should know that Andrea didn't attend the security session. Don't worry, Father.'

'What do you mean *don't worry?* Has everyone gone totally crazy?'

'Take it easy, Andrea,' the doctor said. 'Unfortunately you've been sick for the last forty-eight hours and you haven't been kept up-to-date. Let me fill you in. Raymond Kayn is agoraphobic.'

'So Father Tackler just told me.'

'Besides being a priest, Father Fowler is also a psychologist. Please interrupt me if I leave something out, Father. Andrea, what do you know about agoraphobia?'

'It's a fear of open places.'

'That's what most people think. In reality, people suffering from this affliction exhibit symptoms that are a lot more complex.'

Fowler cleared his throat.

'The thing that agoraphobics fear most is losing control,' the priest said. 'They're afraid of being alone, of finding themselves in places from which there's no escape, or of meeting new people. That's why they stay at home for long periods of time.'

'What happens when they can't control a situation?' Andrea asked.

'It depends on the situation. Mr Kayn's case is particularly severe. If he finds himself in a difficult situation he may well panic, lose touch with reality, begin to suffer dizziness, tremors and heart palpitations.'

'In other words, he couldn't be a stockbroker,' Andrea said.

'Or a neurosurgeon,' Harel joked. 'But sufferers can lead normal lives. There are famous agoraphobics like Kim Basinger or Woody Allen who've fought the illness for years and come out on top. Mr Kayn himself has created an empire out of nothing. Unfortunately, in the last five years his condition has deteriorated.'

'I wonder what the hell provoked such a sick man to risk coming out of his shell?'

'You've hit the nail on the head, Andrea,' Harel said.

Andrea noticed that the doctor was looking at her in a strange way.

They all remained silent for a few moments and then Fowler resumed the conversation.

'I hope you can forgive my excessive force earlier.'

'Maybe, but you almost took my head off,' Andrea said, rubbing her neck.

Fowler looked at Harel, who nodded.

'You'll understand in time, Ms Otero . . . Were you able to see the men getting off the aircraft?' Harel asked.

'There was a young olive-skinned man,' Andrea replied. 'Then a man of about fifty dressed in black who had a huge scar. And finally a thin man with white hair, who I imagine must be Mr Kayn.'

'The young man is Jacob Russell, Mr Kayn's executive assistant,' Fowler said. 'The man with the scar is Mogens Dekker, chief of security for Kayn Industries. Believe me, if you had come any closer to Kayn, given your usual style, Dekker would have become a bit nervous. And you don't want that to happen.'

A warning signal sounded from bow to stern.

'Here we go, time for the introductory session,' Harel said. 'At last the great mystery will be revealed. Follow me.'

'Where are we going?' Andrea asked as they returned to the main deck via the gangway that the reporter had sneaked through some minutes before.

'The whole expedition team will meet for the first time. They'll explain the role each of us is going to play, and most important . . . what it is we're actually looking for in Jordan.'

'By the way, Doc, what is your specialty?' Andrea asked as they entered the meeting room.

'Combat medicine,' Harel said casually.

14

COHEN FAMILY HIDEOUT

February 1943

Jora Myer was sick with worry. There was an acid sensation at the back of her throat that made her nauseous. She hadn't felt that way since she was fourteen and had escaped the 1906 pogroms in Odessa, Ukraine, with her grandfather hanging on to her arm. She had been lucky at such a young age to find work as a servant to the Cohen family, who owned a factory in Vienna. Josef was the eldest of the children. When the *shadchan*, the marriage broker, eventually found him a nice Jewish wife, Jora went with him to look after their children. Their firstborn, Elan, spent his early years in a pampered and privileged environment. The younger one, Yudel, was another story.

Now the child lay curled up in a ball on his makeshift bed, which consisted of two folded blankets on the floor. Until yesterday he had shared the bed with his brother. Lying there, Yudel seemed small and sad, and without his parents, the stifling space seemed huge.

Poor Yudel. Those twelve square feet had been his entire world practically since birth. The afternoon he was born, the entire family, including Jora, had been at the hospital. None of them had returned to the luxury apartment on Rienstrasse.

It was 9 November 1938, the date the world would later come to know as Kristallnacht, the Night of Broken Glass. Yudel's grandparents were the first to perish. The entire building on Rienstrasse burned to the ground, together with the synagogue next door as the firemen drank and laughed. The only things that the Cohens had taken with them were some clothes and a mysterious package that Yudel's father used in a ceremony when the baby was born. Jora didn't know what it was, because during the ceremony, Mr Cohen had asked everyone to leave the room, including Odile, who could barely stand up.

With scarcely any money, Josef was unable to leave the country, but like many others, he believed that the trouble would eventually die down so he sought refuge with some of his Catholic friends. He did not forget about Jora either, something that, in later life, Miss Myer would never forget. Few friendships could withstand the terrible obstacles faced in occupied Austria; there was one, however, that did. The ageing Judge Rath decided to help the Cohens at great risk to his own life. Inside his house he built a hideout in one of the rooms. With his own hands he laid a brick partition, leaving a narrow hole at the base that the family could use to get in and out. Judge Rath then placed a low bookcase in front of the opening to conceal it.

The Cohen family entered their living tomb one December night in 1938, believing that the war would last only a few weeks. There wasn't enough room for all of them to lie down at the same time, and their only comforts were a kerosene lamp and a bucket. Food and fresh air came at one in the morning, two hours after the judge's maid went home. At about half past midnight the old judge would slowly begin to push the bookcase away from the hole. Because of his age, it could take almost half an hour, with frequent rests, before the opening was sufficiently wide to allow the Cohens through.

Together with the Cohen family the judge was also a prisoner of that life. He knew that the maid's husband was a member of the Nazi party, so while he was constructing the hideout, he sent her on holiday to Salzburg for a few days. When she returned he told her that they had had to replace the gas pipes. He didn't dare find another maid because it would have made people suspicious, and he had to be careful about the amount of food he bought. With rationing it became even more difficult to feed an extra five people. Jora felt pity for him since he had sold most of his valuable possessions to buy black market meat and potatoes which he hid in the attic. At night, when Jora and the Cohens came out of their hiding place, barefoot, looking like strange whispering ghosts, the old man would bring down the food from the attic for them.

The Cohens didn't dare stay outside their hiding place for more than a few hours. While Jora made sure that the children washed and moved around a little, Josef and Odile would talk quietly with the judge. During the day they couldn't make the slightest noise and mostly spent their time sleeping or in a state of semi-consciousness, which to Jora was like torture until she began hearing about the concentration camps at Treblinka, Dachau, and Auschwitz. The smallest details of daily life became complicated. Basic needs, drinking or even changing the baby Yudel, were tedious procedures in such a restricted space. Jora was continually amazed by Odile Cohen's ability to communicate. She had developed a complex system of signs that allowed her to carry out long and sometimes bitter conversations with her husband without uttering a word.

Over three years went by in silence. Yudel didn't learn any more than four or five words. Luckily he had a calm disposition and hardly ever cried. He seemed to prefer being held by Jora rather than his mother, but this didn't bother Odile. Odile appeared to care only for Elan, who was suffering the most from being locked up. He had been an unruly, spoiled five-year-old when the November 1938 pogroms exploded and after more than a thousand days in hiding, there was something lost, almost crazy, about his eyes. When it was time to return to the hideout he was always the last to go in. Often he refused, or would remain clinging to the entrance. When that happened, Yudel would go over and take his hand, encouraging Elan to make the sacrifice once more and return to the long hours of darkness.

But six nights ago, Elan couldn't take it any more. He waited until everyone else had gone back into the hole, then slipped away and out of the house. The judge's arthritic fingers only managed to brush the boy's shirt before he disappeared. Josef tried to follow him, but by the time he was out on the street there was no trace of Elan.

The news came three days later in the *Kronen Zeitung*. A young mentally disabled Jewish boy, apparently without family, had been placed in the Kinderspital Am Spiegelgrund. The judge was horrified. When he explained, the words catching in his throat, what would probably happen to their son, Odile became hysterical and refused to listen to reason. Jora felt faint the moment she saw Odile go out the door, carrying that same package they had brought to their hideout, the one they had taken to the hospital years before when Yudel was born. Odile's husband accompanied her, despite her protests, but as he left he handed Jora an envelope.

'For Yudel,' he said. 'He shouldn't open it before his *bar mitzvah*.'

Two terrible nights had passed since then. Jora was anxious for news, but the judge was more silent than usual. The day before, the house had been filled with strange sounds. And then, for the first time in three years, the bookcase began to move in the middle of the day and the judge's face appeared in the entrance hole.

'Quick, come out. We haven't a second to waste!'

Jora blinked. It was difficult to recognise the brightness outside the hideout as sunshine. Yudel had never seen the sun. Frightened, he ducked back in.

'Jora, I'm sorry. Yesterday I found out that Josef and Odile have been arrested. I didn't say anything because I didn't want to upset you further. But you can't stay here. They're going to question them, and no matter how much the Cohens resist, the Nazis will eventually find out where Yudel is.'

'Frau Cohen won't say anything. She's strong.'

The judge shook his head.

'They'll promise to save Elan's life in exchange for revealing where the little one is, or worse. They can always make people talk.'

Jora began to cry.

'There's no time for that, Jora. When Josef and Odile didn't return, I went to see a friend at the Bulgarian embassy. I have two exit visas in the names of Bilyana Bogomil, tutor, and Mikhail Zhivkov, son of a Bulgarian diplomat. The story is that you're returning to school with the boy after spending the Christmas holidays with his parents.' He showed her the rectangular tickets. 'These are train tickets to Stara Zagora. But you won't go there.'

'I don't understand,' Jora said.

'Stara Zagora is your official destination, but you'll get off at Cernavoda. The train stops there for a short while. You'll get out so that the boy can stretch his legs. You'll leave the train with a smile on your face. You won't carry any luggage or have anything in your hands. As soon as you can, disappear. Constanta is thirty-seven miles to the east. You'll either have to walk or find someone willing to take you there by cart.'

'Constanta,' Jora repeated, trying to remember everything in her confusion.

'It was Romania before. Now it's Bulgaria. Tomorrow, who knows? The important thing is that it's a port and the Nazis don't watch it too carefully. From there you can take a ship to Istanbul. And from Istanbul you can go anywhere.'

'But we don't have any money for a ticket.'

'Here are some marks for the trip. And in this envelope there's enough to book passage for the two of you to some-where safe.'

Jora looked around. There was hardly any furniture left in the house. Suddenly she understood what the strange noises the day before had been. The old man had hocked almost everything he owned to give them a chance of escaping.

'How can we ever thank you, Judge Rath?'

'Don't. Your trip will be very dangerous and I'm not sure that the exit visas will protect you. God forgive me, but I hope I'm not sending you to your death.'

Two hours later Jora had managed to drag Yudel to the building's stairway. She was about to go outside when she heard a truck halting on the pavement. Everyone who lived under the Nazis knew exactly what that meant. The whole thing was like a bad melody, beginning with a screech of brakes, followed by someone shouting orders and the dull staccato of boots on snow, which became more precise as the boots hit wooden floors. At that point you prayed for the sounds to fade away; instead there was an ominous crescendo culminating in knocks at a door. After a pause, a chorus of weeping would ensue, punctuated by machine-gun solos. And when the music was over, the lights went on again, people returned to their tables, and mothers would smile and make believe that nothing had happened next door.

Jora, who knew the tune well, hid under the stairs the moment she heard the first notes. While his colleagues broke down Rath's door, a soldier wielding a flashlight paced nervously back and forth at the main entrance. The torch's beam cut through the darkness, barely missing Jora's worn grey shoe. Yudel grabbed her with such animal fear that Jora had to bite her lip in order not to cry out in pain. The soldier came so close to them that they could smell his leather coat and the cold metal and oil of the gun.

A loud shot rumbled down the stairwell. The soldier interrupted his search and rushed upstairs to his companions who were yelling. Jora lifted Yudel in her arms and went out into the street, walking slowly.

15

ON BOARD THE BEHEMOTH

EN ROUTE TO THE GULF OF AQABA, RED SEA

Tuesday, 11 July 2006. 6:03 p.m.

The room was dominated by a large rectangular table set with twenty neatly placed folders. Most of the seats in front of the folders were taken. Harel, Fowler and Andrea were the last ones in and had to sit in the spaces that were left. Andrea ended up between a young African–American woman dressed in some sort of paramilitary uniform and an older man, balding, with a bushy moustache. The young woman ignored her and went on talking to the companions to her left, who were dressed more or less as she was, while the man to Andrea's right offered his hand, with its thick, coarse fingers.

'Tommy Eichberg, driver. You must be Ms Otero.'

'Another person who knows me! It's a pleasure to meet you.'

Eichberg smiled. He had a round, pleasant face.

'I hope you're feeling better.'

Andrea was about to answer but was interrupted by the loud, unpleasant sound of someone clearing his throat. An old man, well over seventy, had just entered the room. His eyes were almost buried in a nest of wrinkles, an impression that was accentuated by the tiny lenses of his glasses. His head was shaved and he had a huge greying beard that seemed to float around his mouth like a cloud of ash. He wore a short-sleeved shirt, khaki trousers and thick black boots. He began to speak, his voice as sharp and unpleasant as a knife scraping teeth, before he reached the head of the table where a portable electronic screen had been placed. Beside it sat Kayn's assistant.

'Ladies and gentlemen, my name is Cecyl Forrester and I'm Professor of Biblical Archaeology at the University of Massachusetts. It's not the Sorbonne, but at least it's a home.'

There was some polite laughter among the professor's assistants, who had heard the joke a thousand times.

'No doubt you have been trying to figure out the reason for this trip ever since you set foot on this ship. I hope you were not tempted to do so beforehand, given that your, or should I say *our*, contracts with Kayn Enterprises require absolute secrecy from the moment they were signed until our heirs rejoice at our death. Unfortunately the terms of my contract also require that I let you in on the secret, which I plan on doing over the course of the next hour and a half. Do not interrupt me unless you have an intelligent question. Since Mr Russell has informed me of your particulars, I am familiar with every detail, from your IQ to your favourite brand of condom. As for Mr Dekker's crew, don't even bother opening your mouths.'

Andrea, who was partially turned towards the professor, heard a threatening whisper from the people in uniform.

'That son of a bitch thinks he's smarter than everyone else. Maybe I'll make him swallow his teeth one at a time.'

'Silence.'

The voice was soft but it had an undertone that was so violent it made Andrea shudder. She turned her head enough to see that the voice belonged to Mogens Dekker, the man with the scar, who was leaning his chair against a bulkhead. The soldiers immediately went quiet.

'Good. Well, now that we're all in one place,' Cecyl Forrester went on, 'I'd better do the introductions. The twenty-three of us have been brought together for what will be the greatest discovery of all time, and each of you is going to play a part in it. You already know Mr Russell to my right. He's the one who selected you.'

Kayn's assistant nodded his head in greeting.

'To his right is Father Anthony Fowler, who will act as the Vatican's observer on the expedition. Beside him are Nuri Zayit and Rani Peterke, cook and assistant cook. Then Robert Frick and Brian Hanley, administration.'

The two cooks were older men. Zayit was skinny, aged around sixty, with a down-turned mouth, while his helper was heavy-set and a few years younger. Andrea couldn't quite tell his age. The two administrators, on the other hand, were both young and almost as dark as Peterke.

'Besides these overpaid workers, we have my idle and syco-phantic assistants. They all have degrees from expensive colleges and think they know more than me: David Pappas, Gordon Durwin, Kyra Larsen, Stowe Erling and Ezra Levine.

The young archaeologists shifted uncomfortably in their chairs and tried to look professional. Andrea felt sorry for them. They must have been in their early thirties, but Forrester had them on a short leash, which made them seem even younger and more insecure than they actually were – which was the complete opposite of the people in uniform seated next to the reporter.

'At the other end of the table we have Mr Dekker and his bulldogs: the Gottlieb twins, Alois and Alryk; Tewi Waaka,

Paco Torres, Marla Jackson and Louis Maloney. They'll be in charge of security, adding a high-calibre component to our expedition. The irony of the phrase is devastating, don't you think?'

The soldiers didn't react, but Dekker righted his chair and leaned across the table.

'We're going into the frontier zone of an Islamic country. Given the nature of our ... mission, the locals could become violent. I'm sure Professor Forrester will appreciate the calibre of our defence if it comes to that.' He spoke with a strong South African accent.

Forrester opened his mouth to respond, but something on Dekker's face must have convinced him that now wasn't the time for any more acid retorts.

'Further to the right you have Andrea Otero, our official reporter. I'm asking you to cooperate with her if and when she requests any information or interviews so that she will be able to tell our story to the world.'

Andrea flashed a smile around the table, which some people returned.

'The man with the moustache is Tommy Eichberg, our head driver. And lastly, on the right, Doc Harel, our official quack.'

'Don't worry if you can't remember everyone's name,' said the doctor, raising her hand. 'We're going to spend a fair amount of time together in a place that's not renowned for its entertainment, so we'll get to know each other pretty well. Don't forget to carry the ID badge the crew left in your cabins—'

'As far as I'm concerned, it doesn't matter if you know everyone's name as long as you do your job,' the old professor interrupted. 'Now, if you would all turn your attention to the screen, I'm going to tell you a story.'

The screen lit up with computer-generated images of an ancient city. Above a valley rose a settlement of red walls and tiled roofs, surrounded by a triple outer wall. The streets were full of people going about their daily routines. Andrea was amazed by the quality of the images, worthy of a Hollywood production, but the voice narrating the documentary was that of the professor. *This guy's got such a huge ego he can't even hear how lousy his voice sounds*, she thought. *He's giving me a headache.* The voiceover began:

Welcome to Jerusalem. It is April in the year AD 70. The city is in its fourth year of occupation by rebel zealots, who have expelled the original inhabitants. The Romans, officially the rulers of Israel, can no longer tolerate the situation and Rome charges Titus to administer a decisive punishment.

The peaceful scene of women filling their water vessels and children playing beside the outer walls near the wells was interrupted as distant banners crowned by eagles appeared on the horizon. Trumpets sounded and the children, suddenly frightened, ran back inside the walls.

Within a few hours the city is surrounded by four Roman legions. This is the fourth attack on the city. Its citizens have repelled the previous three. This time Titus uses a cunning trick. He allows the pilgrims entering Jerusalem for the Easter celebrations to cross the line of battle. After the festivities, the circle is closed, and Titus does not allow the pilgrims to leave. The city now contains twice as many people and its food and water supplies are quickly being depleted. The Roman legions launch an attack from the northern side of the city and knock down the third wall. It is now the middle of May, and the fall of the city is only a matter of time.

The screen displayed a battering ram destroying the outer wall. From the city's highest hill, temple priests witnessed the scene with tears in their eyes.

The city eventually falls in September, and Titus fulfils the promise he made to his father, Vespasian. The majority of the city's inhabitants are executed or dispersed. Their homes are looted and their temple destroyed.

Surrounded by corpses, a group of Roman soldiers carried a gigantic *menorah* out of the burning temple while their general looked on from his horse, smiling.

The second temple of Solomon was burned to its foundations, and remains thus to this day. Many of the temple's treasures were stolen. Many, but not all. After the fall of the third wall in May, a priest by the name of Yirməyáhu had come up with a plan to save at least part of the treasure. He chose a group of twenty brave men, giving packages to the first twelve with precise instructions on where the items should be taken and what should be done with them. These packages contained the temple's more 'conventional' treasures: large amounts of gold and silver.

An old priest with a white beard and dressed in a black robe was talking with two young men as others waited their turn in a large stone cave lit by torches.

Yirməyáhu entrusted the last eight men with a very special mission, ten times more dangerous than that of the others.

Holding a torch, the priest led the eight men, who were carrying a large object with the aid of a litter, through a network of tunnels.

Using the secret passages under the temple, Yirməyáhu led them beyond the walls and away from the Roman army. Although that area, at the rear of the 10th Fretensis Legion, was patrolled from time to time by Roman guards, the priest's men managed to elude them, reaching Yəriho, the modern-day Jericho, with their heavy load the following day. And there the trail disappears for good.

The professor pressed a button and the screen went dark. He turned to the audience, who were waiting expectantly.

'What those men did was quite incredible. They travelled fourteen miles carrying an enormous load in roughly nine hours. And that was only the beginning of their trip.'

'What were they carrying, Professor?' Andrea asked.

'I suppose it was the most valuable piece of treasure,' Harel said.

'All in good time, my dears. Yirməyáhu went back inside the city and spent the next two days writing a very special manuscript on an even more unusual scroll. It was a detailed map with instructions on how to recover the different portions of the treasure that had been salvaged from the temple ... but he couldn't manage the work alone. It was a verbal map, etched into the surface of a copper scroll almost ten feet long.'

'Why copper?' asked someone at the back.

'Unlike papyrus or parchment, copper is extremely durable. It is also very difficult to write on. It took five people to complete the inscription in a single session, at times taking turns. When they had finished, Yirməyáhu divided the document into two parts, giving the first to a messenger with instructions for its safekeeping at a community of Yisseyites who lived near Jericho. The other part he gave to his own son, one of the *kohanim*, a priest like himself. We know this much of the story firsthand because Yirməyáhu wrote it down in its entirety on the copper manuscript. After that, all trace of it was lost for 1,882 years.'

The old man paused to take a sip of water. For a moment he no longer looked like a wrinkled, pompous puppet but seemed more human.

'Ladies and gentlemen, you now know more of this story than most of the experts in the world. Nobody has figured out exactly how the manuscript was written. Nevertheless, it became quite famous when one part of it surfaced in 1952 in a cave in Palestine. It was among the 85,000 or so fragments of text that have been found in Qumran.'

'Is this the famous Copper Scroll of Qumran?' Dr Harel asked.

The archaeologist once again turned on the screen, which now displayed an image of the famous scroll: a curved plate of dark green metal covered in barely legible writing.

'That is how it is referred to. Researchers were immediately struck by the unusual nature of the discovery, as much by the odd choice of writing material as by the inscriptions themselves – none of which could be properly deciphered. What remained clear from the start was that it was a list of treasure containing sixty-four items. The entries gave an idea of what would be found and where. For example, "At the bottom of the cave that is forty paces to the east of Achor Tower, dig three feet. There you will find six bars of gold." But the directions were vague and the quantities described seemed so unreal – something like two hundred tons of gold and silver – that the "serious" researchers thought it had to be some kind of myth, a hoax or a joke.'

'It seems a lot of effort for a joke,' said Tommy Eichberg.

'Exactly! Excellent, Mr Eichberg, excellent, especially for a driver,' said Forrester, who seemed incapable of paying the slightest compliment without an accompanying insult. 'In AD 70 there were no hardware stores. An enormous plate of ninety-nine per cent pure copper must have cost a great deal. Nobody would have chosen to write a piece of fiction on such a precious surface. There was a ray of hope. Item Number sixty-four was, according to the Qumran Scroll, "a text such as this, with instructions and a code for finding the objects described".'

One of the soldiers raised his hand.

'So this old guy, this Yermijacko …'

'Yirməyáhu.'

'Whatever. The old guy cut the thing in two, and each part held the key to finding the other?'

'And both had to be together in order to find the treasure. Without the second scroll there was no hope of figuring things out. But eight months ago, something happened …'

'I'm sure your audience would prefer the shorter version, Professor,' said Father Fowler with a smile.

The old archaeologist stared at Fowler for a few seconds. Andrea noticed that the professor seemed to be finding it difficult to continue and asked herself what on earth had happened between the two men.

'Yes, of course. Well, suffice it to say that the second half of the scroll finally turned up, thanks to the efforts of the Vatican. It had been handed down from father to son as a sacred object. The duty of the family was to keep it safe until the appropriate time. What they did was hide it in a candle, but eventually even they lost track of what was inside.'

'That doesn't surprise me. It was – how many? – seventy, eighty generations? It's a miracle they continued the tradition of protecting the candle all that time,' said someone sitting in front of Andrea. It was the administrator, Brian Hanley, she thought.

'We Jews are a patient people,' said Tommy Eichberg. 'We've been waiting for the Messiah for three thousand years.'

'And you're going to be waiting another three thousand,' said one of Dekker's soldiers. Loud bursts of laughter and slapping of hands accompanied the distasteful joke. But nobody else laughed. Because of the names, Andrea guessed that, with the exception of the hired guards, nearly all the members of the expedition were from a Jewish background. She could feel the tension in the room mounting.

'Let's continue,' said Forrester, ignoring the soldiers' ridicule. 'Yes, it was a miracle. Have a look at it.'

One of the assistants brought over a wooden case about three feet long. Inside it, under protective glass, was a copper plate covered in Hebrew symbols. Everyone, including the soldiers, stared at the object and began commenting on it in low voices.

'It looks almost new.'

'Yes, the Copper Scroll of Qumran must be older. It's not shiny and it's cut into small strips.'

'The Qumran Scroll appears to be more ancient because it was exposed to the air,' the professor explained, 'and it was cut into strips because the researchers couldn't find any other way of opening it to read the contents. The second scroll was protected from oxidation by the wax covering it. That's why the writing is as clear as the day it was written. Our own map of the treasure.'

'So you've managed to decipher it?'

'Once we had the second scroll, figuring out what the first one said was child's play. What wasn't easy was keeping the discovery quiet. Please don't ask me details of the actual process because I'm not authorised to reveal any more, and besides, you wouldn't understand it.'

'So we're going in search of a pile of gold? Isn't that a little trite for such a pretentious expedition? Or for someone who's got money coming out of his ears like Mr Kayn?' asked Andrea.

'Ms Otero, we're not looking for a pile of gold. As a matter of fact, we've already discovered some.'

The old archaeologist signalled to one of his assistants, who spread a piece of black felt on the table and, with some effort, lifted a resplendent object onto it. It was the largest bar of gold Andrea had ever seen: the size of a man's forearm but roughly shaped, it had probably been formed in some millennial foundry. Although its surface was studded with small craters, mounds and imperfections, it was very beautiful. Every eye in the room was glued to the object, and there were whistles of admiration.

'Using the clues from the second scroll we discovered one of the hiding places described in the Copper Scroll of Qumran. That was in March this year, somewhere on the West Bank. There were six bars of gold like this one.'

'How much is it worth?'

'Around three hundred thousand dollars . . .'

The whistles turned into exclamations.

'... but believe me, that's nothing compared to the value of what we're looking for: the most powerful object in the history of mankind.'

Forrester made a gesture and one of the assistants took the bar away, but left the black felt. The archaeologist took out a sheet of graph paper from a file and placed it where the gold bar had lain. Everyone leaned forward, intent on seeing what it was. They all recognised the object sketched on it immediately.

'Ladies and gentlemen, you are the twenty-three people who have been chosen to recover the Ark of the Covenant.'

16

ABOARD THE BEHEMOTH

RED SEA

Tuesday, 11 July 2007. 7:17 p.m.

A ripple of amazement spread through the room. Everyone began to talk excitedly, and then badgered the archaeologist with questions.

'Where is the Ark?'

'What's inside it . . .?'

'How can we help . . .?'

Andrea was shocked by the assistants' reactions as well as by her own. Those words, the Ark of the Covenant, had a magical ring that enhanced the archaeological importance of discovering an object over two thousand years old.

Not even an interview with Kayn could top this. Russell was right. If we find the Ark, it'll be the scoop of the century. Proof of the existence of God . . .

Her breathing quickened. Suddenly she had hundreds of questions for Forrester, but she knew straight away that it would be pointless to ask. The old man had taken them to this point and now he was going to leave them there, begging for more.

A great way to get us to cooperate.

As if confirming Andrea's theory, Forrester was looking at

the group like the cat that had swallowed the canary. He gestured for them to be quiet.

'That's enough for today. I don't want to give you any more than your brains can assimilate. We'll let you know the rest when it's time. For now, I'm going to turn things over to—'

'One last thing, Professor,' Andrea interrupted him. 'You said there were twenty-three of us but I count only twenty-two. Who's missing?'

Forrester turned and consulted with Russell, who nodded that he could go ahead.

'Number twenty-three on the expedition is Mr Raymond Kayn.'

All conversation stopped.

'What the hell does that mean?' one of the hired soldiers asked.

'It means that the boss is going on the expedition. As all of you know, he came on board a few hours ago and he'll be travelling with us. Does that seem strange to you, Mr Torres?'

'Jesus Christ, everybody says the old man's crazy,' Torres replied. 'It's hard enough protecting the sane ones, but the *locos* ...'

Torres appeared to be from South America. He was short, thin, dark-skinned, and spoke English with a strong Latino accent.

'Torres,' said a voice behind him.

The soldier shrank back in his chair, but didn't turn around. Dekker was obviously going to make sure his man didn't continue to stick his foot in his mouth.

In the meantime Forrester had sat down and Jacob Russell had taken the floor. Andrea noticed there wasn't a single wrinkle on his white jacket.

'Good afternoon, everyone. I want to thank Professor Cecyl

Forrester for his moving presentation. And on behalf of myself and Kayn Industries, I want to express my gratitude to all of you for being present. I don't have much to add, except for two very important points. First, from this moment on, all communication with the outside world is strictly forbidden. This includes mobile phones, e-mail and verbal communication. Until we've accomplished our mission, this is your universe. You will understand in time why this measure is necessary to safeguard both the success of such a sensitive mission and our own security.'

There were a few whispered complaints, but they were half-hearted. Everyone already knew what Russell had told them because it had been specified in the lengthy contract each one had signed.

'The second point is a great deal more unpleasant. A security consultancy has given us a report, not yet confirmed, that an Islamic terrorist group knows about our mission and is planning an attack.'

'What ...?'

'... must be a hoax ...'

'... dangerous ...'

Kayn's assistant raised his arms to calm everyone down. He was evidently prepared for the avalanche of questions.

'Don't be alarmed. I just want you to be alert and not to run any unnecessary risks, much less tell anyone outside this group about our final destination. I don't know how the leak could have happened but, believe me, we're looking into it and will take appropriate action.'

'Could it have come from inside the Jordanian government?' Andrea asked. 'A group like ours is bound to attract attention.'

'As far as the Jordanian government is concerned, we're

a commercial expedition doing a preparatory study for a phosphates mine in the Al Mudawwara area of Jordan, close to the Saudi border. None of you will go through Customs, so don't worry about your cover.'

'I'm not worried about my cover, I'm worried about the terrorists,' said Kyra Larsen, one of Professor Forrester's assistants.

'You needn't worry about them as long as we're here to protect you,' flirted one of the soldiers.

'The report isn't confirmed, it's only a rumour. And rumours can't harm you,' said Russell with a broad smile.

But confirmations can, thought Andrea.

The meeting was over a few minutes later. Russell, Dekker, Forrester and some of the others went to their cabins. At the door of the meeting room were two carts with sandwiches and drinks that some crew member had discreetly left there. Evidently, the expedition members were already being isolated from the crew.

Those who stayed behind in the room talked animatedly about the new information as they attacked the food. Andrea spoke at length with Dr Harel and Tommy Eichberg while she wolfed down roast beef sandwiches and a couple of beers.

'I'm glad your appetite is back, Andrea.'

'Thanks, Doc. Unfortunately, after each meal my lungs scream for nicotine.'

'You'll have to smoke on deck,' said Tommy Eichberg. 'Smoking inside the *Behemoth* is prohibited. As you know . . .'

'Mr Kayn's orders,' all three chimed together, laughing.

'Yes, yes, I know. Don't worry. I'll be back in five minutes. I want to see if there's anything stronger than beer on that cart.'

17

ABOARD THE BEHEMOTH

RED SEA

Tuesday, 11 July 2006. 9:41 p.m.

On deck it was already dark. Andrea emerged from the passageway and walked slowly towards the front of the ship. She could have kicked herself for not wearing a sweater. The temperature had dropped quite a bit and a cold wind was blowing her hair around and making her shiver.

She took a wrinkled pack of Camel cigarettes from one pocket of her jeans and a red lighter from another. It was nothing fancy, just a refillable one with flowers stamped on it, and had probably cost no more than seven euros in some department store, but it had been her first gift from Eva.

Due to the wind, it took her ten attempts before she lit her cigarette. But once she had succeeded it was heavenly. Since she had boarded the *Behemoth* she had found it almost impossible to smoke because of her seasickness, and not through lack of trying.

As she relished the sound of the bow cutting through the water, the young reporter searched her mind for anything she could remember about the Dead Sea Scrolls and the Copper Scroll of Qumran. There wasn't much. Fortunately Professor Forrester's assistants had promised to give her a crash course so that she could write more clearly about the importance of the discovery.

Andrea couldn't believe her luck. The expedition was much better than she had imagined. Even if they didn't succeed in finding the Ark, and Andrea felt certain they never would, her report on the second Copper Scroll and the discovery of part of the treasure would be enough to sell an article to any newspaper in the world.

The most sensible thing would be to find an agent to sell the entire story. I wonder if it would be better to sell it as an exclusive to one of the giants like National Geographic *or the* New York Times, *or to make a lot of sales to smaller outlets. I'm sure that kind of money would release me from all my credit card debt,* Andrea thought.

She took a last pull on her cigarette and went to the railing to throw it overboard. She trod carefully, recalling the incident that afternoon with low railing. As she raised her arm to toss the butt she saw a fleeting image of Dr Harel's face reminding her that it was a bad thing to pollute the environment.

Wow, Andrea. There's hope, even for someone like you. Imagine, doing the right thing when no one's looking, she thought as she stubbed out the cigarette against the wall and put the butt in the back pocket of her jeans.

At that moment she felt someone grabbing her around the ankles and the world turned upside down. Her hands pawed the air trying to grab onto something, but with no success.

As she fell, she thought she could see a dark figure watching her from the railing.

A second later her body hit the water.

18

THE RED SEA

Tuesday, 11 July 2006. 9:43 p.m.

The first thing that Andrea felt was the cold water knifing through her extremities. She thrashed her arms around, trying to get back to the surface. It took her two seconds to realise that she didn't know which way was up. The little air that she had in her lungs was running out. She let her breath out slowly to see which direction the bubbles travelled in, but in the total darkness it was useless. She was losing strength and her lungs were desperate for air. She knew that if she inhaled water she was dead. She gritted her teeth, swore not to open her mouth and tried to think.

Fuck. It can't be, not like this. It can't end like this.

She moved her arms again, trusting that she was swimming towards the surface, when she felt something powerful pulling at her.

Suddenly her face was in the air again and she gasped. Someone was holding her up by the shoulder. Andrea tried to turn.

'Easy does it! Breathe slowly!' Father Fowler was yelling in her ear, trying to make himself heard above the roar of the ship's propellers. Andrea was shocked to see how the force of the water was dragging them closer to the back of the ship. 'Listen to me! Don't turn yet or we'll both die. Relax. Take off your shoes. Move your legs slowly. In fifteen seconds we'll be in dead water from the ship's wake. Then I'll let you go. Swim away as hard as you can!'

Andrea used her feet to slip off her shoes, all the while staring at the churning grey foam that could suck them to their deaths. They were barely forty feet from the propellers. She suppressed the impulse to break loose from Fowler and move in the opposite direction. Her eardrums were ringing, and the fifteen seconds seemed like forever.

'Now!' Fowler screamed.

Andrea felt the suction stop. She swam in the opposite direction to the propellers, away from their infernal drone. It was almost two minutes later when the priest, who had followed her closely, grabbed her arm.

'We made it.'

The young reporter turned her eyes towards the ship. It was now quite far away and she could only see one of its sides, which was illuminated by several searchlights aimed at the water. They had started hunting for them.

'Fuck,' Andrea said, as she struggled to stay afloat. Fowler grabbed her before she went completely under.

'Relax. Let me hold you up like I did before.'

'Fuck,' Andrea repeated, spitting out saltwater while the priest supported her from behind in the standard rescue position.

Suddenly a bright light blinded her. The powerful searchlights from the *Behemoth* had found them. The frigate came towards them then maintained its position close by as sailors shouted directions and pointed from the railings. Two of them tossed a couple of lifebelts in their direction. Andrea was exhausted and chilled to the bone now that her adrenalin and fear had subsided. The sailors threw them a line and

Fowler pulled it around her under her arms, then knotted it.

'How the devil did you manage to fall overboard?' said the priest while they were being hauled up.

'I didn't fall, Father. I was pushed.'

19
ANDREA AND FOWLER

'Thank you. I didn't think I was going to make it.'

Wrapped in a blanket and back on board, Andrea was still shivering. Fowler was sitting next to her, watching her with a preoccupied expression. The sailors left the deck, mindful of the prohibition against speaking to members of the expedition.

'You have no idea how lucky we were. The propellers were turning very slowly. The Anderson turn, if I'm not mistaken.'

'What are you talking about?'

'I came out of my cabin to get some air and heard you taking your evening plunge, so I grabbed the nearest ship phone, yelled *man overboard to port*, and dove in after you. The ship had to make a complete circle, which is called the Anderson turn, but it should have been to port, not starboard.'

'Because . . .?'

'Because if the turn is made towards the side opposite where the person fell in, then they'll be chopped into mince-meat by the propellers. That's what almost happened to us.'

'Somehow being turned into fish food wasn't in my plans.'

'Are you sure about what you told me before?'

'As sure as I know my mother's name.'

'Did you see who pushed you?'

'I only saw a dark shadow.'

'Then if what you're saying is true, the ship's turning to starboard instead of port was no accident either . . .'

'They might have misheard you, Father.'

Fowler paused for a minute before answering.

'Ms Otero, please don't tell anyone about your suspicions. When you're asked, just say you fell. If it's true that someone on board is trying to kill you, to reveal it now . . .'

'. . . would warn the bastard.'

'Exactly,' Fowler said.

'Don't worry, Father. Those Armani shoes cost me two hundred euros,' Andrea said, her lips still quivering slightly. 'I want to catch the son of a bitch who sent them to the bottom of the Red Sea.'

20

TAHIR IBN FARIS'S APARTMENT

AMMAN, JORDAN

Wednesday, 12 July 2006. 1:32 a.m.

Tahir entered his home in the dark, shaking with fear. An unfamiliar voice called to him from the living room.

'Come in, Tahir.'

It took the bureaucrat all of his courage to cross the hallway towards the small living room. He searched for the light switch, but it didn't work. He then felt a hand grab his arm and twist it, forcing him to his knees. The voice came from the shadows somewhere in front of him.

'You've sinned, Tahir.'

'No. No, please, sir. I have always lived my life according to *taqwa*, to honesty. The westerners tempted me many times and I never gave in. This has been my only mistake, sir.'

'So you say you are honest, then?'

'Yes, sir. I swear to Allah.'

'And yet you allowed the *kafirun*, the infidels, to own a piece of our land.'

The one who was twisting his arm increased the pressure and Tahir gave a muffled scream.

'Don't scream, Tahir. If you love your family, do not scream.'

Tahir brought his other arm up to his mouth and bit down hard on the sleeve of his jacket. The pressure continued to increase.

There was a terrible dry crack.

Tahir fell, crying in silence. His right arm hung from his body like a stuffed sock.

'Bravo, Tahir. Congratulations.'

'Please, sir. I followed your instructions. No one will go near the excavation zone for the next few weeks.'

'Are you certain of that?'

'Yes, sir. Anyway, nobody ever goes there.'

'And the desert police?'

'The nearest road is just a track around four miles away. The police only visit the area two or three times a year. When the Americans set up camp, they'll be yours, I swear.'

'Good, Tahir. You've done a good job.'

At that point someone switched back the electricity and the lights came on in the living room. Tahir looked up from the floor and what he saw made his blood run cold.

His daughter Myesha and his wife Zayna were tied up and gagged on the sofa. But that wasn't what shocked Tahir. His family had been in the same condition when he'd left five hours before to carry out the hooded men's demands.

What filled him with terror is that the men no longer wore hoods.

'Please, sir,' Tahir said.

The bureaucrat had returned in the hope that everything would be all right. That the bribe from his American friends wouldn't be revealed, and that the hooded men would leave

113

him and his family in peace. That hope had now evaporated like a drop of water on a red-hot frying pan.

Tahir avoided the gaze of the man sitting between his wife and his daughter, their eyes red from crying.

'Please, sir,' he repeated.

The man had something in his hand. A gun. At the end of it was an empty plastic Coca-Cola bottle. Tahir knew exactly what it was: a primitive but effective silencer.

The bureaucrat couldn't control his shaking.

'You have nothing to worry about, Tahir,' said the man, leaning down to whisper in his ear. 'Hasn't Allah prepared a place in Paradise for honest men?'

There was a light report, like a whiplash. The other two shots followed a few minutes apart. Putting on a new bottle and securing it with duct tape takes a little time.

21

ABOARD THE BEHEMOTH

GULF OF AQABA, RED SEA

Wednesday, 12 July 2006. 9:47 a.m.

Andrea woke up in the ship's infirmary, a large room containing a pair of beds, a few glass cabinets and a desk. A worried Dr Harel had made Andrea spend the night there. She probably hadn't slept much, because when Andrea opened her eyes she was already seated at the desk, reading a book as she sipped some coffee. Andrea yawned loudly.

'Good morning, Andrea. You're missing my beautiful country.'

Andrea got out of bed rubbing her eyes. The only thing she could distinguish clearly was the coffee maker on the table. The doctor watched her, amused as the caffeine began working its magic on the reporter.

'Your beautiful country?' Andrea said when she was able to speak. 'Are we in Israel?'

'Technically we're in Jordanian waters. Let's go out on deck and I'll show you.'

When they came out of the infirmary, Andrea lifted her face to the morning sun. It was going to be a hot day. She breathed deeply and stretched in her pyjamas. The doctor leaned on the ship's rail.

'Be careful you don't fall overboard again,' she teased.

Andrea shuddered, aware of how lucky she was to be alive. The night before, with all the excitement of the rescue and her shame at having to lie and say she'd fallen overboard, she hadn't really had the chance to feel afraid. But now, in the light of day, the noise of the propellers and the memory of cold dark water passed through her mind like a waking nightmare. She tried to concentrate on how beautiful everything looked from the ship.

The *Behemoth* was heading slowly towards some piers, pulled by a tugboat from the Port of Aqaba. Harel pointed to the front of the ship.

'That's Aqaba, Jordan. And that's Eilat, Israel. Look at how the two cities face each other, like mirror images.'

'It *is* beautiful. But it's not the only thing . . . '

Harel blushed slightly and looked away.

'You can't really appreciate it from the water,' she went on, 'but if we had come by plane you could see how the Gulf squares off the coastline. Aqaba occupies the eastern corner and Eilat the western one.'

'Now that you mention it, why didn't we come by plane?'

'Because officially, this is not an archaeological dig. Mr Kayn wants to recover the Ark and take it back to the United States. Jordan would never go along with that under *any* circumstances. Our cover is that we're looking for phosphates, so we've come by sea as the other companies do. Hundreds of tons of phosphates are shipped out of Aqaba each day, bound for places all over the world. We're a humble prospecting team. And we're carrying our own vehicles in the hold of the ship.'

Andrea nodded thoughtfully. She was enjoying the peacefulness of the coast. She looked towards Eilat. Pleasure boats floated on the water near the city like white doves around a green nest.

'I've never been to Israel.'

'You should go sometime,' Harel said, smiling sadly. 'It's a beautiful land. Like a garden of fruit and flowers torn out of the blood and sand of the desert.'

The reporter observed the doctor at length. Her curly hair and tanned complexion were even more beautiful in this light, as though any little defects her face might have had been diffused by the sight of her homeland.

'I think I know what you mean, Doc.'

Andrea took out the wrinkled pack of Camels from her pyjama pocket and lit up a cigarette.

'You shouldn't have fallen asleep with them in your pocket.'

'And I shouldn't smoke, drink or sign up for expeditions that have been threatened by terrorists.'

'Evidently we have more things in common than you'd think.'

Andrea stared at Harel, trying to work out what she meant. The doctor reached over and took a cigarette from the pack.

'Wow, Doc. You don't know how happy that makes me.'

'Why?'

'I love seeing doctors who smoke. It's like a chink in their smug armour.'

Harel laughed.

'I like you. That's why it bothers me to see you in this damn situation.'

'What situation?' said Andrea, raising an eyebrow.

'I'm talking about the attempt on your life yesterday.'

The reporter's cigarette stopped midway to her mouth.

'Who told you?'

'Fowler.'

117

'Does anyone else know?'

'No, but I'm glad he told me.'

'I'm going to kill him,' Andrea said, crushing her cigarette against the railing. 'You don't know how ashamed I felt with everybody looking at me ...'

'I know he told you not to tell anybody. But believe me, my case is a little different.'

'Look at that idiot. She can't even keep her balance!'

'Well, that's not entirely untrue. Remember?'

Andrea was embarrassed at the reminder of the previous day when Harel had to grab her by her T-shirt just before the BA-160 showed up.

'Don't worry,' Harel went on. 'Fowler told me for a reason.'

'That only he knows. I don't trust him, Doc. We've run into each other before ...'

'And he saved your life then, too.'

'I see you've been informed about that as well. While we're at it, how the hell did he manage to get me out of the water?'

'Father Fowler was an officer with the US Air Force. Part of an elite Special Ops unit that specialised in pararescue.'

'I've heard of them: they go looking for pilots who've been shot down, isn't that right?'

Harel nodded.

'I think he's taken a liking to you, Andrea. Maybe you remind him of someone.'

Andrea stared thoughtfully at Harel. There was some connection she wasn't getting and she was determined to find out what it was. More than ever, Andrea was convinced that her reporting on a lost relic, or getting an interview with one of the weirdest and hardest to reach multimillionaires, was only part of the equation. On top of that, she had been dumped into the sea from a moving ship.

I'll be damned if I can figure it out, thought the reporter. *I haven't got a clue what's going on but the key must be Fowler, and Harel . . . and how much they're willing to tell me.*

'You seem to know a lot about him.'

'Well, Father Fowler likes to travel.'

'Let's be a little more specific, Doc. The world is a big place.'

'Not the one in which he moves. Are you aware that he knew my father?'

'He was an extraordinary man,' Father Fowler said.

The women both turned around and saw the priest standing a few steps behind them.

'Have you been here long?' asked Andrea. A stupid question that only shows someone you've said something you don't want them to know. Father Fowler ignored it. He had a grave look on his face.

'We have an urgent job,' he said.

22

Offices of Netcatch

SOMERSET AVENUE, WASHINGTON, DC

Wednesday, 12 July 2006. 1:59 a.m.

The CIA agent took a shocked Orville Watson through the reception area of his burnt-out office. There was still smoke in the air but even worse was the smell of soot, dirt and burned bodies. The wall-to-wall carpeting was covered in at least an inch of muddy water.

'Be careful, Mr Watson. We've cut off the electricity supply to avoid short circuits. We'll have to find our way with flashlights.'

Using the powerful beams of their flashlights, Orville and the agent passed through the rows of desks. The young man couldn't believe his eyes. Each time the beam rested on an overturned desk, a sooty face or a smouldering wastebasket, he felt like crying. These people were his staff. This was his life. Meanwhile the agent – Orville thought it was the same one who had called him on his mobile just as he got off the plane, but he couldn't be sure – was explaining every terrible detail of the attack. Orville gritted his teeth in silence.

'The gunmen came in through the main entrance, blew away the receptionist, ripped out the telephone wires, and then opened fire on everyone else. Unfortunately, your employees were all at their desks. There were seventeen of them, is that correct?'

Orville nodded. His horrified eyes fell on Olga's amber necklace. She was in accounting. He had given her the necklace for her birthday two weeks ago. The torchlight gave it an unearthly sheen. In the dark he couldn't even recognise her burnt hands, which were now curved like claws.

'They killed them one by one in cold blood. Your people had no way of getting out. The only exit was through the front door and the office is ... what? A hundred and fifty square metres? There was nowhere to hide.'

Of course. Orville loved open spaces. The whole office was one diaphanous space made of glass, steel and wenge, the dark African wood. There were no doors or cubicles, only light.

'After they were done, they placed a bomb in the closet at the far end and another at the entrance. Homemade explosives; nothing very powerful, but enough to set fire to everything.'

The computer terminals. A million dollars' worth of hardware and millions of extremely valuable pieces of information compiled over the years, all lost. Last month he had changed his data storage back-up to Blu-ray discs. They had used nearly two hundred discs, more than 10 terabytes of information, which they kept in a fireproof cabinet ... which now lay open and empty. How the hell had they known where to look?

'They set off the bombs using cellular phones. We think the whole operation took no more than three minutes, four at most. By the time someone called the police, they were long gone.'

An office in a one-storey building, in a neighbourhood far

from the centre of the city, surrounded by small businesses and a Starbucks. It was the perfect place for an operation – no hassles, no suspicion, no witnesses.

'The first agents to get here cordoned off the area and called the firemen. They kept the snoops away until our damage-control team arrived. We told everyone that there had been a gas explosion and there was one person dead. We don't want anyone to find out what happened here today.'

It could have been one of a thousand different groups. Al Qaeda, Al-Aqsa the Martyrs Brigade, IBDA-C … any of them, alerted to Netcatch's real purpose, would have considered its destruction a priority. Because Netcatch exposed their weak spot: their means of communication. But Orville suspected that this attack had deeper, more mysterious roots: his last project for Kayn Industries. And a name. A very, very dangerous name.

Huqan.

'You were very lucky to have been travelling, Mr Watson. In any case, you needn't worry. You will be placed under full CIA protection.'

On hearing this, Orville spoke for the first time since he crossed the threshold of the office.

'Your fucking protection is like a first-class ticket to the morgue. Don't even think about following me. I'm going to disappear for a couple of months.'

'I can't let that happen, sir,' said the agent, taking a step back and putting a hand on his holster. With his other hand he pointed the flashlight at Orville's chest. The flowery shirt that Orville was wearing clashed with the burnt-out office like a clown at a Viking funeral.

'What are you talking about?'

'Sir, the folks at Langley want to speak to you.'

'I should have known. They're willing to pay me huge sums of money; ready to insult the memory of the men and women who died here, making it out to be some fucking accident instead of murder at the hands of our country's enemies. What they're not willing to do is shut off the information pipeline, isn't that right, agent?' Orville insisted. 'Even if it means risking my life.'

'I don't know anything about that, sir. My orders are to bring you to Langley safe and sound. Please cooperate.'

Orville lowered his head and took a deep breath.

'Fine. I'll go with you. What else can I do?'

The agent smiled, visibly relieved, and shifted the flashlight away from Orville.

'You don't know how pleased I am to hear that, sir. I would've hated to have taken you away in handcuffs. Anyway—'

The agent realised what was happening an instant too late. Orville charged him with all his weight. Unlike the agent, the young Californian had received no training in hand-to-hand combat. He had no triple black belt, nor did he know five different ways to kill a man with his bare hands. The most violent thing Orville had done in his life was to spend time on his PlayStation.

But you can't do much against 240 pounds of pure desperation and fury when it slams you against an overturned desk. The agent crashed down on to the desk, breaking it in two. He twisted round, trying to reach his gun, but Orville was quicker. Leaning over him, Orville slammed him in the face with his flashlight. The agent's arms went limp and he was still.

Suddenly afraid, Orville raised his hands to his face. This was going too far. No more than a couple of hours ago he was getting out of a private plane, master of his own destiny. Now he had assaulted a CIA agent, possibly even killed him.

A quick check of the agent's pulse on his neck told him he had not. Thank heaven for small mercies.

OK now, think. You've got to get out of here. Find a safe place. And above all, stay calm. Don't let them catch you.

With his huge body, his ponytail, and his Hawaiian shirt Orville wouldn't get far. He went over to the window and began to hatch a plan. Some firemen were drinking water and sinking their teeth into slices of orange near the door. Just what he needed. He walked out the door calmly and headed towards a nearby fence, where the firemen had left their coats and helmets, which were too heavy in this heat. The men were busy joking around and had their backs to their clothes. Praying the firemen wouldn't notice him, Orville took one of the coats and a helmet, retraced his steps, and headed back towards the office.

'Hey, buddy!'

Orville turned around anxiously.

'You talking to me?'

'Of course I'm talking to you,' said one of the firemen. 'Where do you think you're going with my coat?'

Answer him, man. Make something up. Something convincing.

'We have to look at the server and the agent said we should take precautions.'

'Your mother never taught you to ask for things before borrowing them?'

'I'm really sorry. Can you lend me your coat?'

The fireman relaxed and smiled.

'Sure, man. Let's see if it's your size,' he said, opening the coat. Orville put his arms through the sleeves. The fireman buttoned it up and put on the helmet. Orville wrinkled his nose briefly at the mixed smells of sweat and soot.

'Perfect fit. Right, guys?'

'He'd look like a real fireman if it wasn't for the sandals,' said another of the crew pointing at Orville's feet. They all laughed.

'Thank you. Thank you so much. But let me treat you to a round of juice to make up for my bad manners. What do you say?'

They gave him the thumbs-up and nodded as Orville walked away. Behind the barrier they had set up five hundred feet away, Orville saw a couple of dozen onlookers and some TV cameras – only a few – trying to get footage of the scene. From that distance the fire must have looked like nothing more than a boring gas explosion, so he guessed they'd soon be leaving. He doubted that the incident would take up more than a minute on the evening news; not even a half a column in tomorrow's *Washington Post*. Right now he had a more immediate problem: getting out of there.

Everything will be fine as long as you don't run into another CIA agent. So just smile. Smile.

'Hi, Bill,' he said, nodding to the policeman guarding the cordoned-off area as if he had known him all his life.

'I'm going to get some juice for the guys.'

'I'm Mac.'

'Right, sorry. I mixed you up with somebody else.'

'You're with the Fifty-fourth, right?

'No, the Eight. I'm Stewart,' Orville said, pointing to the Velcro name-tag on his chest and praying the policeman wouldn't notice his footwear.

'Go ahead,' the man said, moving the Do Not Cross barrier

a little so Orville could pass. 'Bring me back something to eat, OK, buddy?'

'No problem!' Orville replied. He left behind the smoking ruins of his office and disappeared into the crowd.

23

ABOARD THE BEHEMOTH

Wednesday, 12 July 2006. 10:21 a.m.

'I won't do it,' said Andrea. 'It's crazy.'

Fowler shook his head and looked to Harel for support. This was the third time he had tried to convince the reporter.

'Listen to me, dear,' said the doctor, squatting next to Andrea, who was sitting on the floor against the wall, clutching her legs to her body with her left hand and smoking nervously with her right. 'As Father Fowler told you last night, your accident is proof that someone has infiltrated the expedition. Why they attacked you in particular escapes me . . .'

'It may escape you, but it's extremely important to me,' Andrea muttered.

'. . . but what's key for us right now is to get our hands on the same information Russell has. He's not going to share it with us, that's for sure. And that's why we need you to take a look at those files.'

'Why can't I just steal them from Russell?'

'Two reasons. First, because Russell and Kayn sleep in the same cabin, which is under constant surveillance. And second, because even if you managed to get in, their quarters are huge and Russell probably has papers all over the place.

He's brought quite a bit of work with him in order to continue managing Kayn's empire.'

'All right, but that monster ... I've seen the way he looks at me. I don't want to go near him.'

'Mr Dekker can recite the entire works of Schopenhauer from memory. Maybe that will give you something to talk about,' Fowler said in one of his rare attempts at humour.

'Father, you're not helping,' Harel scolded him.

'What's he talking about, Doc?' Andrea asked.

'Dekker cites Schopenhauer whenever he gets worked up. He's famous for it.'

'I thought he was famous for eating barbed wire for breakfast. Can you imagine what he'd do to me if he caught me snooping around in his cabin? I'm out of here.'

'Andrea,' said Harel, grabbing her arm. 'From the very beginning Father Fowler and I have been uneasy about you being on this expedition. We had hoped to convince you to make up some excuse to quit as soon as we docked. Unfortunately, now that they've told us the aim of the expedition, nobody's going to be allowed to leave.'

Damn! Locked up with the exclusive of my life. A life, I hope, that won't be too short.

'You're in this, whether you want it or not, Ms Otero,' Fowler said. 'Neither the doctor nor I can get near Dekker's cabin. They're watching us too closely. But you can. It's a small cabin and he won't have much in it. We're sure that the only files in his cabin are the ones pertaining to the briefing on the mission. They should be black with a gold logo on the cover. Dekker works for a security outfit called DX5.'

Andrea thought for a moment. As much as she feared Mogens Dekker, the fact that there was a killer on board wasn't going to vanish if she simply looked the other way and continued writing her story, hoping for the best. She had to be pragmatic, and teaming up with Harel and Father Fowler wasn't a bad idea.

As long as it suits my purpose and they don't get between my camera and the Ark.

'All right. But I hope that Cro-Magnon doesn't cut me up into tiny pieces, or I'll come back as a ghost and fucking haunt the both of you.'

Andrea headed for the middle of passageway 7. The plan was quite simple: Harel had located Dekker near the bridge and was keeping him busy with questions about vaccinations for his soldiers. Fowler would keep watch on the stairs between the first and second decks – Dekker's cabin was on level two. Unbelievably, his door was unlocked.

Overconfident bastard, thought Andrea.

The small, bare cabin was almost identical to her own. A narrow bunk made up tightly, army style.

Like my father's. Fucking militaristic assholes.

A metal cabinet, a small bathroom, and a desk. On it a pile of black folders.

Bingo. That was easy.

She was reaching her hand towards them when a silky voice almost made her spit out her heart.

'Well, well. To what do I owe the honour?'

24

On Board the Behemoth

Wednesday, 12 July 2006. 11:32 a.m.

Andrea struggled not to scream. Instead she turned around with a smile on her face.

'Hi, Mr Dekker. Or is it Colonel Dekker? I was looking for you.'

The hired hand was so big and stood so close to Andrea that she had to tilt her head backward to avoid speaking to his neck.

'Mr Dekker is fine. Did you need something ... Andrea?'

Think of an excuse, and make it a good one, Andrea thought, widening her smile.

'I came to apologise for showing up yesterday afternoon while you were escorting Mr Kayn from his plane.'

Dekker limited himself to a grunt. The brute was blocking the small cabin door and was so close that Andrea could see more clearly than she wished the reddish scar across his face, his brown hair, blue eyes, and two days' worth of stubble. The smell of his cologne was overpowering.

I can't believe it, he uses Armani. By the litre.

'Well, say something.'

'You say something, Andrea. Or haven't you come to apologise?'

Andrea suddenly recalled a *National Geographic* cover she had seen of a cobra eyeing a guinea pig.

'Forgive me.'

'No problem. Luckily your friend Fowler saved the situation. But you should be careful. Almost all of our sorrows spring out of our relations with other people.'

Dekker took a step forward. Andrea backed up.

'That's very deep. Schopenhauer?'

'Ah, you know the classics. Or are you getting lessons on the ship?'

'I've always been self-taught.'

'Well, the great teacher said: "A man's face as a rule says more, and more interesting things, than his mouth." And your face looks guilty.'

Andrea glanced sideways at the files, although she regretted doing so immediately. She had to avoid suspicion, even if it was too late.

'The great teacher also said: "Every man takes the limits of his own field of vision for the limits of the world."'

Dekker showed his teeth as he smiled in satisfaction.

'Very true. I think you'd better go and get ready – we're going ashore in about an hour.'

'Yes, of course. Excuse me,' said Andrea, attempting to go past him.

At first Dekker didn't budge but finally he moved the brick wall of his body, allowing the reporter to slip through the space between the desk and himself.

Andrea would always remember what happened next as a piece of cunning on her part, an ingenious trick to obtain the information she needed from right under the nose of the South African. The reality was more prosaic.

She tripped.

The young woman's left leg caught on Dekker's left foot, which didn't move an inch. Andrea lost her balance and fell forward, bracing her arms against the desk to avoid slamming her face against the edge. The contents of the files spilled onto the floor.

Andrea looked at the ground in shock and then up at Dekker, who was staring at her, smoke coming out of his nose.

'Oops.'

'. . . so I stuttered an apology and ran out. You should've seen the way he looked at me. I'll never forget it.'

'I'm sorry I wasn't able to stop him,' Father Fowler said, shaking his head. 'He must have come down through some service hatchway from the bridge.'

The three of them were in the infirmary, Andrea seated on a bed with Fowler and Harel looking worriedly at her.

'I didn't even hear him come in. It seems incredible that someone his size could move so quietly. And all that effort for nothing. Anyway, thank you for the Schopenhauer quote, Father. For a moment there he was speechless.'

'You're welcome. He's a pretty boring philosopher. It was hard to recall a decent aphorism.'

'Andrea, do you remember anything you saw when the files fell to the floor?' Harel interrupted.

Andrea closed her eyes in concentration.

'There were photos of the desert, plans of what looked like houses . . . I don't know. Everything was a mess and there was writing all over it. The only folder that was different was yellow with a red logo.'

'What did the logo look like?'

'What difference would it make?'

'You'd be surprised how many wars are won because of unimportant details.'

Andrea concentrated again. She had an excellent memory, but she had glanced at the scattered sheets for only a couple of seconds and had been in a state of shock. She pressed her fingers on the bridge of her nose, screwed up her eyes and made odd little noises. Just when she thought she couldn't remember, the image appeared in her mind.

'It was a red bird. An owl, because of the eyes. Its wings were open.'

Fowler smiled.

'That's unusual. It could help.'

The priest opened his briefcase and took out a mobile phone. He pulled out its thick antenna and proceeded to turn it on while the two women watched in astonishment.

'I thought all contact with the outside world was forbidden,' said Andrea.

'It is,' Harel said. 'He's going to be in real trouble if he's caught.'

Fowler peered closely at the screen, waiting for coverage. It was a Globalstar satellite phone; it didn't use normal signals but instead linked up directly with a network of communication satellites that had a range covering roughly 99 per cent of the earth's surface.

'That's why it's important we check something out today, Ms Otero,' said the priest, as he dialled a number from memory. 'At the moment we're near a big city so a signal from the ship will pass unnoticed among all the others from Aqaba. Once we reach the excavation site, using any kind of phone will be extremely risky.'

'But what—'

Fowler interrupted Andrea by holding up a finger. The call had gone through.

'Albert, I need a favour.'

25

SOMEWHERE IN FAIRFAX COUNTY, VIRGINIA

Wednesday, 12 July 2006. 5:16 a.m.

The young priest jumped out of bed, half asleep. He knew straight away who it was. That mobile rang only in an emergency. It had a different ring tone than the others he used and only one person had the number. A person Father Albert would have given his life for without a second thought.

Of course Father Albert hadn't always been Father Albert. Twelve years ago, when he was fourteen, he was called *Frodo-Poison*, and was the most notorious cyber delinquent in America.

Young Al had been a lonely boy. Mom and Dad both worked and were too busy with their careers to pay much attention to their skinny blond son, despite the fact that he was so frail they had to keep the windows closed in case a draught of air carried him away. But Albert didn't need any draught to soar through cyberspace.

'There's no way to explain his talent,' said the FBI agent in charge of the case after his arrest. 'Nobody taught him. When the kid looks at a computer he doesn't see a device made of copper, silicon and plastic. He just sees doors.'

To begin with, Albert had opened quite a few of those

doors just to amuse himself. Among these were the secure virtual vaults of Chase Manhattan Bank, the Mitsubishi Tokyo Financial Group and the BNP, the national bank of Paris. During the three weeks that his brief criminal career lasted, he stole $893 million by hacking into the banks' programs, redirecting them to credit commissions to a non-existent intermediary bank, called Albert M. Bank, in the Cayman Islands. It was a bank with only one client. Of course giving the bank his own name wasn't the brightest thing to do, but Albert was barely a teen. He noticed his mistake when two SWAT teams broke into his parents' house during supper, ruining the living-room carpet and stepping on the cat's tail.

Albert would never know the inside of a jail cell, confirming the saying that the more you steal the better they treat you. But while he was handcuffed in an FBI interrogation room, the meagre knowledge of the American jail system that he had acquired through watching TV kept running through his head. Albert had a vague notion that jail was a place you could rot in, where you could be *somonised*. And even though he wasn't sure what the second thing meant, he guessed it would hurt.

The FBI agents looked at this vulnerable broken child and sweated uncomfortably. This boy had shaken up a lot of people. It had been incredibly hard to hunt him down, and had it not been for his childish mistake, he would have kept on fleecing the megabanks. The corporate bankers certainly had no interest in bringing the case to trial and having the public find out what had happened. Incidents like that always made investors jittery.

'What do you do with a fourteen-year-old nuclear bomb?' asked one of the agents.

'Teach him not to blow up,' replied another.

And that's why they handed the case over to the CIA, which had use for a raw talent such as his. In order to talk to the boy, they woke up an agent who, in 1994, had fallen from grace inside the Company, a mature Air Force chaplain with experience in psychology.

When the sleepy Fowler entered the interrogation room early that morning and told Albert he had a choice between spending time behind bars or doing six hours of work a week for the Government, the boy was so happy he broke down and cried.

Being babysitter to this boy genius was imposed on Fowler as a punishment, but for him it was a gift. In time the two forged an unbreakable friendship based on mutual admiration, which in the case of Albert entailed embracing the Catholic faith and eventually entering the seminary. After he was ordained a priest, Albert continued to cooperate with the CIA sporadically, but, like Fowler, he did so on behalf of the Holy Alliance, the Vatican's intelligence service. From the start, Albert had got used to receiving calls from Fowler in the middle of the night, which was, in part, pay-back for that night in 1994 when they had first met.

'Hello, Anthony.'

'Albert, I need a favour.'

'Don't you ever call during regular hours?'

'Watch therefore for ye know not what hour—'

'Don't piss me off, Anthony,' said the young priest, walking to the refrigerator. 'I'm exhausted, so talk fast. Are you in Jordan already?'

'Do you know of a security outfit that has a logo of a red owl with its wings spread?'

Albert poured himself a glass of cold milk and went back to the bedroom.

'Are you joking? That's Netcatch's logo. Those guys were the new gurus for the Company. They won a good chunk of the CIA's intelligence contracts for the Department of Islamic Terrorism. They also did consultancy for several private American firms.'

'Why are you referring to them in the past tense, Albert?'

'The Company issued an internal bulletin a few hours ago. Yesterday a terrorist group blew up Netcatch's offices in Washington and wiped out the entire staff. The media knows nothing about it. The whole thing's being passed off as a gas explosion. The Company has been getting a lot of flak for all the anti-terrorist work they've contracted to private outfits. A job like this is going to make them look vulnerable.'

'Any survivors?'

'Only one, someone named Orville Watson, the CEO and owner. After the attack, Watson told the agents he didn't need protection from the CIA, then split. The chiefs at Langley are pretty angry with the jerk who let him get away. Finding Watson and putting him under protective custody is a priority.'

Fowler was silent for a minute. Albert was used to his friend's long pauses and waited.

'Listen, Albert,' Fowler continued, 'we're in a mess and Watson knows something. You have to find him before the CIA does. His life is in danger. And what's worse, so is ours.'

26

ON THE WAY TO THE EXCAVATION

AL MUDAWWARA DESERT, JORDAN

Wednesday, 12 July 2006. 4:15 p.m.

It would be a stretch of the imagination to call the ribbon of hard earth that the expedition convoy was travelling along a road. Viewed from one of the cliffs that dominated the desolate landscape, the eight vehicles must have seemed like nothing more than dusty anomalies. The journey from Aqaba to the excavation site was a little more than a hundred miles, but it took the convoy five hours due to the irregularity of the terrain coupled with the dust and sand thrown up in the wake of each successive vehicle, resulting in zero visibility for the drivers who followed.

At the head of the convoy were two all-purpose Hummer H3s, each containing four passengers. Painted white, with the open red hand of Kayn Industries emblazoned on the doors, these vehicles were part of a limited series built specifically to contend with the harshest conditions on earth.

'It's one hell of a truck,' said Tommy Eichberg at the wheel of the second H3, to a bored Andrea. 'I shouldn't call it a truck. It's a tank. It can go over a fifteen-inch wall, or climb a sixty-degree slope.'

'I'm sure it costs more than my apartment,' said the reporter. Unable to get any photos of the landscape because of the dust, she contented herself with some candid shots of Stowe Erling and David Pappas, who were seated behind her.

'Almost three hundred thousand euros. As long as it has enough fuel, this machine can cope with anything.'

'That's why we brought the gasoline trucks, right?' said David.

He was an olive-skinned young man, with a slightly flattened nose and a narrow forehead. Whenever he opened his eyes wide in surprise – something he did fairly often – his eyebrows nearly touched his hairline. Andrea liked him, in contrast to Stowe, who even though he was tall and attractive, with a neat ponytail, behaved liked something out of a self-help manual.

'Of course, David,' Stowe replied. 'You shouldn't ask questions you already know the answer to. Assertiveness, remember? That's the key.'

'You're very sure of yourself when the professor's not around, Stowe,' David said, sounding slightly hurt. 'This morning, when he was correcting your evaluations, you didn't seem so assertive.'

Stowe raised his chin, making a 'can you believe this?' gesture to Andrea, who ignored him and busied herself changing the memory card of her camera. Each four-gigabyte card had room for 600 high-resolution photos. As soon as each card was full, Andrea transferred the pictures to a special portable hard disk that could store 12,000 stills and had a seven-inch LCD preview screen. She would have preferred to bring her laptop, but only Forrester's team was allowed them on the expedition.

'How much fuel do we have, Tommy?' Andrea asked, turning towards the driver.

Eichberg stroked his moustache thoughtfully. Andrea was amused by how slowly he spoke, and the way he began every other sentence with a long 'W-e-l-l-l-l-l-l'.

'The two trucks behind us are carrying the supplies. Russian Kamaz, military. Hard as nails. The Russians tried them out in Afghanistan. Well ... after that we have the tankers. The one with water is carrying 10,500 gallons. The one with the gasoline is a little smaller and has a little over 9,000 gallons.'

'That's a lot of fuel.'

'Well, we're going to be out here for weeks, and we need electricity.'

'We can always fall back on the ship. You know ... to send more supplies.'

'Well, that's not going to happen. Orders are that once we get to the camp, we're incommunicado. No contact with the outside world, period.'

'What if there's an emergency?' Andrea said nervously.

'We're pretty self-sufficient. We could survive for months on what we've brought, but the planning has taken every aspect into consideration. I know, because as official driver and mechanic, I was in charge of supervising the loading of all the vehicles. Dr Harel has a veritable hospital back there. And, well, if there's anything more than a sprained ankle, we're only forty-five miles away from the nearest town, Al Mudawwara.'

'That's a relief. How many people live there? Twelve?'

'Did they teach you that attitude in your journalism classes?' Stowe cut in from the back seat.

'Yes, it's called Sarcasm 101.'

'I bet it was your best subject.'

Smart arse. I hope you suffer a stroke while you're digging. Then let's see what you think about getting sick in the middle of the Jordanian desert, thought Andrea, who had never got high marks in anything at school. Insulted, she maintained a dignified silence for a short while.

'Welcome to Southern Jordan, my friends,' Tommy said happily. 'Home of the simoon. Population: zero.'

'What's a simoon, Tommy?' Andrea said.

'A giant sand storm. You have to see one to believe it. Right, we're almost there.'

The H3 slowed down and the trucks began to line up at the side of the road.

'I think this is the turn-off,' Tommy said, pointing to the GPS on the dashboard. We only have about two miles to go, but it'll take us a while to cover the distance. These dunes are going to be tough on the trucks.'

When the dust began to settle, Andrea spied an enormous dune of rose-coloured sand. Behind it was Claw Canyon, the place, according to Forrester, where the Ark of the Covenant had lain hidden for over two thousand years. Small whirl-winds chased each other up the side of the dune, beckoning Andrea to join them.

'Do you think I could walk the rest of the way? I'd like to take a few photos of the expedition as it arrives. I'll get there before the trucks do, by the look of it.'

Tommy regarded her with concern. 'Well, I don't think that's a good idea. Climbing that hill isn't going to be easy. It's cool inside the truck. Out there it's 104 degrees.'

'I'll be careful. Anyway, we'll stay in visual contact all the time. Nothing will happen to me.'

'I don't think you should do it, either, Ms Otero,' said David Pappas.

'Come on, Eichberg. Let her go. She's a big girl,' Stowe said, more for the fun of going against Pappas than to back up Andrea.

'I'll have to consult Mr Russell.'

'Then go ahead.'

Against his better judgement Tommy grabbed the walkie-talkie.

Twenty minutes later Andrea was regretting her decision. Before beginning the climb to the top of the dune, she first had to descend some eighty feet from the road, and then stagger slowly up another 2,500 feet, the last fifty of which were at an incline of 25 degrees. The top of the dune seemed deceptively close; the sand, deceptively smooth.

Andrea had taken with her a backpack containing a large bottle of water. Before she had reached the top of the dune she had drunk every drop. She had a headache, even though she was wearing a hat, and her nose and throat hurt. She was wearing only a short-sleeved shirt, shorts and boots and despite the fact she had put on a high factor sunscreen before getting out of the Hummer, the skin on her arms was starting to sting.

Less than a half an hour and I'm ready for the burns unit. Let's hope nothing goes wrong with the trucks or we'll have to walk back, she thought.

That didn't seem likely. Tommy personally drove each truck to the top of the dune, a task that required experience to avoid the risk of overturning the vehicle. First he took care of the two Kamaz supply trucks, leaving them parked on the hill just below the steepest part of the climb. Then he dealt with the two water trucks while the rest of his team watched from the shade of the H3s.

Meanwhile Andrea was observing the whole operation through her telephoto lens. Each time Tommy got out of a vehicle, he waved to the reporter at the top of the dune and Andrea returned the gesture. Tommy then took the H3s to the edge of the final ascent since he was going to use them to tow the heavier vehicles, which, despite their large wheels, did not have enough traction for such a steep sandy climb.

Andrea took a few photos of the first of the trucks as it made its way up to the summit. One of Dekker's soldiers was now driving the all-terrain vehicle, which was connected to the Kamaz via a cable. She observed the enormous effort required to get the truck to the top of the dune but after it rolled past her, Andrea lost interest in the procedure. Instead, she turned her attention to Claw Canyon.

At first the huge rocky gorge looked no different to any other in the desert. Andrea could see two walls about 150 feet apart that stretched out into the distance then split off. On the way there, Eichberg had shown her an aerial photograph of their destination. The canyon looked like the triple talon of a giant hawk.

Both walls were 100 to 130 feet high. Andrea aimed her telephoto lens at the top of the rocky wall, searching for a higher vantage point she could use to shoot from.

That's when she saw him.

It was only for a second. A man dressed in khaki, watching her.

Surprised, she looked up from the lens but the spot was too far away. She aimed the camera at the rim of the canyon once more.

Nothing.

Switching her position, she scanned the wall again, but it was useless. Whoever had seen her had quickly hidden himself, which was not a good sign. She tried to work out what to do.

The most intelligent thing would be to wait and discuss it with Fowler and Harel . . .

She went and stood in the shade of the first truck, which was shortly joined by the second. An hour later the whole expedition had arrived at the top of the dune and was ready to enter Claw Canyon.

27

MP3 File Recovered by the Jordanian Desert Police from Andrea Otero's Digital Recorder after the Moses Expedition Disaster

Title, all caps. *The Ark Recovered.* No, wait, delete that. Title ... *Treasure in the Desert.* No, that's no good. I have to refer to the Ark in the title – that will sell papers. All right, let's leave the title until I've finished writing the article. Lead sentence: *To mention its name is to invoke one of the most prevalent myths of all humanity. The history of Western civilisation began with it, and today it is the object most coveted by archaeologists the world over. We are accompanying the Moses Expedition on its secret journey across the southern Jordanian desert into Claw Canyon, the place where almost two thousand years ago a group of faithful hid the Ark during the destruction of the second Temple of Solomon ...*

This is all too dry. I'd better write it out first. Let's start with the Forrester interview ... Fuck, that old guy gives me the creeps with his wheezing voice. They say it's because of his illness. Note: Look up on the Internet how to spell pneumoconiosis.

QUESTION: Professor Forrester, the Ark of the Covenant has been firing the human imagination from time immemorial. To what do you attribute this interest?

ANSWER: Look, if you want me to give you an introduction, you don't need to go round in circles and tell me what I already know. Just say what you want and I'll talk.

Q: Do you give a lot of interviews?

A: Dozens. So you're not going to ask me anything original, anything I haven't already heard or answered before. If we had an Internet connection on the dig, I'd tell you to look some of them up and copy the answers.

Q: What's the problem? Are you worried about repeating yourself?

A: I'm worried about wasting time. I'm seventy-seven years old. I've spent forty-three of those years searching for the Ark. It's now or never.

Q: Well, I'm sure you've never answered like that before.

A: What is this? An originality contest?

Q: Professor, please. You're an intelligent and passionate man. Why don't you try to reach out to the public and transmit some of your passion to them?

A: (*a brief pause*) You want a master of ceremonies? I'll do what I can.

Q: Thank you. The Ark...?

A: The most powerful object in history. This is no mere coincidence, especially considering it was the beginning of Western Civilisation.

Q: Wouldn't historians say that civilisation began in Ancient Greece?

A: Nonsense. Human beings spent thousands of years worshipping sooty stains in dark caves. Stains they called gods. Time went by and the stains changed in size, shape and colour, but they continued to be stains. We didn't know about the existence of a single deity until it was revealed to Abraham only four thousand years ago. What do you know about Abraham, young lady?

Q: He's the father of the Israelites.

A: Correct. And of the Arabs. Two apples that fell from the same tree, right next to one another. And straight away, the two little apples learned to hate each other.

Q: What has this to do with the Ark?

A: Five hundred years after God revealed himself to Abraham, the Almighty became sick and tired of the fact that people kept turning their backs on Him. When Moses led the Jews out of Egypt, God once again revealed Himself to His people. Only one hundred and forty-five miles from this spot. And it was there that they signed a contract. On the one hand, humanity agrees to comply with ten simple clauses.

Q: The Ten Commandments.

A: On the other, God agrees to give man eternal life. It is the single most important moment in history – the moment at which life acquired its significance. Three thousand five hundred years later, every human being carries that contract somewhere in his consciousness. Some call it natural law, others dispute its existence or meaning and they'll kill and die to defend their interpretation. But the moment Moses received the Tablets of the Law from the hands of God: that is when our civilisation began.

Q: And then Moses puts the tablets in the Ark of the Covenant.

A: Together with other objects. The Ark is the safe that holds the contract with God.

Q: Some say that the Ark has supernatural powers.

A: Nonsense. I'll explain that to everyone tomorrow when we begin work.

Q: So you don't believe in the supernatural nature of the Ark?

A: With all my heart. My mother read to me from the Bible even before I was born. My life has been dedicated to the Word of God, but that does not mean I'm not prepared to disprove any myths or superstitions.

Q: Speaking of superstition, for many years your research has caused controversy in academic circles that are critical of using ancient texts to discover treasure. There have been insults hurled on both sides.

A: Academics ... they couldn't find their own ass with two hands and a flashlight. Would Schliemann have found the treasures of Troy without Homer's *Iliad*? Would Carter have found Tutankhamun's tomb without the obscure Ut papyrus? Both were heavily criticised in their day for using the same techniques I now use. Nobody remembers their critics, but Carter and Schliemann are immortal. I intend to live forever.

[a severe bout of coughing]

Q: Your illness?

A: You can't spend this many years in damp tunnels, breathing dirt, without paying the price. I have chronic pneumoconiosis. I'm never too far from an oxygen tank. Go on, please.

Q: Where were we? Oh, yes. Have you always been convinced of the historical existence of the Ark of the Covenant, or does your belief date back to the time when you began translating the Copper Scroll?

A: I was raised a Christian, but converted to Judaism when I was relatively young. By the 1960s, I could read ancient Hebrew as well as English. When I began to study the Copper Scroll of Qumran I didn't discover that the Ark was real – I already knew that. With over two hundred references to it in the Bible, it is the most frequently described object in the scriptures. What I realised when I held the Second Scroll in my hands was that I would be the one who would finally rediscover the Ark.

Q: I see. How exactly did the second scroll help you to decipher the Qumran Copper Scroll?

A: Well, there's been a lot of confusion over the consonants like *he, het, mem, kaf, vav, zayin,* and *yod . . .*

Q: In layman's terms, Professor.

A: Some of the consonants weren't too clear, which made deciphering the text difficult. And the strangest thing was that a series of Greek letters had been inserted throughout the scroll. Once we had the key to understanding the text, we realised that these letters were the titles of sections, which changed the order and therefore the context. That was the most exciting period of my professional career.

Q: It must have been frustrating to dedicate forty-three years of your life to the translation of the Copper Scroll, and then have the whole matter resolved in the space of three months after the Second Scroll turned up.

A: Absolutely not. The Dead Sea Scrolls, including the Copper Scroll, were brought to light by accident when a shepherd threw a rock inside a cave in Palestine and heard something break. That's how the first of the manuscripts was found. That's not archaeology: that's luck. But without all these decades of in-depth study, we would never have come to Mr Kayn ...

Q: Mr Kayn? What are you talking about? Don't tell me that the Copper Scroll mentions a billionaire!

A: I can't talk any more about that. I've already said too much.

28

𝒯HE 𝒠XCAVATION

AL MUDAWWARA DESERT, JORDAN

Wednesday, 12 July 2006. 7:33 p.m.

The next hours were a frenetic coming and going. Professor Forrester had decided to establish the camp at the entrance to the canyon. The site would be protected from the wind by the two walls of rock that first narrowed then widened out and finally joined once again 800 feet beyond, in what Forrester called the index finger. Two branches of the canyon to the east and south-east made up the middle and ring fingers of the claw.

The group would live in special tents designed by an Israeli company to withstand the desert heat, and it took a good part of the afternoon to erect them. The work of unloading the trucks fell to Robert Frick and Tommy Eichberg, who used the hydraulic winches on the Kamaz trucks to unload the large numbered metal boxes containing the equipment for the expedition.

'Four thousand five hundred pounds of food, two hundred and fifty pounds of medicine, four thousand pounds of archaeological equipment and electrical gear, two thousand pounds of steel rails, a drill and a mini-excavator. What do you think of that?'

Andrea was amazed and made a mental note for her article

as she checked off the items on the list Tommy had given her. Because of her limited experience in pitching tents, she had volunteered to help with the unloading and Eichberg had put her in charge of directing where each box should go. She had done so not out of a desire to help, but because she supposed that the sooner she was finished the sooner she would be able to talk to Fowler and Harel alone. The doctor was busy helping to set up the tent for the infirmary.

'There goes number thirty-four, Tommy,' yelled Frick from the back of the second truck. The chain on the winch was attached to two metal hooks on either side of the box; it made a loud clanking sound as it lowered its cargo towards the sandy soil.

'Be careful, this one weighs a ton.'

The young reporter looked anxiously at the list, fearing she had missed something.

'This list is wrong, Tommy. It only has thirty-three boxes.'

'Don't worry. This particular box is special … and here come the people in charge of it,' Eichberg said, unhooking the chains.

Andrea looked up from her list to see Marla Jackson and Tewi Waaka, two of Dekker's soldiers. They both knelt next to the box and released the locks. The top came off with a slight hiss, as if it had been vacuum-sealed. Andrea glanced discreetly at its contents. The two mercenaries didn't appear to mind.

It's almost as if they were expecting me to look.

The contents of the case couldn't have been more mundane: packets of rice, coffee and beans, arranged in rows of twenty. Andrea didn't understand; especially when Marla Jackson grabbed a packet with each hand and suddenly tossed them at Andrea's chest, the muscles of her arms rippling under her black skin.

'There you go, Snow White.'

Andrea had to drop the clipboard in order to catch the packages. Waaka fought back a snigger while Jackson, ignoring the surprised reporter, stuck her hand into the space left and pulled hard. The layer of packages shifted to reveal a much less prosaic cargo.

Rifles, machine guns, and small firearms rested on layer after layer of trays. While Jackson and Waaka removed the trays – six in total – and placed them carefully on top of the other boxes, Dekker's remaining soldiers as well as the South African himself came over and began to arm themselves.

'Excellent, gentlemen,' said Dekker. 'As a wise man once said, great men are like eagles ... they build their nests on lonely heights. The first watch belongs to Jackson and the Gottliebs. Find cover positions there, there and there.' He pointed to three places at the top of the canyon walls, the second of which wasn't too far from the spot where Andrea thought she had seen the mysterious figure a few hours before. 'Only break radio silence to report in every ten minutes. That goes for you, too, Torres. If you trade cooking recipes with Maloney like you did in Laos, you'll have me to deal with. March.'

The Gottlieb twins and Marla Jackson took off in three separate directions, looking for accessible climbs to the sentry positions from which Dekker's soldiers would continuously guard the expedition during its time at the site. Once they had determined their posts, they secured rope and aluminium ladders to the rock every ten feet to make the vertical ascent easier.

*

Andrea, in the meantime, was marvelling at the ingenuity of modern technology. Not even in her wildest dreams had she imagined that her body would find itself in the vicinity of a shower over the next week. But to her surprise, among the last items to be lowered from the Kamaz trucks were two pre-fabricated showers and two portable toilets, made from plastic and fibreglass.

'What's the matter, beautiful? Aren't you happy you won't have to crap in the sand?' said Robert Frick.

The bony young man was all elbows and knees, and he moved about nervously. Andrea took in his vulgar remark with a loud burst of laughter and began to help him secure the toilets.

'That's for sure, Robert. And from what I can see, we'll even have His and Hers bathrooms . . .'

'That's a little unfair, seeing as there's only four of you and twenty of us. Well, at least you'll have to dig out your own latrine,' Frick said.

Andrea went pale. Tired as she was, even the thought of lifting a shovel made her hands feel blistered. Frick was creasing up.

'I don't see what's so funny.'

'You've gone whiter than my Aunt Bonnie's butt. That's what's so funny.'

'Don't pay any attention to him, honey,' Tommy broke in. 'We'll use the mini-excavator. It'll take us ten minutes.'

'You always spoil the fun, Tommy. You should have let her sweat a little more.' Frick shook his head as he went off to find someone else to bother.

29

ℋUQAN

He was fourteen when he began to learn.

Of course he first had a great deal to forget.

To start with, everything he had learned at school, from his friends, in his home. Nothing was real. Everything was a lie invented by the enemy, the oppressors of Islam. They had a plan, the imam had told him, whispering it in his ear. 'They start by giving women their freedom. They place them on the same level as men to weaken us. They know that we're stronger, more capable. They know that we are more serious in our commitment to God. Then they brainwash us, they take over the minds of holy imams. They try to cloud our judgement with impure images of lust and corruption. They promote homosexuality. They lie, lie, lie. They even lie about the dates. They say it's the twenty-second of May. But you know what day it is today.'

'The sixteenth day of *shawwal*, master.'

'They talk about integration, about getting along with others. But you know what God wants.'

'No, I don't know, master,' said the frightened boy. How could he be inside God's mind?

'God wants to avenge the Crusades; the crusades that took place a thousand years ago and those of today. God wants us to re-establish the Caliphate, which they destroyed in 1924. From that day on, the Muslim community has been broken up into parcels of territory that are controlled by our enemies. You only have to read a newspaper to see how our Muslim brothers live in a state of oppression, humiliation and genocide. And the greatest affront is the stake driven into the heart of Dar al-Islam: Israel.'

'I hate the Jews, master.'

'No. You only think you do. Listen carefully to my words. This hatred you believe you feel now, in a few years' time it will seem to have been no more than a tiny spark compared to the conflagration of an entire forest. Only true believers are capable of such a transformation. And you will be one of them. You are special. I have only to look into your eyes to see you have the power to change the world. To unify the Muslim community. To bring *sharia* to Amman, Cairo, Beirut. And then to Berlin. To Madrid. To Washington.'

'How will we do it, master? How can we bring Islamic Law to the entire world?'

'You're not ready for the answer.'

'Yes, I am, master.'

'Do you want to learn, with all your heart and soul and mind?'

'There is nothing I want more than to carry out the word of God.'

'No, not yet. But soon . . .'

30

THE EXCAVATION

Wednesday, 12 July 2006. 8:27 p.m.

The tents were finally up, the toilets and showers had been installed, the pipes were connected to the water tank and the expedition's civilian personnel was resting inside the small square created by the surrounding tents. Andrea, seated on the ground with a bottle of Gatorade in her hand, had given up trying to find Father Fowler. Neither he nor Dr Harel seemed to be around, so she devoted herself to contemplating the cloth and aluminium structures, which were unlike anything she had ever seen. Each tent comprised an elongated cube with a door and plastic windows. There was a wooden platform that sat about a foot and a half above the ground on a dozen concrete blocks to insulate the inhabitants against the burning heat of the sand. The roof was made of a large curve of cloth that was fastened to the ground on one side in order to improve the refraction of the sun's rays. Each tent had its own electric cable that led to a central generator next to the fuel truck.

Of the six tents, three were slightly different. One was the infirmary, which had a rougher design but was hermetically sealed. Another formed the combined kitchen and mess tent. It had air-conditioning so that expedition members could relax there during the hottest hours of the day. The last tent was Kayn's and was slightly removed from the rest. It had no visible windows and was roped off – a silent warning that the billionaire did not wish to be disturbed. Kayn had stayed inside his H3, driven by Dekker, until they had finished putting up his tent and he had yet to reappear.

I doubt he'll emerge for the rest of the expedition. I wonder if his tent has a built-in toilet, thought Andrea, taking an absentminded sip from her bottle. *Here comes someone who might know the answer.*

'Hello, Mr Russell.'

'How are you?' said the assistant, smiling politely.

'Very well, thank you. Listen, about this interview with Mr Kayn—'

'I'm afraid that's not possible yet,' Russell cut in.

'I hope you haven't brought me out here just to sightsee. I want you to know that—'

'Welcome, ladies and gentlemen,' the disagreeable voice of Professor Forrester interrupted the reporter's complaints. 'Against our predictions, you've managed to install all of the tents on time. Congratulations. Give yourself a big hand.'

His tone was as insincere as the faint applause that followed. The professor always left his listeners feeling slightly uncomfortable, if not humiliated, but the members of the expedition managed to remain seated around him as the sun began to set behind the cliffs.

'Before we get on with supper and the assignment of tents, I want to finish the story,' the archaeologist went on. 'Remember that I told you a chosen few had taken the treasure out of the city of Jerusalem? Well, this group of brave—'

'One question keeps running through my head,' Andrea cut in, ignoring the old man's piercing look. 'You said that

Yirməyáhu was the author of the Second Scroll. That he wrote it before the Romans razed Solomon's temple. Am I mistaken?'

'No, you're not wrong.'

'Did he leave any other writings?'

'No, he did not.'

'Did the men who took the Ark out of Jerusalem leave any?'

'No.'

'Then how do you know what happened? Those men carried a very heavy object covered in gold for, what, almost two hundred miles? All I did was climb that dune carrying my camera and a water bottle, and it was—'

The old man had grown redder with each of Andrea's words until the contrast between his bald head and beard made his face look like a cherry resting on a wad of cotton.

'How did the Egyptians manage to build the Pyramids? How did the natives of Easter Island erect their ten-thousand-ton statues? How did the Nabateans carve the city of Petra out of these same rocks?'

He spat each word out at Andrea, leaning over her as he talked until his face was next to hers. The reporter turned away to avoid his rancid breath.

'With faith. You need faith to cover one hundred and eighty-five miles under a scorching sun and on rough terrain. You need faith to believe you can do it.'

'So other than the Second Scroll, you don't have any proof,' Andrea said, unable to stop herself.

'No, I do not. But I have a theory, and let's hope I'm right, Ms Otero, or we're going home empty-handed.'

The reporter was about to reply, but felt a slight elbowing in her ribs. She turned to see Father Fowler staring at her in warning.

'Where have you been, Father?' she whispered. 'I've been looking everywhere. We have to talk.'

Fowler silenced her with a gesture.

'The eight men who left Jerusalem with the Ark reached Jericho the following morning.' Forrester had backed away and was now addressing the fourteen people who listened with growing interest. 'We're now entering the realm of speculation, but it happens to be the speculation of a man who has spent decades pondering this very question. In Jericho they would have picked up supplies and water. They crossed the Jordan River near Bethany and reached the King's Highway near Mount Nebo. The highway is the oldest uninterrupted communications link in history, the path that led Abraham from Chaldea to Canaan. Those eight Jews walked south on that route until they reached Petra, where they left the highway and headed in the direction of a mythical place that would have seemed like the end of the world to the Jerusalemites. This place.'

'Professor, do you have any idea which part of the canyon we should be looking in? Because this place is huge,' said Dr Harel.

'That's where all of you come in, starting from tomorrow. David, Gordon ... show them the equipment.'

The two assistants appeared, each wearing a strange contraption. They had a harness across their chest, to which a metallic device the shape of a small backpack was attached. The harness had four straps from which hung a square metal structure that framed the body at thigh level. At the front corners of this structure were two lamp-like objects resembling the headlights of a car, which were pointed towards the ground.

'These, good people, will be your summer outfits for the

next few days. The device is called a proton precession magnetometer.

There were whistles of admiration.

'Flashy name, isn't it?' said David Pappas.

'Be quiet, David. We're working on the theory that the men chosen by Yirməyáhu hid the Ark somewhere in this canyon. The magnetometer will let us know the exact location.'

'How does it work?' Andrea asked.

'The instrument sends out a signal that registers the magnetic field of the Earth. Once it is attuned to that, it will pick up any anomaly in the magnetic field, such as the presence of metal. You don't need to understand exactly how it works, because the equipment transmits a wireless signal directly to my computer. If you find something, I'll know before you do.'

'Is it difficult to operate?' asked Andrea.

'Not if you know how to walk. Each of you will be assigned a series of quadrants in the canyon about fifty feet apart. All you have to do is press the start button on the harness and take a step every five seconds. Like this.'

Gordon took a step forward and stopped. Five seconds later, the instrument gave off a low whistle. Gordon took another step and the whistle stopped. Five seconds later the whistle went off again.

'You'll do this for ten hours a day in shifts of an hour and a half, with fifteen-minute rest periods,' Forrester said.

Everyone began to complain.

'What about people who have other duties?'

'Take care of them when you're not working in the canyon, Mr Frick.'

'You expect us to walk ten hours a day in this sun?'

'I suggest you drink plenty of water – at least a litre every hour. With a temperature of 111 degrees, the body dehydrates quickly.'

'What if we haven't completed our ten hours by the end of the day?' another voice piped up.

'Then you'll finish them at night, Mr Hanley.'

'Isn't democracy fucking great,' Andrea muttered.

Evidently not quietly enough, because Forrester heard her.

'Does our plan seem unfair to you, Ms Otero?' the archaeologist said in a silken voice.

'Now that you mention it, yes,' replied Andrea defiantly. She leaned aside, fearing another blow from Fowler's elbow, but it didn't come.

'The Jordanian government has given us a fake licence for one month for the mining of phosphates. Imagine if I imposed a slower pace? We might finish gathering data from the canyon in the third week and then not have enough time to dig up the Ark in the fourth. Would that seem fair?'

Andrea lowered her head in embarrassment. She really hated the man, no question about it.

'Would anyone else care to join Ms Otero's union?' Forrester added, scrutinising the faces of those present. 'No? Good. From now on, you're not doctors or priests or drill operators or cooks. You're my beasts of burden. Enjoy yourselves.'

31

THE EXCAVATION

Thursday, 13 July 2006. 12:27 p.m.

Step, wait, whistle, step.

Andrea Otero had never made a list of the three worst experiences of her life. First, because Andrea hated lists; second, because despite her intelligence she had little capacity for introspection, and third, because whenever problems did happen to hit her in the face, her invariable response was to rush off and do something else. If she had spent five minutes the night before thinking about her worst experiences, the top of the list would undoubtedly have been the incident with the beans.

It had been the last day of school, and she was marching through her teenage years with a firm and determined step. She had left the class with only one idea in mind: to attend the opening of the new swimming pool in the housing complex where her family lived. That's why she'd bolted down her food, aiming to get into her bathing costume ahead of everyone else. Still chewing her last mouthful, she had got up from the table. That's when her mother had dropped the bomb.

'Whose turn is it to do the dishes?'

Andrea didn't even hesitate because it was her oldest brother Miguel Angel's turn. But her three other brothers weren't willing to wait for their leader on such a special day, so they answered in unison: 'Andrea's!'

'Like hell it is. Are you out of your minds? It was my turn the day before yesterday.'

'Sweetheart, please don't make me have to wash your mouth out with soap.'

'Go ahead, Mama. She deserves it,' one of her brothers said.

'But, Mama, it's not my turn,' Andrea whined, stamping her foot on the floor.

'Well, you'll do them anyway, and offer it up to God as penance for your sins. You're going through a very difficult age,' said her mother.

Miguel Angel suppressed a smile and his brothers elbowed each other triumphantly.

An hour later, Andrea, who had never been good at holding back, would think of five good replies to this injustice. But at that moment she could think of only one.

'Mamaaaaaa!'

'Mama nothing! Do the dishes and let your brothers go ahead to the pool.'

Suddenly Andrea understood everything: her mother knew it wasn't her turn.

It would be hard to understand what she did next unless you were the youngest of five children and the only girl, growing up in a traditional Catholic home where you're guilty before you've even sinned; the daughter of a military man of the old school, who made it clear that his sons came first. Andrea had been stepped on, spat at, mistreated and shunted aside merely for being a female – even though she possessed many qualities of a boy, and certainly had the same sensibilities.

That day she said *enough is enough*.

Andrea returned to the table and lifted the lid off the pot of the bean and tomato stew they had just finished eating. It was half full and still warm. Without thinking twice, she poured the remainder over Miguel Angel's head and left the pot sitting there like a hat.

'You do the dishes, you bastard.'

The consequences were dire. Not only did Andrea have to do the dishes, but her father came up with a more interesting punishment. He didn't forbid her to go swimming all summer. That would have been too easy. He ordered her to sit down at the kitchen table, from which she had a perfect view of the swimming pool, and placed upon it seven pounds of dried beans.

'Count them. When you tell me how many there are, you can go down to the pool.'

Andrea spread the beans on the table and one by one began counting them, putting them into a pot. When she reached twelve hundred and eighty-three, she got up to go to the bathroom.

When she returned the pot was empty. Someone had put the beans back on the table.

Dad, your hair will turn grey before you hear me cry, she thought.

Of course she did cry. Over the next five days, no matter the reason for leaving the table, each time she came back she had to start counting the beans all over again, forty-three different times.

The night before, Andrea would have considered the incident of the beans to have been one of the worst experiences of her life, even worse than the brutal beating she'd received in Rome the year before. Now, however, the experience with the magnetometer had risen to the top of the list.

The day had started at five on the dot, three-quarters of an hour before sunrise, with a series of blasts from a horn. Andrea had to sleep in the infirmary with Dr Harel and Kyra Larsen, the two sexes segregated because of Forrester's sanctimonious rules. Dekker's detail was in another tent, the service staff in another, and Forrester's four male assistants and Father Fowler in the remaining one. The professor preferred to sleep alone in a small tent that cost eighty dollars and went with him on all his expeditions. But he didn't sleep much. By five in the morning he was out there among the tents, blasting his air horn until he received a couple of death threats from a crowd of people who were already frazzled.

Andrea got up, cursing in the dark, looking for her towel and her toiletries bag, which she had left next to the inflatable mattress and sleeping bag that served as her bed. She was heading for the door when Harel called her. In spite of the early hour, she was already dressed.

'You're not thinking of showering, are you?'

'Of course.'

'You could find out the hard way, but I should remind you that the showers work using individual codes and each of us is allowed only thirty seconds of water per day. If you waste your share now, you'll be begging us just to spit on you tonight. '

Andrea slumped back on her mattress, defeated.

'Thank you for screwing up my day.'

'True, but I've saved your night.'

'I look terrible,' Andrea said, pulling her hair into a pony-tail, something she hadn't done since college.

'Worse than terrible.'

'Fuck, Doc, you're supposed to say: "Not as bad as me" or "No, you look great". You know, female solidarity.'

'Well, I've never been a conventional woman,' Harel said, looking directly into Andrea's eyes.

What the hell did you mean by that, Doc? Andrea asked herself as she pulled on her shorts and laced up her boots. *Are you what I think you are? And more importantly . . . should I make the first move?*

Step, wait, whistle, step.

Stowe Erling had escorted Andrea to her assigned area and helped her to put on her harness. So there she was, in the middle of a piece of ground fifty foot square, marked off with string attached at each corner to eight-inch spikes.

Suffering.

First there was the weight. Thirty-five pounds didn't seem like much at first, especially when it hung from a harness. But by the second hour, Andrea's shoulders were killing her.

Then there was the heat. By noon, the ground wasn't sand – it was a grill. And her water ran out half an hour into the shift. The rest periods between each shift lasted quarter of an hour, but eight of those minutes were taken up leaving and returning to the quadrants and getting bottles of cold water, and another two reapplying sunscreen. That left roughly three minutes, which consisted of Forrester continuously clearing his throat and looking at his watch.

On top of that, it was the same routine over and over. That stupid step, wait, whistle, step.

Fuck, I'd be better off in Guantánamo. Even though the sun is beating down on them too at least they don't have to carry this stupid weight.

'Good morning. It's kind of hot, isn't it?' said a voice.

'Go to hell, Father.'

'Have some water,' Fowler said, offering her a bottle.

He was dressed in serge trousers and his usual short-sleeved black shirt and clerical collar. He stepped back out of her quadrant and sat on the ground, watching her with amusement.

'Can you explain who you bribed so you don't have to wear this thing?' asked Andrea, thirstily emptying the bottle.

'Professor Forrester has a great deal of respect for my religious duties. He's also a man of God, in his own way.'

'An egotistical maniac, more like.'

'That too. And what about you?'

'Well, at least promoting slavery is not one of my faults.'

'I'm talking about religion.'

'Are you trying to save my soul with half a bottle of water?'

'Would that be enough?'

'I'd need at least a full one.'

Fowler smiled and handed her another bottle.

'If you take small sips it quenches your thirst better.'

'Thanks.'

'You're not going to answer my question?'

'Religion is too deep for me. I prefer riding a bike.'

The priest laughed and took a sip from his own bottle. He seemed tired.

'Come on, Ms Otero; don't be angry with me for not having to do the donkey work now. You don't think that all these squares showed up by magic, do you?'

The quadrants began two hundred feet from the tents. The other members of the expedition were spread out over the surface of the canyon, each one with his own step, wait, whistle, step. Andrea had reached the end of her section and took a step to the right, turned 180 degrees, and then began walking again, her back to the priest.

'And there I was, trying to find the two of you . . . So this is what you and the doc were up to all night.'

'There were other people there too, so you needn't worry.'

'What do you mean by that, Father?'

Fowler didn't say anything. For a long while there was only the rhythm of step, wait, whistle, step.

'How did you know?' said Andrea anxiously.

'I suspected it. Now I know.'

'Fuck.'

'I'm sorry for having invaded your privacy, Ms Otero.'

'The hell you are,' Andrea said and bit her fist. 'I'd kill for a smoke.'

'What's stopping you?'

'Professor Forrester told me that it interferes with the instruments.'

'You know something, Ms Otero? For someone who acts like she's on top of everything you're pretty naïve. Tobacco smoke doesn't affect the magnetic field of the Earth. At least, not according to my sources.'

'The old bastard.'

Andrea dug around in her pockets then lit a cigarette.

'Are you going to tell Doc, Father?'

'Harel is intelligent, much more so than I am. And she's Jewish. She doesn't need advice from an old priest.'

'Do I?'

'Well, you're Catholic, right?'

'I lost confidence in your outfit fourteen years ago, Father.'

'Which one? Military or clerical?'

'Both. My parents really screwed me up.'

'All parents do that. Isn't that how life begins?'

Andrea turned her head and managed to see him out of the corner of her eye.

'So we have something in common.'

'You can't imagine. Why were you searching for us last night, Andrea?'

The reporter looked around before answering. The nearest human being was David Pappas, locked into his harness a hundred feet away. A blast of hot wind gusted from the entrance to the canyon, forming beautiful whirlpools of sand at Andrea's feet.

'Yesterday, when we were at the entrance to the canyon, I climbed up that enormous dune on foot. At the top I began taking shots with my telephoto lens and I saw a man.'

'Where?' Fowler blurted out.

'On top of the cliff behind you. I only saw him for a second. He was wearing light brown clothes. I didn't tell anyone because I didn't know if it had something to do with the person who tried to kill me on the *Behemoth*.'

Fowler squinted and ran his hand over his bald head, taking a deep breath. His face looked troubled.

'Ms Otero, this expedition is extremely dangerous and its success depends on secrecy. If anyone knew the truth about why we're here ...'

'They'd throw us out?'

'They'd kill us all.'

'Oh.'

Andrea lifted her gaze, acutely aware of how isolated the place was and how trapped they would be if someone broke through Dekker's thin line of sentries.

'I need to speak to Albert immediately,' Fowler said.

'I thought you said you couldn't use your satellite telephone here? That Dekker had a frequency scanner?'

The priest simply looked at her.

'Oh, shit. Not again,' Andrea said.

'We'll do it tonight.'

32

2,700 FEET WEST OF THE EXCAVATION

AL MUDAWWARA DESERT, JORDAN

Friday, 14 July 2006. 1:18 a.m.

The tall man was named O and he was crying. He had to get away from the other men. He didn't want them to see him showing his feelings, much less talk about it. And it would have been very dangerous to reveal why he was crying.

It was really because of the girl. She had reminded him too much of his own daughter. He had hated having to kill her. Killing Tahir had been simple, a relief, in fact. He had to admit that he'd even enjoyed playing with him – giving him a preview of hell, but here on earth.

The girl was another story. She was only sixteen years old.

And yet, D and W had agreed with him: the mission was too important. Not only were the lives of the other brothers crowded in the cave at stake, but all of Dar Al-Islam. The mother and daughter knew too much. There could be no exceptions.

'Meaningless shitty war,' he said.

'So you're talking to yourself now?'

It was W, who had come crawling over. He didn't like

running risks and always talked in whispers, even inside the cave.

'I was praying.'

'We have to go back into the hole. They might see us.'

'There's only one sentry on the western wall, and he has no direct line of vision over here. Don't worry.'

'What if he changes position? They have night-vision goggles.'

'I said don't worry. The big black one is on duty. He smokes the whole time and the light from the cigarette stops him seeing anything,' O said, annoyed that he had to talk when he had wanted to enjoy the silence.

'Let's go back inside the cave. We'll play chess.'

That W ... O hadn't fooled him for a moment. W knew he was feeling down. Afghanistan, Pakistan, Yemen. They had gone through a lot together. He was a good comrade. As clumsy as his efforts were, he was attempting to cheer him up.

O stretched out the length of his body on the sand. They were in a hollow area at the foot of a rock formation. The cave, which was at its base, was only about one hundred feet square. O was the one who had found it three months earlier, when he was planning the operation. There was hardly enough room for them all, but even if the cave had been a hundred times bigger, O would have preferred being outside. He felt trapped in that noisy hole, attacked by the snores and farting of his brothers.

'I think I'll stay out here a while longer. I like the cold.'

'Are you waiting for Huqan's signal?'

'It'll be a while before that comes. The infidels haven't found anything yet.'

'I hope they hurry up. I'm tired of being holed up, eating out of tins and pissing into a can.'

O didn't answer. He closed his eyes and concentrated on the breeze on his skin. Waiting was fine with him.

'Why are we sitting around here doing nothing? We're well-armed. I say we go in there and kill them all,' W insisted.

'We'll follow Huqan's orders.'

'Huqan takes too many chances.'

'I know. But he's clever. He told me a story. Do you know how a bushman finds water in the Kalahari when he's far from home? He finds a monkey and watches it all day. He can't let the monkey see him or the game's over. If the bushman is patient, the monkey ends up showing him where to find water. A crack in the rock, a little pool ... places a bushman would never have found.'

'And what does he do then?'

'He drinks the water and eats the monkey.'

33

THE EXCAVATION

AL MUDAWWARA DESERT, JORDAN

Friday, 14 July 2006. 01:18 a.m.

Stowe Erling nibbled nervously on his ballpoint pen and cursed Professor Forrester with all his might. It wasn't his fault that the data from one of the quadrants hadn't gone where it was supposed to. He had been busy enough putting up with the complaints of their indentured prospectors as he helped them into and out of their harnesses, changed the batteries on their equipment, and made sure that nobody went over the same quadrant twice.

Of course, no one was there to help him put on his harness now. And it wasn't as if the operation was easy in the middle of the night, with only the light from a camping gas lantern. Forrester didn't give a damn about anybody – anybody except himself, that is. The moment he had found an anomaly in the data, after supper, he had ordered Stowe to do a new analysis of quadrant 22K.

In vain Stowe had asked – almost begged – Forrester to let him do it the following day. If the data from all the quadrants wasn't linked, the program wouldn't function.

Fucking Pappas. Isn't he supposedly the world's leading archaeological topographer? A qualified software designer, right? Shit is what he is. He should never have left Greece. Fuck!

I bust myself kissing the old man's ass so he'd let me prepare the headings for the magnetometer codes, and he ends up giving them to Pappas. Two years, two whole years researching references for Forrester, correcting his childish errors, buying his medicine, emptying his trash can full of infected bloody tissues. Two years, and he treats me like this.

Fortunately, Stowe had finished the complicated series of movements and the magnetometer was now on his shoulders and working. He picked up the lantern and placed it halfway up the incline. Quadrant 22K covered part of a sandy slope near the knuckle of the index finger of the canyon.

The ground here was different, unlike the spongy pink surface at the base of the canyon or the baked rock that covered the rest of the area. The sand was darker and the slope itself had a gradient of around 14 per cent. As he walked, the sand shifted as though an animal were moving under his boots. Stowe had to hold on tightly to the straps of the magnetometer as he made his way up the incline in order to keep the instrument balanced.

As he leaned over to place the lantern on the ground, his right hand grazed a splinter of iron protruding from the frame. It drew blood.

'Ouch – shit!'

Sucking on the cut, he began moving with the instrument over the terrain in that slow annoying rhythm.

He's not even American. Not even a Jew, dammit. He's a lousy fucking Greek immigrant. Greek Orthodox before he started working for the professor. He only converted to Judaism after three months with us. A fast-track conversion – very convenient. I'm so tired. Why am I doing this? I hope we find the Ark. Then History departments will fight over me and I'll be able to find a tenured position. The old man's not going to last much longer –

probably just enough to steal all the credit. But in three or four years they'll talk about his team. About me. I wish his rotten lungs would just burst in the next few hours. I wonder who Kayn would put at the head of the expedition then? It wouldn't be Pappas. If he craps in his pants each time the professor even looks at him, imagine what he'll do if he sees Kayn. No, they'd need someone stronger, someone with charisma. I wonder what Kayn is really like. They say he's very sick. But then why did he come all the way out here?

Stowe stopped in his tracks, halfway up the incline and facing the canyon wall. He thought he had heard footsteps, but that was impossible. He looked back at the camp. Everything was still.

Of course. The only one not in bed is me. Well, except for the guards, but they're bundled up and probably snoring. Who are they going to protect us from? It'd be better if—

The young man stopped again. He had heard something and this time he knew he hadn't imagined it. He cocked his head in an attempt to hear better, but the annoying whistle went off once more. Stowe felt for the instrument's switch and quickly pressed it once. That way he could turn off the whistle without turning off the instrument (which would set off an alarm on Forrester's computer), something a dozen people would have given an arm and a leg to have known yesterday.

It must be a couple of the soldiers changing shifts. Come on, you're a little too old to be afraid of the dark.

He turned off the instrument and began making his way downhill. Now that he'd thought about it, it would be better if he went back to bed. If Forrester wanted to be pissed off, then that was his business. He'd start first thing in the morning, skipping breakfast.

That's it. I'll get up before the old man, when there's more light.

He smiled, chiding himself for being alarmed over nothing. Now he could finally go to bed, which was all he needed. If he hurried, he'd be able to get three hours' sleep.

Suddenly something was pulling on the harness. Stowe leaned back waving his arms in the air to keep his balance. But just when he thought he was going to fall, he felt someone grab him.

The young man did not feel the point of the knife puncturing the bottom of his spinal column. The hand that had grabbed his harness pulled harder. Stowe suddenly remembered his childhood when he went with his father to Chebacco Lake to fish for black crappies. His father would hold a fish in his hand and then, in one swift motion, gut it. The movement made a wet, whistling sound very similar to the last thing that Stowe heard.

The hand released the young man, who fell to the ground like a rag doll.

Stowe made a broken sound as he died, a brief, dry moan, and then there was silence.

34

THE EXCAVATION

Friday, 14 July 2006. 2:33 a.m.

The first part of the plan was to wake up on time. So far so good. From that moment on, everything was a disaster.

Andrea had put the wristwatch between her alarm clock and her head, with the alarm set for 2:30 in the morning. She would meet with Fowler at quadrant 14B, where she had been working when she told the priest about seeing the man on the cliff. All that the reporter knew was that the priest needed her help in order to neutralise Dekker's frequency scanner. Fowler hadn't told her how he planned to do this.

To make sure she would show up on time, Fowler had given her his wristwatch since her own didn't have an alarm. It was a rough black MTM Special Ops with a Velcro wristband that seemed almost as old as Andrea herself. On the back of the watch was the inscription: *That others may live.*

'*That others may live.*' *What kind of person wears a watch like this? Not a priest, of course. Priests wear twenty-euro watches, at best a cheap Lotus with an imitation leather strap. Nothing with as much character as this*, Andrea thought before falling asleep. When the alarm sounded, she was careful to turn it off straight away and take the watch with her. Fowler had made it clear what would happen to her if she lost it. Besides which, the face had a small LED light that would make it easier to get through the canyon without tripping over one of the quadrant strings and cracking her head open on a rock.

While she searched for her clothes, Andrea listened to see if the alarm had woken anyone up. Kyra Larsen's snores eased the reporter's mind but she decided to wait until she got outside to put on her boots. Creeping towards the door, her customary clumsiness came into play and she dropped the watch.

The young reporter tried to control her nerves and recall the layout of the infirmary. At the far end were two stretchers, a table and the medical instruments cabinet. The three room-mates slept near the entrance on their mattresses and sleeping bags. Andrea in the middle, Larsen to her left, Harel to her right.

Using Kyra's snores to orient herself, she began searching the floor. She felt the edge of her own mattress. A little further on she touched one of Larsen's discarded socks. She made a face and rubbed her hand on the seat of her trousers. She continued over her own mattress. A little further. That must be Harel's mattress.

It was empty.

Surprised, Andrea took the lighter out of her pocket and flicked it on, obscuring the flame by placing her body between it and Larsen. Harel was nowhere in the infirmary. Fowler had told her not to let Harel know what they were planning to do.

The reporter didn't have time to give the matter further thought, so she picked up the watch, which she found lying between the mattresses, and went out of the tent. The camp was as still as a tomb. Andrea was glad that the infirmary was near the north-west wall of the canyon, so she would avoid anyone on their way to or from the toilets.

I'm sure that's where Harel is. I can't understand why we can't tell her what we're doing if she already knows about the priest's satellite telephone. Those two are up to something strange.

A moment later the professor's air horn went off. Andrea froze, fear tearing at her like a trapped animal. At first she thought that Forrester had discovered what she was up to, until she realised that the sound was coming from some distance away. The horn was muffled but it echoed faintly through the canyon.

There were two blasts and then it stopped.

Then it began again and didn't stop.

It's a distress signal. I'd bet my life on it.

Andrea wasn't sure who to call on. With Harel nowhere in sight and Fowler waiting for her at 14B, her best option was Tommy Eichberg. The service personnel tent was the closest to her now and with the help of the watch's light, Andrea found the tent's zipper and burst inside.

'Tommy, Tommy, are you here?'

Half a dozen heads looked up from their sleeping bags.

'For God's sake, it's two in the morning,' said a dishevelled Brian Hanley, rubbing his eyes.

'Get up, Tommy. I think the professor is in trouble.'

Tommy was already climbing out of his sleeping bag.

'What's going on?'

'It's the professor's horn. It hasn't stopped.'

'I don't hear anything.'

'Come with me. I think he's in the canyon.'

'Just a minute.'

'What are you waiting for, Hanukkah?'

'No, I'm waiting for you to turn around. I'm naked.'

Andrea went out of the tent mumbling an apology. Outside the horn was still going but each successive blast was weaker. The compressed air was running out.

Tommy joined her, followed by the rest of the men in the tent.

'Go and check in the professor's tent, Robert,' Tommy said, pointing at the skinny drill operator. 'And you, Brian, go and alert the soldiers.'

This last order wasn't necessary. Dekker, Maloney, Torres and Jackson were already approaching, not fully dressed but with their machine guns at the ready.

'What the fuck is going on?' Dekker said. He had a walkie-talkie in his huge hand. 'My guys say there's someone raising hell at the end of the canyon.'

'Ms Otero thinks the professor is in trouble,' Tommy said. 'Where are your lookouts?'

'That sector's at a blind angle. Waaka is looking for a better position.'

'Good evening. What's going on? Mr Kayn is trying to sleep,' Jacob Russell said as he approached the group. He wore cinnamon-coloured silk pyjamas and his hair was slightly tousled. 'I thought that—'

Dekker interrupted him with a gesture. The walkie-talkie crackled and Waaka's flat voice came over the speaker.

'Colonel, I can see Forrester and a body on the ground. Over.'

'What's the professor doing, Nest One?'

'He's leaning over the body. Over.'

'Copy, Nest One. Remain at your position and cover us. Nests Two and Three, maximum alert. If a mouse farts, I want to know about it.'

Dekker broke off communication and proceeded to give further orders. In the few moments that he had been in contact with Waaka, the entire camp had roused itself. Tommy Eichberg lit one of the powerful halogen floodlights, throwing huge shadows against the canyon walls.

Meanwhile Andrea stood slightly apart from the circle of people crowding around Dekker. Over his shoulder she could see Fowler walking behind the infirmary, completely dressed. He looked around and then went over to stand behind the reporter.

'Don't say anything. We'll talk later.'

'Where's Harel?'

Fowler looked at Andrea and arched his eyebrows.

He has no idea.

Suddenly a suspicion occurred to Andrea and she turned towards Dekker, but Fowler grabbed her arm and held her back. After exchanging a few words with Russell, the huge South African had made a decision. He left Maloney in charge of the camp and together with Torres and Jackson headed for quadrant 22K.

'Let me go, Father! He said there was a body.' Andrea said, trying to free herself.

'Wait.'

'It could be her.'

'Hold on.'

In the meantime Russell had raised his arms and was addressing the group.

'Please, please. We're all very agitated, but running around from one place to another isn't going to help anyone. Take a look around you, and tell me if there's anyone missing. Mr Eichberg? And Brian?'

'He's dealing with the generator. It's low on fuel.'

'Mr Pappas?'

'Everyone's here except Stowe Erling, sir,' said Pappas nervously, his voice cracking with the strain. 'He was going over quadrant 22K again. The headings on the data were wrong.'

'Dr Harel?'

'Dr Harel isn't here,' said Kyra Larsen.

'She's not? Does anyone have an idea where she might be?' said a surprised Russell.

'Where who might be?' said a voice behind Andrea. The reporter turned, relief etched across her face. Harel was standing behind her, her eyes bloodshot, dressed only in boots and a long red shirt. 'You'll have to excuse me, but I took a sleeping pill and I'm still a little groggy. What happened?'

While Russell was getting the doctor up to speed, Andrea confronted mixed emotions. Although she was relieved that Harel was all right, she couldn't understand where the doctor could have been all this time or why she had lied.

And I'm not the only one, Andrea thought, watching her other tent-mate. Kyra Larsen hadn't taken her eyes off Harel. *She suspects the doctor of something. I'm sure she noticed that she wasn't in her bed a few minutes ago. If looks were laser beams, Doc would have a hole in her back the size of a small pizza.*

35
KAYN

The old man got up on a chair and untied one of the knots that held up the sides of the tent. He tied it, untied it, and tied it once more.

'Sir, you're doing it again.'

'Someone's dead, Jacob. Dead.'

'Sir, the knot is fine. Please, come down. You have to take this.' Russell was holding out a small paper cup containing some pills.

'I'm not going to take them. I need to be alert. I could be next. Do you like this knot?'

'Yes, Mr Kayn.'

'It's called a double eight. It's a very good knot. My father showed me how to do it.'

'It's a perfect knot, sir. Please come down from the chair.'

'I just want to make sure—'

'Sir, you're falling back into obsessive compulsive behaviour.'

'Don't use that term on me.'

The old man turned so violently that he lost his balance. Jacob moved to catch Kayn, but he wasn't quick enough and the old man fell.

'Are you all right? I'll call Dr Harel!'

The old man lay crying on the floor, but only a small part of his tears was due to the fall.

'Someone's dead, Jacob. Someone's dead.'

36

THE EXCAVATION

AL MUDAWWARA DESERT, JORDAN

Friday, 14 July 2006. 3:13 a.m.

'Murder.'

'Are you sure, Doctor?'

Stowe Erling's body was lying at the centre of a circle of gas lamps. They gave off a pale light, and the shadows on the surrounding rocks faded into a night that suddenly seemed filled with danger. Andrea fought back a shudder as she gazed at the body on the sand.

When Dekker and his entourage had arrived at the scene only minutes earlier, he'd found the old professor holding the dead man's hand, continuously sounding the now useless air horn. Dekker had prised the professor away and called for Dr Harel. The doctor had asked Andrea to come with her.

'I'd rather not,' Andrea had said. She had felt dizzy and confused when Dekker had said over the radio that they had found Stowe Erling dead. She couldn't help remembering how she'd wished that the desert would simply swallow him up.

'Please. I'm very anxious, Andrea. Give me a hand.'

The doctor had seemed truly disturbed, so without another word Andrea began to walk alongside her. The reporter tried to think of ways she could ask Harel where the hell she'd been when this mess started, but she couldn't do so without revealing that she too was somewhere she shouldn't have been. When they reached quadrant 22K they discovered that Dekker had managed to illuminate the body so that Harel could determine the cause of death.

'You tell me, Colonel. If it wasn't murder, it was a very determined suicide. He has a knife wound at the base of his spine, which is by definition fatal.'

'And very difficult to accomplish,' Dekker said.

'What do you mean?' Russell cut in, standing next to Dekker.

Further away, Kyra Larsen was squatting next to the professor, attempting to console him. She draped a blanket over his shoulders.

'He means that it was a perfectly placed wound. With a very sharp knife. Stowe hardly bled at all,' Harel said, taking off the latex gloves with which she had examined the body.

'A professional, Mr Russell,' added Dekker.

'Who found him?'

'Professor Forrester's computer has an alarm that goes off if one of the magnetometers stops transmitting,' Dekker said, indicating the old man with a nod of his head. 'He came over here to give off to Stowe. When he saw him on the ground, he thought he was sleeping and started sounding the air horn in his ear until he realised what had happened. Then he kept blowing the horn to alert us.'

'I don't want even to imagine how Mr Kayn is going to react when he finds out Stowe was murdered Where the hell were your men, Dekker? How could this have happened?'

'They must have been looking out beyond the canyon, as I ordered. There are only three of them covering a very large terrain on a moonless night. They were doing all they could.'

'Which is not much,' Russell said, pointing at the body.

'Russell, I told you. It is insane coming to this place with only six men. At a push, we have three men doing four-hour guard duty. But to cover a hostile zone like this, we really need at least twenty. So don't blame me.'

'That's out of the question. You know what would happen if the Jordanian government—'

'Will you two stop arguing!' The professor had got up, the blanket hanging from his shoulders. His voice shook with anger. 'One of my assistants is dead. I sent him here. Will you please stop blaming each other?'

Russell went silent. To Andrea's surprise, so did Dekker, although he saved face by turning to Dr Harel.

'Can you tell us anything else?'

'I imagine he was killed up there and then he slid down the incline, given the rocks that came down with him.'

'You imagine?' Russell said, raising an eyebrow.

'I'm sorry, but I'm not a forensic pathologist, just an ordinary physician who specialises in combat medicine. I'm certainly not qualified to analyse a crime scene. In any case, I don't think you're going to find footprints or any other clues with the mixture of sand and rock we have out here.'

'Do you know if Erling had any enemies, Professor?' said Dekker.

'He didn't get on with David Pappas. I was responsible for the rivalry between them.'

'Did you ever see them argue?'

'Many times, but they never came to blows.' Forrester paused and then shook his finger in Dekker's face. 'Wait a minute. You're not suggesting that one of my assistants did this, are you?'

Meanwhile, Andrea had been observing Stowe Erling's

body with a mixture of shock and disbelief. She wanted to walk over into the circle of lamps and pull on his ponytail to show that he wasn't dead, that it was just a sick joke of the professor's. She understood the gravity of the situation only when she saw the frail old man shaking his finger in the gigantic Dekker's face. At that point the secret that she had been withholding for two days cracked like a dam from the pressure.

'Mr Dekker.'

The South African turned to her, his expression clearly not friendly.

'Ms Otero, Schopenhauer said that the first encounter with a face makes a lasting impression on us. For the time being I've had enough of your face – understood?'

'I don't even know why you're here, nobody asked you to come,' added Russell. 'This story is not for publication. Go back to the camp.'

The reporter took a step back, but held the gaze of both the mercenary and the young executive. Ignoring Fowler's advice, Andrea decided to spit it out.

'I'm not leaving. It's possible that this man's death is my fault.'

Dekker came so close to her that Andrea could feel the dry heat from his skin.

'Speak up.'

'When we arrived at the canyon, I thought I saw someone on top of that cliff.'

'What? And it didn't occur to you to say anything?'

'I didn't give it much importance at the time. I'm sorry.'

'Terrific, you're sorry. That makes everything all right then. Fuck!'

Russell was shaking his head, amazed. Dekker scratched

the scar on his face, trying to take in what he had just heard. Harel and the professor were looking at Andrea in disbelief. The only one who reacted was Kyra Larson, who pushed Forrester aside, rushed over to Andrea, and slapped her.

'Bitch!'

Andrea was so stunned that she didn't know what to do. Then, seeing the anguish on Kyra's face, she understood and lowered her arms.

I'm sorry. Forgive me.

'Bitch,' the archaeologist repeated, throwing herself on Andrea and pummelling her face and chest. 'You could have told everyone that we were being watched. Don't you know what we're looking for? Don't you realise how it affects us all?'

Harel and Dekker grabbed Larsen by the arms and pulled her back.

'He was my friend,' she mumbled, moving away slightly.

At that moment David Pappas arrived at the scene. He had been running and sweat was pouring from him. It was obvious he had fallen at least once because there was sand on his face and glasses.

'Professor! Professor Forrester!'

'What is it, David?'

'The data. Stowe's data,' Pappas said, bending over and leaning on his knees to catch his breath.

The professor made a dismissive gesture.

'This isn't the time, David. Your colleague is dead.'

'But, Professor, you have to listen. The headings. I've fixed them.'

'Very good, David. We'll talk tomorrow.'

Then David Pappas did something he would never have done were it not for the tension of that night. Grabbing

Forrester's blanket, he jerked the old man around to face him.

'You don't understand. We have a peak. A 7911!'

At first Professor Forrester didn't react, but then he spoke very slowly and deliberately, in such a low voice that David could hardly hear him.

'How big?'

'Huge, sir.'

The professor fell to his knees. Unable to speak, he leaned backward and forward in mute supplication.

'What's a 7911, David?' asked Andrea.

'Atomic weight 79. Position 11 on the periodic table,' the young man said, his voice breaking. It was as if, in delivering his message, he had emptied himself. His eyes were on the corpse.

'And that is . . .?'

'Gold, Ms Otero. Stowe Erling had found the Ark of the Covenant.'

37

Some Facts about the Arc of the Covenant, Transcribed from the Moleskin Notebook of Professor Cecyl Forrester

The Bible says: 'And they shall make an Ark of shittim wood: two cubits and a half shall be the length thereof, and a cubit and a half the breadth thereof, and a cubit and a half the height thereof. And thou shalt overlay it with pure gold, within and without shalt thou overlay it, and thou shalt make upon it a crown of gold round about. And thou shalt cast four rings of gold for it, and put them in the four corners thereof; and two rings shall be in the one side of it, and two rings in the other side of it. And thou shalt make staves of shittim wood, and overlay them with gold. And thou shalt put the staves into the rings by the sides of the Ark, that the Ark may be borne with them.'

I'll apply the measurements of the regular cubit. I know I'll be criticised because few scholars do; they rely on the Egyptian cubit and the 'sacred' cubit, which are much more glamorous. But I'm right.

This is what we know for sure about the Ark:

- Year of construction: 1453 BC at the foot of Mount Sinai.
- 44 inches long
- 25 inches wide

- 25 inches high
- 84-gallon capacity
- 600 pounds in weight

There are people who would suggest that the weight of the Ark was greater, around 1,100 pounds. Additionally, there is an idiot who dared to insist that the Ark weighed more than a ton. That is crazy. And they call themselves experts. They love to add the weight of the Ark itself. Poor idiots. They don't realise that gold, even though it is heavy, is too soft. The rings could not have supported such weight, nor would the wooden poles have been long enough for more than four men to carry it comfortably.

Gold is a very soft metal. Last year I saw a whole room covered in thin sheets of gold made from one good-sized coin, following methods dating back to the Bronze Age. The Jews were skilled craftsmen, and did not have great amounts of gold in the desert, nor would they have burdened themselves with such a great weight that they left themselves vulnerable to their enemies. No, they would have used a small amount of gold and created thin sheets of it to cover the wood. Shittim wood, or acacia, is a solid wood that could last centuries without being damaged, especially if it was covered by a thin layer of metal that did not rust and was indifferent to the effects of time. It was an object built for eternity. How could it be otherwise, since it was the Timeless One who gave the instructions?

38
THE EXCAVATION

Friday, 14 July 2006. 2:21 p.m.

'So the data had been manipulated.'

'Somebody else had the information, Father.'

'That's why they killed him.'

'I understand the what, where and when. If you'll just give me the how and the who, I'll be the happiest woman in the world.'

'I'm working on it.'

'Do you think it was an outsider? Maybe the man I saw at the top of the canyon?'

'I don't think you're that foolish, young lady.'

'I still feel guilty.'

'Well, you should stop. I was the one who asked you not to tell anyone. But believe me: someone in this expedition is a murderer. That's why it's more important than ever that we talk to Albert.'

'OK. But I think you know more than you're telling me – much more. Yesterday there was an unusual amount of activity in the canyon for that time of night. The doctor wasn't in her bed.'

'I told you . . . I'm working on it.'

'Shit, Father. You're the only person I know who speaks so many languages but doesn't like to talk.'

Father Fowler and Andrea Otero were sitting in the shade of the west wall of the canyon. Since nobody had slept much the night before, after the shock of Stowe Erling's murder, the day had begun slowly and heavily. However, little by little, the knowledge that Stowe's magnetometer had discovered gold began to eclipse the tragedy, altering the mood in the camp. There was a whirlwind of activity around quadrant 22K, with Professor Forrester at its centre: analysis of the composition of the rocks, further tests with a magnetometer and, above all, measurements of the solidity of the ground for digging.

The procedure consisted of running an electric wire through the ground to find out how much current it would handle. A hole filled with earth, for example, has less electrical resistance than the undisturbed ground around it.

The results of the test were conclusive: the ground at this point was very unstable. This infuriated Forrester. Andrea watched as he gesticulated wildly, throwing papers into the air and insulting his workers.

'Why is the professor so angry?' asked Fowler.

The priest was sitting on a flat rock about a foot and a half above Andrea. He had been playing with a small screwdriver and some cables that he had taken from Brian Hanley's toolbox, paying little heed to what was going on around him.

'They've been running tests. They can't simply dig up the Ark,' Andrea replied. She had spoken with David Pappas a few minutes before. 'They believe that it's in a manmade hole. If they use the mini-excavator there's a good chance the hole will collapse.'

'They may have to go around it. That could take weeks.'

Andrea took another series of shots with her digital camera and then looked at them on the monitor. She had some excellent pictures of Forrester literally foaming at the mouth. A frightened Kyra Larsen throwing her head back in shock after the news of Erling's death.

'Forrester is screaming at them again. I don't know how his assistants put up with it.'

'Maybe that's what they all need this morning, don't you think?'

Andrea was about to tell Fowler to stop talking nonsense when she realised that she had always been a fervent believer in using self-punishment as a way of escaping grief.

LB is proof of that. If I practised what I preached, I would have thrown him out of the window a long time ago. Damn cat. I hope he doesn't eat the neighbour's shampoo. And if he does, I hope she doesn't make me pay for it.

Forrester's screams were inducing people to scurry around like cockroaches when the lights are turned on.

'Maybe he's right, Father. But I don't think it shows much respect for their dead colleague to carry on working.'

Fowler glanced up from his work.

'I don't blame him. He has to hurry. Tomorrow's Saturday.'

'Oh, yes. The *Sabbath*. The Jews can't even turn on a light once the sun sets on Friday. It's nonsense.'

'At least they believe in something. What do you believe in?'

'I've always been a practical person.'

'I suppose you mean a non-believer.'

'I suppose I mean practical. Wasting two hours a week in a place full of incense would take up exactly 343 days of my life. No offence, but I don't think it's worth it. Not even for a supposed eternity.'

The priest chuckled.

'Have you ever believed in anything?'

'I believed in a relationship.'

'What happened?'

'I screwed up. Let's just say that she had more faith in it than I did.'

Fowler remained silent. Andrea's voice had sounded slightly forced. She realised that the priest wanted her to unburden herself.

'On top of that, Father ... I don't think that faith is the only motivating factor behind this expedition. The Ark is going to be worth a lot of money.'

'There are roughly 125,000 tons of gold in the world. Do you believe that Mr Kayn needs to go after the thirteen or fourteen inside the Ark?'

'I'm talking about Forrester and his busy bees,' Andrea replied. She loved arguing but hated it when her arguments were so easily refuted.

'All right. Do you want a practical reason? They're in denial. Their work keeps them going.'

'What the hell are you talking about?'

'Dr Kübler-Ross's stages of mourning.'

'Oh, yes. Denial, anger, depression, all that stuff.'

'Exactly. They're all in the first phase.'

'The way the professor is screaming, you'd think he was in the second.'

'They'll feel better tonight. Professor Forrester will conduct the *hesped*, the eulogy. I believe it will be interesting to hear him say something good about someone other than himself.'

'What's going to happen to the body, Father?'

'They'll put it in a hermetically sealed body bag and bury it for the time being.'

Andrea looked at Fowler in disbelief.

'You're joking!'

'It's Jewish law. Everyone who dies has to be buried within twenty-four hours.'

'You know what I mean. Aren't they going to return him to his family?'

'Nothing and nobody can leave the camp, Ms Otero. Remember?'

Andrea put the camera in her backpack and lit a cigarette.

'These people are crazy. I hope this stupid exclusive doesn't end up wiping all of us out.'

'Always going on about your exclusive, Ms Otero. I can't understand what it is that you need so desperately.'

'Fame and fortune. How about you?'

Fowler stood up and stretched his arms. He leaned backward and his spine gave a loud crack.

'I'm just following orders. If the Ark is real, the Vatican wants to know, so they can recognise it as the object that holds God's commandments.'

A very simple answer, quite ingenious. And totally untrue, Father. You're a very bad liar. But let's pretend I believe you.

'Maybe,' Andrea said after a moment. 'But in this case, why didn't your bosses send a historian?'

Fowler showed her what he had been working on.

'Because a historian couldn't have done this.'

'What is it?' Andrea said curiously. It looked like a simple electrical breaker switch with a pair of wires coming out of it.

'We'll have to forget yesterday's plan for contacting Albert. After Erling's murder, they'll be even more on their guard. So this is what we'll do instead ...'

39

THE EXCAVATION

Friday, July 14, 2006. 3:42 p.m.

Father, tell me one more time why I'm doing this.

Because you want to know the truth. The truth about what's going on here. About why they bothered to contact you in Spain when Kayn could have found a thousand reporters more experienced and famous than you are right there in New York.

The conversation continued to ring in Andrea's ears. The question was the same one the weak little voice in her head had been asking for quite some time now. It had been drowned out by the Philharmonic of Pride, accompanied by Mr Visa Debt, baritone, and Ms Fame at Any Cost, soprano. But Fowler's words had given the weak little voice centre stage.

Andrea shook her head, trying to concentrate on what she was doing. The plan was to take advantage of the period when the off-duty soldiers would be trying to rest, taking a nap or playing cards.

'That's where you come in,' Fowler had said. 'On my signal you slip under the tent.'

'Between the wooden floor and the sand? Are you crazy?'

'There's enough space. You'll have to crawl about a foot and a half until you reach the electrical panel. The cable that connects the generator and the tent is the orange one. Pull it out quickly; connect it to the end of my cable and the other end of my cable back into the electrical panel. Then press this button every fifteen seconds for three minutes. After that, get out of there fast.'

'What will that do?'

'Nothing too complicated technologically. It'll produce a slight drop in the electrical current without totally cutting it off. The frequency scanner will only shut off twice: once when you connect the cable, the second time when you disconnect it.'

'And the rest of the time?'

'It'll be in start-up mode, like a computer when it's loading its operating system. As long as they don't look under the tent there won't be any problems.'

Except that there was: the heat.

Crawling under the tent when Fowler gave the signal had been easy. Andrea had squatted, pretending to tie her boot-lace, looked around and then rolled under the wooden plat-form. It was like diving into a vat of hot butter. The air was thick with the heat of the day and the generator next to the tent produced broiling draughts of heat that wafted into the space where Andrea had crawled.

She was now under the electrical panel, and her face and arms were burning up. She took out Fowler's breaker and held it at the ready in her right hand while with her left she pulled sharply on the orange wire. She connected it to Fowler's device then connected the other end to the panel, and waited.

This useless lying watch. It says only twelve seconds have gone by but it seems more like two minutes. God, I can't bear this heat!

Thirteen, fourteen, fifteen.

She pressed the breaker button.

Above her, the tone of the soldiers' voices changed.

Looks like they've noticed something. I hope they don't give it much thought.

She listened more closely to the conversation. It started as a way to distract herself from the heat and keep her from fainting. She hadn't drunk enough water that morning and was now paying for it. Her throat and lips were parched, and her head felt slightly dizzy. But thirty seconds later, what she was hearing made Andrea begin to panic. So much so that, once the three minutes had elapsed, she was still there pressing the button every fifteen seconds, fighting the feeling that she was about to pass out.

40

SOMEWHERE IN FAIRFAX COUNTY, VIRGINIA

Friday, July 14, 2006. 8:42 a.m.

'Do you have it?'

'I think I have something. It hasn't been easy. This guy is very good at covering his tracks.'

'I need something more than guesswork, Albert. People have started to die here.'

'People always die, don't they?'

'This time it's different. It's scaring me.'

'You? I don't believe it. You didn't even get scared with the Koreans. And that time—'

'Albert . . .'

'Sorry. I've called in a few favours. The experts at the CIA have recovered some of the data from the computers at Netcatch. Orville Watson had a lead on a terrorist by the name of Huqan.'

'Syringe.'

'If you say so. I don't know any Arabic. It looks like the guy was after Kayn.'

'Anything else? Nationality? Ethnic group?'

'Nothing. Just vague stuff, a couple of intercepted e-mails. None of the files escaped the fire. Hard disks are very delicate.'

'You have to find Watson. He's the key to everything. It's urgent.'

'I'm on it.'

41

INSIDE THE SOLDIERS' TENT, FIVE
MINUTES BEFORE

Marla Jackson wasn't used to reading newspapers, and that was why she ended up in jail. Of course, Marla didn't see it that way. She thought she had gone to jail for being a good mother.

The truth about Marla's life lay somewhere between these two extremes. She had had a poor but relatively normal childhood – as normal as a person could have in Lorton, Virginia, whose own citizens referred to it as the armpit of America. Marla was born into a lower-class black family. She played with dolls and a skipping rope, went to school, and fell pregnant at the age of fifteen and a half.

Marla had, in fact, tried to prevent the pregnancy. But she had no way of knowing that Curtis had put a pinhole in the condom. She had no choice. She had heard about the crazy practice among some teenage boys who tried to make themselves look big by getting girls pregnant before they were out of high school. But that was something that happened to other girls. Curtis loved her.

Curtis disappeared.

Marla left high school and entered the not very select club of teenage mothers. Little Mae became the centre of her mother's life, for better or worse. Left behind were Marla's dreams of saving enough money to study meteorological photography. Marla took a job at a local factory, which in addition to her responsibilities as a mother, gave her little time for reading newspapers. Which in turn caused her to make a regrettable decision.

One afternoon her boss announced that he wanted to increase her hours. The young mother had already seen women emerging from the factory exhausted, their heads down, carrying their uniforms in supermarket bags; women whose sons had been left alone and had ended up either in reform school or shot up in a gang fight.

To prevent this, Marla signed up for the Army reserves. That way the factory couldn't increase her hours because it would conflict with her instruction at the army base. This would allow her to spend more time with little Mae.

Marla made the decision to join one day after the Military Police Company was notified of its next destination: Iraq. The news item had appeared on page 6 of the *Lorton Chronicle*. In September 2003, Marla waved goodbye to Mae and climbed aboard a truck at the base. The girl, hugging her grandmother, cried at the top of her lungs with all the grief a six-year-old can muster. Both would die four weeks later when Mrs Jackson, who wasn't as good a mother as Marla, pushed her luck by smoking in bed for the last time.

When she was given the news, Marla found she was incapable of returning home and begged her astonished sister to make all the arrangements for the wake and burial. She then requested that her tour of duty in Iraq be extended, and went on to devote herself wholeheartedly to her next stint – as an MP in a prison called Abu Ghraib.

A year later, a few unfortunate photos turned up on a national television programme. They demonstrated that something inside Marla had finally cracked. The good mother from Lorton, Virginia, had become a torturer of Iraqi prisoners.

Of course, Marla wasn't the only one. In her head, losing her daughter and her mother somehow became the fault of 'Saddam's dirty dogs'. Marla was given a dishonourable discharge and sentenced to four years in prison. She served six months. After she got out of jail she went straight to the security firm DX5 and asked for work. She wanted to return to Iraq.

They gave her work, but she didn't return to Iraq straight away. Instead she fell into Mogens Dekker's hands. Literally.

It had been eighteen months and Marla had learned a great deal. She could shoot much better, knew more philosophy, and had experienced making love with a white man. Colonel Dekker had been turned on almost instantly by the woman with the big strong legs and the face of an angel. Marla had found him somewhat comforting, and the remainder of her comfort derived from the smell of gunpowder. She had killed for the first time and she liked it.

A lot.

She also liked her crew ... sometimes. Dekker had chosen them well: a handful of assassins with no conscience who enjoyed killing under the impunity of a government contract. While they were on the battlefield, they were blood brothers. But on a hot sticky afternoon like this, when they had ignored Dekker's orders to get some sleep and instead were playing cards, things took a different turn. They became as irritated and dangerous as a gorilla at a cocktail party. The worst one was Torres.

'You're messing me around, Jackson. And you haven't even given me a little kiss,' said the small Colombian. It made Marla especially uneasy when he played with his small rusty razor. Like him, it was apparently harmless but capable of slitting a man's throat as if it were butter. The Colombian was slicing small white strips off the edge of the plastic table where they were sitting. There was a smile on his lips.

'*Du scheißt' mich an*, Torres. Jackson has a full house and you're full with shit,' said Alryk Gottlieb, who was constantly battling with English prepositions. The taller of the twins had hated Torres with a vengeance ever since they had watched a World Cup match between their two countries. They had said things to each other, fists had flown. In spite of his six foot two frame, Alryk didn't sleep well at night. If he was still alive, it may only have been because Torres wasn't sure he could take down both twins.

'All I'm saying is that her cards are a little too good,' Torres shot back, smiling even more.

'Well, are you going to deal or what?' said Marla, who had cheated but wanted to remain cool. She had already won almost two hundred from him.

This streak can't last much longer. I'll have to start letting him win, or one night I'm going to end up with that blade in my neck, she thought.

Slowly Torres began to deal, making all sorts of faces to distract them.

The truth is, the bastard's cute. If he wasn't such a psycho and didn't smell weird, he'd turn me on big time.

At that moment the frequency scanner, which sat on a table six feet from where they were playing, started to beep.

'What the hell?' said Marla.

'It's the *verdammt* scanner, Jackson.'

'Torres, go look at it.'

'The fuck I will. I bet five bucks.'

Marla got up and looked at the screen on the scanner, a

machine the size of a small video recorder that nobody used any more, except that this one had an LCD screen and cost a hundred times more.

'Seems OK; it's restarting,' Marla said, returning to the table. 'I'll see your five and raise you five.'

'I'm out,' said Alryk, leaning back in his chair.

'Chickenshit. Doesn't even have a pair,' said Marla.

'You think you're the one running the show, Mrs Dekker?' Torres said.

Marla didn't mind the words as much as his tone. Suddenly she forgot about letting him win.

'No way, Torres. I live in coloured land, bro.'

'What colour? Shit brown?'

'Any colour except yellow. Funny ... the coward's colour, same as on the top of your flag.'

Marla was sorry as soon as she said it. Torres might be a filthy degenerate rat from Medellín, but for a Colombian his country and his flag were as sacred as Jesus. Her opponent pressed his lips together so tightly they almost disappeared and his cheeks turned slightly purple. Marla felt both scared and excited; she enjoyed putting Torres down and drinking in his rage.

Now I'll have to lose the two hundred bucks I won from him and another two hundred of my own. This pig is so pissed off he's likely to hit me, even though he knows Dekker would kill him.

Alryk looked at them, more than a little worried. Marla knew how to take care of herself, but at that moment she felt as if she were crossing a mine field.

'Come on, Torres, raise Jackson. She's bluffing.'

'Leave him alone. I don't think he plans to shave any new customers today, right, fucker?'

'What are you talking about, Jackson?'

'Don't tell me it wasn't you who did the white prof last night?'

Torres looked very serious.

'It wasn't me.'

'It had your signature all over it: a small, sharp instrument, low in the back.'

'I'm telling you, it wasn't me.'

'And I'm saying that I saw you arguing with the ponytailed white dude on the ship.'

'Come off it, I argue with a lot of people. Nobody understands me.'

'Then who was it? The simoon? Or maybe the priest?'

'Sure, it could have been the old crow.'

'You're not serious, Torres,' Alryk cut in. 'That priest is only a *warmer bruder*.'

'Hasn't he told you? This big-time hit man is scared shitless of the priest.'

'I'm not scared of anything. I'm just telling you, he's dangerous,' Torres said, pulling a face.

'I think you swallowed the story that he's from the CIA. For Christ's sake, he's an old man.'

'Only three or four years older than your senile boyfriend. And as far as I know, the boss can break a donkey's neck with his bare hands.'

'Damn right, fucker,' said Marla, who loved bragging about her man.

'He's much more dangerous than you think, Jackson. If you'd taken your head out of your ass for one moment you'd have read the report. That guy is Special Ops pararescue. There's nobody better. A few months before the boss picked you up as the group's mascot, we did an operation in Tikrit.

There was a Special Forces para in our unit. You wouldn't believe the things I saw that guy do … they're not normal. Those dudes have death stuck all over them.'

'Paras are bad news. Hard like hammers,' Alryk said.

'Go to hell, the two of you, fucking Catholic babies,' Marla said. 'What do you think he carries in that black briefcase? C4? A gun? You both patrol that canyon with an M4 that can spit out nine hundred bullets a minute. What's he going to do, smack you with his Bible? Maybe he'll ask the doctor for a scalpel to cut off your nuts.'

'I'm not worried about the doc,' Torres said, waving his hand dismissively. 'She's just some Mossad dyke. I can handle her. But Fowler—'

'Forget the old crow. Hey, if all this is an excuse for not admitting that you took care of the white prof—'

'Jackson, I'm telling you it wasn't me. But trust me: nobody here is who they say they are.'

'Then thank God we have an Ypsilon protocol on this mission,' Jackson said, displaying her perfectly white teeth, which had cost her mother eighty double shifts in the diner where she worked.

'As soon as your boyfriend says *sarsaparilla* it's time for heads to roll. The first one I'm going after is the priest.'

'Don't mention the code, fucker. Go ahead and raise.'

'Nobody's going to raise,' Alryk said, motioning to Torres. The Colombian held back his chips. 'The frequency scanner isn't working. It keeps trying to start.'

'Fuck. Something's wrong with the electricity. Leave it alone.'

'*Halt die klappe Affe*. We can't have that thing turned off or Dekker will kick our ass. I'm going to check out the electrical panel. You two go on playing.'

Torres looked as if he was about to continue the game, but then he gave Jackson a cold stare and got up.

'Wait up, white man. I want to stretch my legs.'

Marla realised that she had gone too far in messing with Torres's manhood, and the Colombian had placed her high up on his list of potential hits. She was only a little sorry. Torres hated everybody, so why not give him a good reason?

'I'm going too,' she said.

The three went out into the boiling heat. Alryk squatted near the platform.

'Everything looks OK here. I'm going to check out the generator.'

Shaking her head, Marla went back inside the tent, wanting to lie down for a while. But before going inside she noticed the Colombian kneeling at the end of the platform and digging around in the sand. He picked up an object and looked at it with a weird smile on his lips.

Marla didn't understand the significance of the red lighter decorated with flowers.

42

THE EXCAVATION

AL MUDAWWARA DESERT, JORDAN

Friday, 14 July 2006. 8:31 p.m.

Andrea's afternoon had been a series of close calls.

She had barely managed to escape from under the platform when she heard the soldiers getting up from the table. And not a moment too soon. A few more seconds of the hot air from the generator and she would have passed out for good. She crawled out through the side of the tent opposite the door, stood up, and walked very slowly towards the infirmary, doing her best not to keel over. What she really needed was a shower, but that was out of the question, since she didn't want to go in that direction and run into Fowler. She grabbed two bottles of water and her camera and left the infirmary tent again, looking for a quiet spot on the rocks in the index finger.

She found a hiding place on a small slope above the canyon floor and sat there watching the archaeologists' activities. She didn't know what stage their grief had reached now. At some point Fowler and Dr Harel went by, probably looking for her. Andrea ducked her head behind the rocks and tried to piece together what she had heard.

The first conclusion she came to was that she couldn't trust Fowler – which was something she already knew – and she couldn't trust Doc – which was something that made her even more uncomfortable. Her thoughts about Harel hadn't gone much beyond the tremendous physical attraction

All I have to do is look at her and I'm turned on.

But the idea that she was a spy for Mossad was more than Andrea could handle.

The second conclusion she reached was that she had no choice but to trust the priest and the doctor if she wanted to get out of this alive. Those words about the Ypsilon protocol had totally undermined her sense of who was really in charge of the operation.

On one side there's Forrester and his stooges, all of them much too meek to pick up a knife and kill one of their own. Or maybe not. Then there's the maintenance people, tied to their thankless work – no one pays them much attention. Kayn and Russell, the brains behind this madness. A group of hired soldiers, and a secret code word to start killing people. But to kill who, or who else? What's clear, for better or worse, is that our fate was sealed the moment we joined this expedition. And it seems fairly certain that it is for worse.

Andrea must have fallen asleep at some point because when she woke up, the sun was going down and a heavy grey light had replaced the usual high contrast between sand and shade in the canyon. Andrea was sorry she had missed the sunset. Each day she tried to make sure she went to the open area beyond the canyon at that time. The sun would dive into the sand, revealing layers of heat that looked like waves on the horizon. Its final burst of light was like a gigantic orange explosion that remained in the sky for several minutes after it had disappeared.

Back here in the canyon's index finger, the only twilight scenery was large, bare sandy rock. With a sigh she reached her hand into her trouser pocket and pulled out her packet of cigarettes. Her lighter was nowhere to be found. Surprised, she began searching her other pockets until a voice in Spanish almost made her heart leap into her throat.

'Looking for this, my little bitch?'

Andrea glanced up. Five feet above her, Torres was lying on the slope, his arm outstretched, offering her the red lighter. She guessed that the Colombian must have been there for a while – *stalking her* – and it sent a shiver up her spine. Trying not to betray her fear, she stood up and reached for the lighter.

'Didn't your mother teach you how to speak to a lady, Torres?' Andrea said, controlling her nerves enough to light the cigarette and exhale the smoke towards the mercenary.

'Sure, but I don't see no lady here.'

Torres was staring at Andrea's smooth thighs. She was wearing a pair of trousers that she'd unzipped above the knees to convert them into shorts. With the heat, she had rolled them up even further, and the white skin above her suntan seemed sensual and inviting to him. When Andrea noticed the direction of the Colombian's gaze, her fear increased. She turned towards the end of the canyon. One loud scream would be good enough to get everyone's attention. The crew had started digging some test pits a couple of hours before – almost the same time as her little trip under the soldiers' tent.

But when she turned, she couldn't see anyone. The mini-excavator was sitting there by itself, off to one side.

'Everybody's gone to the funeral, baby. We're all alone.'

'Shouldn't you be at your post, Torres?' Andrea said, pointing to one of the cliffs, trying to appear nonchalant.

'I'm not the only one who's been somewhere they shouldn't, right? That's something we need to correct, no question about it.'

The soldier jumped down to where Andrea was standing. They were on a rocky platform no bigger than a pingpong table, some fifteen feet above the canyon floor. An irregular pile of rocks was heaped up towards the edge of the platform, which had served to conceal Andrea earlier, but now blocked her escape.

'I don't know what you're talking about, Torres,' Andrea said, playing for time.

The Colombian took a step forward. He was now so close to Andrea that she could see the beads of sweat covering his forehead.

'Of course you do. And now you're going to do something for me, if you know what's good for you. It's a shame that such a fine-looking girl has to be a dyke. But I think that's because you've never had a good stiff one.'

Andrea took a step back towards the rocks, but the Colombian placed himself between her and the place where she had climbed on to the platform.

'You wouldn't dare, Torres. The other guards could be watching us right now.'

'Only Waaka can see us . . . and he's not going to do a thing. He'll feel kind of jealous, can't get it up any more. Too many steroids. But don't worry, mine works fine. You'll see.'

Andrea realised that it was impossible to get away, so she made a decision out of pure desperation. She tossed her cigarette to the ground, planted her two feet firmly on the rock and leaned forward a little. She wasn't going to make it easy for him.

'Come on then, you son of a whore. If you want it, come and get it.'

A sudden gleam ran across Torres's eyes, a mixture of excitement at the challenge and anger at the insult to his mother. He lunged forward and grabbed Andrea's arm, pulling her roughly towards him with a strength that didn't seem possible in someone so short.

'I love that you're asking for it, bitch.'

Andrea twisted her body and hit him hard in the mouth with her elbow. Blood spilled down on to the stones and Torres let out a grunt of rage. Pulling violently on Andrea's T-shirt, he ripped it at the sleeve, revealing her black bra. Seeing this excited the soldier even more. He grabbed both of Andrea's arms, intending to bite her breast, but at the last minute the reporter took a step back and Torres's teeth shut on nothing.

'Come on, you're going to like it. You know you want to.'

Andrea tried kneeing him between the legs or in the stomach, but anticipating her moves, Torres turned aside and crossed his legs.

Don't let him throw you to the ground, Andrea said to herself. She remembered a story she had followed two years before on a group of rape victims. She had gone with some other young women to an anti-rape seminar led by an instructor who had almost been raped when she was a teen. The woman had lost an eye but not her virginity. The rapist lost everything. *If he throws you to the ground, he has you.*

Another violent grab from Torres ripped off the bra strap. Torres decided that this was enough and added more pressure to Andrea's wrists. She could barely move her fingers. He twisted her right arm violently, leaving the left one loose. Andrea now had her back to him, but was unable to move because of the Colombian's pressure on her arm. He forced her to bend over and kicked her ankles to open her legs.

The rapist is weakest at two points, the words of the instructor rang in her mind. The words were so strong, the woman had been so sure of herself, so in control that Andrea felt new strength. *When he takes off your clothes and when he takes off his. If you're lucky and he takes his off first, take advantage of it.*

With one hand, Torres undid his belt and his camouflage trousers fell to his ankles. Andrea could see his erect member, hard and menacing.

Wait until he leans over you.

The mercenary leaned over Andrea, searching for the fastening on her trousers. His rough beard scratched the back of her neck, and that was the signal she needed. She lifted her left arm suddenly, shifting all her weight to her right side. Taken by surprise, Torres let go of Andrea's right arm and she tumbled to the right. The Colombian tripped on his trousers and fell forward, hitting the ground hard. He tried to get up, but Andrea was on her feet first. She gave him three swift kicks to the stomach, taking care that the soldier didn't grab her ankle and make her fall. The kicks found their mark and when Torres tried to roll into a ball to protect himself, he left a much more sensitive place open to attack.

Thank you, God. I never get tired of doing this, the youngest and only female of five siblings confessed silently as she pulled back her foot before blasting Torres's testicles. His scream bounced off the canyon walls.

'Let's keep this between us,' Andrea said. 'Now we're even.'

'I'm gonna get you, you bitch. I'm going to get you so bad you're going to choke on my dick,' Torres whined, almost crying.

'On second thoughts …' Andrea began. She had reached the edge of the terrace and was about to climb down but she turned quickly and ran a few steps, aiming her foot once more between Torres's legs. It was useless for him to try to cover up with his hands. This time there was even more force behind the kick and Torres was left gasping for breath, his face red and two big tears running down his cheeks.

'Now we're really good and even.'

43

THE EXCAVATION

AL MUDAWWARA DESERT, JORDAN

Friday, 14 July 2006. 9:43 p.m.

Andrea returned to the camp as fast as she could without running. She didn't look back nor did she worry about her ripped clothing until she approached the row of tents. She felt a strange kind of shame about what had happened, mixed with the fear that someone would find out about her interfering with the frequency scanner. She attempted to look as normal as possible, despite the fact her T-shirt was hanging off her, and headed over towards the infirmary. Luckily she didn't run into anyone. As she was about to enter the tent, she ran into Kyra Larsen, who was carrying her belongings out.

'What's going on, Kyra?'

The archaeologist gave her a cold look.

'You didn't even have the decency to show up at the *hesped* for Stowe. I guess it doesn't matter. You didn't know him. For you he was just a nobody, right? That's why you didn't even care that it's your fault he died.'

Andrea was about to reply that other things had kept her away, but she doubted Kyra would understand so she said nothing.

'I don't know what you're up to,' Kyra went on, barging

past her. 'You know very well that the doctor wasn't in her bed that night. She may have fooled everyone else, but not me. I'm going to sleep with the rest of the team. There's an empty cot, thanks to you.'

Andrea was happy to see her go – she wasn't in the mood for any more confrontations and in her heart she agreed with every one of Kyra's words. Guilt had played an important part in her Catholic education, and sins of omission were as persistent and painful as any other.

She went into the tent and saw Dr Harel, who turned away. It was obvious that she had had an argument with Larsen.

'I'm glad you're all right. We were worried about you.'

'Turn around, Doc. I know you've been crying.'

Harel faced her, rubbing her reddened eyes.

'It's silly really. A simple secretion from tear glands and yet we all feel embarrassed about it.'

'A lie is more embarrassing.'

Then the doctor noticed Andrea's ripped clothing, something that Larsen, in her anger, seemed to have overlooked, or hadn't bothered to comment on.

'What happened to you?'

'I fell down the stairs. Don't change the subject. I know who you are.'

Harel chose each of her words carefully.

'What do you know?'

'I know that combat medicine is highly regarded by Mossad, or so it seems. And that your emergency substitution was not as big a coincidence as you told me.'

The doctor frowned, then went over to Andrea, who was rummaging around in her rucksack for something clean to wear.

'I'm sorry you had to find out this way, Andrea. I'm only a

low-ranking analyst, not a field agent. My government wants to have eyes and ears on every archaeological expedition that's after the Ark of the Covenant. This is the third one I've been on in seven years.'

'Are you really a doctor? Or is that a lie too?' Andrea said as she slipped into another T-shirt.

'I'm a doctor.'

'And how is it that you get along so well with Fowler? Because I've also found out that he's a CIA agent, in case you didn't know.'

'She already knew, and you owe me an explanation,' Fowler said.

He was standing near the door, frowning but relieved after having looked for Andrea all afternoon.

'Bullshit,' Andrea said, pointing her finger at the priest, who stepped back surprised. 'I almost died from the heat under that platform, and on top of that, one of Dekker's dogs just tried to rape me. I'm in no mood to talk to the two of you. At least not yet.'

Fowler touched Andrea's arm, noticing the bruises on her wrists.

'Are you all right?'

'Better than ever,' she said, pushing the hand away. The last thing she wanted was male contact.

'Ms Otero, did you hear the soldiers' conversation while you were under the platform?'

'What the hell were you doing there?' a shocked Harel interrupted.

'I sent her. She was helping me break up the frequency scanner so I could call my contact in Washington.'

'I would have liked to have been informed, Father,' Harel said.

Fowler lowered his voice until it was almost a whisper.

'We need information and we're not going to get it trapped inside this bubble. Or do you think that I don't know you slip away every night to send text messages to Tel Aviv?'

'Touché,' Harel said, pulling a face.

Was that what you were up to, Doc? Andrea wondered, biting her lower lip and trying to work out what to do. *Maybe I was wrong and I should trust you after all. I hope so, because there's no other choice.*

'Fine, Father. I'll tell you both what I heard . . .'

44

ℱOWLER AND ℋAREL

'We have to get her out of here,' whispered the priest.

The shadows of the canyon surrounded them, and the only sounds came from the mess tent, where members of the expedition had begun eating their supper.

'I don't see how, Father. I thought of stealing one of the Hummers, but we'd have to get it over that dune. And I don't think we would get far. What if we told everyone in the group what's really going on here?'

'Suppose we could do that and they believed us … what good would it do?'

In the darkness, Harel fought back a moan of rage and impotence.

'The only thing I can think of is the same answer you gave me yesterday about the mole: wait and see.'

'There is one way,' Fowler said. 'But it'll be dangerous, and I'll need your help.'

'You can count on me, Father. But first explain to me what this Ypsilon protocol is.'

'It's a procedure by which a security detail assassinates all the members of a group they're supposed to protect, if the code word comes over the radio. They kill everybody except the person who hired them and anyone he says should be left alone.'

'I don't understand how something like that can exist.'

'Officially it doesn't. But a few soldiers in mercenary outfits who were in Special Forces, for example, imported the concept from Asian countries.'

Harel stood very still for a moment.

'Is there any way of knowing who's included?'

'No,' the priest said weakly. 'And the worst part is that the person who contracts the military detail is always different to the one who is supposed to be in charge.'

'Then Kayn . . .' Harel said, opening her eyes.

'Exactly, Doctor. Kayn isn't the one who wants us dead. It's someone else.'

45

THE EXCAVATION

AL MUDAWWARA DESERT, JORDAN

Saturday, 15 July 2006. 2:34 a.m.

At first, there was absolute stillness in the infirmary tent. With Kyra Larsen sleeping with the other assistants, the breathing of the remaining two women was the only thing that could be heard.

After a while there was a light scratching. It was the *Hawnvëiler* zip, the most hermetic and secure in the world. Not even dust could penetrate, but nothing could prevent an intruder's access once it had been unzipped twenty inches or so.

What followed was a series of faint sounds: stockinged feet on the wood; the pop of a small plastic box being opened; then an even fainter but more menacing sound: that of twenty-four nervous keratin legs scurrying around inside the little box.

Then there followed a discrete silence because the movements were almost inaudible to the human ear: the partly opened end of a sleeping bag being lifted up, the twenty-four little legs landing on the cloth inside, the end of the cloth being returned to its original position, covering the owners of those twenty-four small legs.

For the next seven seconds, breathing once again dominated the silence. The sliding of the stockinged feet leaving the tent was even quieter than before, and the prowler didn't close the zip when he left. The movement that Andrea made inside the sleeping bag was so brief that it hardly produced a sound. It was, however, enough to provoke the visitors to her sleeping bag into discharging their anger and confusion after being shaken about so much by the prowler before he entered the tent.

The first sting drilled into her and Andrea shattered the silence with her screams.

46

Al Qaeda Training Manual
Found By Scotland Yard in a Hideout
Pages 131 and following.
Translated By WM and SA[1].

Military studies for the Jihad against tyranny

In the name of Allah, the merciful and the compassionate [...]

[1] The original Al Qaeda manual comprises 5,000 pages in several volumes, and contains detailed information concerning operations carried out in the past by the terrorist group, as well as the correct methods for recruiting new members; training; creating cells, preparing and using explosives against military and civilian targets; assassinations with all sorts of firearms, poisons and knives; espionage and counter-espionage; and resistance to interrogation and torture. In terrorist hideouts there is always a smaller version some 180 pages long. It is strictly forbidden to take the manual out of the house and the head of the cell has orders to destroy it at any sign of danger.

Chapter 14: Kidnappings and Assassinations Using Rifles and Pistols

It is better to choose a revolver, because even though it has fewer bullets than an automatic pistol, it doesn't jam and the empty cartridges remain in the cylinder, making it more difficult for investigators.

[...]

Critical parts of the body

The gunman should be familiar with the essential parts on the body or [where] to wound critically in order to aim at these areas on the individual who is to be assassinated. They are:

1. The circle that includes the two eyes, the nose and the mouth is a fatal area, and the gunman should not aim below or to the left or right or he risks having the bullet fail to kill
2. The part of the neck where the arteries and veins meet
3. The heart
4. The stomach
5. The liver
6. The kidneys
7. The spinal column

Principles and Rules for Firing

The biggest mistakes in aiming are due to physical stress or nerves, which can make the hand jump or shake. This can be caused by putting too much pressure on the trigger or by pulling on the trigger instead of squeezing it. This makes the muzzle of the gun shift away from the target.

For that reason, the brothers should follow these rules when aiming and firing:

1. Control yourself when you squeeze the trigger so the gun doesn't move
2. Squeeze the trigger without too much force and without pulling on it
3. Do not let the sound of the shot affect you and do not concentrate on what it will sound like because that will make your hand shake
4. Your body should be normal, not tense, and your limbs relaxed; but not too relaxed
5. When you fire, line up your right eye with the centre of the target
6. Close your left eye if you fire with your right hand and vice versa
7. Do not take too long in aiming or your nerves may fail you
8. Do not feel regret in squeezing the trigger. You are killing an enemy of your God

47

WASHINGTON SUBURB

Friday, 14 July 2006. 8:34 p.m.

Nazim took a sip of Coke but immediately set it aside. It contained too much sugar, as did all the drinks in restaurants where you could refill your cup as many times as you wanted. The Mayur Kebab shop where he had bought dinner was one such place.

'You know, I saw a documentary the other day about this guy who only ate hamburgers from McDonald's for a month.'

'That's disgusting.'

Kharouf had his eyes half closed. He had been trying to fall asleep for a while but couldn't. Ten minutes ago he had given up and tilted the car seat upright again. That Ford was too uncomfortable.

'They said that his liver turned into pâté.'

'That could only happen in the United States. The country with the fattest people in the world. You know it uses up to 87 per cent of the world's resources.'

Nazim didn't say anything. He had been born an American, but a different kind of American. He hadn't learned to hate his country, even though his lips said otherwise. To him, Kharouf's hatred of the United States seemed too all-encompassing. He would prefer to imagine the President kneeling and facing Mecca in the Oval Office than see the White House destroyed by fire. One time he had said something of the sort to Kharouf and Kharouf had shown him a CD containing photos of a small girl. They were photos of a crime scene.

'The Israeli soldiers raped and killed her in Nablus. There isn't enough hatred in the world for such a thing.'

Remembering the images made Nazim's blood boil too, but he tried to keep such thoughts out of his head. In contrast to Kharouf, hatred was not the source of his energy. His motivations were selfish and twisted; they were about getting something for himself. His prize.

Days before, when they had gone into the offices of Net-catch, Nazim had barely been conscious of anything. In a certain way he felt bad because the two minutes they had spent wiping out the *kafirun*[2] had almost been erased from his head. He had tried to remember what had happened, but it was as if they were somebody else's memories, like the crazy dreams in the chic-flicks his sister liked, in which the main character sees herself from the outside. Nobody has dreams in which they see themselves from the outside.

'Kharouf.'

'Talk to me.'

'Remember what happened last Tuesday?'

'Are you talking about the operation?'

'Right.'

Kharouf looked at him, shrugged his shoulders and smiled sadly.

'Every detail.'

Nazim looked away because he felt ashamed of what he was going to say.

'I ... I don't remember too much, you know?'

---

[2] Disbelievers, according to the Koran.

'You should thank Allah, blessed be his name. The first time I killed someone I couldn't sleep for a week.'

'You?'

Nazim opened his eyes wide.

Kharouf tousled the young man's hair playfully.

'That's right, Nazim. You're a jihadist now and we're equals. Don't be so surprised that I went through tough times too. It's sometimes hard to act as God's sword. But you have been blessed with being able to forget the ugly details. The only thing left for you is pride in what you've done.'

The young man felt much better than he had in the last few days. He was quiet for a while, saying a prayer of thanks. He felt the sweat trickling down his back but didn't dare turn on the car's engine so that he could put on the air-conditioning. The wait began to feel endless.

'Are you sure he's in there? I'm beginning to wonder,' said Nazim, pointing to the wall that surrounded the estate. 'Don't you think we should look elsewhere?'

Kharouf thought for a moment, and then shook his head.

'I wouldn't have the slightest idea where to look. How long did we follow him? A month? He only came here once, and was loaded down with packages. He went out with nothing in his hands. That house is empty. For all we know, it could belong to a friend and he was doing him a favour. But it's the only link we have, and we have you to thank for finding it.'

This was true. On one of the days that Nazim had to follow Watson on his own, the guy had started acting strangely, switching lanes on the highway, and taking a route back home that was completely different to the one he usually took. Nazim had turned up the volume on the radio and imagined he was a character in *Grand Theft Auto*, the popular video game in which the main character is a criminal who has to carry out missions such as kidnapping, killing, drug dealing and fleecing prostitutes. There was a part of the game in which you had to follow a car that was trying to get away. It was one of his favourite parts, and what he had learned helped him in following Watson.

'Do you think he knows about us?'

'I don't think he even knows anything about *Huqan*, but I'm sure our leader has good reason to want him dead. Pass me the bottle. I have to piss.'

Nazim passed him a two-litre bottle. Kharouf unzipped his trousers and urinated inside. They had several empty bottles so that they could relieve themselves discreetly inside the car. It was better putting up with the hassle and throwing the bottles out later than having someone notice them pissing in the street or going into one of the local bars.

'You know what? To hell with this,' Kharouf said grimacing. 'I'll get rid of this bottle in the alley and then we'll go look for him in California at his mother's house. To hell with everything.'

'Wait, Kharouf.'

Nazim was pointing at the gate of the estate. A delivery man on a motorcycle was ringing the bell. Seconds later someone appeared.

'He's there! You see, Nazim, I told you. Congratulations!'

Kharouf was excited. He slapped Nazim on the back. The boy felt happy and nervous at the same time, as if a hot wave and a cold wave were colliding deep inside him.

'Excellent, kid. We're finally going to finish what we started.'

48

THE EXCAVATION

AL MUDAWWARA DESERT, JORDAN

Saturday, 15 July 2006. 2:34 a.m.

Harel woke up startled by Andrea's screams. The young reporter was sitting on top of her sleeping bag, grabbing her leg as she cried out.

'God, it hurts!'

The first thing Harel thought was that Andrea had got cramp while she slept. She jumped up, turned on the infirmary lights and grabbed hold of Andrea's leg in order to massage it.

It was then that she saw the scorpions.

There were three of them, at least three that had come out of the sleeping bag and were running around crazily with their tails up, ready to sting. They were a sickly yellow colour. Terrified, Dr Harel jumped on to one of the examination tables. She was barefoot and thus easy prey.

'Doc, help me. Oh God, my leg's on fire ... Doc! Oh, God!'

Andrea's cries helped the doctor to channel her fear and think. She couldn't leave her young friend helpless and suffering.

Let me see. What the hell do I remember about these bastards? They're yellow scorpions. The girl has twenty minutes at most before things turn ugly. If only one of them stung her, that is. If more than one . . .

A terrible thought crossed the doctor's mind. If Andrea was allergic to the scorpion's poison, she was a goner.

'Andrea, listen to me very carefully.'

Andrea opened her eyes and looked at her. Lying on her bedding, clutching her leg and staring blankly ahead of her, the girl was clearly in agony. Harel made a superhuman effort to overcome her own paralysing fear of scorpions. It was a natural fear that any Israeli, as she was, born in Beersheba at the edge of the desert, would have learned as a young girl. She tried to put her foot on the floor but couldn't.

'Andrea. Andrea, on the list of allergies you gave me, were cardiotoxins included?'

Andrea howled again in pain.

'How do I know? I carry the list because I can't remember any more than ten names at a time. Fuuuuuuuuuuuck! Doc, get down from there, for God's sake, or Jehovah's, or whatever. The pain is worse . . .'

Harel tried again to master her fear, putting a foot on the floor, and in two leaps she reached her own mattress.

I hope they're not in here. Please God, don't let them be in my sleeping bag . . .

She kicked the sleeping bag to the floor, grabbed a boot in each hand and returned to Andrea.

'I have to put on my boots and go over to the medicine cabinet. You'll be all right in a minute,' she said, pulling on her boots. 'The poison is very dangerous, but it takes almost half an hour to kill a person. Hold on.'

Andrea did not reply. Harel looked up. Andrea had brought her hand up to her neck and her face was starting to turn blue.

Oh, Holy God! She is *allergic. She's going into anaphylactic shock.*

Forgetting to put on her other boot, Harel knelt next to Andrea, her naked legs exposed to the floor. She had never been so aware of every square inch of her flesh. She looked for the place where the scorpions had stung Andrea and found two spots on the reporter's left calf, two small holes, each surrounded by an inflamed area roughly the size of a tennis ball.

Shit. They really got her.

The tent flap opened and Father Fowler came in. He was also barefoot.

'What's going on?'

Harel was leaning over Andrea, trying to give her mouth-to-mouth resuscitation.

'Father, please hurry. She's in shock. I need epinephrine.'

'Where is it?'

'In the cabinet at the end, second shelf from the top. There are some green vials. Bring me one and a syringe.'

She leaned over and blew more air into Andrea's mouth, but the swelling in her throat was hindering the passage of air into her lungs. If Harel didn't treat the shock straight away, her friend would be dead.

And it'll be your fault, for being such a coward and climbing up on the table.

'What the hell happened?' said the priest, running to the cabinet. 'She's in shock?'

'Get out,' Doc screamed at the half-dozen sleepy heads peering into the infirmary. Harel didn't want one of the scorpions to escape and find some other victim. 'A scorpion stung her, Father. There are three in here right now. Be careful.'

Father Fowler flinched slightly at the news and moved

carefully towards the doctor with the epinephrine and syringe. Harel immediately injected five CCs into Andrea's naked thigh.

Fowler grabbed a five-gallon jar of water by the handle.

'You take care of Andrea,' he told the doctor. 'I'll find them.'

Harel now turned all her attention to the young reporter, although by this point all she could do was observe her condition. It would be the epinephrine that would have to work its miraculous effect. As soon as the hormone entered Andrea's bloodstream, the nerve endings in her cells would start firing. The fat cells in her body would begin to break up the lipids to free extra energy, her heart rate would increase, her blood would carry more glucose, her brain would start producing dopamine, and most importantly, her bronchial tubes would dilate and the swelling in her throat disappear.

With a loud gulp, Andrea took her first breath of air on her own. To Dr Harel, the sound was almost as beautiful as the three dry thuds of Father Fowler's gallon jug that she had heard in the background as the medicine continued to work. When Father Fowler sat down on the floor next to her, Doc had no doubt that the three scorpions were now reduced to three stains on the floor.

'And the antidote? Something to deal with the poison?' asked the priest.

'Yes, but I don't want to inject her just yet. It's made from the blood of horses that have been exposed to hundreds of scorpion stings so that eventually they become immune. The vaccine always carries traces of the toxin, and I don't want to risk another shock.'

Fowler watched the young Spaniard. Her face was slowly starting to look normal again.

'Thank you for everything you've done, Doctor,' he said. 'I won't forget it.'

'No problem,' replied Harel, who was by now all too conscious of the danger they had been through, and began to shake.

'Will there be any after-effects?'

'No. Her body can fight against the poison now.' She raised the green vial. 'This is pure adrenalin, it's like giving her system a weapon. All the organs in her body will double their capacity and prevent her from choking. She'll be all right in a couple of hours, although she will feel like shit.'

Fowler's face relaxed a little. He pointed to the door.

'Are you thinking what I'm thinking?'

'I'm no idiot, Father. I've been in the desert hundreds of times in my country. The last thing I do at night is make sure all the doors are closed. In fact, I double check. This tent is more secure than a Swiss bank account.'

'Three scorpions. All at the same time. In the middle of the night ...'

'Yes, Father. That's the second time someone has tried to kill Andrea.'

49

Orville Watson's Safe House

Friday, 14 July 2006. 11:36 p.m.

Ever since he had started hunting terrorists, Orville Watson had taken a series of basic precautions: making sure he had telephone numbers, addresses and postal codes under different names, then buying a house through an unnamed foreign association that only a genius would have been able to trace to him. An emergency hideout in case things got ugly.

Of course, a safe house only you know of has its problems. For a start, if you want to stock it with supplies then you have to do so on your own. Orville took care of that. Once every three weeks he would take to the house cans, meat for the freezer, and a stack of DVDs of the latest films. He'd then get rid of anything that was out of date, lock up the place and leave.

It was paranoid behaviour ... no question about it. The only mistake Orville had ever made, other than letting himself be followed by Nazim, was that the last time he'd been there he'd forgotten the bag of Hershey bars. It was an unwise addiction, not only because of the 330 calories per bar, but because an emergency order to Amazon might let the terrorists know that you were inside the house they were watching.

But Orville hadn't been able to help himself. He could've done without food, water, internet access, his collection of sexy photos, his books or his music. But when he'd entered the house in the early hours of Wednesday morning, thrown the fireman's coat into the garbage bin and looked into the cupboard where he stored his chocolate and saw that it was empty, his heart had sunk. He couldn't go three or four months without chocolate, having been totally hooked ever since his parents' divorce.

I could've had a worse addiction, he thought, trying to calm himself. *Heroin, crack, voting Republican.*

Orville had never tried heroin in his life, but not even the overwhelming craziness of that drug could compare to the uncontrollable rush he felt when he heard the sound of foil crackling as he unwrapped his chocolate.

If Orville were to go all Freudian, he might have decided that this was because the last thing the Watson family had done together before the divorce was to spend the Christmas of 1993 at his uncle's house in Harrisburg, Pennsylvania. As a special treat his parents took Orville to the Hershey factory, which was only fourteen miles from Harrisburg. Orville grew weak at the knees when they first entered the building and absorbed the aroma of the chocolate. He was even given some Hershey bars with his name on them.

But now Orville was even more worried by another sound: that of breaking glass, if his ears weren't playing tricks on him.

He carefully pushed aside a small pile of chocolate wrappers and got out of bed. He had resisted touching the chocolate for three hours, a personal record, but now that he'd finally given in to his addiction, he planned to go all out. And again, if he'd gone all Freudian about it, he would have worked out that he had eaten seventeen chocolates, one for each member of his company who had died in Monday's attack.

But Orville didn't believe in Sigmund Freud's head trips. For a case of broken glass, he believed in Smith & Wesson. That's why he kept a .38 Special next to his bed.

It can't be. The alarm is on.

He picked up the gun and an object that sat next to it on the night table. It looked like a key chain, but it was a simple remote control with two buttons. The first set off a silent alarm at the police station. The second set off a siren throughout the estate.

'It's so loud it could wake up Nixon and get him tap dancing,' the man installing the alarm had said.

'Nixon's buried in California.'

'Now you know how powerful it is.'

Orville pressed both buttons, not wanting to take any chances. On hearing no siren, he wanted to beat the shit out of the cretin who had installed the system and sworn that it was impossible to disconnect.

Shit, shit, shit, Orville swore to himself, clutching the gun. *What the hell do I do now? The plan was to get here and be safe. What about the mobile . . .?*

It was on the night table on top of an old copy of *Vanity Fair*.

His breathing became shallow and he began to sweat. When he'd heard the breaking glass – probably in the kitchen – he'd been sitting in his bed, in the dark, playing *The Sims* on his laptop and sucking on the chocolate still stuck to the wrappers. He hadn't even realised that the air-conditioning had stopped a few minutes earlier.

They probably cut the electricity at the same time as the supposedly foolproof alarm system. Fourteen thousand bucks. Son of a bitch!

Now, as his fear and the sticky Washington summer drenched him in sweat, his grasp on the gun became slippery and each step he took felt precarious. There was no doubt that Orville had to get out of there as quickly as possible.

He crossed the dressing room and looked out into the hallway of the top floor. Nobody there. There was no way to get down to the first floor other than the stairs, but Orville had a plan. At the end of the hall, on the opposite side to the stairs, there was a small window, and outside a rather puny cherry tree that refused to bloom. No matter. The branches were thick and near enough to the window to allow someone as non-athletic as Orville to try to descend that way.

He got down on all fours and tucked the gun into the tight elastic band of his shorts, then made his large body crawl the ten feet across the rug to the window. Another noise from the floor below confirmed that someone really had broken into the house.

Opening the window, he gritted his teeth the way thousands of people do each day when they are attempting not to make any noise. Fortunately, their lives don't depend on it; unfortunately, his most certainly did. He could already hear footsteps coming up the stairs.

Abandoning all caution, Orville stood up, opened the window, and leaned out. The branches were roughly five feet away, and Orville had to stretch right out even for his fingers to graze one of the thicker ones.

That's not going to work.

Without thinking twice, he put one foot on the window sill, pushed off and made a leap that not even the kindest person watching could have termed graceful. His fingers managed to grab hold of the branch, but in jumping the gun slipped into his shorts, and after a brief, cold contact with what he called 'little Timmy', it slipped down his leg and fell into the garden.

Fuck! What else can go wrong?

At that moment the branch broke.

Orville's full weight landed on his rear end, making quite a bit of noise. More than thirty per cent of the cloth of his shorts didn't survive the fall, as he later realised when he saw the bleeding cuts on his behind. But at that particular moment he didn't notice them because his only concern was to get that same behind as far away as possible from the house, so he headed for the gate of his property, some sixty-five feet down the hill. He didn't have the keys to the gate, but he'd chew his way through it if necessary. Halfway down the hill, the fear attacking him inside was replaced by a sense of accomplishment.

Two impossible escapes in one week. Suck on that, Batman.

He couldn't believe it, but the gate was open. Reaching his arms forward in the dark, Orville headed for the exit.

Suddenly, from the shadows of the wall surrounding the property a dark form emerged and crashed against his face. Orville felt the full force of the blow, and heard a horrible crunching sound as his nose broke. Whimpering and grabbing at his face, Orville fell to the ground.

A figure came running down the path from the house and placed a pistol at the back of his neck. The move was unnecessary since Orville had already passed out. Standing next to his body was Nazim, nervously holding the shovel with which he had hit Orville after assuming the classic stance of a batter facing a pitcher. It had been a perfect swing. Nazim had been a good hitter when he played baseball at school, and in an absurd sort of way he thought that his coach would have been proud to see him make such a fantastic swing in the dark.

'Didn't I tell you?' said Kharouf, between gasps. 'The broken glass works every time. They run like scared little rabbits wherever you want them to go. Come on, put that down and help me get him into the house.'

50

THE EXCAVATION

AL MUDAWWARA DESERT, JORDAN

Saturday, 15 July 2006. 6:34 a.m.

Andrea woke up feeling like she had been chewing on cardboard. She was lying on an examination table next to which Father Fowler and Dr Harel, both in pyjamas, were dozing off on chairs.

She was about to get up to head for the bathroom when the zip on the doorway opened and there was Jacob Russell. Kayn's assistant had a walkie-talkie on his belt and a pensive frown on his face. Seeing that the priest and the doctor were asleep, he tiptoed over to the table and whispered to Andrea.

'How are you?'

'Remember the morning after the day you graduated?'

Russell smiled and nodded.

'Well, the same, but it's as if they substituted brake fluid for the booze,' Andrea said, holding her head.

'We were very worried about you. What happened to Erling, and now this ... We're having a lot of bad luck.'

At that moment Andrea's guardian angels awoke simultaneously.

'Bad luck? That's bullshit,' Harel said, stretching in her chair. 'What happened here was attempted murder.'

'What are you saying?'

'I'd like to know too,' Andrea said, shocked.

'Mr Russell,' Fowler said, standing up and going over to the assistant, 'I'm formally requesting that Ms Otero be evacuated to the *Behemoth*.'

'Father Fowler, I appreciate your concern for Ms Otero's welfare, and normally I'd be the first to agree with you. But doing that would mean breaking the rule about the security of the operation and that's a huge step—'

'Listen—' Andrea broke in.

'Her health is in no immediate danger, is it, Dr Harel?'

'Well ... technically no,' said Harel, forced to concede.

'A couple of days and she'll be as good as new.'

'Listen to me ...' Andrea insisted.

'You see, Father, it wouldn't make sense to evacuate Ms Otero before she's had a chance to accomplish her task.'

'Even when somebody is trying to kill her?' Fowler said tensely.

'There's no proof of that. It was an unfortunate coincidence that the scorpions got into her sleeping bag but—'

'STOP!' Andrea screamed.

Astonished, the three turned towards her.

'Could you stop talking about me as if I wasn't here, and listen to *me* for one fucking moment? Or am I not allowed to give my opinion before you dump me from this expedition?'

'Of course. Go ahead, Andrea,' Harel said.

'First, I want to know how the scorpions got into my sleeping bag.'

'An unfortunate accident,' Russell commented.

'It couldn't have been an accident,' Father Fowler replied. 'The infirmary is a sealed tent.'

'You don't understand,' Kayn's assistant said, shaking his head in frustration. 'Everybody is jumpy about what

247

happened to Stowe Erling. Rumours are flying all over the place. Some people are saying it was one of the soldiers, others that it was Pappas when he found out that Erling had located the Ark. If I evacuate Ms Otero now, a lot of other people will want to leave as well. Every time they see me, Hanley, Larsen and a few others say they want me to send them back to the ship. I've told them that, for their own security, they must remain here, because we simply cannot guarantee that they'll reach the *Behemoth* safely. That argument wouldn't count for much if I evacuated you, Ms Otero.'

Andrea was quiet for a few moments.

'Mr Russell, am I to understand that I'm not free to leave whenever I want?'

'Well, I've come to offer you a proposition from my boss.'

'I'm all ears.'

'I don't think you quite understand. Mr Kayn himself will be the one making you the offer.' Russell took the walkie-talkie from his belt and pressed the call button. 'Here she is, sir,' he said, handing it to Andrea.

'Hello and good morning, Ms Otero.'

The old man's voice was pleasant, although he had a slight Bavarian accent.

Like that governor of California. The one who was an actor.

'Ms Otero, are you there?'

Andrea had been so surprised to hear the old man's voice that it took her a while to get her parched throat going again.

'Yes, I'm here, Mr Kayn.'

'Ms Otero, I would like to invite you to have a drink with me later around lunchtime. We can chat and I can answer your questions if you wish.'

'Yes, of course, Mr Kayn. I would like that very much.'

'Do you feel well enough to come over to my tent?'

'Yes, sir. It's only forty feet from here.'

'Well, I'll see you then.'

Andrea gave the walkie-talkie back to Russell, who politely said goodbye and left. Fowler and Harel didn't utter a word; they simply stared at Andrea disapprovingly.

'Stop looking at me like that,' Andrea said, letting herself fall back on the examination table and closing her eyes. 'I can't let a chance like this slip through my fingers.'

'Don't you think it's an amazing coincidence that he offered you an interview the moment we asked if you could leave,' Harel said with irony.

'Well, I can't pass it up,' Andrea insisted. 'The public has a right to know more about this man.'

The priest waved a hand dismissively.

'Millionaires and reporters. They're all the same, thinking they own the truth.'

'Just like the Church, Father Fowler?'

51

ORVILLE WATSON'S SAFE HOUSE

Saturday, 15 July 2006. 12:41 a.m.

The slaps woke Orville up.

They weren't too hard or too many, just enough to bring him back to the land of the living and make him cough out one of his front teeth, which had been damaged by the blow from the shovel. As Orville spat it out, the pain from his broken nose coursed through his skull like a herd of wild horses. The slaps from the man with the almond-shaped eyes punctuated the rhythm intermittently.

'Look. He's awake,' said the older man to his partner, who was tall and thin. The older man smacked Orville a couple more times until he moaned. 'You're not in good shape, are you, *koondeh*[3]?'

Orville found he was lying on top of the kitchen table, wearing nothing but his wristwatch. Despite never having cooked in the house – in fact, he had never cooked anywhere – he did have a fully equipped kitchen. Orville cursed his need for perfection as he regarded all the utensils lined up next to

---

[3] Homosexual in Arabic.

the sink, wishing he hadn't bought that set of sharp kitchen knives, the corkscrews, the barbeque skewers . . .

'Listen—'

'Shut up!'

The younger man was pointing a pistol at him. The older one, who must have been in his mid-thirties, lifted one of the skewers and showed it to Orville. The sharp tip gleamed briefly in the light from the halogen lamps on the ceiling.

'Do you know what this is?'

'It's a skewer. They cost $5.99 a set in Wal-Mart. Listen . . .' Orville said as he tried to sit up. The other man put his hand between Orville's fat breasts and made him lie down again.

'I told you to shut up.'

He lifted the skewer and, leaning heavily, drove the point right through Orville's left hand. The man's expression didn't change, not even when the sharp metal nailed the hand to the wooden table.

At first Orville was too dazed to realise what had happened. Then, suddenly, the pain ran up his arm like an electric shock. He squealed.

'Do you know who invented skewers?' asked the shorter man, grabbing Orville's face to make him look at him. 'It was our people. In fact, in Spain they were called Moorish skewers. They invented them when it was considered bad manners to eat at a table using a knife.'

That's it, you bastards. I have to say something.

Orville was not a coward, but he wasn't stupid. He knew how much pain he could bear and he knew when he was beaten. He took three noisy breaths through his mouth. He didn't dare breathe through his nose and make it hurt even more.

'OK, enough. I'll tell you what you want to know. I'll sing,

I'll spill the beans, I'll draw a rough diagram, plans. There's no need for violence.'

The last word almost became a scream when he saw the man grabbing another skewer.

'Of course you'll talk. But we're not the torture committee. We're the execution committee. The thing is that we want to do it real slow. Nazim, put the pistol to his head.'

The one called Nazim, his expression a complete blank, sat down on a chair and placed the muzzle of the gun on Orville's skull. Orville went still when he felt the cold metal.

'As long as you're in the mood to talk … tell me what you know about Huqan.'

Orville closed his eyes. He was scared. So this was what it was about.

'Nothing. I've just heard things here and there.'

'Bullshit,' said the short man, slapping him three times. 'Who told you to go after him? Who knows about the thing in Jordan?'

'I don't know anything about Jordan.'

'You're lying.'

'It's the truth. I swear to Allah!'

The words seemed to set something off in his aggressors. Nazim pressed the muzzle of the gun harder into Orville's head. The other one placed the second skewer against his naked flesh.

'You make me sick, *koondeh*. Look how you've used your talent – to drag your religion to the ground and betray your Muslim brothers. And all for a handful of beans.'

He traced the point of the skewer over Orville's chest, stopping for a moment on the left breast. He gently lifted the fold of flesh, then let it drop suddenly, making the fat ripple across his belly. The metal left a scratch on the flesh, the droplets of blood mixing with the nervous sweat on Orville's naked body.

'Except that it wasn't exactly a handful of beans,' the man went on, sinking the sharp steel a little more deeply into the flesh. 'You have several houses, a nice car, employees ... and look at that watch, blessed be the name of Allah.'

You can have it if you let go, thought Orville, but he didn't utter a word because he didn't want another steel rod run through him. *Shit, I don't know how I'm going to get out of this.*

He tried to think of something, anything, he could say to make the two men leave him alone. But the horrible pain in his nose and his hand screamed at him that such words did not exist.

With his free hand, Nazim removed the watch from Orville's wrist and gave it to the other man.

'Hey ... Jaeger LeCoultre. Only the best, isn't that right? How much does the government pay you for being a rat? I'm sure it's a lot. Enough to buy twenty-thousand-dollar watches.'

The man threw the watch to the kitchen floor and started stomping as if his life depended on it, but all he managed to do was scratch the face, which made his theatrical gesture lose all its impact.

'I only go after criminals,' Orville said. 'You don't have a monopoly on Allah's message.'

'Don't you dare say His Name again,' said the short one, spitting in Orville's face.

Orville's upper lip began to shake, but he was no coward. He suddenly realised that he was about to die, so he spoke with as much dignity as possible. '*Omak zanya feeh erd*[4]' he

[4] Your mother committed adultery with a monkey.

253

said, looking straight into the man's face and trying not to stutter. Anger flashed in the man's eyes. It was clear that the two men had thought they could break Orville and would watch him begging for his life. They didn't expect him to be brave.

'You're going to cry like a girl,' the older man said.

His arm went up and came down hard, driving the second skewer into Orville's right hand. Orville couldn't help himself and let out a scream that belied his daring of a few moments before. A spray of blood landed in his open mouth and he began to choke, coughing in spasms that wracked his body with pain as his hands jerked away from the skewers that pinned them to the wooden table.

Slowly the coughing lessened and the man's words came true as two large teardrops rolled down Orville's cheeks onto the table. It seemed to be all that the man needed to free Orville from his torture. He raised a new kitchen utensil: a long knife.

'It's all over, *koondeh*—'

A shot went off, echoing from the metal skillets that hung on the wall, and the man fell to the floor. His partner didn't even turn around to see where the shot had come from. He leapt over the kitchen counter, scratching the expensive finish with his belt buckle, and landed on his hands. A second shot splintered part of the door frame a foot and a half above his head as Nazim disappeared.

Orville, his face smashed, his palms run through and bleeding like some strange parody of the crucifixion, was barely able to turn to see who had saved him from certain death. It was a thin blond man of about thirty, dressed in jeans and what looked like a priest's dog collar.

'Great pose, Orville,' the priest said as he ran past him in pursuit of the second terrorist. He hid behind the door frame and then suddenly leaned out, holding the pistol with both hands. The only thing in front of him was an empty room with an open window.

The priest came back into the kitchen. Orville would have rubbed his eyes with amazement had his hands not been pinned to the table.

'I don't know who you are, but thank you. See what you can do to let me loose, please.'

With his damaged nose, it sounded like 'led be looze, bleaze'.

'Grit your teeth. This is going to hurt,' the priest said, pulling on the skewer in his right hand. Although he tried to draw it straight out, Orville still screamed in pain. 'You know, you're not easy to find.'

Orville interrupted him by raising his hand. The wound on it was clearly visible. Gritting his teeth again, Orville rolled to his left and pulled the second skewer out himself. This time he didn't scream.

'Can you walk?' asked the priest, helping him to stand.

'Is the Pope Polish?'

'Not any more. My car is close by. Any idea where your guest has gone?'

'How the fuck should I know?' Orville said, grabbing a roll of kitchen towels next to the window and wrapping his hands in thick layers of paper, like giant wads of candy floss, which slowly began to turn pink from the blood.

'Leave that and get away from the window. I'll bandage you up in the car. I thought you were an expert on terrorists.'

'And I suppose you're from the CIA? Here I was thinking I'd got lucky.'

'Well, more or less. My name's Albert and I'm an ISL[5].'

'A link? Who with? The Vatican?'

Albert didn't answer. Agents of the Holy Alliance never acknowledged their affiliation with the group.

'Forget it, then,' Orville said, fighting back the pain. 'Look, nobody's going to help us here. I doubt if anyone even heard the shots. The nearest neighbours are half a mile away. Do you have a cell phone?'

'Not a good idea. If the police show up, they'll take you to hospital and then they'll want to question you. The CIA will arrive in your room half an hour later with a bunch of flowers.'

'So you know how to handle that thing?' Orville said, pointing at the gun.

'Not really. I hate guns. You're lucky I hit the guy with the knife, and not you.'

'Well, you'd better start liking them,' Orville said, lifting his candy-floss hands and signalling the gun. 'What kind of agent are you?'

'I've only had basic training,' Albert said, looking baleful. 'My thing is computers.'

'Well, that's just great! I'm beginning to feel dizzy,' Orville said, on the verge of fainting. The only thing that kept him from hitting the floor was Albert's arm.

'Do you think you can make it to the car, Orville?'

Orville nodded, but wasn't too sure.

'How many of them are there?' Albert asked.

'The only one left is the one you scared off. But he'll be waiting for us in the garden.'

---

[5] International Service Liaison, link between international espionage services.

Albert took a brief look out of the window but he couldn't see anything in the dark.

'Let's go, then. Down the hill, close to the wall ... he could be anywhere.'

52

ORVILLE WATSON'S SAFE HOUSE

Saturday, 15 July 2006. 1:03 a.m.

Nazim was very scared.

He had imagined the scene of his martyrdom many times. Abstract nightmares in which he'd die in a great ball of fire, something huge that would be televised all over the world. Kharouf's death turned out to be an absurd anticlimax, leaving Nazim confused and frightened.

He had run off into the garden, afraid that the police would show up at any minute. For a moment he was tempted by the main gate, which was still half open. The sound of crickets and cicadas filled the night with promises and life, and for a moment Nazim hesitated.

No. I've dedicated my life to the glory of Allah and the salvation of my loved ones. What will happen to my family if I run away now, if I grow soft?

So Nazim didn't go out of the gate. He remained in the shadows, behind a row of badly neglected snapdragons that still displayed some yellowish blooms. Attempting to ease the tension in his body, he switched the pistol from hand to hand.

I'm in good shape. I jumped over the kitchen counter. The

bullet that was coming for me missed me by a mile. One is a priest and the other is wounded. I'm more than a match for them. All I have to do is watch the path to the gate. If I hear police cars, I'll go over the wall. It's high but I can do it. There's a place on the right that looks a little lower. It's a shame that Kharouf isn't here. He was a genius at opening doors. The gate to the estate only took him fifteen seconds. I wonder if he's already with Allah. I'm going to miss him. He'd want me to stay and finish Watson off. He'd already be dead if Kharouf hadn't waited so long, but nothing made him angrier than someone who betrayed his own brothers. I don't know how it would help the jihad if I died tonight without taking the koondeh down first. No. I can't think like that. I have to concentrate on what matters. The empire in which I was born is destined to fall. And I will help it to do so with my blood. Even though I wish it were not today.

There was a noise from the path. Nazim listened more attentively. They were coming. He had to be quick. He had to—

'OK. Throw down the gun. Go on.'

Nazim didn't even think. He didn't say a final prayer. He just turned around, pistol in hand.

Albert, who had gone out of the back of the house and had stayed close to the wall so he could reach the gate safely, had found the fluorescent strips on Nazim's Nikes in the dark. It wasn't the same as when he'd fired at Kharouf instinctively, to save Orville's life, and hit him through pure luck. This time he had caught the guy unawares only a few feet away. Albert planted both feet on the ground, aimed at the centre of Nazim's chest, and squeezed the trigger halfway, calling out for him to drop the gun. When Nazim turned, Albert pressed the trigger the whole way, blowing open the young man's chest.

Nazim was only vaguely conscious of the shot. He didn't feel any pain, although he was aware of being knocked to the ground. He tried to move his arms and legs but it was pointless and he couldn't speak. He saw the one who had fired bending over him, checking the pulse on his neck then shaking his head. A moment later, Watson arrived. Nazim saw a drop of Watson's blood fall as he leaned over. He never knew if that drop mixed with his own blood flowing from the wound in his chest. His vision was clouding over by the second, but still he was able to hear the voice of Watson, praying.

'Blessed be Allah, who has given us life and an opportunity to praise him with righteousness and honesty. Blessed be Allah, who has taught us the sacred Quran, which says that even though someone may raise his hand against us to kill us, we shall not raise a hand against him. Forgive him, Lord of the Universe, for his sins are those of the deceived innocent. Protect him from the tortures of Hell, and bring him close to you, oh Lord of the Throne.'

After that, Nazim felt much better. It was as if a weight had been lifted from him. He had given everything for Allah. He allowed himself to be transported to such a state of peace that when he heard the police sirens in the distance he confused them with the sound of the crickets. One of them was singing next to his ear and it was the last thing he heard.

Minutes later, two uniformed policemen leaned over a young man dressed in a Washington Redskins jersey. His eyes were open, looking at the heavens.

'Central, this is Unit Twenty-three. We have a ten fifty-four. Send an ambulance–'

'Forget it. He didn't make it.'

'Central, cancel that ambulance for now. We'll go ahead and rope off the crime scene.'

One of the officers looked at the young man's face, thinking that it was a shame he'd died from his wounds. *He was young enough to be my son.* But the man wouldn't lose any sleep over it. He'd seen enough dead kids on Washington's streets to carpet the Oval Office. Yet none of them wore the expression on this one's face.

For a moment he thought of calling his partner to ask him why the hell this kid had such a peaceful smile. He didn't do it, of course.

He was afraid of looking like a fool.

53

SOMEWHERE IN FAIRFAX COUNTY, VIRGINIA

Saturday, 15 July 2006. 2:06 a.m.

Orville Watson's safe house and Albert's apartment were almost twenty-five miles apart. Orville travelled the distance in the back seat of Albert's Toyota, half asleep and semi-conscious, but at least his hands had been properly bandaged, thanks to the first-aid kit the priest carried in his car.

An hour later, dressed in a towelling bathrobe – the only thing of Albert's that fit him – Orville swallowed several Tylenols with the orange juice the priest had brought him.

'You've lost a lot of blood. This will help stabilise you.'

The only thing Orville wanted was to stabilise his body on a hospital bed, but given his limited options he decided he might as well stick with Albert.

'Would you happen to have a Hershey's bar?'

'No, sorry. I can't eat chocolate – it gives me pimples. But in a while I'll go by a Seven Eleven to get something to eat, some extra large T-shirts, and maybe some candy if you want.'

'Forget it. After what happened tonight I think I'm going to hate Hersheys for the rest of my life.'

Albert shrugged. 'It's up to you.'

Orville pointed at the array of computers that cluttered

Albert's living room. On a table about twelve feet long sat ten monitors connected to a mass of cables as thick as an athlete's thigh that ran along the floor next to the wall. 'You have great equipment, Mr International Liaison,' Orville said, speaking to relieve the tension. Observing the priest, he realised they were both in the same boat. His hands were shaking slightly and he seemed a little lost. 'HarperEdwards System, with TINCom motherboards . . . That's how you tracked me down, right?'

'Your offshore in Nassau, the one you used to buy the safe house. It took me forty-eight hours to track down the server that stored the original transaction. Two thousand one hundred and forty-three steps. You're good.'

'You too,' Orville said, impressed.

The two men looked at each other and nodded, recognising fellow hackers. For Albert, this brief moment of relaxation meant that the shock he had held at bay suddenly invaded his body like a group of hooligans. Albert didn't make it to the bathroom. He vomited into a bowl of popcorn he had left on the table the night before.

'I've never killed anybody before. That kid . . . I didn't even notice the other one because I had to act, I shot without thinking. But the kid . . . he was just a baby. And he looked me in the eye.'

Orville didn't say anything, because there was nothing he could say.

They stood like that for ten minutes.

'I understand him now,' the young priest finally said.

'Who?'

'A friend of mine. Someone who's had to kill, and who's suffered because of it.'

'Are you talking about Fowler?'

Albert eyed him suspiciously.

'How do you know that name?'

'Because this whole mess began when Kayn Industries contracted my services. They wanted to know about Father Anthony Fowler. And I can't help noticing that you're also a priest.'

This made Albert even more nervous. He grabbed Orville by the bathrobe.

'What did you say to them?' he shouted. 'I have to know!'

'I told them everything,' Orville said flatly. 'His training, that he was connected to the CIA, to the Holy Alliance ...'

'Oh God! Do they know his real mission?'

'I don't know. They asked me two questions. The first was, who is he? The second: who would matter to him?'

'What did you find out? And how?'

'I didn't find out anything. I would have given up if I hadn't received an anonymous envelope containing a photo and the name of a reporter: Andrea Otero. A note in the envelope said Fowler would do anything to make sure she wasn't harmed.'

Albert let go of Orville's robe and began pacing around the room as he tried to piece it all together.

'Everything is starting to make sense ... When Kayn went to the Vatican and told them he had a clue to finding the Ark, that it could be in the hands of an old Nazi war criminal, Cirin promised to put his best man on the case. In exchange, Kayn had to take a Vatican observer on the expedition. By giving you Otero's name, Cirin made sure that Kayn would allow Fowler to be part of the expedition because then Cirin could control him through Otero, and that Fowler would accept the mission in order to protect her. Manipulative son of a bitch,' Albert said, restraining a smile that was half disgust, half admiration.

Orville looked at him with his mouth open.

'I don't understand a word you're saying.'

'That's lucky for you: if you did then I'd have to kill you. Only joking. Listen, Orville, I didn't rush out to save your life because I'm an agent with the CIA. I'm not. I'm just a simple link in the chain, doing a favour for a friend. And that friend is in serious danger, in part because of the report you gave Kayn about him. Fowler is in Jordan, on a crazy expedition to recover the Ark of the Covenant. And as strange as it might seem, the expedition may prove a success.'

'Huqan,' Orville said, barely audible. 'I found something out by chance about Jordan and Huqan. I gave the information to Kayn.'

'The guys at the Company retrieved that from your hard disks, but nothing else.'

'I managed to find a mention of Kayn on one of the webmail servers used by terrorists. Do you know much about Islamic terrorism?'

'Only what I've read in the *New York Times*.'

'Then we're not even at square one. Here's a crash course. The media's high opinion of Osama Bin Laden, the villain in this film, makes no sense. Al Qaeda as a super-evil organisation doesn't exist. There's no head to chop off. The *jihad* doesn't have a head. The *jihad* is a commandment from God. There are thousands of cells at different levels. They drive and inspire each other without having anything to do with each other.'

'It's impossible to fight against that.'

'Exactly. It's like trying to cure an illness. There isn't a miracle cure, like the invasion of Iraq, or Lebanon, or of Iran. We can only produce white blood cells to kill the germs one by one.'

'That's your job.'

'The problem is that it's not possible to infiltrate Islamic terrorist cells. They can't be bribed. What motivates them is religion, or at least the twisted notion they have of it. You can understand that, I suppose.'

Albert's expression was sheepish.

'They use a different vocabulary,' Orville went on. 'It's a language that's too complex for this country. They can have dozens of different aliases, they use a different calendar ... a westerner needs dozens of checks and mental codes for each piece of information. That's where I come in. With one click of a mouse I'm right there, in between one of these fanatics and another three thousand miles away.'

'The Internet.'

'It looks much prettier on a computer screen,' Orville said, caressing his flattened nose, which was now orange from the Betadine. Albert had tried to set the nose straight using a piece of cardboard and some tape, but he was aware that if he didn't get Orville to a hospital soon, in a month they'd have to break the nose again to straighten it.

Albert thought for a moment.

'So this Huqan, he was going to go after Kayn.'

'I don't remember too much, other than that the guy seemed pretty serious. The truth is that what I gave Kayn was raw information. I hadn't had a chance to analyse anything in detail.'

'Then ...'

'It was like a free sample, you know. You give them a little then sit back and wait. In time they'll ask for more. Don't look at me like that. People have to earn a living.'

'We have to get that information back,' Albert said, drumming his fingers on his armchair. 'First, because the people who attacked you were worried about what you knew. And second, because if Huqan is part of the expedition—'

'All my files have disappeared or been burned.'

'Not all of them. There's a copy.'

Orville was slow to understand what Albert meant.

'No way. Don't even joke about it. That place is impregnable.'

'Nothing is impossible, except one thing – that I go another minute without eating,' Albert said, picking up his car keys. 'Try to relax. I'll be back in half an hour.'

The priest was about to go out the door when Orville called to him. Just the idea of breaking into the fortress that was Kayn Tower was making Orville feel anxious. There was only one way to overcome his nerves.

'Albert . . .?'

'Yes?'

'I've changed my mind about the chocolate.'

54

ℋUQAN

The imam was right.

He had told him that the jihad would enter his soul and his heart. He had warned him about the ones he called weak Muslims because they called true believers radicals.

'You cannot be afraid of how other Muslims will feel about what we do. God did not prepare them for the task. He didn't temper their hearts and souls with the fire that is within us. Let them think that Islam is a religion of peace. That helps us. It weakens the defences of our enemies; it creates holes through which we can penetrate. Cracks.'

He felt it. He could hear the screams in his heart that were only mumblings on others' lips.

He felt it for the first time when he was asked to be a leader in the jihad. He was asked because he had special talent. Gaining the respect of his brothers had not been easy. He had never been in the fields of Afghanistan or Lebanon. He had not followed the orthodox path, and still the Word had clung to the deepest part of his being like a vine to a young tree.

It happened outside the city, in a warehouse. Some brothers were holding another who had let the temptations of the outside world interfere with God's commandments.

The imam had told him he must remain firm, prove himself worthy. All eyes would be watching him.

On the way to the warehouse he had bought a hypodermic

needle and bent the end of it lightly against the car door. He was supposed to go in and talk with the traitor, with the one who wanted to embrace the comforts that they had been called to erase from the face of the Earth. His job was to convince him of his error. Completely naked, his hands and feet tied, the man was sure to listen.

Instead of talking, he had walked into the warehouse, gone directly to the traitor and plunged the bent syringe into the man's eye. Ignoring the screams, he had yanked out the syringe, lacerating the eye. Without waiting, he had then stabbed the other eye and pulled.

Not even five minutes had passed before the traitor was begging them to kill him. Huqan smiled. The message had been clear. His job was to cause pain and make those who went against God want to die.

Huqan. Syringe.

That day he had earned his name.

55

THE EXCAVATION

AL MUDAWWARA DESERT, JORDAN

Saturday, 15 July 2006. 12:34 p.m.

'A white Russian, please.'

'You surprise me, Ms Otero. I imagined you would drink a Manhattan, something more trendy and post-modern,' Raymond Kayn said, smiling. 'Let me mix it myself. Thank you, Jacob.'

'Are you sure, sir?' said Russell, who didn't seem too happy about leaving the old man alone with Andrea.

'Relax, Jacob. I'm not going to jump on Ms Otero. That is, unless she wants me to.'

Andrea realised she was blushing like a schoolgirl. As the billionaire made the drink, she took in her surroundings. Three minutes before, when Jacob Russell had come to the infirmary to get her, she'd been so nervous her hands were shaking. After a couple of hours spent correcting, polishing, then rewriting her questions, she had ripped out the five pages from her notebook, crushed them into a ball, and stuck them in a pocket. That man wasn't normal and she wasn't going to ask him the normal questions.

When she entered Kayn's tent she had begun to doubt her decision. The tent was divided into two rooms. One was a kind of foyer in which Jacob Russell obviously worked. It contained a desk, a laptop, and, as Andrea had suspected, a shortwave radio.

So that's how you keep in touch with the ship ... I thought you wouldn't be disconnected like the rest of us.

To the right, a thin curtain separated the foyer from Kayn's room, proof of the symbiosis between the young assistant and the old man.

I wonder how far these two take their relationship? There's something I don't trust about our friend Russell, with his metro-sexual attitude and his self-importance. I wonder if I should hint at something like that in the interview.

As she'd come through the curtain, she'd discerned a light aroma of sandalwood. A simple bed – *But definitely more comfortable than the inflatable mattresses we're sleeping on* – took up one side of the room. A smaller version of the toilet/shower that the rest of the expedition used, a small desk without papers – and no visible computer – a small bar and two chairs completed the furniture. Everything was white. A pile of books as tall as Andrea was threatening to tip over if anyone came too close. She was attempting to read the titles when Kayn appeared and came straight over to greet her.

Up close he seemed taller than when Andrea had caught a glimpse of him on the rear deck of the *Behemoth*. Five feet, seven inches of shrivelled-up flesh, white hair, white clothes, bare feet. Still, the overall effect was oddly youthful, until you took a closer look at his eyes, two blue holes surrounded by bags and wrinkles that put his age back in perspective.

He didn't extend his hand, leaving Andrea's hanging in the air as he regarded her with a smile that was more of an apology. Jacob Russell had already warned her that under no circumstances should she try touching Kayn, but she wouldn't have been true to herself if she hadn't tried. In any case, it gave her a certain advantage. The billionaire obviously felt a bit self-conscious as he offered Andrea the cocktail. The reporter, true to her profession, wasn't about to turn down a drink, no matter the time of day.

'You can learn a great deal about a person by what they drink,' Kayn said now, handing her the glass. He kept his fingers near the top, leaving Andrea plenty of room to take it without touching him.

'Really? And what does a White Russian say about me?' Andrea asked as she took a seat and had her first sip.

'Let's see . . . a sweet blend, plenty of vodka, coffee liqueur, cream. It tells me that you like to drink, that you can hold your liquor, that you've spent a while finding what you like, that you're attentive to your surroundings, and that you're demanding.'

'Excellent,' Andrea said, with some irony, her best defence when she was unsure of herself. 'You know what? I'd say that you had me investigated beforehand and knew perfectly well what I like to drink. You don't find a bottle of fresh cream in just any portable bar, let alone one that belongs to an agoraphobic billionaire who rarely has visitors, especially in the middle of the Jordanian desert, and who, from what I can see, drinks Scotch and water.'

'Well, now I'm the one who's surprised,' said Kayn, his back to the reporter as he poured his own drink.

'That's as close to the truth as the difference in our bank balances, Mr Kayn.'

The billionaire turned to her, frowning, but did not reply.

'I would say that this has been more of a test, and I gave you the answer you expected,' Andrea went on. 'Now, please tell me why you're granting me this interview.'

Kayn took the other chair but avoided Andrea's gaze.

'It was part of our agreement.'

'I think I've asked the wrong question. Why me?'

'Ah, the curse of the *g'vir*, of the rich man. Everybody wants to know his hidden motives. Everyone supposes he has an agenda, even more so when he's Jewish.'

'You haven't answered my question.'

'Young lady, I'm afraid you'll have to decide which answer you want – the answer to that question, or all the others.'

Andrea bit her lower lip, angry at herself. The old bastard was sharper than he appeared.

He's thrown me a challenge without even ruffling his feathers. OK, old man, I'll follow your lead. I'm going to open my heart completely, swallow your story and when you least expect it I'll find out exactly what I want to know, even if I have to yank out your tongue with my tweezers.

'Why do you drink if you're on medication?' Andrea said, her voice intentionally aggressive.

'I suppose you have deduced that I use medication because of my agoraphobia,' answered Kayn. 'Yes, I take medication for anxiety and no, I shouldn't be drinking. I do it anyway. When my great-grandfather was eighty years old, my grandfather hated seeing him *shiker*. That's drunk. Please interrupt me if there is a Yiddish word that you don't understand, Miss Otero.'

'Then I'm going to have to interrupt you a lot, because I don't know any.'

'As you wish. My great-grandfather drank and drank, and my grandfather used to say: "You should take it easy, *tateh*". He always replied: "Go fuck yourself, I'm eighty years old and I'll drink if I want to." He died at the age of ninety-eight when a mule kicked him in the gut.'

Andrea laughed. Kayn's voice had changed as he spoke of

his ancestor, enlivening his anecdote like a born storyteller and using different voices.

'You know a lot about your family. Were you close to your elders?'

'No, my parents died during the Second World War. Even though they told me stories I don't remember much because of the way we spent my first years. Almost everything I know about my family has been gathered from a variety of outside sources. Let's just say that when I was finally able to do so, I combed all of Europe in search of my roots.'

'Talk to me about those roots. Do you mind if I record our interview?' Andrea asked, taking her digital recorder out of her pocket. It could hold thirty-five hours of top-quality voice recording.

'Go ahead. This story begins one harsh winter in Vienna, with a Jewish couple walking towards a Nazi hospital . . .'

56

ELLIS ISLAND, NEW YORK

December 1943

Yudel cried quietly in the darkness of the hold. The ship had reached the pier and the seamen were motioning the refugees crowded into every inch of the Turkish freighter to leave. All of them hurried forward in search of fresh air. But Yudel didn't move. He grabbed Jora Myer's cold fingers, refusing to believe that she was dead.

It was not his first contact with death. He had seen plenty of it since leaving the hiding place in Judge Rath's house. Fleeing that small hole, which had been asphyxiating but safe, had been a tremendous shock. His first experience of sunlight had taught him that monsters lived out there in the open. His first experience of the city taught him that any little nook was a hiding place from which he could scan the street before scurrying rapidly to the next. His first experience of trains terrorised him, with their noise and the monsters walking up and down the aisles, looking for someone to grab. Luckily, if you showed them yellow cards they didn't bother you. His first experience of an open field made him hate snow, and the brutal cold made his feet feel frozen as he walked. His first experience of the sea was one of a frightening and impossible vastness, the wall of a prison seen from the inside.

On the ship that took him to Istanbul, Yudel began to feel better as he huddled in a dark corner. It had taken them only a day and a half to reach the Turkish port, but it was seven months before they were able to leave it.

Jora Myer had fought tirelessly to get an exit visa. At that time Turkey was a neutral country and many refugees crowded the piers, forming long lines in front of the consulates or humanitarian organisations such as the Red Crescent. With each new day Great Britain was limiting the number of Jews entering Palestine. The United States refused to allow more Jews to enter. The world was turning a deaf ear to the disturbing news about the massacres in the concentration camps. Even a newspaper as prominent as The Times *of London referred to the Nazi genocide merely as 'horror stories'.*

In spite of all the obstacles, Jora did all she could. She begged in the street and covered the tiny Yudel with her coat at night. She tried to avoid using the money that Dr Rath had given her. They slept wherever they could. Sometimes it was a smelly inn or the crowded entrance hall of the Red Crescent, where at night refugees covered every inch of the grey-tiled floor and being able to get up to relieve yourself was a luxury.

All Jora could do was hope and pray. She had no contacts and could speak only Yiddish and German, refusing to use the first language since it brought unhappy memories. Her health was not getting any better. The morning when she first coughed up blood she decided she couldn't go on waiting. She screwed up her courage and decided to give all their remaining money to a Jamaican sailor who worked aboard a freighter that flew the American flag. The ship was leaving in a few days. The crewman managed to smuggle them into the hold. There they mixed with the hundreds lucky enough to have Jewish relatives in the United States who backed up their requests for visas.

Jora died of tuberculosis thirty-six hours before reaching the

United States. Yudel had not left her side for a moment, despite his own illness. He had developed a severe ear infection and his hearing had been blocked for several days. His head felt like a barrel filled with jam, and any loud noises sounded like horses galloping on its lid. That's why he couldn't hear the sailor who was yelling at him to leave. Tired of threatening the boy, the sailor began to kick him.

'Move it, blockhead. They're waiting for you in Customs.'

Yudel again tried to hold on to Jora. The sailor – a short, pimply man – grabbed him by the neck and prised him away from her violently.

'Somebody will come and get her. You, get out!'

The boy struggled free. He searched Jora's coat and managed to find the letter from his father Jora had told him about so many times. He took it and hid it in his shirt before the seaman grabbed him again and forced him out into the frightening daylight.

Yudel walked down the gangplank and on into the building where customs officials dressed in blue uniforms waited at long tables to receive the lines of immigrants. Trembling with fever, Yudel waited in the queue. His feet were burning in his decrepit shoes, and he was longing to escape, and to hide from the light.

Finally it was his turn. A customs official with small eyes and thin lips looked at him over gold spectacles.

'Name and visa?'

Yudel looked at the floor. He didn't understand.

'I don't have all day. Your name and your visa. Are you retarded?'

Another younger customs official with a bushy moustache tried to calm his colleague.

'Take it easy, Creighton. He's travelling alone and doesn't understand.'

'These Jewish rats understand more than you think. Dammit! This is my last ship today and my last rat. I have a mug of cold beer waiting for me at Murphy's. If it makes you happy, you take care of him, Gunther.'

The official with the large moustache came around the table and squatted in front of Yudel. He began speaking to Yudel, first in French, then German and then Polish. The boy continued to look at the floor.

'He doesn't have a visa and he's a half-wit. We'll send him back to Europe on the next damned ship,' interjected the official with glasses. 'Say something, idiot.' He reached over the table and boxed Yudel on the ear.

For a second Yudel felt nothing. But then pain suddenly filled his head as if he had been stabbed and a stream of hot pus shot out of his infected ear.

He screamed the word for compassion in Yiddish.

'Rakhmones!'

The moustachioed official turned angrily on his co-worker.

'Enough, Creighton!'

'Unidentified child, doesn't understand the language, no visa. Deportation.'

The man with the moustache quickly searched the boy's pockets. There was no visa. In fact, there was nothing in his pockets except some bread crumbs and an envelope with Hebrew writing. He checked to see if it contained any money but there was only a letter, which he put back in Yudel's pocket.

'He understood you, dammit! Didn't you hear his name? He's probably lost his visa. You don't want to deport him, Creighton. If you do that, we'll be here for another fifteen minutes.'

The official with the glasses took a deep breath and gave up.

'Tell him to say his surname out loud so I can hear him, and then we'll go for a beer. If he can't, he'll be heading straight to Deportation.'

'Help me, kid,' whispered the moustached man. 'Believe me, you don't want to go back to Europe or end up in an orphanage. You have to convince this guy that you have people waiting for you outside.' He tried again with the only word he knew in Yiddish. 'Mishpokhe?' meaning: family.

From his trembling lips, scarcely audible, Yudel spoke his second word. 'Cohen,' he said.

Relieved, moustache looked at glasses.

'You heard him. He's called Raymond. His name is Raymond Kayn.'

57

KAYN

Kneeling in front of the plastic toilet inside the tent, he fought back the urge to vomit while his assistant tried in vain to get him to drink some water. The old man finally managed to contain his nausea. He hated vomiting, that relaxing but exhausting sensation of expelling everything that was corroding him inside. It was a faithful reflection of his soul.

'You don't know how much this has cost me, Jacob. You have no idea, that *rechielesnitseh*[6] ... talking to her, seeing myself so exposed. I couldn't stand it any more. She wants another session.'

'I'm afraid you are going to have to put up with her a little longer, sir.'

The old man looked at the bar at the other end of the room. His assistant, aware of the direction of his gaze, stared at him disapprovingly and the old man looked away and sighed.

'Human beings are full of contradictions, Jacob. We end up enjoying what we hate the most. Telling a stranger about my life took a weight off my shoulders. For a moment I felt connected to the world. I had planned to deceive her, maybe mix in lies with some truths. Instead of that, I told her everything.'

---

[6] Gossipy woman in Yiddish.

'You did it because you know it's not a real interview. She won't be able to publish it.'

'Perhaps. Or maybe I just needed to talk. Do you think she suspects anything?'

'I don't think so, sir. In any case, we've almost reached the finish.'

'She's very bright, Jacob. Watch her closely. She could turn out to be more than a minor player in this whole thing.'

58

Andrea and Doc

The only thing she remembered from the nightmare was a cold sweat, being gripped by fear and gasping in the darkness, trying to remember where she was. It was a recurring dream but Andrea never knew what it was about. Everything was erased the moment she woke up, leaving her with only traces of fear and loneliness.

But now Doc was immediately by her side, crawling over to her mattress to sit with her and put a hand on her shoulder. One was afraid of going any further, the other that she wouldn't. Andrea sobbed. Doc embraced her.

Their foreheads touched and then their lips.

Like a car that has struggled uphill for hours and has finally reached the top, the next moment was going to be decisive, the instant of equilibrium.

Andrea's tongue searched desperately for Doc's, and she returned the kiss. Doc pulled off Andrea's T-shirt and traced the moist, salty skin of her breasts with her tongue. Andrea lay back on the mattress. She was no longer afraid.

The car raced headlong downhill, without any brakes.

59

THE EXCAVATION

Sunday, 16 July 2006. 1:28 a.m.

They remained next to each other, talking, for a long time; kissing every few words, as if they couldn't believe that they had found each other and that the other person was still there.

'Wow, Doc. You really know how to take care of your patients,' Andrea said as she caressed Doc's neck and played with the curls in her hair.

'It's part of my hypocritical oath.'

'I thought it was the Hippocratic Oath.'

'I took a different oath.'

'It doesn't matter how much you joke around, you're not going to make me forget that I'm still angry with you.'

'I'm sorry I didn't tell you the truth about myself, Andrea. I guess lying is part of my work.'

'What else is part of your work?'

'My government wants to know what's happening here. And don't ask me any more about it, because I'm not going to tell you.'

'We have ways of making you talk,' Andrea said, shifting her caresses to a different place on Doc's body.

'I'm sure I'll be able to fight off the interrogation,' Doc whispered.

Neither woman spoke for a few minutes until Doc let out a long, almost silent, moan. Then she pulled Andrea to her and whispered in her ear.

'Chedva.'

'What does that mean?' Andrea whispered back.

'It's my name.'

Andrea exhaled her surprise. Doc sensed the joy in her and hugged her tight.

'Your secret name?'

'Never say it out loud. Now you're the only one who knows it.'

'And your parents?'

'They're no longer alive.'

'I'm sorry.'

'My mother died when I was a girl and my father died in a prison in the Negev.'

'Why was he there?'

'Are you sure you want to know? It's a shitty, frustrating story.'

'My life is full of shitty frustrations, Doc. It'd be nice to hear someone else's for a change.'

There was a brief silence.

'My father was a *katsa*, a special agent for Mossad. There are only thirty at any one time, and hardly anyone at the Institute reaches that rank. I've been in it for seven years and I'm only *bat leveyha*, the lowest grade. I'm thirty-six years old, so I don't think I'm going to be promoted. But my father was a *katsa* at the age of twenty-nine. He did a lot of work outside Israel and in 1983 he undertook one of his last operations. He lived in Beirut for several months.'

'You didn't go with him?'

'I only travelled with him when he went to Europe or the United States. Beirut wasn't a good place for a young girl back then. It wasn't a good place for anyone, really. That's where he met Father Fowler. Fowler was on his way to the Beqa'a Valley to rescue some missionaries. My father had a great deal of respect for him. He said rescuing those people was the bravest act he'd ever seen in his life, and there wasn't one word about it in the press. The missionaries simply said they'd been released.'

'I suppose that kind of work doesn't welcome publicity.'

'No, it doesn't. During the mission my father uncovered something unexpected: information suggesting that a group of Islamic terrorists with a truck full of explosives was going to make an attempt on an American installation. My father reported this to his superior, who replied that if the Americans were sticking their noses into Lebanon they deserved everything they got.'

'What did your father do?'

'He sent an anonymous note to the American embassy, to warn them; but without a reliable source to back it up, the note was ignored. The next day a truck full of explosives crashed through the gate of a Marine compound, killing two hundred and forty-one Marines.'

'My God.'

'My father returned to Israel, but the story didn't end there. The CIA demanded an explanation from Mossad and someone mentioned my father's name. A few months later, when he was returning home from a trip to Germany, he was stopped at the airport. The police searched his bags and found two hundred grams of plutonium and proof that he was attempting to sell it to the Iranian government. With that amount of material Iran could have built a medium-sized nuclear bomb. My father went to jail, practically without a trial.'

'Someone had planted the evidence against him?'

'The CIA had its revenge. They used my father to send a message to agents all over the world: if you find out about something like this again, make sure you let us know or we'll make sure you're fucked.'

'Oh, Doc, that must have destroyed you. At least your father knew that you believed in him.'

There was another silence, this time a long one.

'I'm ashamed to say this, but . . . for quite a few years I didn't believe in my father's innocence. I thought he had grown tired, that he wanted to earn some money. He was completely alone. Everyone forgot about him, including me.'

'Were you able to make your peace with him before he died?'

'No.'

Suddenly Andrea embraced the doctor, who began to cry.

'Two months after his death, a highly confidential *sodi beyoter* report was declassified. It stated that my father was innocent and supported this with concrete proof, including the fact that the plutonium had belonged to the United States.'

'Wait . . . are you telling me that Mossad knew all about it from the beginning?'

'They sold him out, Andrea. In order to cover up their duplicity they handed the CIA my father's head. The CIA were satisfied, and life went on – except for the two hundred and forty-one soldiers, and my father in his maximum-security prison cell.'

'The bastards . . .'

'My father is buried in Gilot, to the north of Tel Aviv, à

place reserved for those who have fallen in combat against the Arabs. He was the seventy-first member of Mossad to be buried there, with full honours and acclaimed as a war hero. None of which erases the unhappiness they caused me.'

'I don't understand it, Doc. I really don't. Why the hell are you working for them?'

'The same reason my father put up with jail for ten years: because Israel comes first.'

'Another crazy person, just like Fowler.'

'You still haven't told me how the two of you know each other.'

Andrea's voice darkened. That memory was not exactly pleasant.

'In April of 2005 I went to Rome to cover the death of the Pope. By chance I got hold of a tape in which a serial killer said he had killed a couple of cardinals who were to be part of the conclave electing the successor to John Paul II. The Vatican tried to suppress the story and I ended up on the roof of a building fighting for my life. Let's say that Fowler made sure I didn't end up splattered on the pavement. But in the process, he made off with my exclusive.'

'I understand. That must have been frustrating.'

Andrea didn't have a chance to reply. There was a tremendous blast outside that shook the walls of the tent.

'What was that?'

'For a moment I thought it was ... No, it couldn't be—' Doc stopped in mid-sentence.

There was a scream.

And another.

And then many more.

60

THE EXCAVATION

AL MUDAWWARA DESERT, JORDAN

Sunday, 16 July 2006. 1:41 a.m.

Outside there was chaos.

'Bring the buckets.'

'Take them over there.'

Jacob Russell and Mogens Dekker were shouting contradictory orders in the middle of a river of mud that was flowing from one of the water trucks. A giant hole in the back of the tank was spewing out precious water, turning the ground around it into thick reddish sludge.

Several of the archaeologists, Brian Hanley and even Father Fowler ran from one place to the other in their underwear, attempting to form a chain with buckets in order to salvage as much of the water as they could. Little by little, the rest of the sleepy members of the expedition joined them.

Someone – Andrea wasn't certain who it was because the person was covered in mud from head to toe – was trying to build a wall of sand near Kayn's tent to block the river of mud that was heading towards it. He sank the shovel again and again in the sand but before long he was shovelling mud so he stopped. Luckily the billionaire's tent was on slightly higher ground and Kayn didn't have to leave his retreat.

Meanwhile, Andrea and Doc had dressed quickly and had

joined the chain with the other latecomers. As they handed empty buckets back and sent full ones forward, the reporter realised that what she and Doc had been doing before the explosion was the reason why they were the only ones who had bothered to put on all their clothing before coming out.

'Get me a welding torch,' Brian Hanley was shouting from the front of the chain next to the tanker. The chain passed the command along, repeating his words like a litany.

'There isn't one,' the chain signalled in reply.

Robert Frick was at the other end, well aware that with a torch and a large sheet of steel they could have soldered the hole, but he didn't remember unpacking one and didn't have time to look. He had to find some way of storing the water they were managing to save but couldn't find anything large enough.

Suddenly it occurred to Frick that the large metal containers they had used to transport the equipment could hold water. And if they carried these closer to the river of water, they could collect more. The Gottlieb twins, Marla Jackson and Tommy Eichberg lifted one of the boxes and tried to carry it over towards the leak but the last few feet were impossible as their feet lost traction on the slippery ground. Even so, they did manage to fill two of the containers before the water pressure began to weaken.

'It's emptying out now. Let's try to cover the hole.'

With the water nearing the level of the hole, they were able to improvise a stopper using several feet of waterproof canvas. Three people were pushing on the canvas, but the hole was so large and irregular that all it did was slow down the leak.

After half an hour, the result was disappointing.

'I think we've managed to save about 475 gallons out of the

'8,700 that were left in the tank,' said Robert Frick, dispirited, his hands shaking with exhaustion.

Most of the members of the expedition were milling around in front of the tents. Frick, Russell, Dekker and Harel were next to the tanker.

'I'm afraid there'll be no more showers for anyone,' Russell said. 'We have enough water for ten days if we allocate just over twelve pints per person. Will that be enough, Doctor?'

'It's getting hotter each day. By noon it'll reach 110 degrees. That's going to be suicide for anyone working out in the sun. Not to mention holding at least some back for personal hygiene.'

'And don't forget we have to cook,' said Frick, evidently worried. He loved soup and could envisage himself eating nothing but sausages in the coming days.

'We'll have to manage,' Russell said.

'What if it takes longer than ten days to complete the job, Mr Russell? We should fetch more water from Aqaba. I doubt that it will compromise the success of the mission.'

'Dr Harel, I'm sorry to inform you, but I've learned from the ship's radio that Israel has been at war with Lebanon for the past four days.'

'Really? I had no idea,' Harel lied.

'Every radical group in the region is supporting the war. Can you imagine what would happen if a local merchant happened to tell the wrong person that he'd sold water to some Americans running around in the desert? Being low on water and dealing with the intruders who killed Erling would be the least of our problems.'

'I understand,' Harel said, aware that her opportunity to get Andrea out of there had vanished. 'But don't complain when everyone starts getting heat stroke.'

'Fuck!' said Russell, venting his frustration by kicking one of the truck's tyres. Harel could hardly recognise Kayn's assistant. He was covered in mud, his hair was wild and a disturbing look on his face belied his usual demeanour, *the masculine version of Bree Van de Kamp*[7], as Andrea said, always calm and unflappable. It was the first time she had heard him curse.

'I was just warning you,' Doc replied.

'What's up, Dekker? Do you have any idea what happened here?' Kayn's assistant turned his attention to the South African commander.

Dekker, who hadn't said a word since the pitiful attempt to salvage some of their water supply, was kneeling at the back of the water truck studying the enormous hole in the metal.

'Mr Dekker?' Russell repeated impatiently.

The South African stood up.

'Take a look: a round hole in the middle of the truck. That's easy to do. If that had been our only problem, we could have covered it with something.' He pointed to an irregular line that ran across the hole. 'But this line complicates matters.'

'What do you mean?' Harel asked.

'Whoever did this put a thin line of explosives on the tank which, together with the pressure of the water inside, made the metal bend out instead of bending in. Even if we'd had a welding torch, we couldn't have covered the hole. This is the work of an artist.'

'Terrific! We're dealing with fucking Leonardo da Vinci,' Russell said, shaking his head.

[7] A neurotic housewife who is obsessive about cleanliness, what others might think, and good manners in the series *Desperate Housewives*.

61

MP3 File Recovered by the Jordanian Desert Police from Andrea Otero's Digital Recorder after the Moses Expedition Disaster

QUESTION: Professor Forrester, there's something I'm very curious about, and it's the supposed supernatural occurrences that have been associated with the Ark of the Covenant.

ANSWER: We're back to that.

Q: Professor, there is a series of unexplained phenomena cited in the Bible, like that light—

A: It's not 'that light'. It's the *Shekinah*, God's presence. You must speak respectfully. And yes, Jews believed that there was a luminescence that appeared between the cherubim from time to time, a clear sign that God was within.

Q: Or the Israelite who fell dead after touching the Ark. Do you really believe God's power resides in the relic?

A: Ms Otero, you have to understand that 3,500 years ago, human beings had a different conception of the world and an entirely different way of relating to it. If Aristotle, who is closer to us by more than a thousand years, saw the Heavens as a bunch of concentric spheres, imagine what the Jews thought about the Ark.

Q: I'm afraid you've lost me, Professor.

A: It's merely a question of scientific method. In other words, a rational explanation – or rather, the absence of such a thing. The Jews couldn't explain how a golden chest could appear to shine with its own independent light, so they limited themselves to giving a name and a religious explanation for a phenomenon that was beyond Antiquity's comprehension.

Q: And what is the explanation, Professor?

A: Have you heard of the Baghdad Battery? No, of course not. It's not something you'd hear about on TV.

Q: Professor . . .

A: The Baghdad Battery is a series of artefacts found in a museum in the city in 1938. It was composed of clay vessels, inside of which were copper cylinders, held in place by asphalt, each containing an iron rod. In other words, the whole thing was a primitive but effective electrochemical instrument that was used to coat different objects in copper through electrolysis.

Q: That's not so surprising. In 1938 that technology was almost ninety years old.

A: Ms Otero, if you'd let me continue, you wouldn't sound like such an idiot. The researchers who analysed the Baghdad Battery discovered that it originated in ancient Sumer, and managed to date it back to 2500 BC. That is a thousand years before the Ark of the

Covenant and forty-three centuries before Faraday, the man who supposedly invented electricity.

Q: And the Ark was similar?

A: The Ark was an electrical condenser. The design was very intelligent, allowing the accumulation of static electricity: two gold plates separated by an insulating layer of wood, but joined by the two golden cherubim that acted like positive and negative terminals.

Q: But if it was a condenser, how did it store electricity?

A: The answer is fairly prosaic. The objects in the Tabernacle and the Temple were made of leather, linen and goat hair, three of five materials that can generate the greatest amount of static electricity. Under the right conditions, the Ark could release about two thousand volts. It makes sense that the only ones who could touch it were the 'chosen few'. You can bet the chosen few had very thick gloves.

Q: So you insist that the Ark didn't come from God?

A: Ms Otero, nothing could be further from my intention. What I'm saying is that God asked Moses to keep the commandments in a safe place so they could be venerated for centuries to come and be the central aspect of the Jewish faith. And that human beings have invented artificial ways of keeping the legend of the Ark alive.

Q: What about other disasters, like the collapse of the walls of Jericho, the storms of sand and fire that wiped out whole cities?

A: Invented stories and myths.

Q: So you reject the idea that the Ark can bring disasters in its wake?

A: Absolutely.

62

THE EXCAVATION

AL MUDAWWARA DESERT, JORDAN

Tuesday, 18 July 2006. 1:49 p.m.

Eighteen minutes before she died, Kyra Larsen was thinking about baby wipes. It was a kind of mental reflex. Not long after she had given birth to little Bente two years before, she had discovered the advantages of the little towels that were always moist and left a nice smell.

The other advantage was that her husband hated them.

It wasn't that Kyra was a bad person. But for her, one of the fringe benefits of marriage consisted in noticing small cracks in her husband's defences and sticking a few barbs in them to see what would happen. Right now Alex would be contending with quite a few baby wipes because he had to take care of Bente until the expedition was over. Kyra would return triumphant, with the satisfaction of having scored real points against Mr They've-made-me-a-partner-at-the-law-firm.

Am I a bad mother for wanting to share the responsibility for our baby with him? Am I? Shit, no!

Two days before, when an exhausted Kyra had heard Jacob Russell say that they would have to step up the work and that there would be no more showers, she had thought she could put up with anything. Nothing would get in the way of her making a name for herself as an archaeologist. Unfortunately, reality and what a person imagines do not always coincide.

Stoically, she had put up with the humiliation of the search that took place after the attack on the water truck. She had stood there, covered in mud from head to toe, and watched as the soldiers went through her papers and her underwear. Many people on the expedition had protested, but they had all been relieved when the search was over and nothing had been found. The morale of the group had been greatly altered by recent events.

'At least it's not one of us,' David Pappas had said, once the lights went out and fear invaded every shadow. 'We can take comfort in that.'

'Whoever it was probably doesn't know what we're doing here. It could be Bedouins, angry at us for invading their turf. They won't do anything more with all those machine guns up on the cliffs. '

'Not that the machine guns did Stowe much good.'

'I still say Dr Harel knows something about his death,' Kyra insisted.

She had told everyone that, despite pretending otherwise, the doctor hadn't been in her bed when Kyra woke up that night, but no one paid her much attention.

'Be quiet, all of you. The best thing you can do for Erling, and for yourselves, is to work out how we're going to dig that tunnel. I want you to think about that even when you're asleep,' said Forrester, who, at Dekker's insistence, had left his private tent on the opposite side of the camp and joined the others.

Kyra was frightened, but she was inspired by the professor's fierce indignation.

Nobody is going to chase us away from here. We have a

mission to accomplish, and we will complete it, whatever the cost. After that everything will be better, she thought, without realising that she had zipped her sleeping bag up to the top in a ridiculous attempt to protect herself.

Forty-eight exhausting hours later, the group of archae-ologists had outlined the route they would follow, digging down at an angle in order to reach the object. Kyra wouldn't permit herself to call it anything other than 'the object' until they were sure it was what they had expected and not . . . not just something else.

By the crack of dawn on Tuesday, breakfast was already a memory. All the members of the expedition had helped to build a steel platform that would allow the mini-excavator to find a point of attack on the side of the mountain. Otherwise, the uneven ground and the steep angle of the slope would have meant there was a risk of the small but powerful machine tipping over as it began the work. David Pappas had designed the structure so that they could begin digging the tunnel some twenty feet above the canyon floor. Fifty feet tunnelling in, then a diagonal in the opposite direction towards the object.

That was the plan. Kyra's death would be one of the unfore-seen consequences.

Eighteen minutes before the accident, Kyra Larsen's skin was so sticky she felt as though she was wearing a smelly rubber suit. The others had used part of their ration of water to clean themselves up as best they could. Not Kyra. She'd been incredibly thirsty – she had always sweated a lot, especially after her pregnancy – and was even stealing little sips from other people's bottles when they weren't looking.

She closed her eyes for a moment and in her mind she could see Bente's room: on top of the chest of drawers there was a box of baby wipes that would have felt heavenly on her skin just then. She fantasised about rubbing them over her body, removing the dirt and dust that had accumulated in her hair, the insides of her elbows, and along the edges of her bra. And afterwards she would hug her baby girl, play with her on the bed as she did each morning, and explain to her that Mummy had found buried treasure.

The best treasure of all.

Kyra was carrying several planks of wood that Gordon Durwin and Ezra Levine were using to shore up the walls of the tunnel to prevent a cave-in. It was to be ten feet wide and eight feet high. The professor and David Pappas had argued for several hours about the dimensions.

'It'll take us twice as long! Do you think this is archaeology, Pappas? It's a damned rescue operation, and we have a limited amount of time, in case you haven't noticed!'

'If we don't make it wide enough we won't be able to get the earth out of the tunnel easily, the excavator will bang against the walls and the whole thing will cave in on us. That's assuming we don't hit the rock base of the cliff, in which case the net result of all this effort will be to lose two more days.'

'To hell with you, Pappas, and your Master's from Harvard.'

In the end David had won and the tunnel measured ten feet by eight.

Kyra absentmindedly brushed a beetle from her hair as she made her way to the far end of the tunnel, where Robert Frick was struggling with the wall of earth in front of him. Meanwhile, Tommy Eichberg was loading the conveyor belt that ran along the floor of the tunnel and ended a foot and a half from the platform, throwing a steady cloud of dust over the canyon floor. The mountain of earth that had been excavated from the side of the hill was now nearly as high as the tunnel opening.

'Hello, Kyra,' Eichberg greeted her. He sounded tired. 'Have you seen Hanley? He was supposed to take over from me.'

'He's below trying to rig up some electric lights. Soon we won't be able to see anything in here.'

They had dug almost twenty-five feet into the side of the mountain, and by two o'clock in the afternoon the daylight no longer reached the back of the tunnel, making it nearly impossible to work. Eichberg cursed out loud.

'Am I going to have to keep shovelling like this for another hour? Bullshit,' he said, throwing his spade down.

'Don't go, Tommy. If you leave, Frick can't continue either.'

'Well, you take over, Kyra. I have to take a piss.'

Without another word, he left.

Kyra looked at the ground. Shovelling earth on to the conveyor was a horrible job. You were constantly bending down, you had to do everything quickly, and keep an eye on the arm of the excavator to make sure it didn't hit you. But she didn't want to imagine what the professor would say if they took a break for an hour. He'd blame her, as usual. Kyra was secretly convinced that Forester hated her.

Maybe he resented my involvement with Stowe Erling. Maybe he would like to have been in Stowe's place. Dirty old man. I wish you were in his place right now, she thought as she bent down to pick up the shovel.

'Look out back there!'

Frick had reversed the excavator a little and the cabin almost slammed into Kyra's head.

'Be careful!'

'I warned you, beautiful. I'm sorry.'

Kyra made a face at the machine because it was impossible to get angry with Frick. The big-boned operator was vile-tempered, cursed constantly, and farted while he worked. He was a human being in every sense of the word, a real person. Kyra appreciated that most of all, especially when she compared him to the pale imitations of life that were Forrester's assistants.

The Ass-kissers' Club, Stowe called them. He had wanted nothing to do with them.

She began to shovel debris onto the conveyor belt. In a little while they'd have to add another section to the belt as the tunnel went deeper into the mountain.

'Hey, Gordon, Ezra! Quit shoring up and bring another section for the conveyor, please.'

Gordon Durwin and Ezra Levine mechanically obeyed her command. Like everyone else, they felt they had already reached the limits of their endurance.

As useless as tits on a frog, as my grandfather would've said. But we're so close; I can taste the hors d'oeuvres at the welcoming reception in the Jerusalem museum. One more shovelful and I'll be keeping all the journalists at bay. Another shovelful and Mr I'm-working-late-with-my-secretary will have to look up to me for once. I swear to God.

Durwin and Levine were carrying another section for the conveyor. The machinery was made up of a dozen flat sausages about a foot and a half long, connected by an electrical cable. They were no more than rollers with a strong plastic band around them, but they displaced a large quantity of material per hour.

Kyra dug her shovel in one more time, just so the two men would have to hold the heavy conveyor section a little longer.

The shovel made a loud, metallic, clanking sound.

For a second, an image of a freshly opened tomb flashed through Kyra's brain.

After that the ground tilted. Kyra lost her balance and Durwin and Levine tripped, losing their hold on the section, which fell against Kyra's head. The young woman screamed, but it was not a scream of terror. It was a scream of surprise and fear.

The ground moved again. The two men disappeared from Kyra's side like two children sledding down a hill. Perhaps they shouted, but she didn't hear them, nor did she hear the huge chunks of earth splitting off from the walls and hitting the ground with a dull thud. Nor did she feel the sharp rock that fell from the ceiling and left her temple a bloody mess; nor hear the crumpling metal of the mini-excavator, which went crashing down from the platform and hit rocks thirty feet below.

Kyra wasn't aware of anything because her five senses were focused on her fingertips, or, more precisely, on the four and a half inches of cable that she was using to help her cling on to the conveyor module, which had fallen almost parallel to the edge of the precipice.

She tried to kick her legs to find a hold but it was useless. Her arms were on the edge of the chasm and the ground was beginning to cede under her weight. The sweat on her hands meant Kyra couldn't hold on and the four and a half inches of cable became three and a half. Another slip, another pull of gravity, and now there were barely two inches of cable left.

In one of those weird tricks of the human mind, Kyra cursed having made Durwin and Levine wait a little longer than necessary. If they had left the section lying against the tunnel wall the cable wouldn't have got caught up under the conveyor's steel rollers.

Finally, the cable disappeared and Kyra fell into the darkness.

63

THE EXCAVATION

AL MUDAWWARA DESERT, JORDAN

Tuesday, 18 July 2006. 2:07 p.m.

'Several people are dead.'
  'Who?'
  'Larsen, Durwin, Levine and Frick.'
  'Shit no, not Levine. They pulled him out alive.'
  'The doctor's up there.'
  'Are you sure?'
  'I'm fucking telling you.'
  'What happened? Another bomb?'
  'It was a cave-in. Nothing mysterious.'
  'It was sabotage, I swear. Sabotage.'

A circle of pained faces gathered around the platform. There was anxious whispering as Pappas came out of the entrance to the tunnel, followed by Professor Forrester. Behind them were the Gottlieb brothers who, due to their skill at abseiling, had been appointed by Dekker to rescue any possible survivors.

The German twins were carrying out the first body on a stretcher covered by a blanket.

'It's Durwin; I recognise his boots.'

The professor approached the group.

'There's been a collapse due to a natural cavity in the earth that we hadn't reckoned with. The speed at which we dug the tunnel didn't allow us to …' He stopped, unable to continue.

I guess that's the closest he'll come to admitting a mistake, thought Andrea as she stood in the middle of the group. She had her camera in her hand, ready to take photos, but when she found out what had happened she put the lens cap back on.

The twins carefully laid the body on the ground, then slid the stretcher from under it and went back to the tunnel.

An hour later, the bodies of the three archaeologists and the operator were lying near the edge of the platform. The last one out was Levine. It had taken twenty minutes longer to get him out of the tunnel. Although he was the only one who had survived the initial fall, Dr Harel could do nothing for him.

'He suffered too much internal damage,' she whispered to Andrea once she'd emerged. The doctor's face and arms were covered with dirt. 'I would have preferred …'

'Don't say any more,' Andrea said, squeezing her hand furtively. She let go of it to cover her head with her cap, as did the rest of the group. The only ones who didn't follow the Jewish custom were the soldiers, perhaps out of ignorance.

The silence was absolute. A warm breeze drifted over from the cliffs. Suddenly the silence was broken by a voice that sounded deeply perturbed. Andrea turned her head and couldn't believe her eyes.

The voice belonged to Russell. He was walking behind Raymond Kayn, and they were no more than a hundred feet from the platform.

The billionaire was advancing towards them barefoot, his

shoulders stooped and his arms crossed. His assistant followed, his face like thunder. He quietened down when he realised that the others could hear him. It was obvious that seeing Kayn there, outside his tent, made Russell extremely nervous.

Slowly everybody turned to watch the two figures approaching. Aside from Andrea and Dekker, Forrester was the only other spectator to have seen Raymond Kayn in person. And that had happened only once, during a long tense meeting at Kayn Tower, when Forrester had agreed to the strange demands of his new boss without thinking twice. Of course, the reward for accepting had been huge.

As was the cost. It was lying there on the ground, covered by blankets.

Kayn stopped a dozen feet from them, a shaking, hesitant old man, his head bearing a yarmulke as white as the rest of his clothing. Out in the open his thinness and slight stature made him look even frailer, but, despite this, Andrea found herself fighting the urge to kneel. She perceived how the attitude of the people around him changed, as though they were affected by some invisible magnetic field. Brian Hanley, who was less than three feet from her, began to shift his weight from one foot to the other. David Pappas bowed his head, and even Fowler's eyes seemed oddly bright. The priest stood off to one side, slightly apart from the others.

'My dear friends, I haven't had the chance to introduce myself. My name is Raymond Kayn,' the old man said, his clear voice belying his fragile appearance.

Some of those present nodded, but the old man didn't notice and continued speaking.

'I regret that we had to meet for the first time under such terrible circumstances, and I'd like to ask that we join in prayer.' He lowered his eyes, bowed his head, and recited, '*El maley rachamim shochen bam'romim hamtzey menuchah nechonah al kanfey haschechinah bema'alot kedoshim ute'ho-rim kezohar harakia me'irim umazhirim lenishmat.*[8] Amen.'

Everyone repeated the Amen.

Strangely, Andrea felt better, even though she did not understand what she had heard, nor was it part of her child-hood faith. An empty, lonely silence hung over the group for a few moments until Dr Harel spoke up.

'Should we return home, sir?' She extended her arms in a gesture of silent supplication.

'We shall now comply with the *halaká*[9] and bury our brothers,' Kayn replied. His tone was calm and reasonable, in contrast to Doc's hoarse exhaustion. 'Afterwards, we'll rest for a few hours and then continue our work. We cannot allow the sacrifice of these heroes to be in vain.'

Having said this, Kayn returned to his tent, followed by Russell.

Andrea looked around and saw nothing but agreement on the faces of the others.

'I can't believe these people are buying this shit,' she whispered to Harel. 'He didn't even come near us. He stood several yards away, as if we were suffering from the plague or were going to do something to him.'

'We aren't the ones he was afraid of.'

'What the hell are you talking about?'

Harel didn't answer.

---

[8] Oh, merciful God, who art in Heaven, permit the souls of our friends to rest in the wings of your divine presence; in the divine heights of your purity and holiness accept the bright spirit that approaches you.

[9] Jewish Law.

But the direction of her gaze did not escape Andrea, nor the look of complicity that passed between the doctor and Fowler. The priest nodded.

If it wasn't us, then who was it?

64

Document Recovered from the e-mail Account of Kharouf Waadi, used as a Letter Box for Communications Between Terrorists Belonging to the Syrian Cell

Brothers, the chosen moment has arrived. Huqan has asked that you prepare yourselves for tomorrow. A local source will provide you with the necessary equipment. Your trip will take you by car from Syria to Amman, where Ahmed will give you more instructions. K.

Salaam Aleikum. I only wanted to remind you before departure of the words of Al Tabrizi, which have always served as an inspiration to me. I hope that you will draw similar comfort in them prior to setting out on your mission. W

> 'God's messenger said: a martyr has six privileges before God. He pardons your sins on shedding the first drop of your blood; He delivers you to a place in paradise, redeeming you from the torments of the grave; He offers you salvation from the terror of hell and sets upon your head a crown of glory, each ruby of which is worth more than the entire world and all that exists within it; He will wed you to seventy-two *houris* with the blackest eyes; and He

will accept your intercession on behalf of seventy-two of your kin.'

Thank you, W. Today my wife blessed me and bid me goodbye with a smile on her lips. She said to me: 'From the day I met you I knew that you were made for martyrdom. Today is the happiest day of my life.' Blessed be Allah for having bequeathed me someone like her. D

Blessings upon you, D. O

Isn't your soul filled to bursting? Would that we could share it with someone, shout it to the four winds. D

I too would like to share it, but I do not feel your euphoria. I find myself strangely at peace. This is my final message, since I leave in a few hours with my two brothers for our appointment in Amman. W

I share W's sense of peace. Euphoria is understandable but dangerous. In a moral sense, because it is the daughter of pride. In a tactical sense, because it can cause you to commit mistakes. You should purify your thoughts, D. When you find yourself in the desert you'll have to wait many hours in the hot sun for Huqan's signal. Your euphoria could quickly turn to desperation. Search for the things that will fill you with serenity. O

What would you recommend? D

Think of the martyrs who have gone before us. Our struggle, the struggle of the *umma*, is composed of small steps. The brothers who slaughtered the infidels in Madrid achieved one small step. The brothers who destroyed the Twin Towers achieved ten such steps. Our mission signifies a thousand steps. It aims to bring the invaders to their knees forever. Do you realise? Your life, your blood, will bring about an end that no other brother can even aspire to. Imagine an ancient king who has led a virtuous life multiplying his seed in an enormous harem, defeating his enemies, expanding his kingdom in the name of God. He can look around himself with the satisfaction of someone who has fulfilled his duty. That is how you should feel. Take refuge in that thought and transmit it to the warriors you will take with you to Jordan. P

I've meditated for many hours on what you told me, O, and I am thankful. My spirit is different, my state of mind closer to God. The only thing that still causes me distress is that these will be our last messages to each other, and that, although we will triumph, our next meeting will be in another life. I've learned so much from you and have passed on that knowledge to the others.

Until forever, brother. *Salaam Aleikum.*

65

THE EXCAVATION

AL MUDAWWARA DESERT, JORDAN

Wednesday, 19 July 2006. 11:34 a.m.

Hanging from the ceiling in a harness twenty-five feet above the ground in the same place where four people had lost their lives the day before, Andrea couldn't help feeling more alive than she ever had in her life. She couldn't deny that the imminent possibility of death excited her and in a strange way it obliged her to waken from a dream she had been stuck in for the last ten years.

Suddenly questions about who you hate more, your father for being a homophobic bigot or your mother for being the stingiest person in the world, begin to fade before questions like, 'Is this rope going to hold my weight?'

Andrea, who had never learned to abseil, asked that she be lowered to the bottom of the cave slowly, partly through fear and partly because she wanted to try out different camera angles for her shots.

'C'mon, guys. Slow down. I have a good one,' she yelled, leaning back her head and looking up at Brian Hanley and Tommy Eichberg, who were lowering her with the aid of a hoist.

The rope stopped moving.

Below her lay the wreck of the excavator, like a toy smashed by an angry child. Part of the arm stuck out at a strange angle and there was still dried blood on the shattered windscreen. Andrea pointed her camera away from the scene.

I hate blood, hate it.

Even her lack of professional ethics had limits. She focused on the bottom of the cave, but just as she was about to push the shutter she began to spin on the rope.

'Can you make it stop? I can't focus.'

'Miss, you're not made of feathers, you know?' Brian Hanley shouted down to her.

'I think it's better that we keep lowering you,' Tommy added.

'What's the matter? I only weigh eight and a half stone – can't you deal with that? You seem a lot stronger,' Andrea said, always knowing how to manipulate men.

'She weighs a lot more than eight stone,' complained Hanley in a low voice.

'I heard that,' said Andrea, pretending to be insulted.

She was so excited by the experience that it was impossible for her to be angry with Hanley. The electrician had done such a great job in lighting the cave that she didn't even need to use the flash on her camera. Opening up the lens more allowed her to get great shots of the final stage of the dig.

I can't believe it. We're a step away from the greatest discovery of all time, and the photo that'll appear on every front page will be mine!

The reporter observed the inside of the cave closely for the first time. David Pappas had calculated that they needed to build a diagonal tunnel down towards the presumed location of the Ark, but the route – in the most abrupt manner possible – had come across a natural chasm in the earth that bordered the canyon wall.

'Imagine the walls of the canyon thirty million years ago,' Pappas had explained the day before, drawing a small sketch in his notebook. 'Back then there was water in this area, which is what created the canyon. When the climate changed, the rock walls began to wear away, producing this terrain of compacted earth and rocks that surrounds the canyon walls like a giant coating, sealing off the type of cave that we hit on by chance. Unfortunately, my mistake cost several lives. If I'd checked to make sure the ground was solid on the floor of the tunnel . . .'

'I wish I could say I know how you feel, David, but I have no idea. I can only offer you my help, and to hell with the rest of it.'

'Thank you, Ms Otero. That means a lot to me. Especially since some members of the expedition are still blaming me for Stowe's death just because we argued all the time.'

'Call me Andrea, OK?'

'Sure.' The archaeologist pushed his glasses back shyly.

Andrea noticed that David was almost exploding with the stress of it all. She thought of giving him a hug, but there was something about him that made her increasingly uneasy. It was like seeing a painting you'd been staring at suddenly illuminated, revealing a completely different picture.

'Tell me, David, do you think that the people who buried the Ark knew about these caves?'

'I don't know. It's possible there's an entrance in the canyon that we haven't discovered yet because it's covered with rocks or dirt – somewhere they used when they first put the Ark down there. We'd probably have found it by now if this damned expedition wasn't being run in such a crazy way, making things up as we go along. Instead, we've done what no archaeologist should ever do. Maybe a treasure-hunter, yes, but it's certainly not how I was taught.'

Andrea had been taught how to take photos and that's exactly what she was doing. Still contending with the spinning rope, she reached her left arm overhead and grabbed a piece of rock that was jutting out, while her right hand aimed the camera towards the back of the cave: a high but narrow space with an even smaller opening at the far end. Brian Hanley had installed a generator and powerful lights that now cast the large shadows of Professor Forrester and David Pappas against the rough rock wall. Each time one of them moved, fine grains of sand fell from the rock and floated down through the air. The cave smelled dry and acrid, like a clay ashtray left in the kiln too long. The professor kept coughing, even though he was wearing a dust mask.

Andrea took a few more shots before Hanley and Tommy grew tired of waiting.

'Let go of the rock. We're going to lower you down.'

Andrea did as she was told and a minute later she was standing on solid ground. She undid her harness, and the rope went back up. It was now Brian Hanley's turn.

Andrea approached David Pappas, who was trying to help the professor to sit down. The old man was shaking and his forehead was drenched in sweat.

'Drink some of my water, Professor,' David said, offering him his canteen.

'Idiot! You drink it. You're the one who has to go into the cave,' the professor said. The words brought on another bout of coughing. He ripped off his mask and spat a huge glob of blood on the ground. Even though his voice had been damaged by his illness, the professor could still hurl a sharp insult.

David put the canteen back on his belt and went over to Andrea.

'Thank you for coming to help us. After the accident, the professor and I are the only ones left ... and he's not much help in his state,' he added, lowering his voice.

'My cat's shit looks better.'

'He's going to ... well, you know. The only way he could delay the inevitable would be to get on the first plane to Switzerland for treatment.'

'That's what I meant.'

'With the dust inside that cave—'

'I may not be able to breathe, but my hearing is perfect,' said the professor, although each word ended in a wheeze. 'Stop talking about me and get to work. I'm not going to die until you get the Ark out of there, you useless idiot.'

David looked furious. For a moment Andrea thought he was going to answer back, but the words seemed to die on his lips.

You're totally screwed, aren't you? You hate his guts but you can't confront him ... He hasn't just cut off your nuts, he made you fry them for breakfast, thought Andrea, feeling some pity for the assistant.

'Well, David, tell me what I have to do.'

'Follow me.'

About ten feet into the cave the surface of the wall changed a little. Were it not for the thousands of watts lighting up the space Andrea probably wouldn't have noticed it. Instead of bare solid rock, there was an area that seemed to be formed of bits of rock piled up on top of one another.

Whatever it was, it was manmade.

'My God, David.'

'What I don't understand is how they managed to make such a solid wall without using any mortar and without being able to work on the other side.'

'Maybe there's an exit on the other side of the chamber. You said that there had to be one.'

'You could be right, but I don't think so. I've taken new readings with the magnetometer. Behind this block of stones is the unstable area we identified with our initial readings. In fact, the Copper Scroll was found in a hole just like this one.'

'Coincidence?'

'I doubt it.'

David knelt and touched the wall gently with his fingertips. When he found the slightest crack between the stones he tried pulling with all his might.

'There's no way,' he went on. 'This hole in the cave has been sealed on purpose; and for some reason, the stones have become even more tightly compacted than when they were first put there. It could be that in two thousand years there's been downward pressure on the wall. Almost as if . . .'

'As if what?'

'As if God himself had sealed the entrance. Don't laugh.'

I'm not laughing, Andrea thought. *None of this is funny.*

'Can't we pull away the stones one at a time?'

'Not without knowing how thick the wall is and what's behind it.'

'And how are you going to do that?'

'By looking inside.'

Four hours later, with Brian Hanley and Tommy Eichberg helping him, David Pappas had managed to drill a small hole through the wall. They'd had to take apart the motor of the large rock drill – which they hadn't used as yet, since they'd only had to dig through earth and sand – and lower it part by part into the tunnel. Hanley put together a strange-looking contraption from the pieces of the wrecked mini-excavator at the entrance to the cave.

'Now that's recycling!' Hanley said, pleased with his creation.

The result, besides being ugly, was not very practical. It took all four of them to hold it in place, pushing with all their strength. To make matters worse, only the smallest drill bits could be used, to avoid subjecting the wall to excessive vibration. 'Seven feet,' Hanley yelled, above the clanking sound of the motor.

David pushed a fibre-optic camera connected to a small view-finder through the hole, but the cable attached to the camera was too stiff and short and the ground on the other side was full of obstacles.

'Shit! I won't be able to see anything like this.'

Feeling something graze her, Andrea brought her hand up to the back of her neck. Someone was throwing small stones at her. She turned around.

Forrester was trying to get her attention, unable to make himself heard above the din of the motor. Pappas went over and leaned his ear towards the old man.

'That's it,' David yelled, both agitated and overjoyed. 'That's what we'll do, Professor. Brian, do you think you can make the hole a little bigger? Say about three-quarters of an inch by an inch and a quarter?'

'Don't even joke about it,' Hanley said, scratching his head. 'We don't have any small drill bits left.'

Wearing thick gloves he was removing the last of the smoking drill bits, which had bent out of shape. Andrea remembered when she'd tried to hang a beautiful framed photo of the Manhattan skyline in her apartment on a weight-bearing wall. Her drill bit had been about as useful as a pretzel stick.

'Frick would probably have known what to do,' said Brian sadly, looking at the corner where his friend had died. 'He had a lot more experience of this kind of thing than I do.'

Pappas didn't say anything for a couple of minutes. The others could almost hear him thinking.

'What if I let you use the medium-sized drill bits?' he finally said.

'Then there wouldn't be a problem. I could have it done in two hours. But the vibration is going to be that much greater. The area is clearly unstable ... it's a big risk. You're aware of that?'

David laughed, without a drop of humour.

'You're asking me if I'm aware that four thousand tons of rocks might come crashing down, pulverising the greatest object in the history of the world? That it would destroy many years of work and an investment of millions of dollars? That it would render pointless the sacrifice of five people?'

Fuck! He's completely different today. He's as ... contaminated by the whole thing as the professor, Andrea thought.

'Yes, I'm aware, Brian,' David added. 'And I'm going to take that risk.'

66

THE EXCAVATION

AL MUDAWWARA DESERT, JORDAN

Wednesday, 19 July 2006. 7:01 p.m.

Andrea took another photo of Pappas kneeling in front of the stone wall. His face was in shadow, but the device he was using to look through the hole was clearly visible.

Much better, David ... not that you're exactly a great beauty, Andrea observed wryly to herself. In a few hours she would regret having that thought, but at that moment there was nothing closer to the truth. That machine was amazing.

'Stowe used to call it an ATER. Annoying Terrain Explorer Robot, but we call it Freddie.'

'Any special reason?'

'Just to fuck with Stowe. He was an arrogant prick,' David replied. Andrea was surprised at the anger displayed by the usually timid archaeologist.

Freddie was a mobile camera system with a remote control that could be used in places where human access would be dangerous. It had been developed by Stowe Erling, who would sadly not be there to witness his robot's debut. In order to navigate obstacles such as rocks, Freddie had been equipped with treads similar to those used on tanks. The robot was also submersible for periods of up to ten minutes. Erling had copied the idea from a group of archaeologists working in Boston and had recreated it with the help of some engineers from MIT – who were suing him for going off on this mission with the first prototype, although this was something that would no longer trouble Erling.

'We'll put it through the opening to obtain views of the grotto's interior,' said David. 'That way we'll be able to figure out if it's safe to knock down the wall without damaging what's on the other side.'

'How can the robot see in there?'

'Freddie is equipped with night-vision lenses. The central mechanism throws out an infrared beam that only the lens can pick up. The images aren't very good quality, but they're good enough. The only thing we have to watch for is that it doesn't get stuck or tip over. If that happens, we're finished.'

The first few feet were fairly straightforward. The initial stage, although narrow, gave Freddie sufficient room to get into the cave. Crossing the uneven area between the wall and the ground was a little more difficult as it was rough and full of loose rocks. Luckily the robot's treads could be operated independently, enabling it to turn and circumnavigate lesser obstacles.

'Sixty degrees to the left,' said David, focusing on the screen, where he could see little more than a field of rocks in black and white. Tommy Eichberg was manipulating the controls at David's request, since he had a steady hand despite his chubby fingers. Each tread was operated by means of a small wheel on the controls, connected to Freddie via two thick cables that provided power and could also be used to haul in the machine manually should something go wrong.

'We're almost there. Oh no!'

The screen jumped around as the robot nearly tipped over.

'Shit! Be careful, Tommy,' David yelled.

'Take it easy, kid. These wheels are more sensitive than a nun's clit. Excuse the language, miss,' Tommy said, turning to Andrea. 'My mouth is straight out of the Bronx.'

'Don't worry about it. My ears are from Harlem,' said Andrea, going along with the joke.

'You have to stabilise the thing a little more,' said David.

'I'm trying!'

Eichberg turned the wheel carefully and the robot began to cross the uneven ground.

'Any idea how much distance Freddie has covered?' Andrea asked.

'About eight feet from the wall,' David replied, drying the sweat on his brow. Each minute the temperature was increasing because of the generator and the intense lighting.

'And it has— Wait!'

'What?'

'I think I saw something,' Andrea said.

'Are you sure? It's not easy turning this thing around.'

'Tommy, please, go to the left.'

Eichberg looked at Pappas, who nodded. Slowly, the picture on the screen began to move, revealing a dark, round-ish contour.

'Go back a little.'

Two triangles with thin ridges appeared, one next to the other.

A row of squares grouped together.

'A little further back. You're too close.'

Finally, the geometry was transformed into something recognisable.

'Oh, Lord. It's a skull.'

Andrea looked at Pappas with satisfaction.

'There's your answer: that's how they managed to seal the chamber from the inside, David.'

The archaeologist wasn't listening. He was focused on the screen, mumbling, his hands clutching it like an insane fortune-teller looking into a crystal ball. A drop of sweat slid from his greasy nose and landed on the image of the skull where the dead person's cheek would have been.

Just like a teardrop, thought Andrea.

'Quickly, Tommy! Go around it and then go forward a little more,' Pappas said. His voice sounded even more strained. 'To the left, Tommy!'

'Easy, kid. Let's do this calmly. I think there's—'

'Let me do it,' David said, grabbing for the controls.

'What are you doing?' Eichberg said angrily. 'Fuck! Let go.'

Pappas and Eichberg struggled over the controls for a few seconds, knocking the wheel in the process. David's face was a vivid red and Eichberg was breathing heavily.

'Be careful!' Andrea yelled as she stared at the screen. The image was lurching around madly.

Suddenly it stopped moving. Eichberg let go of the controls and David fell back, cutting himself on the temple as he hit the corner of the monitor. But at that moment he was more concerned with what he'd just seen than with the cut on his head.

'That's what I was trying to tell you, kid,' Eichberg said. 'The ground is uneven.'

'Shit. Why didn't you let go?' David yelled. 'The machine's tipped over.'

'Just shut up,' Eichberg yelled back. 'You're the one rushing things.'

Andrea screamed for both of them to be quiet.

'Stop arguing! It hasn't fallen over completely. Take a look.' She was pointing at the screen.

Still angry, the two men approached the monitor. Brian Hanley, who had gone outside to get some tools and had been abseiling down during the brief fight, drew closer as well.

'I think we can fix that,' he said, studying the situation. 'If we all pull on the cable at the same time we can probably get the robot back on its treads. If we pull on it too gently all we'll do is drag it and it'll get stuck.'

'That won't work,' Pappas said. 'We'll yank the cable off.'

'We've nothing to lose by trying, right?'

They lined up, each one holding the cable with both hands, as close as possible to the opening. Hanley pulled the cable taut.

'On my count pull hard. One, two, three!'

The four of them yanked the cable at the same time. Suddenly it felt too loose in their hands.

'Shit. We've disconnected it.'

Hanley continued pulling on the cable until the end appeared.

'You're right. Shit! I'm sorry, Pappas ...'

The young archaeologist turned away, exasperated, ready to pound whoever or whatever was in front of him. He lifted a wrench and was about to hit the monitor, maybe in retaliation for the cut he'd received two minutes before.

But Andrea came closer and then she understood.

No.

I can't believe it.

Because I never really believed in it, did I? I never thought it was possible you could exist.

The transmission from the robot had remained on the screen. When they had pulled on the cable Freddie had righted himself before the cable had become disconnected. In another position without the skull blocking the way, the image on screen showed a flash of something that Andrea could not understand at first. Then she realised that it was the infrared beam reflecting off a metallic surface. The reporter thought she could see the irregular edge of what appeared to be a huge box. On top of it she thought she saw a figure but she couldn't be sure.

The person who was sure was Pappas, who was gazing at it, hypnotised.

'It's there, Professor. I've found it. I've found it for you ...'

Andrea turned towards the professor and took a photo without thinking. She was trying to get his first reaction, whatever it was – surprise, joy, the culmination of his long search and dedication and emotional isolation. She took three shots before she really looked at the old man.

There was no expression in his eyes and from his mouth there was only a bloody trickle that ran down into his beard.

Brian ran over to him.

'Shit! We have to get him out of here. He's not breathing.'

67

LOWER EAST SIDE

NEW YORK

December 1943

Yudel was so hungry he could hardly feel the rest of his body. He was aware only of dragging himself through Manhattan's streets looking for shelter in the doorways and alleys, never staying long in one place. There was always a sound, a light or a voice that frightened him and he would run, clutching the ragged change of clothes that was the only thing he owned. Except for his stay in Istanbul, the only homes he'd known were the hideout he'd lived in with his family, and the hold of the ship. For the boy, the chaos, noise and bright lights of New York were all part of a frightening jungle that was filled with danger. He drank from public fountains. At one point a drunken beggar grabbed the boy's leg as he passed. Later, a policeman called to him from a corner. His uniform reminded Yudel of the monster with the flashlight who had searched for them while they hid under the stairs at Judge Rath's house. He ran to hide.

The sun was setting on the afternoon of his third day in New York when the exhausted boy collapsed in a pile of rubbish in a dirty alleyway near Broome Street. Above him, the tenements were filled with the sound of pots and pans, arguments, sexual encounters, life. Yudel must have passed out for a few moments. When he came to, something was crawling over his face. He knew what it was before he opened his eyes. The rat paid him no attention. It was headed for an overturned bin, where it had scented a piece of dry bread. It was a large piece, too big to carry off, so the rat gnawed at it voraciously.

Yudel crawled over to the bin and grabbed a can, his fingers shaking from hunger. He hurled it at the rat and missed. The rat looked up at him briefly and then went back to gnawing the bread. The boy grabbed a broken umbrella handle and shook it at the rat, which finally ran off in search of an easier way to satisfy its hunger.

The boy grabbed the piece of stale bread. He opened his mouth hungrily, but then immediately closed it and put the bread on his lap. He pulled out a filthy rag from his bundle, covered his head and blessed the Lord for the gift of the bread.

'*Baruch Atah Adonai, Eloheynu Melech ha-olam, ha motzee lechem min ha-aretz.*'[10]

In the alley, a door had opened a moment before. An old rabbi, unnoticed by Yudel, had witnessed the boy battling the rat. When he heard the blessing of the bread from the lips of the starving child, a tear rolled down his cheek. He had never seen anything like it. There was no desperation or doubt in that faith.

The rabbi continued to look at the child for a long while. His synagogue was very poor and he could barely find enough money to keep it open. For that reason even he did not understand his decision.

[10] Blessed art thou, oh God, the Eternal, Universal Presence, who makes bread grow from the earth.

After eating the bread Yudel instantly fell asleep among the rotting detritus. He didn't wake up until he felt the rabbi carefully lift him up and carry him inside the synagogue.

The old stove will keep the cold out for a few more nights. Then we'll see, thought the rabbi.

As he removed the dirty clothing from the boy and covered him with his only blanket, the rabbi found the blue-green card the officers had given Yudel on Ellis Island. On the card the boy was identified as Raymond Kayn, with family in Manhattan. He also found the envelope, on which was written in Hebrew:

For my son, Yudel Cohen

Not to be read until your bar mitzvah in November 1951

The rabbi opened the envelope, hoping that it would give him a clue to the boy's identity. What he read left him shocked and confused, but it reaffirmed his conviction that the Almighty had guided the boy's footsteps to his door.

Outside, the snow began to fall heavily.

68

Josef Cohen's Letter to His Son, Yudel

Vienna,

Tuesday, 9 February 1943

Dear Yudel,

I write these hurried lines in the hope that the affection and love that we feel for you will fill some of the emptiness left by the urgency and inexperience of your correspondent. I have never been one to show much emotion, your mother knows this very well. Ever since you were born, the enforced intimacy of the space in which we have been imprisoned has eaten away at my heart. It saddens me that I have never seen you play in the sun, and never will. The Eternal One has forged us in the crucible of a trial that has proved too difficult for us to bear. It is up to you to carry out what we have not been able to accomplish.

In a few minutes we will go in search of your brother and we will not return. Your mother won't listen to reason and I cannot allow her to go out there alone. I am aware that I am walking towards a certain death. When you read this letter you will be thirteen years old. You will ask yourself what madness drove your parents to walk straight into the arms of the enemy. Part of the purpose of this letter is so that I myself can understand the answer to that question. When you grow up you will know that there are some things we must do even though we know that the results may go against us.

Time is running out but I must tell you something very important. For centuries the members of our family have been custodians of a sacred object. It is the candle that was present when you were born. Through an unfortunate set of circumstances, it is now the only thing we own of any value, and that is why your mother is forcing me to risk it in order to rescue your brother. It will be as pointless a sacrifice as that of our own lives. But I don't mind. I would not do it if you did not remain behind. I trust in you. I would like to explain to you why this candle is so important, but the truth is I do not know. I only know that it was my mission to keep it safe, a mission that has been passed from father to son for generations, and a mission in which I have failed, as I have failed in so many aspects in my life.

Find the candle, Yudel. We're going to give it to the doctor who is holding your brother at the Am Spiegelgrund Children's Hospital. If it at least serves to purchase your brother's freedom, then you can search for it together. If not, I pray to the Almighty to keep you safe, and that by the time you read this the war will finally be over.

There is something else. Very little is left of the large inheritance that was destined for you and Elan. The factories that belonged to our family are in Nazi hands. The bank accounts that we had in Austria have also been confiscated. Our apartments were burned during Kristallnacht. But luckily we can leave you something.

We have always kept a family fund for emergencies in a bank in Switzerland. We have added to it little by little, making trips every two or three months, even if what we were bringing only amounted to a few hundred Swiss francs. Your mother and I enjoyed our little trips and would often stay there for the weekend. It's not a fortune, about fifty thousand marks, but it will help with your education and getting started wherever you are. The money is deposited in a numbered account at Credit Suisse, Number 336923348927R, under my name. The bank manager will ask for the password. It is 'Perpignan'.

That's it. Say your prayers every day and do not abandon the light of the Torah. Always honour your home and your people.

Blessed be the Eternal One, He who is our only God, Universal Presence, True Judge. He commands me and I command you. May He keep you safe!

Your father,
Josef Cohen

69

ℋUQAN

He had spent so long holding back that when they finally found it, the only thing he felt was fear. Then the fear turned into relief, relief at being able to rid himself at last of that horrible mask.

It would be the next day, in the morning. They would all be in the dining tent for breakfast. Nobody would suspect a thing.

Ten minutes ago, he had crawled under the mess tent's platform and planted it. It was a simple device but very powerful, perfectly camouflaged. They would be above it, unawares. A minute later they would be explaining themselves to Allah.

He wasn't sure if he should give the signal after the explosion. The brothers would come and crush the arrogant little soldiers. The ones who had survived, of course.

He decided to wait a few more hours. He'd give them time to finish their work. No options and no way out.

Remember the bushmen, he thought. The monkey had found the water, but it hadn't yet retrieved it ...

70

KAYN TOWER

NEW YORK

Wednesday, 19 July 2006. 11.22 p.m.

'You too, pal,' said the thin blond plumber. 'It's all the same to me. I get paid whether I work or not.'

'Amen to that,' agreed the fat plumber with the ponytail. The orange uniform fit him so tightly that from behind it looked as if it was going to burst.

'Maybe it's better this way,' said the guard, agreeing with them. 'You come back tomorrow and that's it. Don't complicate my fucking life. I have two men out sick and I can't assign anyone to babysit the two of you. Those are the rules: without a babysitter no outside personnel after eight p.m.'

'You don't know how grateful we are,' said the blond one. 'With a bit of luck the next shift will have to take care of the problem. I don't feel like fixing busted pipes.'

'What? Wait, wait,' said the guard. 'What are you talking about, busted pipes?'

'Just that. They're busted. The same thing happened at Saatchi and Saatchi. Who dealt with that one, Bennie?'

'I think it was Louie Pigtails,' said the fat one.

'Great guy, Louie. God bless him.'

'Amen to that. Well, see you later, Sarge. Have a good night.'

'Should we go to Spinato's, buddy?'

'Do bears shit in the woods?'

The two plumbers picked up their gear and headed towards the exit.

'Wait,' the guard said, getting more anxious with each minute. 'What happened to Louie Pigtails?'

'You know, he had an emergency like this one. One night he couldn't get into the building because of an alarm or something. Anyway, the pressure built up in the drain pipes and they started bursting and, you know, there was shit all over the fucking place.'

'Yeah . . . like fucking Vietnam.'

'Dude, you never set foot in Vietnam, right? My father was there.'

'Your father spent the seventies stoned.'

'The thing is that Louie Pigtails is now Bald Louie. Think about what a fucked-up scene that was. What I'm hoping is that there's nothing too valuable up there, because by tomorrow everything's gonna be shit brown.'

The guard looked again at the central monitor in the lobby. The emergency lights in room 328E were flashing insistently with a yellow light, which meant there was a problem with the water or gas pipes. The building was so smart it could tell you when your shoes were untied.

He checked the directory to verify the location of 328E. When he realised where it was, he went pale.

'Fuck, it's the principal board room on the thirty-eighth floor.'

'Bad deal, huh, buddy?' said the fat plumber. 'I'm sure it's full of leather furniture and Van Gongs.'

'Van Gongs? What the fuck! You ain't got no culture at all. It's Van Gogh. Gogh. You know.'

'I know who he is. The Italian painter.'

'Van Gogh was a German and you're a jerk. Let's split and go to Spinato's before they close. I'm starving over here.'

The guard, who was an art lover, didn't bother maintaining that Van Gogh was actually Dutch because at that moment he remembered that there really was a Cézanne hanging in the board room.

'Guys, wait a minute,' he said, coming out from behind the reception desk and running after the plumbers. 'Let's talk about this …'

Orville flopped down in the president's chair in the board room, a chair that the owner hardly ever used. He thought he might take a nap there, surrounded by all the mahogany panelling. Once he'd recovered from the adrenalin of acting in front of the building guard, the tiredness and the pain in his hands washed over him again.

'Fuck, I thought he'd never leave.'

'You did a great job convincing the guy, Orville. Congratulations,' Albert said, pulling out the top level of his tool box from which he extracted a laptop computer.

'It's a simple enough procedure to get in here,' Orville said, pulling up the huge gloves that covered his bandaged hands. 'It's a good thing you were able to punch in the code for me.'

'Let's get started. I think we have about half an hour before they decide to send someone up to check on us. At that point, if we haven't managed to get in, we'll have another five minutes or so before they reach us. Show me the way, Orville.'

The first panel was simple. The system was programmed to recognise only Raymond Kayn's and Jacob Russell's palm prints. But it had an error common to all systems that rely on an electronic code using a lot of information. And an entire palm print is definitely a whole lot of information.

To expert eyes, the code was easy to detect in the system's memory.

'Bim bam here goes the first one,' Albert said, closing the laptop when the orange light on the black screen lit up and the heavy door opened with a buzz.

'Albert ... they're going to realise something's up,' Orville said, pointing to the area around the plate where the priest had used a screwdriver to pry open the lid in order to get at the system's circuits. The wood was now cracked and splintered.

'I'm counting on it.'

'You're joking.'

'Trust me, OK?' the priest said, going into his pocket.

A mobile phone was ringing.

'Do you think it's a good idea to answer a call right now?' Orville queried.

'I agree,' said the priest. 'Hello, Anthony. We're inside. Call me in twenty minutes.' He hung up.

Orville pushed open the door and they entered the narrow, carpeted hallway that led to Kayn's private lift.

'I wonder what kind of trauma a man has to suffer to lock himself up behind so many walls,' Albert said.

71

MP3 File Recovered by the Jordanian Desert Police from Andrea Otero's Digital Recorder after the Moses Expedition Disaster

QUESTION: I want to thank you for your time and your patience, Mr Kayn. This is proving to be a very difficult task. I really appreciate the way you have shared the more painful details of your life, such as your flight from the Nazis and your arrival in the United States. Those incidents add real human depth to your public persona.

ANSWER: My dear young lady, it's not like you to beat around the bush before asking me what you want to know.

Q: Great, everyone seems to be giving me advice on how to do my job.

A: I'm sorry. Go ahead, please.

Q: Mr Kayn, I understand that your illness, your agora-phobia, was caused by the painful events of your child-hood.

A: That's what the doctors believe.

Q: Let's proceed chronologically, even though we may need to make certain adjustments when the interview is broadcast on the radio. You lived with Rabbi Menachem Ben-Schlomo until you came of age.

A: That's correct. The rabbi was like a father to me. He fed me even if he had to go hungry. He gave purpose to my life so that I could find the strength to overcome my fears. It took over four years before I was able to go out into the street and interact with other people.

Q: That was quite an accomplishment. A child who couldn't even look another person in the eye without having a panic attack became one of the greatest engineers in the world ...

A: It only happened because of the love and faith of Rabbi Ben-Schlomo. I give thanks to the All Merciful for placing me in the hands of such a great man.

Q: Then you became a multimillionaire, and finally a philanthropist.

A: I prefer not to discuss the last point. I don't feel very comfortable talking about my charitable work. I always feel it's never enough.

Q: Let's go back to the last question. When did you realise that you could lead a normal life?

A: Never. I've struggled against this affliction all my life, my dear. There are good days and bad days.

Q: You've run your business with an iron hand, and it's among the top fifty of the Fortune Five Hundred. I guess you could say that there have been more good days than bad ones. You also married and had a son.

A: That's right, but I'd rather not speak about my personal life.

Q: Your wife left and went to live in Israel. She's an artist.

A: She's done some very fine paintings, I can assure you.

Q: What about Isaac?

A: He ... was great. Quite something.

Q: Mr Kayn, I imagine it's very difficult for you to talk about your son but it's an important point and I want to pursue it. Especially seeing the look on your face. It is clear you loved him a great deal.

A: Do you know how he died?

Q: I know that he was one of the victims of the attack on the Twin Towers. And as a result of ... fourteen, almost fifteen hours of interviews, I understand that his death triggered the return of your illness.

A: I'm going to ask Jacob to come in now. I want you to leave.

Q: Mr Kayn, I think that deep down you really do want to talk about this; you need to. I'm not going to bombard you with cheap psychology. But do whatever you think best.

A: Turn off your tape recorder, young lady. I want to think.

Q: Mr Kayn, thank you for continuing with the interview. Whenever you're ready . . .

A: Isaac was everything to me. He was tall and slender, and very handsome. Look at his photo.

Q: He has a nice smile.

A: I think you would have liked him. In fact, he was quite similar to you. He would rather ask for forgiveness than for permission. He had the strength and energy of a nuclear reactor. And everything he achieved, he did by himself.

Q: With all due respect, it's difficult to accept such a statement about a person who was born to inherit such a fortune.

A: What's a father supposed to say? The Almighty said to the prophet David that he 'would be His son forever'. After such a display of love, my words . . . but I can see you're simply trying to provoke me.

Q: Forgive me.

A: Isaac had many faults, but taking the easy way out was not one of them. He never worried about going against my wishes. He went off to study at Oxford, a university to which I had not made a contribution.

Q: And that's where he met Mr Russell, is that correct?

A: They were in a Macroeconomics class together, and after Jacob completed his studies, Isaac recommended him to me. In time, Jacob became my right hand.

Q: The position you would have wanted Isaac to have had.

A: And which he never would have accepted. When he was very young ... [fighting back a sob]

Q: We're continuing with the interview now.

A: Thank you. Forgive me for becoming emotional at that recollection. He was only a child, no more than eleven. One day he came home with a dog he had found in the street. I became very angry. I don't like animals. Do you like dogs, my dear?

Q: A great deal.

A: Well, then you should have seen this one. It was an ugly mongrel, filthy, and it had only three legs. It looked as if it had been out on the streets for years. The only rational thing to do with such an animal would have been to take it to a veterinarian and end its misery. I said this to Isaac. He looked at me and replied: 'You were picked up in the street too, Father. Do you think the rabbi should have ended your misery?'

Q: Ouch!

A: I felt an inner blow, both of fear and of pride. This child was my son! I gave him permission to keep the dog if he took responsibility for it. And he did. The creature lived another four years.

Q: I think I understand what you said before.

A: Even when he was a boy, my son knew that he didn't want to live in my shadow. On his ... last day he went to a job interview at Cantor Fitzgerald. He was on the hundred and fourth floor of the North Tower.

q: Do you want to stop for a while?

a: *Nichtgedeiget*. I'm all right, dear. Isaac called me that Tuesday morning. I was watching what was happening on CNN. I hadn't spoken to him all weekend so it never occurred to me that he might be there.

q: Have some water, please.

a: I picked up the phone. He said, 'Papa, I'm in the World Trade Center. There's been an explosion. I'm very scared.' I stood up. I was in shock. I think I screamed at him. I don't remember what I said. He said to me, 'I've been trying to call you for ten minutes. The network must be overloaded. Papa, I love you.' I told him to stay calm, that I'd call the authorities. That we'd get him out of there. 'We can't go down the stairs, Papa. The floor below us has collapsed, and the fire's coming up through the building. It's very hot. I want to …' And that was it. He was twenty-four years old. *[A long pause.]* I stared at the receiver, caressing it with my fingertips. I didn't understand. The connection had been cut off. I think that was the moment my brain short-circuited. The rest of the day has been completely erased from my memory.

q: You never found out anything more?

a: I wish it had been that way. The next day I opened the papers looking for news of survivors. Then I saw his photo. There he was, up in the air, free. He had jumped.

Q: Oh my God. I'm so sorry, Mr Kayn.

A: I'm not. The flames and the heat must have been unbearable. He found the strength to break the windows and choose his destiny. It might have been his destiny to die that day, but nobody was going to tell him how. He embraced his fate like a man. He died strong, flying, master of the ten seconds he was in the air. The plans that I had made for him all those years were over.

Q: My God, that's terrible.

A: All of this would have been for him. All of it.

72

KAYN TOWER

NEW YORK

Wednesday, 19 July 2006. 11:39 p.m.

'Are you sure you don't remember anything?'

'I'm telling you. He made me turn around and then he punched in some numbers.'

'We can't go on like this. There are still about sixty per cent of the combinations to go through. You have to give me something. Anything.'

They were next to the lift doors. This panel was certainly more of a challenge than the last one. Unlike the panel operated by a palm print, this was a simple number pad like an ATM machine and it was virtually impossible to extract a short numerical sequence from any sizable memory. To open the lift doors, Albert had connected a long, thick cable to the entry panel, intending to crack the code using a basic but brutal method. In the broadest terms this consisted of having the computer try all possible combinations, from all zeroes to all nines, which could take quite some time.

'We have three minutes to get into this lift. It's going to take the computer at least another six to go through the sequence of twenty digits. That's if it doesn't crash in the meantime because I've shifted all the processor's power into the deciphering program.'

The fan in the laptop was making an infernal racket, like a hundred bees trapped in a shoebox.

Orville tried to remember. He turned around, faced the wall and looked at his watch. No more than three seconds had gone by.

'I'm going to limit it to ten digits,' Albert said.

'Are you sure?' Orville said, turning back.

'Absolutely. I don't think we have any other option.'

'How long will it take it?'

'Four minutes,' Albert said, scratching his chin nervously. 'Let's hope it's not the last combination it tries, because I can hear them coming.'

At the other end of the hall someone was banging on the door.

73

THE EXCAVATION

AL MUDAWWARA DESERT,
JORDAN

Thursday, July 20. 6:39 a.m.

For the first time since they had reached Claw Canyon eight days earlier, dawn found most of the members of the expedition asleep. Five of them, under six feet of sand and rocks, would never wake again.

Others were shuddering in the early-morning cold beneath a camouflage blanket. They looked at the place where the horizon was supposed to be and waited for the sun to burst into day, turning the cold air into the hell of what would become the hottest day of the Jordanian summer in over forty-five years. From time to time they gave a worried nod, and that in itself frightened them. For every soldier the night watch is the hardest; and for the one who has blood on his hands it's the time when the ghosts of those he has killed might come to whisper in his ear.

Halfway between the five resting underground and the three doing guard duty up on the cliff, fifteen people turned over in their sleeping bags; perhaps they missed the blasts from the air horn that Professor Forrester had used to get them out of bed before dawn. The sun came up at 5:33 a.m., and was greeted by silence.

Towards 6:15 a.m., roughly the same time that Orville Watson and Father Albert were entering the lobby of Kayn Tower, the first member of the expedition to rouse himself was Nuri Zayit the cook. He prodded his assistant Rani with his foot and stepped outside. As soon as he got to the mess tent he began to prepare instant coffee using evaporated milk instead of water. There weren't many cartons of milk or juice left, since people were drinking them to compensate for the lack of water, and there was no fruit, so the only thing the chef could do was make omelettes and scrambled eggs. The old mute threw all his energy and a handful of the remaining parsley into the meal, communicating, as he had always done, through his culinary skills.

In the infirmary tent, Harel untangled herself from Andrea's embrace and went to check on Professor Forrester. The old man was connected to an oxygen tank, but his condition had only worsened. The doctor doubted that he would last beyond that night. Shaking her head to dispel the thought, she returned to wake Andrea with a kiss. As they caressed and made small talk, both of them began to realise that they were falling in love. Finally they got dressed and headed for the mess tent to have breakfast.

Fowler, who now shared a tent with just Pappas, started his day by going against his better judgement and made a mistake. Thinking that everyone in the soldiers' tent was asleep, he slid outside and made a call to Albert on his satellite phone. The young priest answered and impatiently told him to call back in twenty minutes. Fowler hung up, relieved that the call had been so brief but worried about having to try his luck again so soon.

As for David Pappas, he woke up a little before six thirty and went to see Professor Forrester, hoping that he would be better but also hoping to rid himself of the guilt he felt following last night's dream, in which he was the only archaeologist left alive when the Ark finally saw the light of day.

In the soldiers' tent, Marla Jackson was watching the back of her commander and lover from her mattress – they never slept together when they were on a mission but would sneak off together once in a while on 'reconnaissance'. She wondered what the South African was thinking.

Dekker was one of those for whom dawn brought the breath of the dead, making the hairs on the back of his neck stand on end. In a brief moment of wakefulness between two successive nightmares, he thought he had seen the frequency scanner screen display a signal, but it was too quick to fix a position. Suddenly he leapt up and started giving orders.

In Raymond Kayn's tent, Russell was laying out his boss's clothes and urging him at least to take his red pill. Reluctantly Kayn agreed then spat it out when Russell wasn't looking. He felt strangely calm. At last, the whole purpose of his sixty-eight years would be fulfilled.

In a more modest tent, Tommy Eichberg discreetly stuck his finger in his nose, scratched his behind, and walked to the bathroom looking for Brian Hanley. He needed his help to fix a piece they needed for the drill. They had to get through eight feet of wall but if they drilled from the top they could reduce some of the vertical pressure and then remove the stones by hand. If they worked quickly, they could be finished in six hours. Of course, it didn't help that Hanley was nowhere to be found.

As for Huqan, he checked his watch. Over the past week he had worked out the best place from which to get a good view over the whole site. Now he waited for the soldiers to change shift. Waiting suited him fine. He had waited a lifetime.

74

KAYN TOWER

Wednesday, 19 July 2006. 11:41 p.m.

7456898123

The computer found the code in exactly two minutes and forty-three seconds. This was fortunate because Albert had been wrong in his calculations about how long it would take the guards to show up. The door at the end of the hall opened almost at the same time as that of the lift.

'Hold it!'

Two of the guards and a policeman entered the hallway frowning, their guns drawn. They were not too happy about all the excitement. Albert and Orville threw themselves into the lift. They could hear the sound of feet running on the carpet and saw a hand reaching in to try to stop the lift. It missed by a few inches.

The door closed with a scratching noise. Outside they could make out the muffled voices of the guards.

'How do you open this thing?' the policeman said.

'They won't get far. This lift needs a special key to operate it. Nobody can make it go without it.'

'Activate the emergency system you told me about.'

'Yes, sir. Right away. It'll be like shooting fish in a barrel.'

Orville felt his heart pounding as he turned to Albert.

'Fuck, they're going to get us!'

The priest was smiling.

'What the hell's the matter with you? Think of something,' Orville hissed.

'I already have. When we went into Kayn Tower's computer system this morning, it was impossible to get to the electronic key in their system that makes the lift doors open.'

'Fucking impossible,' agreed Orville, who didn't like being beaten by anything, but on this occasion had run into the mother of all firewalls.

'You may be a great spy and you certainly know a few tricks … but you lack the one thing that is essential in a great hacker: lateral thinking,' Albert said. He crossed his arms behind his head, as if he were relaxing in his living room. 'When the doors are locked, you use the windows. Or in this case you change the sequence that determines the lift's position, and the order of the floors. A simple step that wasn't blocked. Now the Kayn computer thinks that the lift's on the thirty-ninth floor instead of the thirty-eighth.'

'So?' said Orville, slightly annoyed by the priest's bragging, but also curious.

'Well, my friend, in this kind of situation all the emergency systems in this city make the lifts go down to the last available floor and then open the door.'

At that very moment, after a brief shudder, the lift started going up. They could hear the shocked guards yelling outside.

'Up is down and down is up,' Orville said, clapping his hands in the middle of a cloud of mint disinfectant. 'You're a genius.'

75

THE EXCAVATION

AL MUDAWWARA DESERT,
JORDAN

Thursday, 20 July 2006. 6:43 a.m.

Fowler wasn't ready to risk Andrea's life again. Using the satellite phone without any precautions was insane.

It made no sense for someone with his experience to make the same error twice. This would be the third time.

The first had been the previous night. The priest had raised his eyes from his prayer book as the excavation team came out of the cave carrying the half-dead body of Professor Forrester. Andrea came running over to him and told him what had happened. The reporter said they were certain that a gold box lay hidden inside the cave, and Fowler no longer had any doubts. Taking advantage of the general excitement caused by the news, he had called Albert, who explained that he was going to try one last time to get information on the terrorist group and Huqan around midnight in New York, a couple of hours after dawn in Jordan. The call lasted exactly thirteen seconds.

The second one had taken place earlier that morning, when Fowler had jumped the gun and called. That call lasted six seconds. He doubted the scanner had time to work out where the signal came from.

The third call would take place in six and a half minutes' time.

Albert, for God's sake, don't fail me.

76

KAYN TOWER

Wednesday, 19 July 2006. 11:45 p.m.

'How do you think they'll get in?' Orville asked.

'I guess they'll bring a SWAT team and abseil down from the roof, probably shoot out the glass windows and all that shit.'

'A SWAT team for a couple of unarmed burglars? Don't you think that's like using a tank to go after a couple of mice.'

'Look at it this way, Orville: two strangers have broken into the private offices of a paranoid multimillionaire. You should be happy they're not going to drop a bomb on us. Now let me concentrate. To be the only one who has access to this floor, Russell must have a very secure computer.'

'Don't tell me that after everything we've been through to get here you can't get into his computer!'

'I didn't say that. I'm just saying it will take me at least ten more seconds.'

Albert wiped the sweat from his forehead then let his hands fly over the keyboard. Not even the best hacker in the world can get into a computer if it's not linked to a server. That had been their problem from the beginning. They had tried everything to locate Russell's computer within the Kayn network. It was impossible because in terms of systems, the computers on this floor didn't belong to Kayn Tower. To his surprise, Albert found out that not only Russell but also Kayn used computers that were connected to the Internet and each other using 3G cards, two of the hundreds of thousands that were operating in New York City at the time. Without that crucial bit of information, Albert could have spent decades searching the Internet for two invisible computers.

They must pay more than five hundred dollars a day for their broadband usage not to mention the calls, Albert thought. *I suppose that's nothing when you're worth millions. Especially when you can keep people like us at bay using such a simple trick.*

'I think I've got it,' said the priest as the screen changed from a black background to the bright blue of the system's start-up. 'Any luck finding that disk?'

Orville had gone through the drawers and the only cupboard in Russell's neat and elegant office, pulling out files and dumping them on the carpet. He was now tugging paintings off the wall in a frenzy, looking for a safe, and slicing through the bottom of chairs with a silver letter opener.

'Looks like there's nothing to find,' Orville said, pushing one of Russell's chairs over with his foot so that he could sit next to Albert. The bandages on his hands were once again covered in blood and his round face was pale.

'Paranoid son of a bitch. They only communicated with each other. No external e-mails. Russell must use another computer to run the business.'

'He must have taken it to Jordan.'

'I need your help. What do we look for?'

A minute later, after keying in all the passwords he could think of, Orville gave up.

'It's useless. There's nothing. And if there was, he's already erased it.'

'That gives me an idea. Wait,' said Albert, taking from his pocket a USB flash drive no bigger than a stick of chewing gum, and connecting it to the CPU of the computer so that it would interface with the hard drive. 'The little program in this baby will let you retrieve information from erased sections on the hard drive. We can go from there.'

'Terrific. Look for Netcatch.'

'Right!'

With a little buzz, a list of fourteen files appeared in the program's search window. Albert opened all of them at once.

'They're html files. Saved websites.'

'Do you recognise anything?'

'Yes, I saved them myself. They're what I call server conversations. Terrorists never send each other e-mails when they're planning an attack. Any idiot knows that e-mail can go through twenty or thirty servers before reaching its destination, so you never know who's watching your communication. What they do is give everyone in the cell the same password to a free account and they write whatever they need to pass on as a draft e-mail message. It's like you're writing to yourself except that it's a whole cell of terrorists communicating with each other. The e-mail is never sent. It never goes anywhere because each one of the terrorists is using the same account and—'

Orville stood paralysed in front of the screen, so stunned that for a moment he forgot to breathe. The unthinkable, what he had never imagined, suddenly became obvious before his very eyes.

'This isn't right,' he said.

'What is it, Orville?'

356

'I . . . hack through thousands and thousands of accounts every week. When we copy files from a web server, we only keep the text. If we didn't, the images would quickly fill up our hard drives. The result is ugly, but you can still read it.'

Orville pointed a bandaged finger at the computer screen, where a conversation between terrorists on the e-mail account Maktoob.com could be seen with coloured buttons and images that would not have been the case had this been one of the files he had hacked into and saved.

'Somebody went into Maktoob.com from the browser in this computer, Albert. Even though they erased it after they finished, the images remained in the memory cache. And to get into Maktoob . . .'

Albert understood even before Orville could finish.

'Whoever was here had to know the password.'

Orville agreed.

'It's Russell, Albert. Russell is Huqan.'

At that moment shots rang out, shattering the large window.

77

THE EXCAVATION

AL MUDAWWARA DESERT, JORDAN

Thursday, 20 July 2006. 6:49 a.m.

Fowler looked carefully at his watch. Nine seconds ahead of the agreed time, the unexpected happened.

Albert was calling.

The priest had gone to the canyon entrance to make his call. There was a blind spot there that the soldier watching from the southern end of the cliff couldn't see. The moment he turned on the phone, the call came. Fowler knew straight away that something was wrong.

'Albert, what's happened?'

On the other end of the line he heard a number of voices yelling. Fowler tried to understand what was going on.

'Throw down the phone!'

'Officer, I *have* to make this call!' Albert's voice sounded far away, as if he didn't have the phone next to his ear. 'It's really important. It's a question of national security.'

'I told you to drop the fucking phone.'

'I'm going to lower my arm slowly and talk. If you see me do something suspicious, then shoot me.'

'This is my last warning. Drop it!'

'Anthony,' Albert's voice was steady and clear. He'd finally put the earpiece in. 'Can you hear me?'

'Yes, Albert.'

'Russell is Huqan. Confirmed. Be careful—'

The connection was cut off. Fowler felt a wave of shock wash over his body. He turned around to run towards the camp, then everything went black.

78

INSIDE THE DINING TENT,
FIFTY-THREE SECONDS BEFORE

Andrea and Harel stopped at the entrance to the mess tent when they saw David Pappas running towards them. Pappas was carrying a bloody T-shirt and he seemed to be disoriented.

'Doctor, Doctor!'

'What the hell's going on, David?' answered Harel. She had been in the same bad mood ever since the water incident had made proper coffee a thing of the past.

'It's the professor. He's in bad shape.'

David had volunteered to stay with Forrester while Andrea and Doc went to breakfast. The only thing that had delayed the demolition of the wall to get to the Ark was Forrester's condition, although Russell had wanted to go ahead with the job the previous night. David had refused to open the cavity until the professor had had a chance to recover and could join them. Andrea, whose opinion of Pappas had gone from bad to worse over the past few hours, suspected that he was simply waiting for Forrester to be completely out of the way.

'OK.' Doc sighed. 'You go ahead, Andrea. It doesn't make sense for both of us to miss breakfast.' She began jogging back towards the infirmary.

The reporter took a quick peek inside the mess tent. Zayit and Peterke waved back at her. Andrea liked the mute cook and his assistant but the only people sitting at the tables at that moment were two of the soldiers, Alois Gottlieb and Louis Maloney, who were eating from their trays. Andrea was surprised there were only two of them, because the soldiers normally had breakfast together, leaving only one lookout posted on the southern ridge for half an hour. In fact, breakfast was the only time she ever saw the soldiers together in one place.

Since she didn't care for their company, Andrea had decided she would go back and see if she could help Harel.

Even though my medical knowledge is so limited I'd probably put a hospital gown on backwards.

Then Doc turned around and yelled: 'Do me a favour, and bring me a large coffee, OK?'

Andrea put one foot inside the mess tent, trying to work out the best route to avoid the sweaty soldiers, who were leaning over their food like apes, when she almost banged into Nuri Zayit. The cook must have seen the doctor running back to the infirmary because he handed Andrea a tray with two cups of instant coffee and a plate of toast.

'Instant coffee dissolved in milk, is that right, Nuri?'

The mute smiled and shrugged his shoulders to say it wasn't his fault.

'I know. Perhaps tonight we'll see water springing from a rock and all that biblical stuff. Anyway, thank you.'

Slowly, making sure she didn't spill the coffee because she knew she wasn't the most coordinated person in the world, even though she would never admit it out loud, she headed for the infirmary. Nuri waved to her from the entrance to the mess tent, still smiling.

And then it happened.

Andrea felt as if a giant hand were lifting her up from the ground and throwing her six and a half feet into the air before flinging her back down. She felt a sharp pain in her left arm and a terrible burning on her chest and her back. She turned just in time to see thousands of small pieces of burning cloth falling from the sky. A column of black smoke was all that was left of what, two seconds ago, had been the mess tent. Up high the smoke seemed to mix with another much blacker smoke. Andrea couldn't work out where it was coming from. Carefully, she touched her chest and realised that her shirt was covered in a hot sticky liquid.

Doc came running over.

'Are you all right? Oh God, are you OK, darling?'

Andrea was aware that Harel was shouting even though she sounded far away due to the whistling in Andrea's ears. She felt the doctor checking her neck and arms.

'My chest.'

'You're OK. It's only coffee.'

Andrea stood up carefully and saw that she had spilled the coffee over herself. Her right hand was still clutching the tray, while her left arm had banged against a rock. She moved her fingers, afraid that she had suffered more injuries. Luckily nothing was broken but her whole left side felt as if it were paralyzed.

While a few members of the expedition tried to put out the fire using buckets of sand, Harel concentrated on taking care of Andrea's wounds. The reporter had cuts and scratches to the left side of her body. Her hair and the skin on her back had been slightly burned and there was a constant buzzing in her ears.

'The buzzing will disappear in three to four hours,' Harel said as she put her stethoscope back into her trouser pocket.

'I'm sorry . . .' Andrea said, almost shouting without realising it. She was crying.

'You have nothing to be sorry for.'

'He . . . Nuri . . . brought the coffee out to me. If I had gone inside to get it, I'd be dead right now. I could've asked him to come out and smoke a cigarette with me. I could've saved his life in return.'

Harel pointed to the surroundings. Both the mess tent and a fuel truck had been blown up – two separate explosions at the same time. Four people had been turned to nothing but ash.

'The only one who should feel anything is the son of a bitch who did this.'

'Don't worry about it, lady, we have him,' Torres said.

He and Jackson were dragging a person in handcuffs by the feet. They deposited him in the middle of the area by the tents while the other expedition members looked on in shock, unable to believe what they were seeing.

79

THE EXCAVATION

AL MUDAWWARA DESERT,
JORDAN

Thursday, 20 July 2006. 6:49 a.m.

Fowler put his hand up to his forehead. It was bleeding. The explosion from the truck had thrown him to the ground and he had hit his head against something. He had tried to get up and head back towards the camp with the satellite phone still in his hand. In the middle of his hazy vision and the thick cloud of smoke, he saw two soldiers approaching with their guns aimed at him.

'It was you, you son of a bitch!'

'Look, he still has the phone in his hand.'

'That's what you used to set off the explosions, wasn't it, you bastard?'

The butt of a rifle hit his head. He fell to the ground but didn't feel the kicks or the other blows to his body. He had lost consciousness long before that.

'This is ridiculous,' Russell screamed, joining the group that had crowded around Father Fowler: Dekker, Torres, Jackson and Alryk Gottlieb on the soldiers' side; Eichberg, Hanley and Pappas from what was left of the civilians.

With Harel's help, Andrea was trying to stand up and go

over to the group of threatening faces that were black with soot.

'It's not ridiculous, sir,' said Dekker, throwing down Fowler's satellite phone. 'He was carrying this when we found him near the fuel truck. Thanks to the scanner, we know he made a brief phone call this morning, so we were already suspicious of him. Instead of going to breakfast, we took our positions and watched him. Luckily.'

'It's only—' Andrea began, but Harel yanked her arm.

'Quiet. That's not going to help him,' she whispered.

Exactly. What was I going to say, that it's the secret phone he uses to communicate with the CIA? That's not the best way of defending his innocence, idiot.

'It's a telephone. Certainly something that's not allowed on this expedition, but it's not enough to accuse this man of causing the explosions,' Russell said.

'Maybe not just the phone, sir. But look what we found in his briefcase.'

Jackson tossed the ruined briefcase in front of them. It had been emptied and the bottom cover ripped off. Glued to the base was a secret compartment containing small bars that looked like marzipan.

'It's C4, Mr Russell,' Dekker went on.

The information made them all hold their breath. Then Alryk pulled out his pistol.

'This pig killed my brother. Let me put a bullet through his fucking skull,' he screamed, out of his mind with rage.

'I've heard enough,' said a soft but steady voice.

The circle opened and Raymond Kayn approached the unconscious body of the priest. He leaned over him, one figure in black and the other in white.

'I can't understand what made this man do what he did.

But this mission has been delayed for too long, and it cannot be delayed any more. Pappas, please get back to work and knock down the wall.'

'Mr Kayn, I can't do that without knowing what's going on here,' Pappas answered.

Brian Hanley and Tommy Eichberg folded their arms and went and stood next to Pappas. Kayn didn't even look at them twice.

'Mr Dekker?'

'Sir?' said the large South African.

'Please, exercise your authority. The time for niceties is over.'

'Jackson,' said Dekker, signalling.

The soldier lifted her M4 and aimed it at the three rebels.

'You've got to be joking,' complained Eichberg, whose large red nose was a couple of inches from the muzzle of Jackson's automatic.

'It's no joke, honey. Start walking or I'll shoot you a new asshole.' Jackson cocked her weapon with an ominous metallic click.

Ignoring the others, Kayn walked over to Harel and Andrea.

'As for you young ladies, it has been a pleasure to be able to rely on your services. Mr Dekker will guarantee your return to the *Behemoth*.'

'What are you saying?' howled Andrea, who despite her difficulty in hearing had caught some of what Kayn had said. 'Damned son of a bitch! They're going to extract the Ark in a few hours' time. Let me stay until tomorrow. You owe me.'

'Are you saying that the fisherman owes the worm? Take them away. Oh, and make sure they leave only with what they're wearing. Have the reporter hand over the disk containing her photos.'

Dekker pulled Alryk aside and spoke to him quietly.

'You take them.'

'Bullshit. I want to stay here and deal with the priest. He killed my brother,' said the German, his eyes bloodshot.

'He'll still be alive when you get back. Now do as you're told. Torres will keep him nice and warm for you.'

'Fuck, Colonel. It takes at least three hours to go from here to Aqaba and back, even if we're driving at top speed in the Humvee. If Torres gets his hands on the priest, there'll be nothing left of him by the time I get back.'

'Believe me, Gottlieb. You'll be back in an hour.'

'What are you saying, sir?'

Dekker looked at him seriously, annoyed by his subordinate's slowness. He hated having to spell things out.

'Sarsaparilla, Gottlieb. And make it quick.'

80

THE EXCAVATION

Thursday, 20 July 2006. 7:14 a.m.

Sitting in the back of the H3, Andrea half closed her eyes in a vain attempt to deal with the dust that was pouring in through the windows. The explosion of the fuel tanker had blown out the vehicle's windows and cracked the windscreen, and even though Alryk had repaired some of the holes with duct tape and a few shirts, he had worked so quickly that there were still places where the sand blew in. Harel complained, but the soldier didn't reply. He was holding the steering wheel with both hands, his knuckles white and his mouth tense. He had raced over the large dune at the entrance to the canyon in only three minutes and was now stepping on the accelerator as if his life depended on it.

'It won't be the most comfortable trip in the world, but at least we're going home,' Doc said, putting her hand on Andrea's thigh. Andrea grasped her hand firmly.

'Why did he do it, Doc? Why did he have explosives in his briefcase? Tell me they planted them on him,' said the young reporter, almost pleading.

The doctor leaned closer, so that Alryk couldn't hear her, although she doubted he could hear anything with the noise of the engine and the wind flapping the temporary covers on the windows.

'I don't know, Andrea, but the explosives were his.'

'How do you know?' asked Andrea, her eyes suddenly serious.

'Because he told me. After you heard the soldiers talking when you were under their tent, he came to me for help with a crazy plan to blow up the water supply.'

'Doc, what are you saying? You knew about that?'

'He came here because of you. He saved your life once before, and according to the code of honour his kind live by, he believes he must assist you any time you need help. In any case, for reasons I don't quite understand, it was his boss who got you involved in the first place. He wanted to make sure Fowler was on the expedition.'

'Is that why Kayn mentioned the thing about the worm?'

'Yes. For Kayn and his people you were just a way of controlling Fowler. Everything's been a lie from the very start.'

'And what will happen to him now?'

'Forget about him. They'll interrogate him and then … he'll disappear. And before you say anything, don't even think about going back there.'

The reality of the situation left the reporter stunned.

'Why, Doc?' Andrea pulled away from her in disgust. 'Why didn't you tell me, after all we've been through? You swore you'd never lie to me again. You swore while we were making love. I don't know how I could have been so stupid …'

'I say a lot of things.' A tear slid down Harel's cheek, but when she continued her voice was steely. 'His mission is different from mine. For me, this was just another of the silly expeditions that take place from time to time. But Fowler knew it could be the real thing. And if it was, he knew he had to do something about it.'

'And what was that? Blow us all up?'

'I don't know who set off the explosion this morning, but believe me, it wasn't Anthony Fowler.'

'But you didn't say anything.'

'I couldn't say anything without implicating myself,' Harel said looking away. 'I knew they would get us out of there ... I ... wanted to be with you. Away from the excavation. Away from my life, I suppose.'

'What about Forrester? He was your patient and you left him there.'

'He died this morning, Andrea. Just before the explosion, as a matter of fact. He's been ill for years, you know that.'

Andrea shook her head.

If I was American I'd win the Pulitzer, but at what price?

'I can't believe it. So many deaths, so much violence, and all for a ridiculous museum piece.'

'Fowler didn't explain it to you? There's much more at stake here ...' Harel stopped talking as the Humvee slowed down.

'This isn't right,' she said, looking out through the cracks in the window. 'There's nothing here.'

The vehicle came to a rough stop.

'Hey, Alryk, what are you doing?' Andrea said. 'Why are we stopping?'

The big German didn't say anything. Very slowly, he took the keys out of the ignition, pulled up the handbrake, and got out of the Hummer, slamming the door.

'Shit. They wouldn't dare,' Harel said.

Andrea saw the fear in the doctor's eyes. She could hear

Alryk's footsteps in the sand. He was coming around to Harel's side.

'What's going on, Doc?'

The door opened.

'Get out,' Alryk said coldly, his face impassive.

'You can't do this,' Harel said, not moving an inch. 'Your commander doesn't want to make an enemy of Mossad. We're very bad enemies to have.'

'Orders are orders. Get out.'

'Not her. At least let her go, please.'

The German brought his hand to his belt and pulled his automatic pistol from the holster.

'For the last time. Get out of the vehicle.'

Harel looked at Andrea, resigned to her fate. She shrugged and with both hands grabbed hold of the passenger handle above the side window to exit the vehicle. But suddenly she tensed her arm muscles and, still gripping the handle, swung her feet out, hitting Alryk in the chest with her heavy boots. The German let go of the pistol, which fell to the ground. Harel lunged head first at the soldier, knocking him down. The doctor leapt up immediately and kicked the German in the face, splitting his eyebrow and damaging his eye. Doc lifted her foot over his face, ready to finish the job but the soldier came to, grabbed her foot with his huge hand and spun her violently to the left. There was a loud sound of breaking bone as Doc fell.

The mercenary stood up and turned around. Andrea was coming at him, ready to strike, but the soldier disposed of her by smacking her with the back of his hand, leaving an ugly red welt on her cheek. Andrea fell backwards. As she hit the sand she felt something hard beneath her.

Alryk now bent over Harel. He grabbed the big mane of

curly black hair and pulled, lifting her up as if she were a rag doll until his face was next to hers. Harel was still reeling from the shock but managed to look the soldier in the eye and spat at him.

'Fuck you, you piece of shit.'

The German spat back at her, and then lifted his right hand, which was holding a combat knife. He sank it into Harel's stomach, enjoying the sight of his victim's eyes rolling back and her mouth opening as she fought to breathe. Alryk turned the knife in the wound and then pulled it out roughly. Blood gushed out, splashing the soldier's uniform and boots. He let go of the doctor, a look of disgust on his face.

'Nooo!'

The mercenary now turned to Andrea, who had landed on the pistol and was trying to find the safety catch. She screamed with all her might and pressed the trigger.

The automatic jumped in her hands, leaving her fingers numb. She had never fired a gun before and it showed. The bullet whistled past the German and slammed into the door of the Hummer. Alryk yelled something in German and charged at her. Almost without looking, Andrea fired three more times.

One bullet missed.

Another punctured a tyre on the Humvee.

The third went into the German's open mouth. Because of the momentum of his 200-pound body, he continued plunging towards Andrea, although his hands were no longer intent on taking her pistol and choking her. He fell, face up, trying to talk, blood gurgling from his mouth. Horrified, Andrea saw that the shot had ripped out some of the German's teeth. She stepped aside and waited, still aiming the pistol at him – although if she hadn't managed to wound him through sheer luck, this would have been pointless as her hand was shaking too much and her fingers had no strength left in them. Her arm ached from the pistol's kick.

It took the German almost a minute to die. The bullet had gone through his neck, destroying his spinal cord and leaving him paralysed. He choked on his own blood as it flooded his throat.

When she was sure that Alryk was no longer a threat, Andrea ran over to Harel, who lay bleeding on the sand. She sat down and cradled Doc's head, avoiding looking at the wound as Harel tried helplessly to hold her guts in with her hands.

'Hold on, Doc. Tell me what I have to do. I'll get you out of here, even if it's just so I can kick your butt for lying to me.'

'Don't bother,' Harel answered in a weak voice. 'I've had it. Believe me. I'm a doctor.'

Andrea let out a sob and leaned her forehead against Harel's. Harel took a hand away from the wound and grabbed one of the reporter's.

'Don't say that. Please don't.'

'I've told you enough lies. I want you to do something for me.'

'Name it.'

'In a minute I want you to get into the Hummer and head west on this goat track. We're about ninety-five miles from Aqaba, but you should be able to reach the road in a couple of hours.' She paused and gritted her teeth in pain. 'The vehicle has a GPS direction finder. If you see anybody, get out of the Hummer and ask for help. What I want you to do is get away from here. Swear to me you'll do that?'

'I swear.'

Harel twisted in pain. Her grip on Andrea's hand was weakening by the second.

'You see, I never should have told you my real name. I want you to do something else for me. I want you to say it out loud. Nobody has ever done that.'

'Chedva.'

'Scream it out.'

'CHEDVA!' Andrea yelled, her anguish and pain shattering the stillness of the desert.

A quarter of an hour later Chedva Harel's life was extinguished for ever.

Digging a grave in the sand with her bare hands was the most difficult thing Andrea had ever done. Not because of the effort it required, but because of what it meant. Because it was a senseless gesture, and because in part Chedva had died because of the events she had set in motion. She dug the shallow grave, and marked it with the aerial from the Hummer and a circle of rocks.

When she finished, Andrea searched the Hummer for water but with little success. The only water she could find was in the soldier's canteen hanging from his belt. It was three-quarters full. She also took his cap, even though to keep it on she had to adjust it with a safety pin she found in her pocket. She also pulled out one of the shirts stuffed into the broken windows and grabbed a steel tube from the trunk of the Hummer. She ripped out the windscreen wipers and stuck them into the pipe, draping them with the shirt to make an improvised umbrella.

She then went back to the track the Hummer had left. Unfortunately, when Harel had asked her to swear to return to Aqaba, she didn't know about the stray bullet that had destroyed the front tyre because she had had her back to the vehicle. Even if Andrea had wanted to keep her promise, which was not the case, it would have been impossible for her to change the tyre on her own. As much as she looked she couldn't find the jack. On that kind of rocky road the vehicle would not have been able to go a hundred feet without a functioning front wheel.

Andrea looked to the west, where she could see the faint line of the main road snaking in and out of the dunes.

Ninety-five miles to Aqaba in the noonday sun, almost sixty to the main road. That's at least several days' walking in 100–degree heat, hoping I'll find someone, and I don't even have enough water to last me six hours. And that's assuming I don't get lost trying to find an almost invisible road, or that those sons of bitches haven't already taken the Ark and come across me on their way out of here.

She looked to the east, where the Hummer's tracks were still fresh.

Eight miles in that direction were vehicles, water and the scoop of the century, she thought as she started to walk. *Not to mention a whole crowd of people who want me dead. The upside? I still have a chance to get my disk back and help the priest. I have no clue how, but I'll give it a shot.*

ℛELICS ℂRYPT

VATICAN CITY

Thirteen days earlier

'Do you want some ice for that hand?' Cirin asked. Fowler took a handkerchief out of his pocket and used it to bandage his knuckles, which were bleeding from several cuts. Avoiding Brother Cesáreo, who was still trying to repair the niche that he had destroyed with his fists, Fowler approached the Chief of the Holy Alliance.

'What is it you want from me, Camilo?'

'I want you to bring it back, Anthony. If it truly exists, the place for the Ark is here, in a reinforced room one hundred and fifty feet under the Vatican. Now isn't the time for it to go floating around the world in the wrong hands. Let alone for the world to know of its existence.'

Fowler gritted his teeth at the arrogance of Cirin and whoever it was above him, maybe even the Pope himself, who felt they could decide the fate of the Ark. What Cirin was asking of him was much more than a simple mission; it weighed like a tombstone over his whole life. The risks were incalculable.

'We will keep it,' Cirin insisted. 'We know how to wait.'

Fowler nodded.

He'd go to Jordan.

But he too was capable of making his own decisions.

THE EXCAVATION

Thursday, 20 July 2006. 9:23 a.m.

'Wake up, Padre.'

Fowler came to slowly, not knowing exactly where he was. He only knew that his whole body hurt. He was unable to move his arms because they were handcuffed above his head. The cuffs were somehow pinned to the wall of the canyon.

When he opened his eyes he verified this, as well as the identity of the person who had been trying to wake him up. Torres was standing in front of him.

A big smile.

'I know you understand me,' said the soldier in Spanish. 'I prefer to talk in my own language. I can handle the subtle details much better that way.'

'There's nothing subtle about you,' said the priest in Spanish.

'You're wrong, Padre. On the contrary, one of the things that made me famous in Colombia was the way I've always used nature to help me. I have small friends who do my work for me.'

'So you're the one who put the scorpions in Ms Otero's sleeping bag,' Fowler said, trying to pull the handcuffs loose without Torres noticing. It was useless. They were fastened to the canyon wall with a steel nail that had been driven into the rock.

'I appreciate your efforts, Padre. But no matter how hard you pull, those handcuffs are not going to move,' said Torres. 'But you're right. I wanted to get your little Spanish bitch. It didn't work. So now I have to wait for our friend Alryk. I think he's abandoned us. He must be enjoying himself with your two whore friends. I hope he screws them both before he blows their heads off. Blood is so difficult to wash off your uniform.'

Fowler yanked at the cuffs, blind with anger and unable to control himself.

'Come here, Torres. You come here!'

'Hey, hey! What's up?' said Torres, enjoying the fury on Fowler's face. 'I like seeing you pissed off. My little friends are going to love this.'

The priest looked in the direction Torres was pointing. Not far from Fowler's feet was a mound on the sand with a few red forms moving about on top of it.

'*Solenopsis catusianis*. I don't really know any Latin, but I do know that these ants are fucking serious, Padre. I was very lucky to find one of their hills so close by. I love to watch them work and I haven't seen them do their thing for a while . . .'

Torres squatted down and picked up a rock. He stood up, played with the rock for a few moments, then stepped back a few paces.

'But today it looks as if they're going to work extra hard, Padre. My little friends have teeth like you wouldn't believe. But that's not all. The best part is when they stick their stinger into you and inject the poison. Here, let me show you.'

He brought back his arm and lifted his knee like a baseball pitcher, then hurled the rock. It hit the mound, destroying the top of it.

It was as if a red fury had come alive on the sand. The ants swarmed out of the nest in their hundreds. Torres stepped back a little further and threw another rock, this time in an arc so that it landed halfway between Fowler and the nest. The red mass was still for a moment and then charged at the rock, making it disappear beneath its anger.

Torres stepped back even more slowly and threw another rock, which landed about a foot and a half from Fowler. Once again the ants advanced on the rock until the mass was no more than eight inches from the priest. Fowler could hear the crackling of the insects. It was an ugly, frightening sound like someone shaking a paper bag full of bottle caps.

They use movement to guide themselves. Now he'll throw another rock closer to me so that I move. If I do that, I'm done for, Fowler thought.

And that's exactly what happened. The fourth rock fell at Fowler's feet and the ants converged on it immediately. Slowly, Fowler's boots were covered by a sea of ants that grew by the second as new ones emerged from the nest. Torres threw more rocks at the ants which became even angrier, as if the smell of their smashed brothers added to their desire for vengeance.

'Admit it, Padre. You're fucked,' Torres said.

The soldier threw another rock, this time not aiming at the ground but at Fowler's head. It missed by two inches and fell on the red tide that was moving like an angry vortex.

Torres bent down once more and chose a smaller rock, which he could throw more easily. He aimed carefully and let it fly. The rock hit the priest on the forehead. Fowler fought back the pain and the urge to move.

'You'll give up sooner or later, Padre. I plan to spend the morning like this.'

He bent down again, looking for ammunition, but had to stop as his walkie-talkie crackled into life.

'Torres, Dekker here. Where the fuck are you?'

'Taking care of the priest, sir.'

'Leave that to Alryk, he'll be back soon. I promised him, and as Schopenhauer said, a great man treats his promises as divine laws.'

'Roger, sir.'

'Report to Nest One.'

'With all due respect, sir, it's not my turn.'

'With all due respect, if you're not up at Nest One in thirty seconds I'll find you and skin you alive. Do you copy?'

'I copy, Colonel.'

'I'm glad to hear it. Over and out.'

Torres returned the walkie-talkie to his belt and slowly began walking back. 'You heard him, Padre. Since the explosion, there are only five of us, so we're going to have to postpone our game for a couple of hours. When I get back you'll be in worse shape. Nobody can sit still for that long.'

Fowler watched as Torres rounded the bend of the canyon near the entrance. His relief didn't last long.

Some of the ants on his boots were beginning to inch their way up his trouser leg.

83

ᴀʟ-ǫᴀʜɪʀᴀ
ᴍᴇᴛᴇᴏʀᴏʟᴏɢɪᴄᴀʟ
ɪɴsᴛɪᴛᴜᴛᴇ

CAIRO, EGYPT

Thursday, 20 July 2006. 9:56 a.m.

It wasn't even ten in the morning and the junior meteor-ologist's shirt was already soaked through. He had been on the phone the whole morning doing someone else's job. It was the height of the summer season and everyone who was anyone had left and was on the shore of Sharm El Sheikh, pretending to be an expert diver.

But this was one task that could not be postponed. The beast that was approaching was too dangerous.

For what seemed like the thousandth time since he had confirmed the readings on his instruments, the official picked up the phone and called another of the areas due to be affected by the forecast.

'Port of Aqaba.'

'*Salaam aleikum*, this is Jawar Ibn Dawud, from the Al-Qahira Meteorological Institute.'

'*Aleikum salaam*, Jawar, this is Najjar.' Even though the two men had never met they had spoken on the phone a dozen times. 'Can you call me back in a few minutes? I'm really busy this morning.'

'Listen to me, this is important. Early this morning we spotted a huge air mass. It's extremely hot and it's headed your way.'

'A simoon? Coming this way? Shit, I'll have to call my wife and tell her to bring in the laundry.'

'You'd better stop joking. This is one of the biggest I've ever seen. It's off the charts. Extremely dangerous.'

The meteorologist in Cairo could almost hear the harbour-master swallowing hard on the other end of the line. Like all Jordanians, he had learned to respect and fear the simoon, a sandstorm that moved in a circular motion like a tornado, with speeds of up to 100 miles per hour and temperatures of 120 degrees Fahrenheit. Anyone unlucky enough to witness a simoon in full force out in the open died instantly of cardiac arrest due to the intense heat, and the body was robbed of all moisture, leaving an empty, dried-out carcass where only minutes before there had been a human being. Luckily, modern weather forecasts gave civilians sufficient time to take precautions.

'I understand. Do you have a vector?' said the harbour-master, now clearly worried.

'It left the Sinai desert a few hours ago. I think it's just going to graze Aqaba, but it will feed on the currents there and explode over your central desert. You'll have to call every-one so they can relay the message.'

'I know how the network works, Jawar. Thank you.'

'Just make sure that nobody sails before tonight, OK? If not, you'll be collecting mummies in the morning.'

84

THE EXCAVATION

AL MUDAWWARA DESERT,
JORDAN

Thursday, 20 July 2006. 11:07 a.m.

David Pappas pushed the head of the drill through the opening for the last time. They had just finished drilling a slit in the wall some six feet wide and three and a half inches high, and thanks to the Everlasting the ceiling of the chamber on the other side of the wall had not collapsed, although there had been a slight tremor caused by the vibrations. They could now remove the rocks by hand without having to break them apart. Lifting them and setting them aside was another matter, since there were quite a few.

'It's going to take another two hours, Mr Kayn.'

The billionaire had come down into the cave half an hour earlier. He had stood in the corner with both hands behind his back, as he often did, simply watching and seemingly relaxed. Raymond Kayn had been afraid of the descent into the hole, but only in a rational way. He had spent the entire night preparing himself mentally, and had not felt the usual fear gripping his chest. His pulse had raced, but no more than usual for a sixty-eight-year-old man who had been strapped into a harness and lowered into a cavern for the first time.

I don't understand why I feel so good. Is it being close to the

Ark that is making me feel like this? Or is it this narrow uterus, this hot well that soothes me and suits me?

Russell approached him and whispered that he had to go and fetch something from his tent. Kayn nodded, distracted by his own thoughts, but proud to have freed himself from his dependence on Jacob. He loved him like a son, and was grateful for his sacrifice, but he could hardly recall a minute when Jacob was not on the other side of the room, ready to offer a helping hand or a piece of advice. How patient the young man had been with him.

If it hadn't been for Jacob, none of this could ever have happened.

85

Transcript of the communication between the crew of the *Behemoth* and Jacob Russell

20 July 2006

MOSES 1: Behemoth, Moses 1 here. Do you read me?

BEHEMOTH: Behemoth. Good morning, Mr Russell.

MOSES 1: Hello, Thomas. How are you?

BEHEMOTH: You know, sir. A lot of heat, but I think those of us born in Copenhagen can never get enough of it. How can I help?

MOSES 1: Thomas, Mr Kayn needs the BA-609 in a half-hour. We have to make an emergency pick-up. Tell the pilot to carry the maximum payload of fuel.

BEHEMOTH: Sir, I'm afraid that is going to be impossible. We've just received a communication from the Aqaba harbourmaster informing us that a giant sandstorm is moving across the area between the port and your location. They've suspended all air traffic until 1800 hours.

MOSES 1: Thomas, I'd like you to clarify something for me. Does the side of your ship bear the insignia of the port of Aqaba or of Kayn Industries?

Behemoth: Kayn Industries, sir.

Moses 1: I thought so. Another thing. Did you happen to hear me when I told you the name of the person who requires the BA-609?

Behemoth: Hmm, yes, sir. Mr Kayn, sir.

Moses 1: Very well, Thomas. Then please be so kind as to follow the orders I have given you, or you and the entire crew of that tub will be out of a job within the month. Have I made myself clear?

Behemoth: Perfectly clear, sir. The aircraft will be heading your way immediately.

Moses 1: Always a pleasure, Thomas. Over and out.

86

HUQAN

He began by praising the name of Allah the Wise, the Holy, the Compassionate, the one who would let him triumph over his enemies. He did so kneeling on the floor, dressed in a white robe that covered his entire body. In front of him was a basin of water.

To make sure that the water reached the skin below the metal, he removed the ring inscribed with the date when he had finished his studies. It had been a gift from the brotherhood. He then washed both of his hands up to the wrists, concentrating on the areas between his fingers.

He cupped his right hand, the one which under no circumstances had ever been used to touch his private parts, and scooped up some water, then vigorously rinsed out his mouth three times.

Once again he collected water in his hand, brought it to his nose and inhaled forcefully in order to cleanse his nostrils. He repeated the ritual three times. With his left hand he cleaned out the remaining water, sand and mucus.

Using his left hand again, he moistened his fingertips and cleaned the tip of his nose.

He lifted his right hand and held it in front of his face, then lowered it in order to dip it into the basin and cleaned his face from his right ear to his left ear three times.

Then from his forehead to his throat three times.

He removed his watch and vigorously washed both fore-arms, first the right and then the left, from wrist to elbow.

Wetting the palms of his hands, he rubbed his head from the forehead to the back of his neck.

He placed his wet index fingers inside his ears, washing behind the ears and then the lobes with his thumbs.

Finally, he washed both feet up to the ankles, beginning with his right foot and making sure to wash between the toes.

'*Ash hadu an la ilaha illa Allah wahdahu la shariika lahu wa anna Muhammadan 'abduhu wa rasuluh,*' he recited fervently, stressing the central tenet of his faith that there is no God but Allah, who has no equals, and that Mohammed is his servant and Messenger.

That concluded the ritual of ablution, which would mark the beginning of his life as a declared warrior of the Jihad. Now he was ready to kill and die for the greater glory of Allah.

He grasped the pistol, allowing himself a brief smile. He could hear the plane's engines. It was time to give the signal.

With a solemn gesture, Russell left the tent.

87

THE EXCAVATION

Thursday, 20 July 2006. 1:24 p.m.

The pilot of the BA-609 was Howell Duke. In twenty-three years of flying he had logged 18,000 hours in various types of aircraft under all possible weather conditions. He had survived a blizzard in Alaska and an electrical storm in Madagascar. But he had never felt true fear, that cold sensation that made your nuts shrivel up and your throat go dry.

Until today.

He was flying in a cloudless sky with optimum visibility, squeezing every last drop of horsepower from his engines. The plane wasn't the fastest or the best he had piloted, but it certainly was the most amusing. It could reach a velocity of 315 miles per hour and then hover majestically in place like a cloud. Everything was going perfectly.

He lowered his eyes to check on the altitude, the fuel gauge, and the distance to his destination. When he looked up again his mouth fell open. There was something on the skyline that had not been there before.

At first it looked like a wall of sand one hundred feet high and a couple of miles wide. Given the few landmarks in the desert, Duke thought at first that what he was seeing was still.

Slowly, he realised that it was moving, and it was doing so quickly.

I see the canyon up ahead. Fuck. Thank God this didn't happen ten minutes ago. It must be the simoon they warned me about.

He would need at least three minutes to land the plane, and the wall was less than twenty-five miles away. He made a quick calculation. It would take the simoon another twenty minutes to reach the canyon. He pressed the helicopter conversion mode and felt the motors slow down immediately.

At least it's working. I'll have time to set down this bird and squeeze myself into the smallest space I can find. If half the things they say about this thing are true . . .

Three and a half minutes later, the landing gear of the BA-609 was settling on the flat ground between the camp and the excavation. Duke cut the engine and for the first time in his life he didn't bother to go through his final safety check but got out of the plane as if his pants were on fire. He glanced around but couldn't see anyone.

I have to let everyone know. Inside that canyon they won't see this thing until it's thirty seconds away.

He ran towards the tents, although he wasn't so sure that being inside a tent was the safest place to be. Suddenly a figure dressed in white was walking towards him. Before long he recognised who it was.

'Hey, Mr Russell. I see you've gone native,' Duke said, feeling nervous. 'I hadn't seen you—'

Russell was twenty feet away. At that moment the pilot noticed that Russell had a pistol in his hand and stopped in his tracks.

'Mr Russell, what's going on?'

The executive said nothing. He simply aimed at the pilot's

chest and fired three quick shots. He stood over the fallen body and fired three more times into the pilot's head.

In a nearby cave, O heard the shots and alerted the group. 'Brothers, that's the signal. Let's go.'

88

THE EXCAVATION

Thursday, 20 July 2006. 1:39 p.m.

'Are you drunk, Nest Three?'

'Colonel, I repeat that Mr Russell just blew off the pilot's head and then ran towards the excavation. What are your orders?'

'Fuck. Does anyone have a visual on Russell?'

'Sir, this is Nest Two. He's climbing the platform. He's dressed kind of strange. Should I fire a warning shot?'

'Negative, Nest Two. Don't do anything until we know more. Nest One, do you read me?'

'. . .'

'Nest One, do you read me?'

'Nest One. Torres, pick up the fucking radio.'

'. . .'

'Nest Two, do you have a visual of Nest One?'

'Affirmative, sir. I have a visual, but Torres isn't there, sir.'

'Shit! You two, don't take your eyes off the entrance to the excavation. I'm on my way.'

89

AT THE ENTRANCE TO THE CANYON,
TEN MINUTES BEFORE

The first sting had been on his calf, twenty minutes ago.

Fowler had felt a sharp pain, but luckily it didn't last long, fading into a dull ache, more like a hard slap than the initial bolt of lightning.

The priest had planned to suppress any screams by gritting his teeth, but forced himself not to do so yet. He'd try that with the next sting.

The ants had gone no higher than his knees, and Fowler didn't have the slightest idea if they knew what he was. He tried his best to seem like something that wasn't edible or dangerous, and for both reasons there was one thing he could not do: move.

The next sting hurt a great deal more, maybe because he knew what would come next: the swelling in the area, the inevitability of it all, the feeling of helplessness.

After the sixth sting he lost count. Perhaps he had been stung twelve times, perhaps twenty. Not many more, but he couldn't take it much longer. He had used up all his resources – gritting his teeth, biting his lips, flaring his nostrils wide enough for a truck to enter. At some point, feeling desperate, he had even risked twisting his wrists in the hand-cuffs.

The worst thing was not knowing when the next sting

would come. Up to that point he had been lucky, since most of the ants had gone half a dozen feet to his left and only a couple of hundred covered the ground beneath him. But he knew that at the slightest movement they would attack.

He needed to concentrate on something other than the pain, or he would go against his better judgement and start trying to crush the insects with his boots. Maybe he'd even manage to kill a few, but it was clear that they had the numerical advantage and in the end he would lose.

A new sting was the last straw. The pain ran up his legs and exploded in his genitals. He was on the verge of losing his mind.

Strangely, it was Torres who saved him.

'Padre, your sins are attacking you. One by one, just like they eat away the soul.'

Fowler looked up. The Colombian was standing almost thirty feet away, watching him with an amused expression on his face.

'I got tired of being up there, you know, so I came back to see you in your own private Hell. Look, this way we won't be disturbed,' he said, turning off the walkie-talkie with his left hand. In the right hand, he was holding a rock about the size of a tennis ball. 'Now, where were we?'

The priest was grateful that Torres was there. It gave him someone to focus his hatred on. Which in turn would buy him a few more minutes of remaining still, a few more minutes of life.

'Oh, yes,' Torres went on. 'We were trying to work out if you were going to make the first move or if I was going to make it for you.'

He threw the rock and hit Fowler on the shoulder. The stone tumbled over to where most of the ants were massing, once more the pulsating lethal swarm that was ready to attack whatever it was that threatened their home.

Fowler closed his eyes and attempted to control the pain. The rock had hit him in the same place a psychopathic killer had shot him sixteen months before. The whole area still hurt at night, and now he felt as if he were reliving the whole ordeal. He tried to concentrate on the pain in his shoulder to block out the ache in his legs, using a trick that an instructor had taught him what seemed a million years ago: *the brain can only handle one sharp pain at a time.*

When Fowler opened his eyes again and saw what was happening behind Torres, he had to make an even bigger effort to control his emotions. If he betrayed himself for one moment, he was finished. Andrea Otero's head had appeared from behind the dune that lay just past the exit to the canyon where he was being held prisoner by Torres. The reporter was very close, and without doubt in a few moments she would see them, if she hadn't already done so.

Fowler understood that he had to make absolutely sure that Torres didn't turn around to look for another rock. He decided to give the Colombian what the soldier least expected.

'Please, Torres. Please, I beg you.'

The expression on the Colombian's face changed completely. Like all killers, few things excited him more than the control he thought he had over his victims when they began to beg.

'What are you begging for, Padre?'

The priest had to force himself to concentrate and find the right words. Everything depended on making sure that Torres didn't turn around. Andrea had seen them, and Fowler was sure that she was close, although he'd lost sight of her because Torres's body was blocking the way.

'I'm begging for my life. My miserable life. You're a soldier, a real man. Compared to you I'm nothing.'

The mercenary was smiling broadly, revealing his yellowish teeth. 'Well said, Padre. And now—'

Torres never got a chance to finish his sentence. He didn't even feel the blow.

Andrea, who had had a chance to take in the scene as she drew near, had decided not to use the pistol. Remembering what a bad shot she had been with Alryk, the most she could hope for was that a stray bullet wouldn't find Fowler's head the same way one had hit the tyre of the Hummer earlier. Instead, she pulled the windscreen wipers out of her make-shift umbrella. Holding the steel pipe like a baseball bat, she crept forward slowly.

The pipe wasn't too heavy, so she had to choose her line of attack carefully. Only a few steps behind him, she decided to aim for the side of his head. She could feel the sweat on the palm of her hands, and prayed that she wouldn't screw this up. If Torres turned around she was fucked.

He didn't. Andrea planted her feet firmly on the ground, swung her weapon and hit Torres with all her strength on the side of his head near the temple.

'Take that, you bastard!'

The Colombian dropped into the sand like a stone. The mass of red ants must have felt the vibration because immediately they turned and headed for his fallen body. Unaware of what had happened, he started to get up. Still semi-conscious from the blow to his temple, he staggered and fell again as the first ants reached his body. When he felt the first stings,

Torres brought his hands to his eyes in absolute terror. He tried to get up on to his knees but this provoked the ants even more and they swarmed over him in greater numbers. It was as if they were passing on a message to each other through their pheromones.

Enemy.

Kill.

'Run, Andrea!' Fowler yelled. 'Get away from them.'

The young reporter took several steps back, but very few ants turned to follow the vibrations. They were more concerned with the Colombian, who was covered in them from head to toe, howling in agony, every fibre of his body under attack from the sharp jaws and needle-like stings. Torres managed to stand up again and take a few steps, the ants covering him like a strange skin.

He took one more step, then fell, and didn't get up again.

Andrea, in the meantime, had retreated to the place where she had dropped the wipers and the shirt. She wrapped the wipers in the cloth. Then, making a wide detour around the ants, she approached Fowler and lit the shirt with her lighter. When the shirt was burning she traced a circle with it on the ground around the priest. The few ants that hadn't joined the attack on Torres scurried away from the heat.

Using the steel pipe, she pried Fowler's handcuffs and the spike that held them away from the rock.

'Thank you,' said the priest, his legs shaking.

When they had gone about a hundred feet away from the ants and Fowler considered they were safe, they collapsed on the ground, exhausted. The priest rolled up his trousers to check on his legs. Other than the small reddish sting marks, the swelling, and the continuous but dull pain, the twenty-odd bites hadn't inflicted too much damage.

'Now that I've saved your life, I suppose your duty to me has been repaid?' Andrea said sarcastically.

'Did Doc tell you about that?'

'That, and a lot of other things I want to ask you about.'

'Where is she?' the priest asked, but he already knew the answer.

The young woman shook her head and began to sob. Fowler held her gently.

'I'm so sorry, Ms Otero.'

'I loved her,' she said, burying her face in the priest's chest. As she sobbed, Andrea realised that Fowler had suddenly gone tense and was holding his breath.

'What's wrong?' she asked.

In answer to her question, Fowler pointed at the horizon, where Andrea saw a deadly wall of sand heading towards them as inevitably as night.

THE EXCAVATION

AL MUDAWWARA DESERT,
JORDAN

Thursday, July 20, 2006. 1:48 p.m.

You two, don't take your eyes off the entrance to the excavation site. I'm on my way.

Those were the words that caused, albeit indirectly, the demise of Dekker's remaining crew. When the attack came, the eyes of the two soldiers were looking everywhere but the place from which the danger came.

Tewi Waaka, the huge Sudanese, only glimpsed the intruders dressed in brown when they were already in the camp. There were seven of them, armed with Kalashnikov rifles. He alerted Jackson on the radio and the two opened fire. One of the intruders fell under the hail of bullets. The others hid behind the tents.

Waaka was surprised that they didn't return fire. In reality that was his last thought, because a few seconds later two terrorists who had climbed the cliff ambushed him from behind. Two bursts from the Kalashnikov and Tewi Waaka joined his ancestors.

On the other side of the canyon in Nest 2, Marla Jackson saw Waaka being shot through the scope of her M4 and understood that she was heading for the same fate. Marla knew the cliffs well. She had spent so many hours there with nothing to do other than look around and touch herself through her trousers when no one was watching, counting the hours until Dekker would come and take her off on a private reconnaissance mission.

During the hours of sentry duty she had imagined hundreds of times how hypothetical enemies might climb up and surround her. Now, peering over the edge of the cliff, she saw two very real enemies only a foot and a half away. She immediately plugged them with fourteen bullets.

They made no sound as they died.

There were now four of the enemy left that she knew of, but she could do nothing from her position without cover. The only thing she could think of was to join Dekker down at the excavation so they could decide on a plan together. It was a shitty option, because she'd lose the advantage of height and an easier escape route. But she had no choice, because she now heard three words on her walkie-talkie:

'Marla . . . help me.'

'Dekker, where are you?'

'Down below. At the base of the platform.'

Unconcerned for her own safety, Marla climbed down the rope ladder, and ran towards the excavation. Dekker was lying next to the platform with a very ugly wound to the right side of his chest and with his left leg twisted under him. He must have fallen from the top of the scaffolding. Marla examined the wound. The South African had managed to stop the bleeding but his breathing was . . .

Fucking whistling.

. . . worrying. He had a punctured lung, and that was bad

news unless they got to a doctor straight away.

'What happened to you?'

'It was Russell. That son of a bitch ... he caught me by surprise as I came in.'

'Russell?' Marla said, surprised. She tried to think. 'You'll be all right. I'll get you out of here, Colonel. I swear.'

'No way. You have to get yourself out of here. I'm finished. The master said it best: "Life to the great majority is a constant struggle for mere existence, with the certainty of being overcome at last."'

'Could you please leave fucking Schopenhauer out for once, Dekker?'

The South African smiled sadly at his lover's outburst and made a slight gesture with his head.

'Behind you, soldier. Don't forget what I told you.'

Marla turned and saw the four terrorists converging on her. They had fanned out, and were using the rocks as cover, while her only protection would be the heavy tarpaulins protecting the hydraulic system and steel bearings of the platform.

'Colonel, I think we're both finished.'

Strapping the M4 on her shoulder she tried to drag Dekker under the scaffolding, but could only move him a few inches. The South African's weight was too much, even for a strong woman like her.

'Listen to me, Marla.'

'What the hell do you want?' Marla said, trying to think as she squatted next to the scaffolding's steel supports. While she wasn't sure if she should open fire before she had a clear shot, she *was* sure they'd have one much sooner that she would.

'Give yourself up. I don't want them to kill you,' Dekker said, his voice growing weaker.

Marla was about to swear at her commander again when a quick glance towards the canyon entrance told her that giving herself up might be the only way out of this absurd situation.

'I give up!' she screamed. 'Are you listening, you pricks? I give up. Yankee she go home.'

She threw her rifle several feet in front of her, followed by her automatic pistol. Then she stood and put up her hands.

I'm counting on you, bastards. This is your chance to inter-rogate a woman prisoner in depth. Don't fucking shoot me.

Slowly the terrorists approached, their rifles aimed at her head, each Kalashnikov muzzle ready to spit out lead and end her precious life.

'I give up,' Marla repeated, watching them advance. They formed a semi-circle, their knees bent, faces covered by black scarves, about twenty feet apart from each other so they wouldn't be an easy target.

The hell I give up, you sons of bitches. Enjoy your seventy-two virgins.

'I give up,' she yelled one last time, hoping to drown out the growing noise of the wind that turned into an explosion when the wall of sand swept over the tents, swallowing up the plane then hurtling towards the terrorists.

Two of them turned in shock. The others never knew what hit them.

All of them died instantly.

Marla threw herself next to Dekker and pulled the tarpaulin over them as an improvised kind of tent.

You have to get down. Cover yourself with something. Don't fight the heat and the wind or you'll dry up like a raisin.

Those had been Torres's words, always the braggart, when

he had talked to his companions about the myth of the simoon while they played poker. Maybe it would work. Marla grabbed hold of Dekker and he tried to do the same, although his grip was weak.

'Hang in there, Colonel. In half an hour we'll be far away from here.'

THE EXCAVATION

AL MUDAWWARA DESERT,
JORDAN

Thursday, 20 July 2006. 1:52 p.m.

The hole was no more than a crack at the base of the canyon, but it was large enough for two people pressed together. They had just managed to squeeze themselves in before the simoon hit the canyon. A small outcrop of rock protected them from the first wave of heat. They had to yell in order to be heard above the roar of the sandstorm.

'Relax, Ms Otero. We'll be here for at least twenty minutes. This wind is deadly, but luckily it doesn't last too long.'

'You've been in a sandstorm before, haven't you, Father?'

'A few times. But I've never seen a simoon. I've only read about it in a Rand McNally atlas.'

Andrea went quiet for a while, trying to catch her breath. Luckily, the sand that was blowing through the canyon barely penetrated their refuge, even though the temperature rose dramatically and Andrea was finding it difficult to breathe.

'Talk to me, Father. I feel like I'm going to faint.'

Fowler tried to shift his position so he could rub the pain in his legs. The bites needed disinfectants and antibiotics as soon as possible, although that wasn't a priority. Getting Andrea out of there was.

'As soon as the wind dies down we'll run over to the H3s and create a distraction so that you can get out of here and head for Aqaba before anyone starts shooting. You know how to drive, don't you?'

'I'd be in Aqaba already if I'd been able to find a jack in that damn Hummer,' Andrea lied. 'Somebody took it.'

'It's under the spare tyre in that kind of vehicle.'

Which is where I didn't look, of course.

'Don't change the subject. You used the singular. Aren't you coming with me?'

'I have to complete my mission, Andrea.'

'You came here because of me, didn't you? Well, now you can leave with me.'

The priest took a few seconds before answering. Finally he decided that the young reporter should know the truth.

'No, Andrea. I was sent here to bring back the Ark, no matter what, but it was an order I never planned on carrying out. There's a reason why I had explosives in my briefcase. And that reason is inside that cave. I never really believed it existed and I never would have accepted the mission if you hadn't been involved in it. My superior used us both.'

'Why, Father?'

'It's very complicated, but I'll try to explain as briefly as I can. The Vatican has thought through the possibilities of what might happen if the Ark of the Covenant was returned to Jerusalem. People would see it as a sign. In other words, as a sign that the Temple of Solomon should be reconstructed in its original place.'

'Where the Dome of the Rock and the Al Aqsa Mosque are located.'

'Exactly. The religious tension in the region would increase a hundredfold. It would provoke the Palestinians. The Al

Aqsa Mosque would end up being knocked down so that the original temple could be rebuilt. This isn't just speculation, Andrea. It is a fundamental idea. If one group has the power to crush another and they believe they have justification, eventually they do it.'

Andrea remembered one of the stories she had worked on towards the beginning of her professional career, seven years earlier. It was September 2000, and she was working on the international section of a newspaper. The news came that Ariel Sharon was going for a walk, surrounded by hundreds of anti-riot police, on the Temple Mount – on the border between the Jewish and Arab sectors, in the heart of Jerusalem, one of the most sacred and disputed territories in history, site of the Temple of the Rock, the third most important place in the Islamic world.

That simple walk had led to the Second Intifada, which was still going on. To thousands of dead and wounded; to suicide bombings on one side and military attacks on the other. To a never-ending spiral of hatred that promised little chance of reconciliation. If discovering the Ark of the Covenant meant rebuilding the Temple of Solomon on the spot where the Al Aqsa Mosque now stood, every Islamic country in the world would rise up against Israel, unleashing a conflict with unimaginable consequences. With Iran on the verge of realising its nuclear capacity, there would be no limit to what might happen.

'Is that the justification?' Andrea said, her voice cracking with emotion. 'The holy commandments of the God of Love?'

'No, Andrea. It is the right of ownership to the Promised Land.'

The reporter shifted uncomfortably.

'Now I remember what Forrester called it ... the people's

contract with God. And what Kyra Larsen said about the original meaning and power of the Ark. But what I don't understand is what Kayn has to do with all this.'

'Mr Kayn has a mind that is obviously disturbed but at the same time is deeply religious. From what I understand, his father left him a letter asking him to fulfil his family's mission. That's all I know.'

Andrea, who knew the whole story in greater detail because of her interview with Kayn, didn't interrupt.

If Fowler wants to know the rest, let him buy the book I'm planning to write as soon as I get out of here, she thought.

'Kayn made it clear ever since his son was born,' Fowler continued, 'that he would put all of his resources into finding the Ark, so that his son . . .'

'Isaac.'

'. . . so that Isaac could fulfil his family's destiny.'

'To restore the Ark to the Temple?'

'Not quite, Andrea. According to a certain interpretation of the Torah, the one who is able to recover the Ark and rebuild the Temple – the latter being relatively easy given Kayn's fortune – would be the Promised One: the Messiah.'

'Oh, God!'

Andrea's face was completely transformed as the last piece of the puzzle fell into place. It explained everything. The hallucinations. The obsessive behaviour. The terrible trauma of having grown up locked away in that narrow space. Religion as absolute fact.

'Exactly,' said Fowler. 'Additionally, he saw the death of his own son, Isaac, as the sacrifice required by God so that he himself could achieve that destiny.'

'But, Father . . . if Kayn knew who you were, why the hell did he allow you to come on the expedition?'

'You know, it's ironic. Kayn couldn't carry out this mission without the blessing of Rome, a seal of approval that the Ark was real. That's how they were able to get me involved in the expedition. But someone else infiltrated the expedition too. Someone with a lot of power who decided to work for Kayn after Isaac told him about his father's obsession with the Ark. I'm only guessing, but at first he probably just took the job to gain access to confidential information. Later, when Kayn's obsession changed into something more concrete, he made his own plans.'

'Russell!' Andrea gasped.

'That's right. The man who threw you into the sea and killed Stowe Erling in a clumsy attempt to hide his discovery. Maybe he planned to dig up the Ark himself later on. And either he or Kayn – or both – is responsible for the Ypsilon protocol.'

'*And* he put the scorpions in my sleeping bag, the bastard.'

'No, that was Torres. You have a very select fan club.'

'Only since you and I have known each other, Father. But I still don't understand why Russell wants the Ark.'

'Perhaps to destroy it. If that's the case, although I doubt it, I'm not going to stop him. I think he may want to get it out of here to use it in some crazy scheme to blackmail the government of Israel. I still haven't figured out that part, but one thing is clear: nothing is going to stop me from carrying out my decision.'

Andrea tried to scrutinise the priest's face. What she saw left her frozen.

'You're really going to blow up the Ark, Father? Such a sacred object?'

'I thought you didn't believe in God,' said Fowler with an ironic smile.

'My life has taken a lot of strange turns lately,' Andrea replied sadly.

'God's law is engraved here and here,' said the priest, touching his forehead and then his chest. 'The Ark is only a wood and metal box that would cause the death of millions of people and a hundred years of war if it resurfaces. What we've seen in Afghanistan and Iraq is only a pale shadow of what might happen then. That's the reason it's not leaving that cave.'

Andrea didn't reply. Suddenly there was silence. The wailing of the wind among the rocks in the canyon had finally ceased.

The simoon was over.

92

THE EXCAVATION

Thursday, 20 July 2006. 2:16 p.m.

Cautiously they stepped out from their hiding place and entered the canyon. The landscape before them was a scene of devastation. The tents had been ripped from their platforms and what had been inside was now scattered throughout the surrounding area. The windscreens on the Hummers had been cracked by small rocks that had come loose from the canyon's cliffs. Fowler and Andrea were walking towards the vehicles when suddenly they heard the motor of one of the Hummers roar into life.

Without warning, an H3 was heading for them at full speed.

Fowler shoved Andrea out of the way and jumped aside. For a fraction of a second he saw Marla Jackson behind the wheel, her teeth gritted in anger. The huge rear tyre of the Hummer passed inches in front of Andrea's face, spraying her with sand.

Before the two of them could get up, the H3 had rounded the curve out of the canyon and disappeared.

'I think there's just us,' the priest said as he helped Andrea to her feet. 'That was Jackson and Dekker leaving like the devil himself was after them. I don't think many of their companions are left.'

'Father, I don't think they're the only things to have disappeared. It looks like your plan to get me out of here has gone up in smoke,' said the reporter, pointing to the three remaining all-purpose vehicles.

All twelve tyres had been slashed.

They walked around the wreckage of the tents for a couple of minutes, looking for water. They found three half-full canteens and a surprise: Andrea's backpack with her hard disk, almost buried in the sand.

'Everything's changed,' Fowler said, looking around suspiciously. He seemed unsure of himself and was creeping about as if an assassin on the cliffs might mow them down at any moment.

Andrea followed him, crouched down in fear.

'I can't get you out of here, so stay close until we work something out.'

The BA-609 was turned on its left side like a bird with a broken wing. Fowler entered the cabin and reappeared thirty seconds later holding a few cables.

'Russell won't be able to use the plane to carry the Ark,' he said, throwing the cables far away then jumping back down. He grimaced as his feet hit the sand.

He's still in pain. This is crazy, Andrea thought.

'Do you have any idea where he could be?'

Fowler was about to answer but instead he stopped and went around to the back of the plane. Next to the wheels sat a dull black object. The priest picked it up.

It was his briefcase.

The top cover looked as if it had been sliced open so you could see the space where the plastic explosives that Fowler had used to blow up the water tank had been. He touched the briefcase in two places and the secret compartment opened.

'It's a shame they ruined the leather. This briefcase has been with me for a long time,' the priest said as he collected the four remaining packages of explosives and another object, which was about the size of a watch face with two metal clasps.

Fowler wrapped the explosives up in the nearest piece of clothing that had been blown out of the tents during the sandstorm.

'Put this in your backpack, OK?'

'No way,' Andrea said, taking a step back. 'Those things scare the hell out of me.'

'Without the detonator connected, it's harmless.'

Andrea conceded, reluctantly.

As they headed towards the platform, they saw the bodies of the terrorists who had surrounded Marla Jackson and Dekker before the simoon hit. Andrea's first reaction was to panic, until she realised that they were dead. When they reached the corpses Andrea couldn't help gasping. The bodies were laid out in strange positions. One of them seemed to be trying to get up – one of his arms was in the air, and his eyes were opened wide *as if he was looking into Hell*, Andrea thought, with an expression of disbelief.

Except that he didn't have any eyes.

The eye sockets of the corpses were all empty, their open mouths were nothing but black holes, and their skin was grey like cardboard. Andrea pulled her camera out of the backpack and took some photos of the mummies.

I can't believe it. It's as if the life was yanked right out of them without any warning. Or as if it's still happening. God, how horrible!

Andrea turned around and her backpack grazed the head of one of the men. Before her very eyes the man's body suddenly disintegrated, leaving only a mixture of grey dust, clothes and bones.

Feeling nauseous, Andrea turned to the priest. She saw that he didn't suffer from the same scruples when it came to the dead. Fowler had noticed that at least one of the bodies served a more utilitarian purpose, and had pulled out from under it a clean Kalashnikov. He checked the weapon and saw that it was still in good working order. He took some extra clips from the terrorist's clothes and put them in his pockets.

With the muzzle of the rifle he pointed at the platform leading to the cave entrance.

'Russell's up there.'

'How do you know?'

'When he decided to reveal himself, he clearly called his friends,' Fowler said, inclining his head towards the bodies. 'These are the people you spotted when we first arrived. I don't know if there are others or how many there could be, but it's fairly clear that Russell is still around because there are no tracks in the sand leading away from the platform. The simoon has covered everything. If they had come out, we'd be able to see tracks. He's in there and so is the Ark.'

'What are we going to do?'

Fowler thought for a few seconds, his head bowed.

'If I were smart I'd blow up the entrance to the cave and let them starve to death. But I'm afraid there might be others in there. Eichberg, Kayn, David Pappas . . .'

'Then you're going in?'

Fowler nodded. 'Give me the explosives, please.'

'Let me go with you,' Andrea said, handing him the package.

'Ms Otero, you stay out here and wait until I come out. If you see them coming out instead, don't say anything. Just hide. Take some photos if you're able to, and then get out of here and tell the whole world the story.'

93

INSIDE THE CAVE, FOURTEEN MINUTES
EARLIER

Getting rid of Dekker had been easier than he'd dared imagine. The South African had been taken aback by the fact he'd shot the pilot and had been so anxious to talk to him that he hadn't taken the least precaution as he came into the tunnel. What he found was a bullet that sent him rolling off the platform.

Contracting the Ypsilon protocol behind the old man's back had been a brilliant stroke, thought Russell, congratulating himself.

It had cost almost ten million dollars. Dekker had been suspicious at first, until Russell had agreed to pay him seven figures up front and another seven if he was forced to use the protocol.

Kayn's assistant smiled with satisfaction. Next week the accountants at Kayn Industries would notice that the money was missing from the pension fund and questions would be raised. By then he'd be far away and the Ark would be in a safe place in Egypt. It would be very simple to lose himself there. And then accursed Israel, which he hated, would have to pay the price for the humiliation they had caused the house of Islam.

Russell walked the length of the tunnel and looked into the cave. Kayn was there, watching with interest as Eichberg and

Pappas removed the last rocks that blocked the access to the chamber, alternating between use of the electric drill and their hands. They hadn't heard the shot when he'd fired at Dekker. The moment he knew that the path to the Ark was clear and he no longer needed them, they'd be dispatched.

As for Kayn . . .

No words could describe the torrent of hatred that Russell felt for the old man. It seethed in the depths of his soul, fuelled by the humiliations that Kayn had made him suffer. Being at the old man's side for the past six years had been excruciating, torture.

Hiding in the bathroom to pray, spitting out the alcohol that he was forced to pretend he was drinking so that people wouldn't suspect him. Taking care of the old man's sick and fearful mind at all hours of the day and night. Feigning concern and affection.

It was all lies.

Your best weapon will be taqiyya, *the deception of the warrior. The jihadist can lie about his faith, he can make believe, pretend, hide and twist the truth. He can do this with an infidel without sinning*, the imam had said fifteen years before. *And don't believe it will be easy. You will cry each night because of the pain in your heart, to the point that you will not recognise who you are.*

Now he was himself again.

With all the agility of his young and well-trained body, Russell climbed down the rope without the aid of a harness the same way he had come up it a couple of hours before. His white robe fluttered as he descended, attracting Kayn's attention as he looked at his assistant in shock.

'What's the meaning of the disguise, Jacob?'

416

Russell didn't answer. He went towards the cavity. The space they had opened up was about five feet high and six and a half feet wide.

'It's in there, Mr Russell. We've all seen it,' Eichberg said, so excited that at first he did not notice the way Russell was dressed. 'Hey, what's with the outfit?' he said finally.

'Be quiet and call Pappas.'

'Mr Russell, you should be a little more—'

'Don't make me say it again,' the assistant said, pulling the pistol out of his clothes.

'David!' Eichberg screeched like a child.

'Jacob!' yelled Kayn.

'Shut up, you old bastard.'

The blood drained out of Kayn's face at the insult. No one ever talked to him like that, much less the person who up to now had been his right hand. He didn't have time to reply, because David Pappas came out of the cave, blinking as his eyes adjusted to the light.

'What the hell . . .?'

When he saw the pistol in Russell's hand, he understood immediately. He was the first of the three to understand, although not the one who was most disappointed and shocked. That role belonged to Kayn.

'You!' exclaimed Pappas. 'Now I understand. You had access to the magnetometer's program. You're the one who changed the data. You killed Stowe.'

'A small error that almost cost me dearly. I thought I had better control of the expedition than I really had,' Russell admitted with a shrug. 'And now a quick question. Are you ready to bring out the Ark?'

'Go fuck yourself, Russell.'

Without a thought, Russell aimed at Pappas's leg and fired.

Pappas's right knee turned into a bloody mess and he fell to the ground. His screams echoed off the walls of the tunnel.

'The next bullet is for your head. Now answer me, Pappas.'

'Yes, it's ready to come out, sir. The path is clear,' Eichberg said, his hands up in the air.

'That's all I wanted to know,' Russell replied.

There were two shots in quick succession. His arm moved down and there were two more shots. Eichberg fell on Pappas, both of them shot in the head, their blood now mingling on the stony ground.

'You've killed them, Jacob. You have killed both of them.'

Kayn was cowering in a corner, his face a mask of fear and incomprehension.

'Well, well, old man. For such a mad old bastard you're fairly good at stating the obvious,' Russell said. He peered into the cave, still aiming the gun at Kayn. When he turned back there was a look of satisfaction on his face. 'So we've finally found it then, Ray? The work of a lifetime. It's a shame yours will be cut short.'

The assistant walked towards his boss, taking slow measured steps. Kayn shrank back into his corner even more, totally trapped. His face was covered in sweat.

'Why, Jacob?' cried the old man. 'I loved you like my own son.'

'You call that love?' yelled Russell, drawing near to Kayn and striking him several times with the gun, first on the face, then on his arms and across his head. 'I've been your slave, old man. Every time you cried like a girl in the middle of the night, I ran to you, having to remind myself why I was doing it. I had to think of the moment when I'd finally defeat you and you would be at my mercy.'

Kayn dropped to the ground. His face was swollen, almost

unrecognisable from the blows. Blood trickled out of his mouth and from his shattered cheekbones.

'Look at me, old man,' Russell went on, lifting Kayn by the front of his shirt so that they were eye to eye.

'Look at the face of your own failure. In a few minutes my men will come down into this cave and remove your precious Ark. We'll give the world the punishment it deserves. Things will be the way they should always have been.'

'Sorry, Mr Russell. I'm afraid I'm going to have to disappoint you.'

The assistant turned sharply. At the other end of the tunnel Fowler had just lowered himself down on the rope and was aiming a Kalashnikov at him.

The Excavation

AL MUDAWWARA DESERT,
JORDAN

Thursday, 20 July 2006. 2:27 p.m.

'Father Fowler.'

'Huqan.'

Russell had positioned Kayn's limp body between himself and the priest, who was still aiming the rifle at Russell's head.

'It appears you have disposed of my men.'

'It wasn't me, Mr Russell. God took care of that. He turned them into dust.'

Russell looked at him in shock, trying to figure out if the priest was bluffing. The help of his acolytes was essential to the execution of his plan. He couldn't understand why they hadn't shown up yet and was trying to stall for time.

'So you've managed to get the upper hand, Father,' he said, going back to his usual ironic tone. 'I know how good a shot you are. At this distance you can't miss. Or are you afraid of hitting the unproclaimed Messiah?'

'Mr Kayn is just a sick old man who believes he is doing God's will. From my point of view the only difference between the two of you is your age. Drop the gun.'

Russell was clearly outraged at the insult but powerless to do anything in the situation. He was holding his own gun by the muzzle after he'd used it to beat Kayn, and the old man's body did not offer him sufficient protection. Russell knew that one false move would produce a hole in his head.

He opened his right fist and let the pistol drop, then opened his left and released Kayn.

The old man collapsed in slow motion, crumpling as if his joints weren't connected to each other.

'Excellent, Mr Russell,' Fowler said. 'Now, if you don't mind, please take ten steps back . . .'

Mechanically, Russell did as he was told, hatred burning in his eyes.

For every step that Russell took back, Fowler took one forward, until the former had his back to the wall and the priest was standing beside Kayn.

'Very good. Now put your hands on top of your head and you'll come out of this with your life.'

Fowler squatted down next to Kayn, feeling for his pulse. The old man was shaking, and one of his legs seemed to be in spasm. The priest frowned. Kayn's condition worried him – he was showing all the signs of having had a stroke and his life-force seemed to be evaporating with every moment.

In the meantime Russell was looking around, trying to find something to use as a weapon against the priest. Suddenly, he felt something beneath him on the ground. He looked down and noticed that he was standing on some cables that ended a foot and a half to his right and were connected to the generator that was providing electricity in the cave.

He smiled.

Fowler took Kayn's arm, ready to pull him further away from Russell if he needed to. Out of the corner of his eye he saw Russell jump. Without the least hesitation he fired.

Then the lights went out.

What was meant to be a warning shot ended up destroying the generator. The equipment started shooting off sparks every few seconds, illuminating the tunnel with a sporadic blue light that grew weaker, like a camera flash gradually losing power.

Fowler crouched down immediately, a position that he had taken hundreds of times when he had parachuted into enemy territory on moonless nights. When you didn't know the position of your enemy, the best thing to do was sit still and wait.

Blue spark.

Fowler thought he saw a shadow running along the wall to his left and fired. It missed. Cursing his luck, he moved several feet in a zigzag to make sure that the other wouldn't know his position after the shot.

Blue spark.

Once again a shadow, this time to his right, although longer and right up against the wall. He fired in the opposite direction. Again he missed and there was more movement.

Blue spark.

He was against the wall. He couldn't see Russell anywhere. This could mean he—

With a scream, Russell threw himself at Fowler, hitting him repeatedly on the face and neck. The priest felt the other's teeth biting down on his arm like an animal. Unable to do otherwise, he let go of the Kalashnikov. For a second he felt the other's hands. They struggled and the rifle was lost in the darkness.

Blue spark.

Fowler was on the ground and Russell was trying his best to choke him. The priest, finally able to see his enemy, closed his fist and punched Russell in the solar plexus. Russell groaned and rolled to one side.

One last, weak blue flash.

Fowler managed to see Russell disappearing into the chamber. A sudden dull gleam told him that Russell had found his pistol.

A voice to his right called out.

'Father.'

Fowler crept towards the dying Kayn. He didn't want to offer Russell an easy target in case he decided to try his luck and aim randomly in the dark. The priest finally felt the old man's body in front of him and put his mouth to his ear.

'Mr Kayn, hold on,' he whispered. 'I can get you out of here.'

'No, Father, you can't,' Kayn replied, and although his voice was weak he spoke with the firm tone of a small child. 'It's better like this. I'm going to see my parents, my son and my brother. My life began in a hole. It makes sense that it will end the same way.'

'Then entrust yourself to God,' the priest said.

'I have. Would you give me your hand while I leave?'

Fowler said nothing but felt for the dying man's hand, holding it between his own. Less than a minute later, in the middle of a whispered Hebrew prayer, there was a death rattle and Raymond Kayn was still.

By now the priest knew what he had to do.

In the middle of the darkness he brought his fingers to the buttons on his shirt and undid them, then pulled out the package containing the explosives. He felt for the detonator, stuck it into the bars of C4 and pressed the buttons. In his mind he counted the number of beeps.

After setting it, I have two minutes, he thought.

But he couldn't leave the bomb outside the cavity where the Ark rested. Maybe it wouldn't be powerful enough to seal the cave once more. He wasn't sure how deep the hollow was, and if the Ark was behind an outcrop of rock it might survive without a scratch. If he was going to prevent this insanity happening again, he had to place the bomb next to the Ark. He couldn't throw it in like a grenade because the detonator might come loose. And he had to have enough time to escape.

The only option was to overcome Russell, put the C4 in position and then run like hell.

He crawled around, hoping to avoid making too much noise, but it was impossible. The ground was covered in small rocks that shifted as he moved.

'I can hear you coming, priest.'

There was a red flash and a shot rang out. The bullet missed Fowler by quite a long way, but the priest remained wary and rolled quickly to his left. A second bullet hit the place where he had been just seconds before.

He's using the flash from the gun to orientate himself. But he can't do that too many times or he'll run out of ammunition, Fowler thought, mentally counting the wounds he'd seen on Pappas and Eichberg's bodies.

He probably shot Dekker once, Pappas maybe three times, Eichberg twice, and he's fired at me twice. That's eight bullets. The gun has fourteen bullets, fifteen if there's one in the chamber. That means he has six, maybe seven, bullets left. He'll have to reload soon. When he does, I'll hear the clicking of the magazine. Then . . .

He was still calculating when two more shots lit up the opening to the cave. This time Fowler rolled away from his original position just in time. The shot missed him by about four inches.

Four or five left.

'I'm going to get you, Crusader. I'm going to get you because Allah is with me.' Russell's voice sounded ghostly inside the cave. 'Get out of here while you still can.'

Fowler grabbed a rock and threw it inside the hole. Russell took the bait and fired in the direction of the noise.

Three or four.

'Very clever, Crusader. But it won't do you any good.'

He hadn't finished speaking when he fired again. This time there were not two but three shots. Fowler rolled to his left and then to the right, banging his knees against the sharp rocks.

One bullet or an empty magazine.

Just before he rolled the second time the priest lifted his head for a moment. It was maybe only half a second but what he saw in the brief light from the shots would remain in his memory for ever.

Russell was standing behind a golden box of giant proportions. On top of it two roughly sculpted figures shone brightly. In the flash from the pistol, the gold appeared uneven, creased.

Fowler took a deep breath.

He was almost inside the chamber itself, but he didn't have enough space to manoeuvre. If Russell shot again, even if it was just a shot to see where he was, he would almost certainly hit him.

Fowler decided to do what Russell least expected.

In one quick motion he jumped up and ran into the hole. Russell tried firing, but the hammer made a loud click. Fowler took a flying leap and, before the other man could react, the priest had thrust the whole of his body weight against the top of the Ark, which fell towards Russell, the lid opening and the contents spilling out. Russell jumped back and narrowly avoided being crushed.

What followed was a blind struggle. Fowler was able to hit Russell several times on the arms and chest but Russell somehow managed to stick a full magazine into his pistol. Fowler heard the weapon being reloaded. He felt around in the dark with his right hand, holding Russell's arm with his left.

He found a flat rock.

With all his might he slammed it against Russell's head and the young man dropped to the ground, unconscious.

The force of the blow shattered the rock into pieces.

Fowler tried to regain his footing. His whole body hurt and his head was bleeding. Using the light from his watch, he tried to find his bearings in the dark. He directed the thin but intense shaft of light on to the overturned Ark, producing a soft glimmer that filled the chamber.

He had very little time to admire it. At that moment Fowler heard a sound that, in the struggle, he hadn't noticed . . .

Beep.

. . . and understood that while he had been rolling around to evade the shots . . .

Beep.

. . without meaning to . . .

Beep.

. . . he had activated the detonator . . .

. . . that only sounded in the last ten seconds before exploding . . .

Beeeeeeeeeeeeeeeeeeeep.

Driven by instinct, not reason, Fowler leaped into the blackness outside the chamber, beyond the Ark's faint light.

At the foot of the platform, a nervous Andrea Otero was

biting her nails. Then suddenly the ground shook. The scaffold swayed and groaned as the steel absorbed the impact of the blast but didn't collapse. A cloud of smoke and dust billowed out of the opening to the tunnel, covering Andrea with a fine layer of grit. She ran several feet away from the scaffold and waited. For half an hour her eyes remained glued to the entrance to the smoking cave, although she realised the wait was futile.

Nobody came out.

95

ON THE ROAD TO AQABA

AL MUDAWWARA DESERT,
JORDAN

Thursday, 20 July 2006. 9:34 p.m.

Andrea reached the H3 with the shot tyre where she'd left it, more exhausted than she had ever been in her life. She found the jack exactly where Fowler had said, and mentally recited a prayer for the dead priest.

He is certain to be in Heaven, if such a place exists. If you exist, God. If you're up there, why don't you send a couple of angels to give me a hand?

Nobody showed up, so Andrea had to do the work herself. When she had finished, she went to say goodbye to Doc, who was buried no more than ten feet away. The farewell lasted a while, and Andrea was aware that she had howled and cried out loud several times. She felt she was on the verge – in the middle – of a nervous breakdown after what had happened during the last few hours.

The moon was starting to rise, lighting up the dunes with its silvery blue light when Andrea finally got the strength to say goodbye to Chedva and climb into the H3. Feeling faint, she closed the door and turned on the air-conditioning. The cold air hitting her sweaty skin felt delicious, but she couldn't let herself enjoy it for more than a few minutes. The fuel tank was only a quarter full, and she'd need everything she had to reach the road.

If I'd noticed that detail when we climbed into the vehicle this morning I would've realised the real purpose of the trip. Maybe Chedva would still be alive.

She shook her head. She had to concentrate on driving. With a little luck she'd reach the road and find a town with a petrol station before midnight. If not, she'd have to walk. The important thing was to find a computer with a connection to the Internet as soon as possible.

She had a story to tell.

96

$\mathcal{E}$PILOGUE

The dark figure walked slowly on his journey back home. He had very little water, but it was enough for a man like him, who had been taught to survive under the worst conditions, and to help others survive.

He had managed to find the route through which the chosen of Yirməyáhu had entered the caves over two thousand years ago. This was the darkness into which he had flung himself just before the explosion. Some of the rocks that had covered it had been blown away with the blast. It took a ray of sunlight and several hours of backbreaking effort for him to emerge into the open again.

He slept during the day wherever he found shade. He breathed only with his nose, through an improvised scarf he had made from discarded clothing.

He walked at night, resting ten minutes every hour. His face was completely covered with dust, and now as he saw the outline of the road a few hours' away, he grew increasingly conscious of the fact that his 'death' could finally provide the liberation he had been seeking all these years. He would no longer have to be a soldier of God.

His freedom would be one of two rewards he had received from this undertaking, even though he could never share either of them with anyone.

He reached into his pocket for the fragment of rock, no

bigger than the palm of his hand. This was all that was left of the flat stone with which he had hit Russell in the dark. Across its surface were the profound but perfect symbols that had been etched by no human hand.

Two tears ran down his cheeks, leaving tracks in the dust that covered his face. His fingertips traced over the symbols on the stone and his lips turned them into words.

Loh Tirtzach.

Thou shall not kill.

In that instant, he asked for forgiveness.

And was forgiven.

Acknowledgements

I want to thank the following people:

My parents, for avoiding the bombs during the Civil War and for giving me a childhood so different from their own.

To Antonia Kerrigan, for being the best literary agent on the planet with the best team: Lola Gulias, Bernat Fiol and Víctor Hurtado.

To you, the reader, for making *God's Spy*, my first novel, a success in thirty-nine countries. I truly thank you.

In New York, to James Graham, my 'brother'. To Rory Hightower, Alice Nakagawa and Michael Dillman.

In Barcelona, Enrique Murillo, editor of this book, both untiring and tiring since he has one unusual virtue: he always told me the truth.

In Santiago de Compostela, Manuel Soutiño, who lent his considerable understanding of engineering to descriptions of the Moses Expedition.

In Roma, Giorgio Selano for his knowledge of the catacombs.

In Milan, Patrizia Spinato, word tamer.

In Jordan, Samir Mufti, Bahjat al-Rimaui and Abdul Suheiman, who know the desert like nobody else and who taught me the *gahwa* ritual.

In Vienna, nothing would have been possible without Kurt Fischer, who provided me with information on the real butcher of Spiegelgrund, who died on 15 December of a heart attack.

And to my wife, Katuxa, and my children, Andrea and Javier, for being understanding about my trips and my schedule.

Dear reader, I don't want to end the book without requesting a favour. Go back to the beginning of these pages and reread the poem by Samuel Keen. Do it until you memorise every word. Teach it to your children; send it to your friends. Please.